FENBY ON DELIUS

Collected writings on Delius
To mark Eric Fenby's 90th birthday

Edited by Stephen Lloyd

Thames Publishing
London

Thanks and Acknowledgements

Many people have assisted in different ways in the preparation of this volume, and the Editor would particularly like to thank the following for their help and willing co-operation: Felix Aprahamian, John Bishop, Lionel Carley, Paul Chennell, David Cox, Denham Ford, Lewis Foreman, Thomas Gunn, Marjorie Halstead, Alice Jones, Richard Kitching, Lyndon Jenkins, Robert Layton, Michael Lester, Tasmin Little, Rodney Meadows, Raymond Monk, Brian Radford, Neil Somerville (Senior Assistant, BBC Written Archives Centre, Caversham Park, Reading), Robert Threlfall, Malcolm Walker and Eric Fenby himself.

The publication of this book was made possible by the financial support of The Delius Trust and The Delius Society, to both of which organisations grateful acknowledgement is made.

CONTENTS

Part One : Articles and Talks

Part Two : The Works of Delius

1. Works for Orchestra

2. Works for Solo Instrument(s) and Orchestra

3. Works for Voices and Orchestra

4. Works for Solo Voice

Illustrations between pages 128-129

INTRODUCTION 1: Tasmin Little

I remember the first time I became aware of the name Eric Fenby. It was when I was about eleven years old and was a pupil at the Yehudi Menuhin School. Every morning there was a general meeting and, during this, excerpts of books were frequently read to us. Generally, at that young age, many of the books were way above my level of comprehension and the morning meeting was just something to be 'sat through'. However, when the Director of Music announced during the coming week he would be reading passages from Eric Fenby's book *Delius as I knew him*, I sat upright and decided that this would be worth concentrating on!

I was already familiar with Delius's music, as my parents had often played recordings of his orchestral works at home and, as that week progressed and the story of Eric's years with Delius unfolded, I sat moved almost to tears.

Imagine my utter delight some months later to hear that he was due to visit the school to talk to us and hear some of the pupils play. Having heard so much about this man, we were so excited finally to see him in the flesh! I was very disappointed that I had not been chosen to play to him but enjoyed listening to him take two of my friends through the Delius Cello Sonata.

Shortly after this, my parents joined the Delius Society and through the Society met Eric. For a long time since his visit to the school, I had been begging my teacher to let me learn Delius's Third Violin Sonata and when she finally agreed, I asked my father to see if Eric would be prepared to help me with it. He was delighted to do so, and my father and I met him at a rehearsal studio in central London.

Eric took me through the sonata, bar by bar. He talked eagerly of the way Delius's music should be played and approached - it was as though the essence of Delius's music permeated his whole being and, through him, was being slowly passed to me. The whole experience thrilled me and I couldn't wait to learn more Delius. When we had finally finished working that day, my father asked Eric if he could reimburse him for his time and for the rehearsal studio. Eric would accept nothing at all, saying that it was his pleasure to help me and to share his thoughts with a young devotee of Delius's music. His total generosity of spirit touched both my father and myself.

Even though this experience was a long time ago, I still vividly remember details of the afternoon that I spent with Eric; the things he told me have proved invaluable, both with regard to the Third Violin Sonata and in preparing other works by Delius.

Over the years I have had the pleasure of meeting Eric and Rowena on a number of occasions and of counting them among my friends. It is a privilege for me to write this introduction for Eric's 90th birthday celebration book, and I wish both him and Rowena health and happiness in years to come.

INTRODUCTION 2: Felix Aprahamian, Vice-President, Delius Society, and Adviser to the Delius Trust

The English musical world invariably associates the name of Eric Fenby with that of Frederick Delius, the Bradford-born composer to whom, in 1928, the young man from Scarborough offered his services as musical amanuensis. The ageing, blind and paralysed Delius had lived for years in France; the story of the young Fenby's musical collaboration with him made a news item in the British press at the time. Much later, it became the subject of a dramatic documentary film by Ken Russell. *Song of Summer* still serves to remind those susceptible to the spell of Delius's music of that touching and fruitful episode in which a young English musician went to France to assist an older fellow Yorkshireman.

In 1929, when Frederick Delius came to London for the Festival organised in his honour by Sir Thomas Beecham, the twenty-three-year-old Eric Fenby accompanied Frederick and Jelka to the Festival concerts. Sir Thomas had asked Philip Heseltine to supply programme notes for the Festival, but what the young amanuensis could more practically achieve for the ailing Delius in his remaining years was limited by Delius's infirmity. Fenby returned to his native Scarborough, and although he was at Grez-sur-Loing at times during the next five years, he was not present when I visited the Deliuses in 1933 with Ernest Chapman and Donald Peart. In 1934, Jelka Delius called for Fenby to return to Grez when her own illness prevented her from looking after her dying husband. Fenby's own memoir and Russell's film have perpetuated this final period in Delius's life.

The Delius Trust came into existence a year later. It was created in 1935 on her death-bed by Jelka Delius, on the advice of Sir Thomas Beecham. Having chosen Delius's final resting-place at Limpsfield in the previous year, she accompanied Delius's body to England in 1935, when she herself was already a dying woman. Too ill to be at Limpsfield on that unforgettable Sunday afternoon, she lived only long enough to hear a recording of the service. In the church, Sir Thomas conducted a contingent from the London Philharmonic Orchestra, and gave a valedictory address at Delius's graveside. The following Thursday Jelka Delius was laid to rest in the same grave.

It must have been later during the 1930s, when Eric Fenby occasionally worked as an arranger and consultant for Boosey & Hawkes, that I first met him personally through Ernest Chapman. Ernest was Ralph Hawkes's assistant at the time, and it was Hawkes who had asked Delius to receive Ernest and his two friends in 1933.

As I wrote in the issue (No 89) of the *Delius Society Journal* which marked Eric Fenby's eightieth birthday, long before he became aware of some of us who had come under the spell of Delius's music soon after Fenby himself, we were quite aware of what the world of music owed to him.

I remember that day in 1931 when Ernest Chapman 'phoned from Boosey & Hawkes to tell me that the manuscript of a new Delius work had arrived. That night it had not been locked up in the safe, so Ernest and I deciphered it on the piano in the old Boosey studio at the back of the building later occupied by the new showroom. It was the full score, in Fenby's hand, of the movingly beautiful *Idyll* with its unaltered *Margot La Rouge* Prelude, which, being easier to read than the rest, we played over and over again.

It was not until that sunlit day in Limpsfield churchyard, when Delius was finally laid to rest, that I identified a worried Eric Fenby in serious conversation with Sir Thomas Beecham. One sensed the traumatic experience he had undergone.

Hitler's war intervened before Beecham could take up the cause of Delius again, with more recordings and, eventually, the book on Delius that he had promised to write. Having returned to, then abandoned, the London Philharmonic, in order to found another (not self-governing) London orchestra, the Royal Philharmonic, he ordained in 1946, among its earliest engagements, his second Delius Festival, for which he asked me to write the programme notes. When Sir Thomas chose to drop the last of the *Songs of Farewell* as unauthentic, Fenby was very much in my mind, but he was not around at the time to give chapter and verse about its dictation, and who was I to argue about it with the greatest Delius conductor? I met Eric Fenby sporadically in the following years, but it was not until he himself asked me to give two of the five lectures at the

1962 Delius Centenary Festival in Bradford that I felt that I had won his, as well as Beecham's, approval: it was a proud moment.

My devotion to Sir Thomas, as Delius's unrivalled interpreter, had never led me to swerve from the belief that, after his years at Grez-sur-Loing, Eric more truly represented the Delius 'conscience', something distinct from Beecham's ability to distil magic from the printed symbols. Long before the present happy constitution of the Delius Trust's advisory body, and even before Sir Thomas's death, I was urging Philip Emanuel, his bluff and golden-hearted solicitor, joint Delius Trustee with Barclays Bank, to consult Eric Fenby on every possible occasion regarding Delius affairs. More at home in police court and at races than in the concert room, dear Philip, whose office in Bloomsbury Square was round the corner from mine in Montague Street, would 'phone me because he needed someone closer at hand and more readily available than Beecham, to help him deal with an ever-increasing volume of Delius correspondence. Happily, Eric became more involved in Delius matters in the years following Sir Thomas's death than in the years immediately after Delius's.

This was made possible after 1964, when Eric became a Londoner. In 1961, after Beecham's death, Philip Emanuel had asked me whether I would act formally as Adviser to the Delius Trust. But, since the Trust was a Charity, my personal enthusiasms were not good enough for the Commissioners; the Senior Adviser had to be a more 'official' person. When Philip asked me whom I would most welcome, I had no doubt. Thomas Armstrong, Principal of the Royal Academy of Music, was the obvious man: he knew his Delius and loved the music. His name was put forward, and he was duly accepted as Senior Adviser to the Delius Trust. Joining him in 1961 were Norman Millar (known to Philip Emanuel as, formerly, Manager of Beecham's RPO) and myself. But it was Thomas Armstrong's initial advice that set the Delius Trust on the flourishing path it has maintained ever since, and it was he who, by inviting Fenby to teach at the RAM, made him a valuable Londoner, easily accessible to officials of the Delius Trust and a consulted arbiter of what Delius himself would have wanted. If, previously, Beecham had his private reasons for advising the Trust, without any specific consideration of Fenby's views, it was now clear that Fenby's views should be considered. On the other hand, with hindsight, it is now equally clear that, had Fenby been officially appointed as an Adviser to the Trust, he would have been placed in the invidious position of having to commission work from himself. For this, the post-Beecham Delius Trust was happily responsible.

Already ten years ago, in a tribute to Eric Fenby on the occasion of his eightieth birthday, I was able to record what a privilege it was to see more of Delius's amanuensis in London. Some memorable social occasions combined pleasure with Delius affairs. I remember how his *imprimatur* was sought on the recording of *The Magic Fountain*. Until then, despite Beecham, who first instigated the reinstatement of Delius's second opera in the canon, Fenby resisted, because Delius himself had regarded it as superseded. His reasons for this, Eric Fenby probably sensed as well as anyone: Delius had pillaged it for *Koanga*; it was overtly Wagnerian in its use of *leitmotiv* at a time when this might have been criticised as imitative; and, probably more important, it contained autobiographical elements. Conscientious as ever, Eric came over with the Delius Archive full score for us to follow as we listened to the tapes after dinner. Our worries were allayed by his instant reaction: 'I cannot imagine a better performance.' And so, I like to think, the evidence of the music itself won him over to approve the issue.

What Eric Fenby did for Delius in his lifetime is now musical history. His editorial labours for the Delius Trust added another chapter to that, and then, his recordings provided a crowning glory. From the time of the Bradford Delius Festival of 1962, Eric Fenby's unique position in the Delius saga came to be recognised so that he could continue to play an active part in the cause of Delius's music. Now in his tenth decade, the young man from Scarborough lives to witness the humble gratitude of his juniors for it.

INTRODUCTION 3: Lyndon Jenkins, Chairman of The Delius Society

The greatest stroke of luck the infant Delius Society ever had occurred when Eric Fenby agreed to become its President. This did not come about straightaway. Very few of us who were involved in founding the Society knew him at all, and he certainly did not know us. We knew *of* him, naturally, through his famous book, and some of us had observed his important comings-and-goings as Artistic Director of the Delius Festival held in Bradford in 1962. But by the time a surge of interest in Delius led to us gathering in London later that same year to inaugurate the Society, he once again seemed remote. He was not present, nor do I remember his name being mentioned.

Yet almost immediately afterwards came the announcement that he had agreed to become the Society's President. To me who, like most of the others present, had retired to await developments (perhaps idly wondering whether there would be any), this news was a clarion call. If such a remarkable man, I thought, has put his weight behind it, surely the Society has a real chance of success. And so it proved, beyond our wildest dreams.

Once having got him, of course, we were like children with a new toy. I expect we tried him unmercifully. On one occasion we thought to please him with a rare recording of a Delius work. 'Wrong pitch!' came his pained cry at the first sound, and that was the end of that. A friendly word from him at an early gathering emboldened me to write to ask if he would come to Birmingham to give a talk. Instead of a polite note of refusal, he rang up. He sounded terrifying: 'I will do this for you', - I can still hear the voice rising - 'but it must be the last!' was what he said. By the fateful day I was riddled with guilt. I paced the room. Who was I to ask this famous man to do anything? But he came, was affability itself, and presided over an evening that nobody who was present will ever forget.

Nor was it, as he had threatened, the last. Rather was it the first of many, many such occasions when we have sat avidly at his feet as he brought to life for us people we never knew: Gardiner, Beecham, Maclean, Grainger, Laughton, Kempe; or given us priceless insights into the man who was Delius; and, most important of all, helped us through his own devoted example to a greater understanding and love for the marvellous music that has been our focus for more than thirty years,

All through those years he has been the most loyal, caring and *interested* President any society could have. No distant figurehead he, but a hands-on friend who has always given much, much more of his time than we had any reasonable right to expect. Only Rowena and the family, to whom we feel the same sense of devotion and gratitude, know the extent of it. To them we might say, echoing the very sentence that began Delius's letter to Eric's parents in 1931: 'These are only a few words to thank you once more for letting us have Eric so long.'

And to Eric we say, with an affection that comes from the bottoms of our hearts: Thank you for lending us your name and your distinction so generously and devotedly. It is impossible to imagine that without you the Delius Society would have been anything like so interesting, so enjoyable or so influential as it has been.

EDITOR'S INTRODUCTION

*I marvel when I think of his courage and stamina, sometimes
dictating no more than a bar or two of orchestration a day, never
discussing the work but keeping at it day by day with an iron
determination and will, retaining details in his mind and going
back, correcting, improving it. It was quite incredible.*

Elsewhere in this book it is with these very words that Eric Fenby has
described his admiration for Delius's resolve while he himself, at the
composer's dictation, painstakingly took down, note by note, the *Songs of
Farewell*. Can we any less marvel at the courage and stamina of that
young Yorkshireman who, with his own determination and will, achieved
something surely unparalleled in the history of music? Is his own
achievement any less incredible? And should any reminder be necessary,
let the reader play Eric's own recording of *Songs of Farewell*, or take out
the score, and try to imagine the sheer effort involved.

There have been many whose great privilege it has been to know
Eric Fenby and - dare we presume? - to count him as a friend. They will
wish to join in sending him warmest greetings on his 90th birthday. There
can be no more fitting way to honour this happy occasion than with the
publication of a book which celebrates a lifetime's devotion to the music
and the memory of a great composer.

The story of Eric's time with Delius has long been known to anyone
interested in the composer through what has rightly been acclaimed as a
classic of its kind, his own account in *Delius as I knew him*, first
published in 1936 (coincidentally the same year in which W H Reed's
Elgar as I knew him appeared). But through the medium of television it
reached a wider audience when it was adapted for Ken Russell's
remarkable 1968 BBCTV film *Song of Summer*. A more personal account
of that same period was given in the 1982 Yorkshire TV documentary
Song of Farewell, for which Eric specially revisited Delius's house in
Grez-sur-Loing. A year earlier, largely at the instigation of Christopher
Palmer and with the support of the Delius Trust, he was invited to record
for Unicorn-Kanchana all those dictated orchestral works that form *The
Fenby Legacy*, a project that was later extended to include some works
outside the canon.

Eric was born in Scarborough in 1906. His father was second tenor
in a well-known male-voice quartet. A largely self-taught musician and
blessed with perfect pitch, he once astonished his father by saying that it

was 'thundering in E flat'. His early training was as an organist, and already at the age of 12 he was appointed to Holy Trinity Church. At his school in Scarborough, Eric founded a small orchestra and composed his first piece of music, which was performed at Speech Day in 1921. On leaving school at 16, he was articled to Claude Keeton, organist of St Martin's Church, whose pupils had also included Malcolm Sargent and Thomas Armstrong, and he was soon busy rehearsing local choral societies and amateur orchestras. While his preference was for the organ rather than the piano, his keyboard skills put him much in demand as an accompanist for singers. Neither did he neglect his compositional gifts, and Alick Maclean, the renowned conductor of the Scarborough Spa Orchestra, allowed him to conduct one or two of his youthful works at the morning concerts in the Grand Hall.

It was one of those curious strokes of fate, the switching on of a radio during a stagnating game of chess, that first introduced Eric to the music of Delius. After reading of the composer's condition, he wrote first a 'fan letter' and then, several weeks later, one that was to alter the course of his life, in which he offered his assistance to the blind and paralysed composer who still had music within him. To the former came a warm acknowledgement, in Jelka Delius's handwriting, dated 9 June 1928:

My dear young friend,

Your sympathetic & appreciative letter gave me the greatest pleasure.

I am always so glad when I hear that my music appeals to the young!

I know Scarborough quite well; when a school-boy I used to spend my summer holidays at Filey and my memories of all the happy days on that coast are still very green.

Most likely the Philharmonic choir will give the Mass of Life again under Kennedy Scott next year[1], when perhaps you may be able to hear it.

---

[1]   In his letter, Eric had probably referred to a recent performance of *A Mass of Life*, on 16 May 1928 at Queen's Hall, with Charles Kennedy Scott conducting the Philharmonic Choir and the London Symphony Orchestra. This was only the work's fourth British hearing, earlier ones having been under Beecham in 1909 and 1913, and Paul von Klenau in 1925, all in London. The next British performance, with the Philharmonic Choir, would be under Beecham at the 1929 Delius Festival.

With warm greetings I remain
Sincerely yours
Frederick Delius

His second letter, dated 29 August, brought a prompt and searching reply:

Dear Mr Fenby,

I am greatly touched by your kind and sympathetic letter and I should love to accept your offer.

Come here by all means as soon as you can and see if you like it before deciding anything.

How old are you? And would I not be taking you away from your profession? What is your occupation? How much of a musician are you?

You know, this is a lovely spot, just a quiet little village and our house is in a big garden going down to the river, but of course we live very much alone.

Should you not have travelling money, please let me know at once and I will send it to you.

Perhaps the best way for you would be to travel from London during the night; for instance by Newhaven-Dieppe, leaving Victoria at 8.20 p.m. and arriving at Paris at 5.25 a.m. There you have to take a taxi to the Gare de Lyon, where you can have a nice breakfast in the Café of the station and you take the train at 9.10 a.m. to Bourron, our station, where you will be at 11 and where we will have you fetched if we know when to expect you.

With kind regards from my wife,
Frederick Delius[2]

We live very simply here - No grand clothes needed.

In a subsequent post-card, Jelka informed Eric of a forthcoming performance of *Sea Drift* at the Leeds Triennial Festival, on 3 October 1928. But, although he travelled to Leeds, 'owing to the stupidity of a minor official on the door' he was not even allowed to stand at the rear of

---

[2]   These letters are two of 22 from the Deliuses to Eric Fenby (from a correspondence of 141 letters and postcards in the Delius Trust Archive) reproduced in the second volume of Lionel Carley's *Delius: A Life in Letters*, Scolar Press 1988 (henceforth referred to as *DLL2*). None of Eric's letters to the Deliuses seems to have survived.

the Town Hall to hear the work. When Beecham later heard of this, he characteristically remarked, 'My dear boy, if I had only known I would have put you on the platform!'

Eric left Scarborough six days later, arriving at Grez-sur-Loing the following day. So began his association with Delius. Over the next six years his time was to be divided between France and England, and it was during such periods back at home that he returned to his own composing. On 3 April 1931 Delius, informing Eric that the first performance of the completed *Songs of Farewell* had been held back until the following year, suggested that

> this will give you breathing time and time to continue your own work, which you must, of course, not neglect, especially when the spirit moves you. . . I consider you now a thoroughly well equipped musician and you have an excellent idea of the orchestra and chorus and I am expecting that you will do something very original. Don't be disheartened if the first attempts do not come off exactly as you want, but go at it again. Don't get tired over a work, but in that case lay it aside and forget it for a while and then take it up again.[3]

Again, on 3 July Delius wrote: 'I am now greatly interested in the progress of your own Cello Concerto', and on 23 August Jelka was enquiring: 'Do tell me how your Cello Concerto is getting on. And are you meditating something else too?' (Amongst other accomplishments, Eric had learned to play the cello.) Yet again, on 14 January 1932, she wrote: 'I am delighted to hear you are working, and working well at your own music.'

However, with the exception of the pastiche overture *Rossini on Ilkla Moor*, Eric later destroyed all his compositions. As he has remarked, with the humility that is one of his most endearing characteristics: 'I came to the conclusion that I had not the talent for really original composition. It is a very salutary thing for a young man to come into contact with genius, and as far as composition is concerned, only genius matters.'[4] Among those works he destroyed was a symphony, a string quartet, and a choral setting of Francis Thompson's *The Hound of Heaven*. For someone whose alternative to going to Grez had once been entering a Benedictine monastery, this last work would seem to offer a striking contrast to a saturation in Nietzschean ideals.

---

3   *DLL2, op. cit.*, 380.

4   *DLL2, op. cit.*, 381-2.

Although at their first attempt Eric's collaboration with Delius seemed to meet an impasse, his musical gifts were never in doubt. Even before the first year was out, Jelka was writing about him to friends as being 'very gifted' and 'very musical', and, from a practical point of view, able to play the piano parts 'for any virtuosi who come'. More importantly, Delius was beginning 'to think of his music again'. By 1931 all the dictation work was effectively completed, and Jelka wrote a letter of deep appreciation to Eric's parents for the 'loan' of their son:

> These are only a few words to thank you once more for letting us have Eric so long! The work he has done for my husband is absolutely unique and it is almost a miracle that he came at all and then, that he worked so admirably.
>
> I want you to know how deeply we feel and appreciate what he has done. He has always been so steadfast and so painstaking and with his wonderful musical gift added to all those good qualities he has achieved it. It seems so glorious that all these works, that but for him would have remained mere sketches are now actually brought to Life and in the Publishers hands.
>
> We both hope that now Eric will start his own work and achieve great things![5]

Delius himself wrote[6]: 'Yes, my dear Eric, you have accomplished a really great work in helping me so splendidly all these last years. Without you all these works would never have seen the light.'

Thereafter, Eric's visits to Grez were shorter and less frequent[7], with his time there increasingly spent on caring for Delius. After Delius's death he was, as he himself put it, 'completely burnt out', so he was only too ready to accept the invitation from some friends to spend several weeks with them in Sweden. He returned to England in time to attend Beecham's memorable performances of *An Arabesque* and *Songs of Sunset* at the 1934 Leeds Festival. Sir Thomas, planning to stage *Koanga*

---

[5]   12 February 1931. *DLL2, op. cit.,* 379.

[6]   3 July 1931. *DLL2, op. cit.,* 381

[7]   Briefly summarised, the periods of Eric's time at Grez were: from his arrival on 10 October 1928 until 7 September 1929, from the end of January until October 1930, from mid-October 1931 for 6 weeks, from 1 September until 1 November 1932, from January until May 1933, and from 19 May 1934. Delius died on 10 June 1934.

the following year, asked Eric to prepare a vocal score. By December he was back at Grez, there to be somewhat startled at Jelka's suggestion that he should stay for the rest of her life. But as she wrote the following May to a friend[8]: '[Eric] has been staying with me since Xmas. But of course it can not go on and I *must* advise him to follow his musical career in England.' As it turned out, she had only a few days remaining to live. Already seriously ill, she caught a chill on the Channel crossing on her way to Delius's reinterment at Limpsfield in Surrey that same month, and was buried alongside her husband only four days after the ceremony.

In September 1935, to help promote the Covent Garden production of *Koanga*, Eric gave his first public lecture on Delius. On the opening night (which was broadcast) he gave his first radio talk[9], following which he was encouraged to write the book that Ernest Newman had been urging him to undertake, *Delius as I knew him*. This was accomplished within the space of about three months and was largely written 'out of his head'. Although he had started a diary at Grez, it became increasingly difficult to keep it up on top of his many duties and, besides, he had soon felt it unwise in case Delius got to know of it!

From 1936 until the war, Eric was music adviser to Boosey & Hawkes, the firm that had published all the Delius-Fenby dictated works. He had been asked by Ralph Hawkes to build up the orchestral catalogue, but after rejecting numerous scores because of their poor quality, Eric was almost on the point of resigning the post when John Ireland (the vocal score of whose *These things shall be* he had prepared at Ireland's request and whose *London Overture* was one of the works to be selected) mentioned the then little-known Benjamin Britten as the coming man in English music. Britten's *Variations on a theme of Frank Bridge* was the first score that Eric submitted to Hawkes.

At about this time Eric's composing led him in another direction. Through his friendship with Scarborough hotelier Tom Laughton and his more famous brother Charles, he was invited to provide the music for Alfred Hitchcock's 1939 film, *Jamaica Inn*. This would have been followed by at least one more film score, had not war intervened. Instead, the next few years were to be spent mainly in music educational work.

The early war months found Eric teaching at the Howard-Jones School of Music in London. Once he had received his call-up papers, he

---

8   To Marie Clews, 12 May 1935. *DLL2, op. cit.,* 455.

9   see pages 206-210.

joined the Royal Artillery, 231st Searchlight Regiment, and was stationed at a training camp in Blandford, Dorset, for what he has described as 'the most ghastly year in my life'. There he endured the rigours of 'square-bashing' as well as having the dubious distinction of being in charge of the white-lining and road-making squad - and the camp incinerator! All the same, while at Blandford he managed to form a garrison military band. Relief eventually came via the camp adjutant who, as luck would have it, had been a neighbour in London of those great friends of the Deliuses, Norman and Adine O'Neill. Through him, Eric was invited to lecture on Delius at the Southern Command Headquarters, as a result of which he was soon transferred to the Army Education Corps at Bulford, Wiltshire, under the auspices of ENSA. There he also conducted the Southern Command Orchestra, made up of many familiar faces from the London orchestras. Before long he received a commission that led to him running courses at the Royal Army Education Corps at Cuerdon Hall, Preston, preparing personnel for civilian life on demobilisation. But the most notable event of that period was neither musical nor military, but the occasion of his marriage to Rowena, then a nurse at the Scarborough hospital whom he 'rescued from the x-ray department'.

After the war, back in his native Yorkshire, he founded and directed the music department of the North Riding Training College, in Filey Road, Scarborough, from 1948 until 1962. On the death of Sir Thomas Beecham in 1961, Eric was appointed Artistic Director of the Delius Centenary Festival in Bradford. For his work in this connection he was awarded an OBE. Then, in 1964, Sir Thomas Armstrong invited him to join the staff of the Royal Academy of Music as Professor of Composition, a post he held with distinction until 1978. Further recognition came his way when in 1968 he became chairman of the Composers' Guild of Great Britain, and in 1972 he joined the committee of the Royal Philharmonic Society. In 1984 he was made an Honorary Member of the RPS, a rare honour which he valued highly.

In the years following Beecham's death, the reputation of Delius (as of many other British composers) was at a comparatively low ebb, and Eric did much to restore the balance by giving lecture recitals on the composer all over the country, occasionally broadcasting, and sometimes performing in public as accompanist. At a time when recordings of Delius's music were much less frequent than they are today, it was invariably to Eric that the gramophone companies turned for an authoritative sleeve note. In 1971 he contributed a volume on Delius to

Faber's 'The Great Composers' series, and he continued to enrich the catalogue with his arrangements of Delius's works.

When the Delius Trust was engaged on the completion of the Collected Edition of the Works of Frederick Delius begun by Beecham, Eric's collaboration was eagerly sought in connection with the editing of certain works because of his unique knowledge of those scores. But his experience was put to its severest test in 1979-80. Just as in 1930, when the full score of *Koanga* was thought to be lost and Eric had set about reconstructing it from the orchestral parts, so fifty years later, with the full score of the unperformed *Margot La Rouge* missing, he was commissioned by the Trust to re-orchestrate the complete opera. With no orchestral parts and working from Ravel's piano score, he had largely to rely on his memory of playing the opera to Delius from the full score. Only after the task had been completed and his version had received its first performance (in a BBC studio recording that was subsequently issued on disc) was the original score found. And only then could one marvel at the closeness of the correspondence between the two scores.

In 1976, as a 70th birthday tribute, Christopher Redwood, then Editor of the *Delius Society Journal*, assembled a collection of essays entitled *A Delius Companion* (John Calder 1976) 'to honour the young man from Scarborough on his seventieth birthday on behalf of us all', as Felix Aprahamian wrote in his introduction. At the time of his 75th birthday, Eric recorded for Unicorn-Kanchana *The Fenby Legacy*, its initial LP release coinciding with a revised edition of *Delius as I knew him* (Faber Paperbacks 1981). His appearance on disc as conductor was followed by several notable concert engagements, in England and in America, including *Appalachia* with the London Symphony Orchestra in London and at Daytona Beach, Florida, in 1982, *Songs of Farewell* at Jacksonville, Florida, in 1983, *A Song of Summer* on several occasions, the première staged production of *Margot La Rouge* at St Louis in 1983, and the Requiem at a Royal Philharmonic Society concert in London in 1984. He has also conducted at the Annual Delius Festival in Jacksonville, Florida where he is always a much honoured guest and in whose name the Fenby Lecture has been instituted. Since the inauguration in 1962 of the Delius Society, he has carried out his role as its President over and beyond the call of duty. His loyalty to Delius has been unwavering, and he has not hesitated to voice his opposition to the performance of early immature works that do not show their composer in the best light.

And so to this present volume. Five years ago, as Editor of the *Delius Society Journal*, I wanted to mark Eric's 85th birthday with a special issue consisting of a selection of his writings on Delius. He and Rowena had by then moved from their London flat and returned once more to his native Scarborough. I duly set about collecting all his articles on Delius, his record and programme notes, and even the scripts of his broadcast talks held at the BBC's Written Archive Centre, at Caversham. This turned out to be a far richer harvest than I had anticipated, but I also learned that Eric had been hoping to publish his writings in a more permanent form, and so the birthday issue of the *Journal* instead took on another form[10]. Eric then asked me if I would assist him in the publication of his writings. Unfortunately, a period of poor health prevented his active participation in the project, but the approach of his 90th birthday seemed the ideal occasion for the appearance of such a book, and this opportunity was quickly seized by John Bishop of Thames Publishing. All this would not have been possible without the financial support of the Delius Trust and the Delius Society, two organisations which readily acknowledge their debt to Eric and which are proud to be associated with this project. It is appropriate, too, that there should also be a contribution from the Estelle Palmley Memorial Fund, established in memory of a former and much-loved secretary of the Delius Society.

This book gathers together all of Eric's significant writings and talks on Delius. The first half contains articles of a general nature, arranged chronologically, while the second half is concerned solely with the works of Delius, arranged by category. Inevitably, there is occasionally some repetition of detail from one article or note to another, but these have generally been left untouched so as not to upset the structure of their context. More importantly, these essays can be enjoyed on more than a purely musical level. Few commentators on music write with such an exquisite command of the English language, and readers of *Delius as I knew him* will need no reminder of Eric's skill, sensitivity and fluency with the written word.

What more can one add, except to say that this book is dedicated to Eric, in profound admiration and gratitude, in the name of all lovers of the music of Delius.

Stephen Lloyd
March 1996

---

[10] In addition to three items reprinted in this volume (the interviews with Robert Layton and Fred Calland, and the talk on Visitors to Grez), that issue consisted of an '85th Birthday Documentation' which has been updated and amended as appendices to this book.

Part One

Articles and Talks

FREDERICK DELIUS

Sir,- So much utter nonsense has been written lately in the Press about Frederick Delius, his music, his illness, and his recent inclusion in the New Year's Honours list, that I make no apology for writing in an effort to correct the false impressions created and to give the truth to musical readers.

The following is an example: According to the British United Press, Delius, on hearing the news of the Honour, at Grez-sur-Loing, said: 'This has made me the happiest man in the world. It is wonderful. It is good to know they still remember me in England.'

Now this is pure invention. Delius never made such statements. For the last six months I have been living with Delius as his secretary, and during that time there has been only one Press interview, which was given last Friday to a Daily Express reporter at which I was present, and as Delius never saw anyone from the British United Press I am amazed to read this cutting, which I received from England today. Whilst Delius appreciates the honour conferred on him, yet he strongly resents the publication of things which he has never said.

Again, in a recently published book, 'A Musical Pilgrimage in Yorkshire,'[11] nearly everything written with reference to Delius and his work is entirely wrong. On Page 85 we learn that 'in 1887 he was living in Harrogate, and in this year played a violin solo at a Knaresborough concert,' and on Page 22 a further reference to this event is made:- 'Mr Delius, of Harrogate, charmed the audience with his violin solos.' Mr Delius never lived in Harrogate nor did he go to Knaresborough to charm the audience on this occasion.

Similarly, on Page 86, we are invited 'to consider his "Brigg Fair," his "Sea-drift," his "Eventyr," and other musical dramas! (the interjection is mine), or his many fine songs (published under the pseudonym of Peter Warlock), we are always convinced of a certain original expression, etc.'

Now this is deplorable; it reveals an unbelievable ignorance, for Peter Warlock is the pen-name of Philip Heseltine, and, although the author corrects his error in the Errata column, it is difficult to understand a mentality which does not even take the trouble to make sure of the facts before rushing into print.

Lastly, I quote another example of this sort of reference from an

---

[11] J Sutcliffe Smith, Mus. Doc., *A Musical Pilgrimage in Yorkshire*, Richard Jackson Ltd., Leeds n.d.

article, 'Frederick Delius,' by the same author, which appeared in the January issue of 'Yorkshire Homes.' Here we are told that 'Sea-drift' is best described by the term 'elusive': and later on we rub our eyes when we read that the composer is 'lonely and melancholy.' Obviously this sort of musical journalism cannot be said to add to Delius's pleasure when, apart from its intrinsic worth, its essential implications are definitely false.

Delius, despite his illness, still goes on working, and retains his wonderful spirits to such a degree that one cannot but admire his heroism.- Yours, etc.,

ERIC FENBY.

Grez-sur-Loing, March 6.

Yorkshire Post, 9 March 1929

DELIUS'S LAST YEARS

by Eric Fenby

(The Musical Times, July 1934)

I have been asked to write a few words about the last years of Frederick Delius's life, and upon the conditions of the work which it was my privilege to do as his musical assistant. I find myself assenting with mixed feelings, even reluctance, for in my heart I feel that silence would have been the nobler tribute. I am too near the painful and heart-breaking events that preceded his death, when it seemed so often that the height of human endurance had been reached, only to find that still more demands were to be made on his frail spirit. The shock of his wife's recent illness undoubtedly hastened the end. For nearly forty years her loyalty and devotion never failed him. From 1928 to 1933 his condition remained much the same; but this year he became considerably thinner and more pathetically feeble: yet, four days before he died there was no indication that death was imminent.

Delius was a most complicated and contradictory personality. He was a man of the utmost truthfulness in all things. Everything and everybody was subservient to his ruthless devotion to his art. It was his life. There was no nonsense about him, nor would he tolerate it in others. He possessed a fine common sense, an extraordinary insight, and a keen wit. Fearless, he was often outspoken to an alarming degree, and even in his last years, though he was but the relic of a man physically, a few minutes in his presence was sufficient to reveal his exceptional vitality. No more proof of this is needed than a moment's reflection on the almost unbelievable difficulties under which he composed his last works. Surely it is no exaggeration to say that never was music written so laboriously. It was impossible for him to work longer than an hour and a half a day. He used to be carried to the music room at 4 p.m. and brought away exhausted at 5.30 p.m., and was rarely able to continue on the next day. Thus it took days for him to dictate in full score what in his prime would have been accomplished in an hour. In 1928-29 he completed by dictation two works for the Delius Festival - *A Late Lark* (poem by Henley) for tenor and orchestra, and *Cynara* (poem by Dowson) for baritone and orchestra. In the following year he wrote *A Song of Summer* for orchestra, the Violin and Pianoforte Sonata No 3, and *Caprice and Elegy* for cello and chamber orchestra; but these works were child's play compared with the task of dictating *Songs of Farewell* (Walt Whitman) for double chorus and orchestra. Next followed the *Idyll* for soprano, baritone and orchestra, and the short *Fantastic Dance*. Whatever the merits of these works they are at least a monument to his supreme courage, wonderful patience, and heroism. No one will ever know what Sir Thomas Beecham has done for Delius in editing his scores, nor the amount of deep thinking and industry he has put into their preparation for performance. We have not to be reminded of the results. But we have all to be reminded of the splendid pioneer work of the late Dr Hans Haym, of Elberfeld. Without his untiring efforts Delius would have had to wait years longer for recognition in Germany.

May all young artists imitate his artistic integrity. His death is a great loss to the world of music, and, may I add, to me personally.

Edited by Richard Capell
THE WORLD OF MUSIC

THE YOUNG DELIUS
AN IDYLL OF THE 'NINETIES

By ERIC FENBY

(The Daily Telegraph, Saturday, 19 October 1935)

The Frederick Delius existing in most people's minds is the tragic figure and relic of a man represented by the awful photographs taken of him during the last years of his life. This was the Delius whom Londoners saw in the flesh when he came over from France to attend the festival of his music given in his honour by Sir Thomas Beecham in 1929.

I want here to give some idea of the man he was at the time of the composition of *Koanga* - I mean the Delius of the late nineties.

To judge by one or two unpublished photographs taken about that time, and by chance remarks made by the composer to me when I caught him in reminiscent mood, I am able to piece together a picture of him in those days, a necessarily imperfect picture, but one by which I should prefer him to be remembered, for the picture by which he is most likely to be remembered is but the shadow of the man.

Delius must have been a tall, handsome young fellow, aristocratic in bearing, meticulous in dress, fond of sports - he was a very keen cricketer and often played for an English XI in Paris. He must have been a very wilful, restless, self-centred young man -very sure of himself - a man who knew all there was to be known about food and wine, not to speak of the fair sex. A prodigious reader, a stimulating and entertaining talker with a dry wit curiously his own; often, I am sure, a very trying companion - in short, a most unusual young man.

* * * *

As a young musician, he knew his Wagner inside out, and worshipped Chopin, Grieg and Bizet - particularly the delicacy of the latter's scoring - and if, at times, he found himself writing music coloured by theirs he did not mind, for he believed in working through his influences, not avoiding them. His was a slow development, and he had to dig very deep for his musical gold. Such, then, was the young composer who set to work on the score of *Koanga*.

He had contemplated the writing of a Negro opera for a long time, and, finding a subject that appealed to him in Cable's novel, *The Grandissimes*, he even tried to make his own libretto. His previous attempts in this direction had failed, and consequently he had wasted a good deal of beautiful music, particularly in the case of *Irmelin*, his first opera, in which much of the music has unmistakable charm and freshness. Those who saw *Koanga* at Covent Garden will remember a charming little piece for orchestra, which Sir Thomas found it necessary to interpolate during a change of scenery. This was an unpublished prelude which Delius dictated to me, developing it from a few musical ideas that he had always liked in that very early opera *Irmelin*.

Delius, however, came to the point of seeing that he had neither the time nor the literary gift for the task of making his own libretto, and he therefore turned to his friend Keary, with whom he shared a flat in Paris, to write it for him. Keary set to work on it at a little village near Fontainebleau called Bourron, 20 minutes' walk over the fields from Grez, the village where Delius was in the following year to settle down for life. When the book of the first act was completed, Keary sent for Delius, who was in Paris, asking him to come to Bourron the next day to read it through. Trivial though it may seem, this incident influenced the whole course of the composer's life.

* * * *

It must be explained that shortly before this, Delius had met a young painter, Jelka Rosen, who appeared to be very enthusiastic about his music and not a little solicitous for his future well-being. Delius had confided to her that, his father having refused to make him an allowance to enable him to devote himself to composition, he would have to earn his living by teaching.

Miss Rosen was now at Grez, staying with her friend Ida Gerhardi, another young painter, at the Hôtel Chevillon, then a great rendezvous for artists; and hearing that Delius was at Bourron with Keary, she invited him over to lunch. It was lovely summer weather, and those who have not seen Grez on such a day cannot realise the beauty of the old church, the ruin, the gardens going down in terraces to the river, the old bridge, the light on the lines of poplars, the plain edged by a distant stretch of wood. The young couple took a boat from the hotel landing-stage and, going under the bridge, landed and walked up what appeared to be an overgrown garden. Skirting the pond they eventually found themselves in a courtyard of a rambling house looking on to the street. The young woman, with prompt intuition, decided that this was the very place for Delius to work in, and from that moment she resolved that by hook or crook she would buy the property.

Meanwhile, Delius returned to Paris and worked hard on the first act of *Koanga*. It was his habit in those days to work through the night and sleep during the day. He used to tell me that he smoked incessantly as he worked, that a bottle of red wine was never out of reach, and that he sometimes would leave his work in the middle of the night and steal out for a chat at some café table with his painter friends.

The music for Act II was finished by the end of 1896, and in the New Year Delius decided to return to Florida for a few months to put his orange-grove in order. Keary, having completed the libretto, handed over the last act to the composer, who wrote the greater part of the music for it on that second visit to Florida.

Miss Rosen, in Delius's absence, and unknown to him, had persuaded her mother to buy her the property at Grez. She was now installed there, but had had little or no news of Delius. However, the day after he returned to Paris from Florida she received a postcard announcing his intention of coming down for a week-end. From that week-end Grez became his home, and it was here that *Koanga* was completed and all his finest music conceived.

Delius had set his heart on a first performance of the opera in London, but after repeated efforts to interest people in its production here he returned home to France disheartened and discouraged. The composer had to wait seven years before *Koanga* was eventually performed in Germany, at Elberfeld, in 1904.

To judge by the number of mistakes in the autograph score - wrong notes, missing accidentals, miscalculations in the dynamic markings, all of which had been faithfully copied into the orchestral parts and not corrected at the rehearsals - those Elberfeld performances must have been pretty bad. But Delius, inexperienced and, I understand, pathetically helpless at rehearsals, was too absorbed by the general effect produced by his music and too thrilled by the wonderful experience of at last hearing it on the orchestra to bother about details.

* * * *

Delius believed that the composer, no less than the poet, has something to say about life. For him music was an outburst of the soul. He regarded life as a tragedy made liveable by those rare moments of supreme happiness which come and go, never more to return. At the thought of the 'never-more', music would well up within him, and a few words:

'But my mate no more, no more with me . . .
We two together, no more, no more' -

a few words such as these, and often very undistinguished words, would draw from his music of such intense feeling as to be almost unbearable.

In *Sea Drift*, in *Songs of Sunset, A Village Romeo and Juliet, Cynara, Songs of Farewell* - it is always the same - that same longing for the perpetuation of impossible bliss. It mattered not whether it was an opera, a song, an orchestral or a choral work; it was always that same longing that was uppermost in him, inspiring his finest conceptions.

Was it a coincidence that Delius's most cherished possession was Gauguin's *Nevermore*, which he bought direct from the painter? Delius was only interested in the story of Koanga and Palmyra in so far as the 'never-more' was concerned; hence the complete lack of dramatic action, the absurd situations, and the tameness of his musical characterisations.

A detail or two about the incorporation of music of earlier date may interest the composer's admirers. The dance music in the second act was borrowed from an orchestral suite called *Florida*, written in 1889. The original orchestration he retained throughout, and he added voice parts for Palmyra and the chorus to suit the jolly situation. The short prelude to Act III Delius borrowed from his discarded opera, *The Magic Fountain*.

DELIUS
BBC Radio Script by ERIC FENBY

Rehearsal: 0900 Friday 8 March 1946
Transmission: 1040-1100 Friday 8 March 1946
Light Programme (Forces Educational Broadcast)

[Passages of text in square brackets were omitted for the actual broadcast]

ANNOUNCER:

This is a Forces Educational Broadcast. We have had a number of requests for a programme about Delius, and Eric Fenby, who knew the composer well, is in the studio to talk to you about the man and his music.

FENBY:

I remember as a boy being struck by some words of Emerson[12] which seemed to describe the ideal mental state of an artist: 'If you would write to any purpose, you must be perfectly free from within. Give yourself the natural rein; think of no pattern, no patron, no paper, no press, no public. Think of nothing, but follow your own impulses. Give yourself as you are, what you are, and how you see it. Every man sees with his own eyes or does not see at all. Bring out what you have. If you have nothing, be an honest beggar, rather than a respectable thief.'

As a youth, I went to France in 1928 to help Delius to finish his uncompleted works, by dictation, for he had then become blind and paralysed. Once I had crossed the threshold of Delius's house in the tiny hamlet of Grez-sur-Loing, on the edge of the forest of Fontainebleau, I found myself in another world, peaceful and self-sufficient, which centred around the figure of Delius. It was a world with its own laws, its own standards, its own particular sense of beauty and its own music. It had been made for music-making, and there was an unheard of reverence for work. If you were pausing on the bridge at Grez, and gazing on that cluster of cottages, their garden walls green with climbing vines, and quiet homeliness about their tiny wash-houses under the trees by the water's edge, you could hardly imaging that over that wall between the church and ruined castle there existed a world such as this. A painter's paradise, to be sure, but hardly the sort of place in which a great composer would choose to spend his life. But then, Delius had always disliked the society of musicians. He had found them such a dull and uninspiring lot, they talked about nothing but 'technique, technique'. [The world of beauty was a closed book to them, it seemed. He had much preferred the more vital companionship of painters, and Grez had always been a haunt of painters. There were old men still living who recalled how they had stood as cheeky little boys behind Corot as he worked at his easel, puffing at his pipe under a great umbrella down by the mill. Writers, too, had felt its charm. Strindberg had once stayed for several weeks at the Hôtel Chevillon, then a famous rendezvous for artists, and had not Robert Louis Stevenson proposed to Fanny Osborne on the bridge?] Here in Grez, Delius and his wife, also a gifted artist, had lived contentedly for over thirty years, jealously guarding their little world from intrusion.

---

12   Ralph Waldo Emerson (1803-1882), American poet and essayist.

Nothing can ever dim the memory of my first meeting Delius, as I stood, a little nervous and hesitating at the door. There was Delius, gaunt, pale, his fine classical head proud and erect as he sat upright in his chair surrounded by a great screen. He wore a white shirt open at the neck, and a checked rug hung loosely about his knees. He was obviously a sick man and I wished I had known him in his prime. We talked about Yorkshire, the wolds and moors, Filey Bridge, Festival cricket at Scarborough, and conversation flowed pleasantly and easily enough until suddenly turned to music - how, I cannot remember. But I shall never forget the change that came over him when, in my innocence, I ventured an opinion on English music. He frowned, then pursed his lips in a contemptuous smile, a smile I grew to anticipate whenever visitors began skating on this ice! In the awkward silence which followed, I realised something of his complete intellectual isolation.

Frederick Delius was born in Bradford in 1862, his father, a merchant of considerable affluence, being of German-Dutch extraction and his mother English. The Delius household must have been unique. Delius would often recall how his father would regularly engage notable quartets to play his favourite works in his drawing-room, and how he himself had played second violin in the family quartet. [Possibly this accounted for his violent dislike of chamber music in later years; certainly during the time I knew him he used to say with dry humour that he had had enough of the quartets of the great masters. I remember our sitting in readiness to hear a performance of his own quartet by a celebrated American string quartet who had asked if they might come down from Paris to play it to him in the garden. When the tuning was done, the leader approached the old man sitting there aloof and silent in his carriage and said, 'Sir, before playing your own quartet, we will play you one of the last quartets of Beethoven, Op. No. . . .' 'Oh no you won't,' interrupted Delius. 'My quartet, please, or nothing at all.']

Now great as was his father's love of music, he had no idea of young Frederick becoming a professional musician. He had other plans for him. Frederick was determined that he was meant for music and that all obstacles must be overcome. Eventually he persuaded his father to set him up as an orange-planter in Florida, and once there, left the orange-growing to a Negro servant and devoted his time to writing music under the critical eye of Thomas Ward, an organist in Jacksonville. Then there came one day when the excellent Ward confessed to his pupil that he had taught him all he knew, and suggested his going to Leipzig to study. Delius again had his own way with his father. A few weeks in the pedantic atmosphere of the Conservatoire convinced him that Ward had been wrong; [the professors, unlike Ward, taught with no imagination] but Leipzig did at least offer opportunities for hearing music. The chief event of these Leipzig days was his meeting Grieg, with whom he quickly became friendly. From this time dates Delius's love of Scandinavian literature and his yearly holiday in Norway, where in later years he built a house in the mountains. After three years at Leipzig, Delius again found himself at the cross-roads. Fortunately his uncle in Paris offered him a home [and means of subsistence] so that he might work at composition. From that time onwards to the day of his death in 1934, France became his home, and he rarely left it except for his visits to Norway, or to attend performances of his works in Germany and England. Finding Paris too distracting, he finally settled at Grez, the country retreat I have described, and here all his greatest works were written. He was then in his early thirties and already working on his third opera, *Koanga*, in which the music is coloured by Delius's feeling for Negro life on a slave plantation.

(Record : *Koanga*)

So far Delius had laboured under one very severe handicap. Only twice had he heard the sound of his music on the orchestra, once at the age of twenty-six, and again when he was thirty-one. He had to wait until he was thirty-seven before he was able to profit to the utmost by such a necessary experience, and that on the occasion of the Delius concert at St James's Hall, London, in 1899, which he gave at his own expense. He told me that after the concert he was so conscious of the faults of his music that he could not rest, but left for Grez early the next morning, so eager was he to take up his sketches of the orchestral work *Paris* and apply the technical knowledge that he had just acquired. Certainly *Paris - the Song of a Great City* is greatly in advance of anything he had written hitherto. [Had there been the same opportunities in his day as in ours for the young composer of talent to get a hearing, I doubt whether Delius would have found himself any the sooner. No matter how technically proficient a man may be, his inner development can never be hurried. If a man has something worth saying, he will manage to say it somehow, no matter how clumsily. It is having that something worth saying that is the important thing. Some of us think that Delius had that gift in the highest degree.]

(Record : *Paris*)

What, then, was his particular contribution to music? It was a greatness of mind which ranged in a purely personal art of contemplation. Music, he thought, should be a simple and intimate thing, direct and immediate in its appeal, a thing of instinct rather than of learning, of the heart rather than of the head; he held that the amateur musician is better without a knowledge of the science of music. 'When you see a lovely rose, you treasure it as it is,' he used to say; 'you don't pull it to pieces to appreciate its beauty and find out where its delicious perfume comes from. So it should be with music.'

(Record : *A Village Romeo and Juliet*)

Music, then, was little more than a habit of feeling convincingly in sounds. It would hardly be an exaggeration to say that life for him was entirely a matter of feeling, for he was contemptuous of learning [and completely anti-metaphysical]. For him the power to stir, or to be stirred, was always measured by the harmonic intensity of a work. Instead of tunes, his sketchbooks contain long processions of chords which move in a constant rising and falling movement like this (piano illustration). They defy analysis in terms of text-book grammar, and satisfy by instinct rather than rule. Here and there a few chords are ringed with the comment 'good' beside them and often contain in them the germs of a lovely passage. For instance, takes these chords - (plays) - Delius would then weave delightful arabesques round them in this way (plays). Then from these crude beginnings he would bring the music to life in his sensitive colourings of orchestral sound.

(Record : *Song before Sunrise*)

Notice how the music ebbs and flows in its own particular sense of melody and cadence. Sometimes the melody is formal in shape moving in lyric phrases of equal length as in verse. Here is an example from an interlude taken from his last opera, *Fennimore and Gerda*.

(Record)

Later in *Fennimore and Gerda* we find the melody shaping itself into phrases of irregular length, rather like poetic prose, and becoming more and more ornamental as the emotion intensifies. Listen to this exquisite rhapsodising between flute and oboe:

(Record)

Delius's will to work was not broken by his illness. A choral work, several orchestral works and a violin sonata were composed by dictation during his last years. The technique of dictation varied, often considerably, with each work. Much depended on the extent to which Delius had already arranged and sifted in his mind the musical matter of what he was going to say before calling for me to note it down. The final test was always the sound of his musical thought when transferred to the piano. Delius dictated with great rapidity and the accompanying mood was usually one of frenzied activity as he wriggled about in his chair, gesticulating wildly with his hands until, bathed in perspiration, he could go on no longer. If you had peeped into the music room on one of these occasions this is what you might have heard as I sat at the piano feverishly scribbling the notes down on MS paper:

(piano illustrations)

['A whole-note chord at the new bar; C, A violas; octave F# second violins; A, F# firsts; move each voice down a tone except the first halves of the first fiddles and hold for a dotted half-note and tell me what you've got.'

'Bb, G violas; octave Es, seconds; and G in the second halves of the firsts.'

'Good. Now add octave C in the first halves; mark it 'Divisi'. Next chord - violas, F#, Eb; seconds, octave Cs; Eb, second halves of firsts, and move the divisi octave to Bb. Hold it seven beats.'] 'Now play what you've got there. Good - good. Now a semi-quaver run up in tones in the solo flute from top D to A, three beats on A and then come down - (sings) - ti, er - ti, er - hold it for the rest of the bar.'

'Is that ti-er in the flute a G natural, Delius?'

'Yes, that flute figure suggests a seagull gliding by. Now horns, fourth beat of the last bar (sings phrase).' And so on.

It is impossible to do justice to so prolific a composer as Delius in so short a time. Among his [most] enduring achievements are his magnificent choral works [*A Mass of Life*, *Songs of Sunset*, *The Song of the High Hills*, *Sea Drift*, *Appalachia*, the lovely opera *A Village Romeo and Juliet* and his fine orchestral works *Paris*, *Brigg Fair*, *In a Summer Garden*, *On hearing the first cuckoo in Spring* and *Summer Night on the River*.

Delius was unique, a lonely figure, unaffected by theories and schools of thought, and all the vast paraphernalia of musical artifice; proud, refined, a self-absorbed aristocrat, giving musical expression to emotions common to all sensitive souls, - a poet's musician. No artist could be so poignant as he:]

(Record : 'O past! O happy life!' from *Sea Drift*)

ANNOUNCER:
That ends our Forces Educational broadcast on Delius. The speaker was Eric Fenby.

DELIUS AS I KNEW HIM

Speaker and script-writer: Eric Fenby
Producer: Michael Bell
BBC Third Programme
Wednesday 1 January 1947 6.40 - 7.00 p.m.
Rehearsal 5.10 p.m.

ANNOUNCER:
Mr Eric Fenby, who was closely associated with Delius for many years, is going to give an illustrated talk on 'Delius as I knew him'. Eric Fenby:-

FENBY:
It is good for a young artist to come into occasional contact with genius. He learns humility in a flash, and sees himself and his own efforts as never before. I said 'occasional' contact, for constant association with creative genius is fraught with danger for the younger man. Unless he is fortunate in differing in certain points of view, and has a slightly obstinate streak in his nature, he is sure to be absorbed completely into the mental world of the older man.

So strong and unique was the personality of Frederick Delius that, had I fallen entirely under his spell, he would have effaced me within a month. It was well that this was not so, for I was in daily contact with him for close on six years.

I have told elsewhere of the circumstances which led me as a youth to offer my services to him in the belief that some way might be found to enable him to finish his life's work, now that he was stricken with blindness and paralysis. I had expected to meet a great artist, but not a man so strangely different from his fellows.

There was nothing of the conventional musician about him. Had he been compelled to earn his bread professionally, I cannot think of any musical activity in which he would have succeeded. Breadth of outlook on all forms and styles of musical essential to the teacher he had none, nor was he able to explain any technical matter verbally. He would have been useless as an adjudicator because of his difficulty in making a decision, and probably would have got up and condemned the test pieces as drivel, and the competitors for wasting their time. He was opposed to the whole system of academic training in music, and certainly could not have passed any of the Associated Board of Music examinations himself.

I have never heard Delius play an instrument, of course, but his wife explained the manner in which he used to improvise at the keyboard in strings of chords which came to him by instinct, moving in emotional curves, something like this: (plays).

Anything in the nature of continuous runs he detested, and dismissed the music of the classical masters dryly as 'Scales and Arpeggios!' I can see him now, leaning back in his chair, surrounded by a great screen, and bored with the book I was reading aloud. 'Put it down, and see what's on the wireless,' he would say. If by chance the strains of Mozart or Beethoven came floating into the room, his usual comments were, 'Turn it off and go on reading' or 'Leave it on a minute, and listen . . . listen! Banal! Banal! Just listen. Fillings, my boy, fillings! Turn it off.' The truth is that he could not bear to hear any music but his own, apart from the first performances of new works by younger men. Here he showed astonishing interest, tolerance and concern. It was typical of his supreme individualism, however, that he should upbraid me severely for buying a miniature score of a Sibelius symphony. 'Throw the thing away,' he exclaimed, in slowly deliberate censurings. 'Go out into the woods, and listen to the music of Nature, and don't bother your young head about [the] symphony. It was played out long ago! Elgar, Sibelius, Bruckner, Mahler and the rest of 'em all spending their energies on long drawn-out movements padded with dull development. Twenty bars of deeply felt original music, true and beautiful, are worth pages of such note-spinning.'

This attitude towards composition has caused some to maintain that Delius's world represented a frame of mind rather than that of a composer. If the musical ancestry of such works as *Eventyr*, *Summer Night on the River*, *A Village Romeo and Juliet*, *Sea Drift* and the *Mass of Life* is untraceable, one cannot deny Delius's mastery of the purely technical problems he encountered in their composition. At his best, few composers have written so well. The new world of sound he created was kindled by a most unusual frame of mind, the sovereign influence of which, as he often admitted, was Nietzsche; though it must not be imagined that he subscribed to everything Nietzsche said.

At Christmas 1929, Delius presented me with a copy of Nietzsche's *Thus Spake Zarathustra*, asking his wife to mark the passages on which he had meditated since early manhood. I instance three:-

'New paths do I tread, a new speech cometh unto me; tired have I become - like all creators - of the old tongues. No longer will my spirit walk on worn-out soles.'

'Slow is the experience of all deep fountains: long have they to wait until they know what hath fallen into their depths.'

'I love the great despisers because they are the great adorers.'

Quick though I was to appreciate Nietzsche's lofty poetry which the composer recreated in terms of music in his noblest and grandest work, *The Mass of Life*, I was unresponsive to its philosophy. My own religious faith, steeped in the Christian mystics, was contrary to the mysticism of the pagan tone-poet. That was a fundamental difference of view to which I have referred. I think Delius often despaired of me, for he upheld the virtue of human masterfulness,

Ernest Newman, writing on the recent broadcast performances of the *Mass*, said 'There is a vigour in this work that one may commend to those who regard Delius as a nostalgic singer of the wistful and the drooping.' There was nothing wistful or drooping about Delius's personality. Nietzsche would have hailed certain aspects of his character - his disdain, his severity, his serenity, his extreme refinement - as attributes of his higher mortals. These qualities were tempered by a dry wit, a peculiar charm, a fastidious delight in the pleasures of the table, a boyish love of good detective stories, and, to the end, a dandyish love of clothes.

What excuses he made to have a bottle of wine brought up from the cellar at lunch! And what a barrage of questions he put to his man-servant! Had he got the right vintage; the right year? Was the bottle on ice? At what angle? Had he opened it yet? He would tell him the precise moment to uncork it! and so on. He couldn't eat the soup; it was not salted enough in the cooking. To add salt afterwards was unthinkable! In future he would taste it himself. They were to bring it to him down the garden the next morning whilst his wife read the letters.

He seldom praised anything or anybody, so that to earn his praise set the blood tingling. It was the same with his music to which he listened by highly powered wireless. I have seen him writhing in his chair in pained annoyance during certain performances of his works. 'Turn it off, and take pen and paper' he would order. 'Begin. Dear So-and-so. Your rendering of my music this evening was execrable, Punkt. (He always used the German for Full Stop.) You don't seem to understand my intentions, Punkt.' and he would thunder on like God Thor, hammering his points home with unanswerable forthrightness.

Letters from admirers he answered with touching simplicity, even humbleness, and his pleasure on hearing that his music was loved was unconstrained. There was a bigness and distinction about his nature grounded in an absolute sincerity touching all things, such as I have never seen in any man. No beggar who knocked at the door was turned away empty. I remember one, in particular, who was wined and dined to such repletion that afterwards he became so rowdy in the village that he had to be locked up, and kicked the prison door down in the night. Delius paid for the damage without a word.

His home life at Grez-sur-Loing, the tiny hamlet near Fontainebleau, where he lived in retirement for over forty years, was governed by the clock. His orderly routine, he told me, differed only in certain respects from the regular habits to which he had been accustomed before his illness. Everything and everybody were subservient to the main purpose of his life, music, and though much of it is dreamy in mood, there was little to suggest the dreamer. He had a good business head, and managed his affairs with astuteness and foresight. All his music, prior to the First World War, was published in Austria and Germany. Between 1914 and 1918 many of his copyrights were sold and resold by his publishers, unknown to him. At the end of the war he spent a small fortune defraying the costs of the prolonged litigation which ensued. This was a heavy blow to him, but he was singularly fortunate in his friends, and his shrewdness saved him from real hardship.

It can be imagined that I heard very little music during those six years. In the intervals of rest between his work on new compositions, we used to play records of his music to him which he always insisted that I should follow from the orchestral scores. No music was allowed throughout the actual period of composition, sometimes lasting many months. This was understandable. What was trying, and especially for an exuberant young man, was the abstention from all but the most necessary conversation at these times. I was a little puzzled by this until one day Delius happened to say, 'One should never live in a city to compose. There is too much talk. Nothing dissipates a composer's energy more than talk.' It would have been no hardship for me to join a Trappist order at the end of the year in which he wrote his last choral work, *Songs of Farewell*!

Whenever he felt well enough to dictate, Delius used to be carried to the music room, propped up in an armchair beside me at the pianoforte, and we were left alone until he could go on no longer. I can only say that it seemed helpless at first. Perhaps I had been to rash in venturing to help? My initiation could not have been more unpromising. If I failed in the early attempts, I know that nobody on earth could have made head or tail of the drawling monotone I was expected to decipher. When I had suggested that it might be helpful if he would sing it again, he repeated this amazing recital; on another note! It was fantastic!

There was a tremendous distance to travel before Delius was able to dictate with comparative ease. The technique of dictation varied, often considerably, with each work. Much depended on the extent to which Delius had already arranged and sifted in his mind the musical matter he wished me to put on paper. Sometimes he had no more than the roughest idea until that rough idea had been played over to him. The final test was always the sound of his musical thought when heard on the piano. It must not be assumed that composition by dictation proceeded in a calm and leisurely manner. On the contrary, Delius dictated with great rapidity and nervous excitement. He was quite incapable of pitching a note accurately, and this didn't make things any easier for me. The wonder is that having already written so much that is enduring, he had the courage to go on. His only real happiness, he contended, was the happiness of creating.

The opening bars of his Third Sonata for Violin and Piano were dictated something like this:-

'Are you ready?' 'Yes.' 'Ter-ter-ter-ter ter--ter-ter-ter-ter. Start on G in the bass. No, an octave lower. That's it. D, B flat ter - E, A ter-ter-ter-ter. Got it?' 'I'll play it.' 'Good, 4 beats in a bar. Ter-ter-ter-ter ter (second beat) ter-ter-ter-ter (fourth beat).' 'Is that the second beat tied over?' 'Yes, and tie the first four notes through the phrase. Play it.' 'These are to be tied?' (Piano) 'Yes; that's it. Now repeat it an octave higher.' (Piano) 'Now second beat, second bar, violin, ter-ter-ter-ter ter-ter-ter-ter - play it. (Piano) Now ter-ter-ter ter-ter-ter ti - in the accompaniment two triplets in the first beat, same chord. (Piano) No. Vary the second one. (Piano) That's it, and go on as before. Now play what you've got, and sing the melody. (Piano) No. Go on up in the fiddle part ter-ter-ter ter. (Piano) No, no. B natural. Ter - ter-ter-ter-ter.' 'Is that tied again?' 'Yes, after the third beat. Chord of D. Ter-ter-ter-ter-ter. No, sorry, higher. (piano: E) Yes. Ter-ter-ter-ter. (Piano) Yes. Now, inner part. Ti-er. (Piano) That's it. Now move down chromatically in the bass. (Piano) No, no, no . . . a quaver. That's right. Tar-da-da in bass. (Piano) Same again, ter-ter-ter-ter

ter on B. Ter-ter-ter-ter ti - F sharp. Tar tar, inner part down. (Piano) No. The other one . . . '

And so it went on. This was easy compared with the task of taking down his orchestral music, for even the roughest sketches were dictated instrumentally. For instance he would say:-

'Flute, third beat, top C sharp same rhythm as the opening figure, ti te ter-ter ter-te ti . . . hold it . . . now play it. (Piano) Right. Double it in the clarinet. (Piano) Yes. Harmony ter ter in first horn, C sharp second horn, D in bass clarinet, and change on the ti te, go down chromatically in the bass; horns a fifth. (Piano) Yes. Horns downwards A flat; yes, first horn to D.'

This is an actual passage from A *Song of Summer*. Every bar in each instrumental part was afterwards checked with the utmost care. I had to make the necessary transpositions in the case of English horn, clarinets and French horns, of course, to avoid complication, for it will be realised that there was much that might lead to misunderstanding. All this was child's play in comparison with the detailed work involved in *Songs of Farewell* for Double Chorus and Orchestra, the full score of which was actually engraved and on sale before the first performance.

The enormous strain of those years of work served to deepen our friendship. Despite his physical weakness, he seemed ageless, and I was unprepared for his end. It is twelve years since he died. Mercifully, he was spared the anguish of another world war which he prophesied as early as 1930.

I often wonder whether the spirit still lives at Grez amid that cluster of houses nestling round the church, the old bridge and ruined castle; and whether that lovely garden down by the river blooms in summer like the Paradise Garden he knew.

(Record : *The Walk to the Paradise Garden*)

ANNOUNCER:
Eric Fenby, who was closely associated with Delius for many years, has been giving an illustrated talk on 'Delius as I knew him'.

AS I KNEW HIM: A Personal Portrait 'DELIUS'

by Eric Fenby

Transmission:
Monday 26 November 1951 : 0830-0845
Tuesday 27 November 1951 : 1900-1915
Thursday/Friday 29/30 November 1951 : 0000-0015
Friday 30 November 1951 : 1345-1400

ANNOUNCER:

'As I Knew Him'. Today we give the twelfth in a series of personal portraits of famous men and women of yesterday. Today's portrait is of the composer, Delius, and it is drawn for us by Eric Fenby, who lived with him for six years and to whom Delius dictated a number of his later works.

ERIC FENBY:

Twenty-three years have passed since my first encounter with Delius - but the memory of it is still vivid. The sensitive strangeness of his music had led me to expect something unusual when, a young man, I set out from my home in Yorkshire to cross the English Channel for France - where Delius was then living. But when I eventually reached his house in the little village of Grez-sur-Loing, I was quite unprepared for what I found there - and for the sudden impact of Delius's appearance and personality. I can still see him - as I saw him for that first time - framed by a great screen, sitting like a marble statue of a Roman aristocrat, propped up in a chair. A white shirt, open at the neck, emphasised his gauntness, and a checked rug loosely about his knees. On his wife's announcing me, a long arm was thrust out towards me, the elegant fingers hanging limply. A sudden jerk of the head (a characteristic I was to know well later on) and he greeted me in a strong, yet slightly drawling voice of pleasant tenor quality. Like myself, he was a Yorkshireman and it was of Yorkshire that we started to talk, I remember - about the wolds and moors, about Filey and cricket at Scarborough - and in his dry, humorous way, he told me a good deal about his happy childhood in Bradford. Over lunch I warmed to this strange man and told him without embarrassment how much his music meant to me. He received this with surprising humility. So far so good. But I went on, in my innocence. to make a fatal mistake: I ventured a remark on the subject of English music. 'English music,' he said with biting contempt, 'English music. I've never heard of any.' And the rest of the meal we ate in silence.

I would gladly have said good-bye to him then and there and gone back to England, leaving my promise unfulfilled. The promise was this. Sometime before, I had heard that Delius had been stricken with blindness and paralysis. I wrote to offer my services to him - as a musician - and in the hope that in some way I might help him to continue to compose his music. Delius had accepted my offer. And now, here I was, in his house - how could I go back on my offer? Well, of course, I stayed - in spite of the chilly reception and the doubts I began to have on that first day about whether we could ever get along together. And in the days that followed I began to understand more and more what I was up against. I saw that the virtue of human masterfulness which he upheld in life had kindled a supremely individual attitude to music. Everything and everybody was subservient to this his one purpose, and though much of his music is dreamy in mood, there was little in the man himself to suggest the dreamer. I saw, too, that he managed his business affairs with astuteness and foresight.

It was a strong and lonely life there at Grez-sur-Loing. The household not only of a great composer but of a sick man, with a strict time-table. At six o'clock in the morning he was washed and exercised by his German man-servant. His wife then read aloud to him until eight, and the servant returned with his breakfast and took over the reading until ten o'clock, when a household conference was held to decide whether he was to go into the garden. If the weather was favourable he was dressed and carried downstairs to his invalid carriage and wheeled to the most sheltered spot, where the letters and daily newspapers were read to him. Each item of news was rejected or accepted according to his whim. Anything conjectural was dismissed unread. I was often sent for when his bewildered wife failed to render the abbreviations of cricket scores into intelligible English. These sessions were always interrupted by the ritual of tasting the soup to ensure its seasoned preparation in the kitchen. To have added salt at the table would have been unthinkable!

Lunch at twelve-thirty and Delius rested whilst his wife wrote business letters to publishers. After tea, at four o'clock, Delius worked with me at his music, usually for about two hours. He then rested until supper at seven, after which, in all weathers, and in all seasons, and in flat contradiction to his cautious habits of the morning, he insisted on being pushed in his carriage up the road which led out of the village to Marlotte. Night after night, armed with umbrella and lantern, I wheeled him over the ground on which, for close on forty years, he had contemplated his greatest works. Here, as our friendship grew, I shared his confidences and silences. It pained him deeply that I was unresponsive to his philosophy of life, but on these nocturnal outings he called a truce in his constant fight to shatter my allegiance to organised religion. Of his illness, despite excruciating episodes, he never complained, nor was there a trace of bitterness or self-pity. Stoical, unflinching, he had lived fearlessly and to the full, believing dullness to be the mortal sin of humanity. Truth in all things, as he saw it, was his touchstone, admitting no concessions to conventional behaviour.

If musicians came to play his works and failed to realise his intentions, he stopped then performance and told them so. If visitors bored him, he would call to his servant 'Take me away!' or 'Begin to read!' Once, when a famous string quartet made the uncomfortable journey from Paris to give Delius a private recital, the leader proposed that, before playing Delius's own quartet, they would begin with a Beethoven quartet. 'Oh no, you won't', came the tart reply. 'Play my quartet, - then play the quartet Van Dieren has dedicated to me. I have the parts here!' The truth is that he could no longer bear to hear the music of the Old Masters. Apart from his curiosity about new works by younger men, he had no interest in any music but his own. I often wondered in what capacity he would have succeeded had he been compelled to earn his living as a performer or teacher. He had no breadth of outlook on all styles of music essential to a teacher. Nor could he explain a technical point verbally, nor make a decision in matters practical to the performance of music. Delius was opposed to the whole system of academic training and certainly could not have passed any of the Associated Board of Music Examinations himself. As far as he was concerned, music was little more than the habit of feeling logically in sounds, an outburst of the soul, simple intimate and immediate in its appeal to the listener. He had no time for theories or intellectual speculations about art, and his library of music (other than his own) could have been held in one hand.

Whenever Delius felt well enough to dictate, he was carried into the music room to an armchair beside me at the piano, and we were left alone until he could go on no longer. I can only say that it seemed helpless at first. If I failed in the early attempts, I know that nobody on earth could have made head or tail of the drawling monotone I was expected to decipher. When I suggested that it might be helpful if he would sing it again, he repeated this amazing recital; on another note! It was fantastic.

PART ONE : ARTICLES AND TALKS

There were months of preliminary work before Delius was able to dictate with comparative ease and accuracy. The technique of dictation varied, often considerably, with each work. Much depended on the extent to which Delius had already arranged and sifted in his mind the musical matter he wished me to put on paper. Sometimes he had no more than the roughest idea until that rough idea had been played over to him. The final test was always the sound of his musical thought when heard on the piano. Delius dictated with great rapidity and nervous excitement, calling out the names and time value of the notes, and singing phrases to indicate the instrumental medium in which he wished them to sound. The possibilities of misunderstanding each other were infinite, considering the complexity of his musical texture, which seldom moves in less than five or six parts; the difference between sounds written and those played by the transposing instruments; the problems of orchestral balance; the constant question as to where the next step was going to lead us; and above all, the taking up of the threads again on the morrow.

[The wonder is that he had the courage to go on. But as he always said, that was his only happiness - the happiness of creating. Now this is an idea of how we used to work together in the music-room at Grez.

For instance, he would say: 'Flute, third beat, top C sharp. [Plays] Yes. Now then, same note as we had at the beginning of the piece. [Sings] Now B. Yes, A, F sharp, yes, and then repeat. Keep the C. No, no, repeat the F sharp. [Sings and plays] Yes, then take it down to C, no E in between. [Sings and plays] Now, yes, now then, double it with the clarinet. [Sings and plays] Yes. [Sings and plays] That's it. Now then, harmony, harmony. Horns G sharp and F. Yes. Play it. D bass clarinet. [Plays] That's it. Now then. [Sings and plays] Now change chord - that beat. Now down to C. Yes, and a fifth in the horns, F to E. [Sings and plays] Like that, yes, that's it. Now then. [Sings and Plays] Yes, B, B, that's right. B, G sharp, that's right, in the horns. [Sings] Now then, clinch that low C. Go down to A, bass clarinet. [Sings and Plays] Oh that's it. Now then, G and B natural. Ah, that's it. Now play that.']

The first work I took down in this laborious way was *A Song of Summer*, written in 1929. This was child's play compared to the *Songs of Farewell* for double chorus and orchestra [when only about four or five bars existed on bill heads which he had jotted down on a walking tour in Norway before he was attacked by his last illness]. Nine works occupied us six years.

So strong and unique was the personality of Frederick Delius even in this, the last phase of his life, that, had I fallen entirely under his spell, he could have effaced me within a month. Happily for me, certain aspects of his character - his disdain, severity, aloofness, serenity, his extreme refinement - were tempered by a dry wit, peculiar charm, a fastidious delight in the pleasures of the table, a boyish love of good detective stories, and a wealth of enchanting reminiscence in which Grieg, Ibsen, Strindberg, Gauguin, Busoni, Sibelius and many other artists figured in intimate mood. It was his supreme artistry and the integrity with which he cherished and pursued his ideals, wholly indifferent to the whims of fashion and popular regard that made my fight for him so worth while.

[The last fortnight of his life we read the complete works of Mark Twain. Finally he came to and it was evident to me that the end is near, and Delius, this great friend and wonderful composer, died in my arms.]

And now, let me end these memories of Delius as I knew him with the opening bars of that first work in which I was able to help him: *A Song of Summer.*

[Passages of text in square brackets interpolated from a later broadcast talk.]

The musician who wrote for a blind composer surveys

DELIUS AFTER TWENTY YEARS
by ERIC FENBY

Frederick Delius, still one of the most controversial figures in British music, died twenty years ago this month. During his last years Eric Fenby lived with the blind composer in France and took down the music that Delius dictated.

(*Music and Musicians,* June 1954)

It will be 20 years on June 10 since Delius died at his home at Grez-sur-Loing, the hamlet near Fontainebleau in France where he had worked in seclusion for 40 years. The publicity given to his last works, written by dictation, had revealed to admirers of his music the tragic collapse of his physical powers. Yet it had seemed that he might linger on for many years.

Unable to face once more the laborious effort of dictating a new work, and, no doubt, content that his life's work was done, his end came sooner than I had expected and released me from a service which had long become a burden to my youth.

Helpless Witness

Looking back now, I marvel how I endured those six years of helpless witness to harrowing suffering and constant grappling with new problems and complexities encountered in the technique of dictating music. I shall always be grateful to Ernest Newman for his kindly interest in advising me to write the Delius episode out of my system. The result, my book *Delius as I knew him*[13], probably shocked him - if I can flatter myself that he has ever read it - but, although I cannot now peruse it without a sense of revulsion, is at least a truthful understatement of a strange experience.

Surface memories alone remain. I often recall the good food and good wine of the Delius household, and the silence, particularly the silence imposed at meals during periods of composition. It would have been no hardship to me to have joined a Trappist order after helping Delius to complete the score of his last choral work, *Songs of Farewell*.

Whenever I hear a performance of one of the nine works taken down at his dictation I find my musical attention suspended momentarily and a visual image of the composer awakened by the sound of some detail in the score. Then I am back in the music-room at Grez, with Delius propped in a chair, his head thrown back, calling out the notation and instrumentation in German time-names; or singing an inner part in a cracked tenor voice and straightway repeating it at a different pitch with a confident 'Have you got that?' - and all this with great rapidity and frenzied excitement.

Who can wonder that every detail of those works still lives in my mind! I had 'thumbed out' at the keyboard every phrase in every instrument or vocal part countless times, and these had been checked and rechecked as each strand of harmonic progression was being considered in relation to the total effect which Delius intended. There was often much revision before he was finally satisfied. Otherwise my usual non-musical recollection is of the composer in sunhat, and white shirt open at the neck,

---

13 G Bell & Sons 1936; reprinted Quality Press 1947; new edition revised and edited by the author with an Introduction by Sir Malcolm Sargent and the author's notes to the first and revised editions, Icon Books 1966; new and revised edition with additional material, including 18 photographs, a biographical sketch of Eric Fenby by Christopher Palmer and an 'Author's afterword to 1981 edition', but omitting seven pages of full-score extracts from *A Song of Summer* and *Songs of Farewell* and the reproduction of James Gunn's portrait of Delius, Faber Paperbacks 1981.

sitting in his wheeled chair in his garden about to make some dry quip or acrid remark.

Scoring for Wind

These 20 years have brought no change in my affection for the bulk of Delius's music even after so complete a saturation in its idiom. Some works - *Appalachia* for one - have grown in stature, and I never tire of the rich autumnal tints of his riper work. The evocative magic of his scoring for wind in the slow movement of the Double Concerto is surely unsurpassed in modern music.

Perhaps my strongest reaction to my Delius experience, along with other contributory causes, is that the music of my choice now inclines to chamber music, preferably the last quartets of Beethoven, but Delius would have merely dismissed this as an affectation!

The subtle art of Delius seems to remain a closed book to most musicians. Insensitive performances of his works are still praised in the press despite the superb example by Beecham.

It has been said that Delius must be a freakish composer if one man alone possesses his secret. If convincing lyrical rhapsody is most difficult to sustain in the field of composition, it is not unreasonable to suppose that its execution will demand an equally high degree of lyrical perception, and this, so far as Delius's music is concerned, our younger conductors are clearly unable to convey.

Little Understanding

Too often the full orchestra is made to sound like a great harmonium; or, in more reflective passages, the pointing of the phrasing reveals little understanding of its musical content; or the conductor, having no feeling for Delius's personal sense of flow, loses himself in applied *ritartandos* which are foreign to its continuity.

In his book, *Reflections on Life and Religion*, the late Sir James Baillie suggested that 'the time may come when the present trend of prejudice in the direction of the so-called education of the intellect by books may pass and give place to another, the prejudice in favour of educating the sentiments and emotions, and training the senses to accurate manipulation of the objects of Nature.'

Such a society would breed no lack of performers in the true Delius tradition. Meanwhile we have the growing number of Delius Society[14]

---

[14]   The Delius Society (not to be confused with the present organisation of the same name, inaugurated in 1962) was formed in May 1933 under the auspices of the Columbia Graphophone Company, Ltd. for the issue of

records and Neville Cardus in the *Manchester Guardian* acclaiming their superlative worth.

Delius taught me to love music more than the knowledge of music. That is not the amateur in him speaking, but the artist.

BEECHAM CROWNS HIS SERVICE TO DELIUS

by Eric Fenby

Last month Sir Thomas Beecham published (Hutchinson 30s.) his long-awaited and definitive biography of his friend Frederick Delius, whose music he has championed in a lifetime of effort. Eric Fenby, musical secretary to Delius during the last years of the composer's life, describes the book as 'an imperishable monument', to Beecham as well as to Delius.

(*Music and Musicians*, December 1959)

'I am inclined to think that of all those rare spirits, who sooner or later have found a true understanding of themselves as well as the range and potentiality of their gifts, and who, after much zigzagging to and fro of mind and intention, have fashioned for themselves the one inevitable medium for the embodiment of the spirit moving within them, the most singular and baffling is Frederick Delius . . .'

'If Frederick had prolonged his ten-year residence in Paris indefinitely, and without the choice of an outlet elsewhere, the creation of *Sea Drift, A Mass of Life* or *A Village Romeo and Juliet* might not have been wholly thwarted, but I question if we should have had these absolute

---

gramophone recordings of Delius's music. With Sir Thomas Beecham conducting the London Philharmonic Orchestra, three volumes of 78s, each of seven records, were recorded between April 1934 and June 1938: Volume 1 (issued December 1934), *Paris, Koanga* Closing Scene, *Eventyr, Hassan* Serenade, two songs with piano; Volume 2 (issued December 1936), *Sea Drift,* Intermezzo from *Fennimore and Gerda, Over the Hills and Far Away, In a Summer Garden*; Volume 3 (issued December 1938), *Appalachia, Hassan* Closing Scene, *Irmelin* Prelude, *La Calinda.* Unfortunately, Delius did not live long enough to hear any of them, test-pressings of the first work to be recorded, *Paris,* being held up by French customs (*Delius as I knew him,* 221-2).

expressions of his individuality in quite the shape they took, and with the quality of workmanship bestowed upon them. Happily for its salvation the High Gods took his affairs in hand just as with Richard Wagner, and worked out his future for him, though with less stress and antagonism than for the great German master. They chose the more agreeable agency of feminine influence, and gradually guided it to ends which the gentle instrument of this design could never have foreseen.'

'Brilliant Young Man'

These are key passages in an enthralling account of the strange and adventurous life of Frederick Delius by one whose timely meeting with the composer was no less propitious in its way than that of Jelka Rosen who ultimately became his wife, and 'whose profound belief in his artistic future never faltered for a moment'.

I cannot resist quoting an entry from my diary: Sunday January 13, 1929. Grez-sur-Loing.

Suzanne Haym to lunch. Amusing reminiscences about her father rehearsing D.'s music at Elberfeld. D. talked of Haym, Cassirer and his first making himself known to Beecham after hearing him conduct; D. in middle forties, B. in late twenties; B. was such a brilliant young man that D. feared he might squander his gifts. B. had already formed the best 'orchester' of the time - (D. always says 'orchester'!) - in London.

So began a friendship between these two remarkable men lasting until the composer's death in 1934. Thus for over half a century Sir Thomas has been known as friend and advocate of Delius, and as supreme interpreter of his music in every country where orchestral music is played.

Now, in fulfilment of a personal pledge to Jelka, he has crowned his endeavours with a long-awaited biography of her husband, of a quality and veracity unlikely to be surpassed.

Written with a light and felicitous touch it, abounds in delicious quips and delightful turns of phrase; and the book is illustrated by reproductions of drawings by James Gunn, ARA, an engraving by Ouvré, and photographs of Grez, several of which are of more recent date than Delius's day.

Access to Letters

It is clear that the passage of time has given Sir Thomas a perspective of his subject not enjoyed by previous biographers. Further, as head of the Delius Trust he has had access to the great number of letters kept by Jelka until her death in support of his researches.

He has taken nothing on trust, checking the facts of Delius's life wherever possible and admitting when the trail is lost.

'A small accumulation of legendary lore has always clung to the name, and there is a widening desire to find out how much truth there may be in it. To satisfy that desire is the modest aim of the present work.' This Sir Thomas achieves superbly, presenting for the first time a complete and authentic view of the composer unprejudiced by the poignant incidents of his later years.

The fictitious elements of the tale are investigated and disposed of with amiability and fair judgement. The New York period is the most baffling of all. That Delius was an organist at some time is certain. But where? How I wish I had questioned more often, instead of leaving him to his recollections when and as he chose!

Upon my remarking one day that I thought it rather odd that the composer of *Sea Drift* should house an ancient volume of Bach's organ chorales in his meagre library of music, he replied that he had held casual organ posts in America, and went on to ridicule his feeble technique on the pedal board.

Accepting Sir Thomas's whimsical definition of biography as opposed to autobiography, I cannot believe that Frederick was embellishing the truth here! His own markings in pencil in that score suggest that Delius had more respect for Bach than to attempt anything but works for manuals only.

One is always wiser after the event, but usually I was too preoccupied with the problems of getting his music down on paper than in extracting the facts of his life.

Misguided Influence

From the evidence of Sir Thomas's business-like scrutiny of Delius's troubled relationship with his father, Frederick emerges with credit on the whole, if not with his due. A more bewildering side to his character arouses frank criticism in a penetrating chapter on his misguided influence on that gifted but wayward young man, Philip Heseltine. More agreeable aspects are also revealed by Grieg and Jelka, hers at the author's request.

Beecham rightly apportions to Delius some of the blame for the neglect of his early works written between 1889 and 1900. 'He viewed with indifference the publication of virtually all the output of the period above-mentioned; an indifference due to the realisation of a steadily growing development within himself which rejected the accomplishment of each succeeding lustrum as unrepresentative.'

Discussing the fate of the opera *The Magic Fountain*, Beecham is guilty of a slight exaggeration in asserting that 'No one today knows what it is about, no one knows the characters in it, and no one living has heard a note of the music.'

At the risk of being dubbed a 'pernickety fellow', I must comment that for weeks I laboured to attain some fluency in deciphering the orchestral score of this work at the keyboard, to enable Delius to hear it again, however imperfectly.

This was part of a plan with which he charged me, involving similar efforts with other unpublished works, including the opera *Irmelin*. His idea of dictating the short Prelude of that name was a direct result of one of these encounters.

There is much to ponder in the lucid dissertations on music in general, and the music of Delius in particular, with which Sir Thomas enlivens his narrative.

Beyond a word of warning that 'it is imperative to maintain a tight control over the motion of the melodic line' there is no attempt to 'explain' his interpretations of Delius. The secret of giving flight to the line is his alone, and cannot be imparted. Beecham has already 'explained' the art of Delius for posterity in terms of music alone through the medium of the gramophone.

His book, by virtue of its intrinsic worth, stands in line with the artistry and insight of that achievement, as an imperishable monument to himself no less than to the 'last great apostle in our time of romance, emotion and beauty in music' - Frederick Delius.

DELIUS WAS NO DROOPING DREAMER

by Eric Fenby

Beginning on March 29, Bradford will honour its most famous musical son with a festival in honour of Frederick Delius, born there 100 years ago. Many of his famous works will be given and Sadler's Wells will stage his opera A Village Romeo and Juliet. *Eric Fenby, musical secretary to Delius in the last years of his life, writes about this strange figure in British music.*

(*Music and Musicians*, March 1962)

The unusual musical association which I formed with Frederick Delius from 1928 until his death in 1934, and which led eventually to his regarding me almost as a son, has its own particular memories for me in this year of Centenary celebrations of his birth.

Choral rehearsals of his *Songs of Farewell* which I have attended in Bradford in preparation for the forthcoming Delius Festival have already stirred vivid recollections of the struggle I had 30 years ago to take down the work at Delius's dictation, when all that existed were a few phrases he had jotted down on old bill-heads during a walking tour in Norway, before the onset of his illness in 1922.

At rehearsals for the Birthday Concert at Cartwright Memorial Hall, Bradford, pausing between movements of the Third Violin Sonata while Ralph Holmes tuned his violin, I happened to glance up at James Gunn's full-length portrait of Delius which dominated the platform.

There he sat, a chequered rug thrown over his knees - I remembered posing for Gunn with the rug - just as he had called me that unforgettable Sunday night in 1928 and asked me to write down the first tune he ever dictated to me, the tune we were about to play in the second movement. And what a mess I had made of it! How thrilled Delius was to hear the Sonata for the first time when May Harrison brought her violin to play it to him at his rural home in France!

As the products of our musical collaboration became known, much inquisitiveness was aroused as to his methods of dictation. This in turn gave rise to the inevitable sentimental outpourings which represented the composer as a mawkish weakling.

It was to correct these impressions, and following Ernest Newman's advice to 'write this experience clean out of your system or you'll go on living in the past', that I wrote my *Delius as I knew him* in 1935. It has been out of print for some time, but will be reprinted in September by Arlington Books.[15]

I realised, too, that Delius, like Gesualdo, a similarly isolated composer in the late 16th century, was destined to become a unique figure in musical history, that a dozen of his works would be likely to survive as his achievement was seen in clearer perspective, and that at least one episode in his life, the last, could be written at first hand.

Sir Thomas Beecham has described my book as 'a poignant and sometimes painful account by a highly sensitive youth of an elderly man, blind and paralysed.'

Without exaggeration I can affirm that my narrative of these last six years of Delius's life is an understatement of what happened.

---

[15]   *Delius as I knew him* was not, in fact, reprinted until 1966, by Icon Books.

There was nothing of the drooping dreamer about Delius. It was well for me that I did not fall entirely under his spell, for he would have effaced me within a month,. I found that from the beginning I had to learn how to stand up to him fearlessly and without musical or moral prejudice, for his severity was ruthless.

He was outspoken to an alarming degree, and insisted on the utmost truthfulness in all things. His severity was tempered by a dry wit, a peculiar charm, a fastidious delight in the pleasures of the table, a boyish love of good detective stories and, to the end, a dandyish love of clothes.

Similarly I have attempted in my book to picture his easier methods of dictating the simplest passages when he had already sifted in his mind exactly what he wanted me to write down in the different instruments in the orchestral score.

A recital of his struggles at composition without premeditation, so to speak, would have been unreadable, even had it been in my power to disclose it, so frenzied and faltering was the process. Had I no been blessed with natural gifts of quick perception, an accurate ear - for he had no sense of perfect pitch despite his early training as a violinist - and had I not been schooled thoroughly in the mechanics of music, I should have been useless to him as an amanuensis.

The idea of Delius as an unskilled, meandering composer still persists widely amongst professional musicians. I was soon to find the truth of Deryck Cooke's recent verdict, when, in a brilliant article in *The Listener* of January 25,[16] after spending 'a good deal of time analysing his finest works', he expresses his amazement at Delius's 'endless resource within such a restricted orbit'.

This study revealed that Delius pursued as close a thematic rhythmic and formal logic as Debussy, and a further positive quality - 'the fascination of his original thematic, rhythmic and formal methods, within his limited range.'

It was this inner logic that I was continually ferreting out during our sessions at dictation; and on days when he was too ill to work I would analyse every bar and phrase of what he had already succeeded in

---

[16]   'Delius: A Centenary Evaluation', *The Listener*, 25 January 1962, 195-6. Reprinted in *Vindications: Essays on Romantic Music by Deryck Cooke, with a memoir of the author by Bryan Magee*, Faber and Faber, 1982, together with 'Delius and Form' from *The Musical Times*, June 1962, 392-3, and July 1962, 460-5.

conveying to me so that I could be completely at one with him at the next composing session.

So concentrated are some of Delius's finest melodic lines that I have often used them along with Bach's unaccompanied Sonatas in teaching composition. Delius would have had a seizure with annoyance had I demonstrated these variform symmetries of invention, for he was always scathing about such operations. 'You don't pull a rose to pieces to discover its perfume,' he would say.

Nevertheless, mindful of contemporary fashions, it would seem that unless present-day musicians can be convinced of this inner logic - and I hope that one day Deryck Cooke will publish such 'meticulous analyses' of Delius's best works - his neglect will continue. A new generation has grown up that knows little of the music, much of which is out of print or in short supply in public libraries, a state of affairs that must be remedied by both publishers and the Delius Trust.

Before I went to Delius I had read the essays on his music by Philip Heseltine, Cecil Gray, Van Dieren and Robert Nichols, who, by the time I came to know them, had arrived at more sober judgements. Thus I felt fortified in my own 'obstinacies', as Mrs Delius used to call them.

I had much opposition to overcome at first in the Delius camp, but from the moment of my arrival at Grez she gave me her full support, as did Balfour Gardiner, Delius's closest friend.

If ever a woman sacrificed her own interests completely to a man it was Jelka Delius. She was a gifted painter, a brilliant linguist, a superb cook, a skilled gardener and, like her husband, a firm Nietzschean in her outlook on life.

For years she sat at her desk for two hours every afternoon while he rested, and wrote his letters, signing them in his name in her own hand. Together they were the most original couple I have known, living by themselves, for themselves, utterly self-sufficient and devoted to one aim - Frederick's music.

Much tact had been needed to live in a household in which no other music past or present was given a hearing without withering censure. One work only by Delius met the same fate, the early Piano Concerto, which he detested as his one complete failure and often threatened to withdraw from publication. By the autumn of 1932 it upset him so much to hear it that thereafter he was not told of performances.

For a different reason - his immaturity - he resisted all attempts during his lifetime to persuade him to allow performances of the works of his apprenticeship.

The claims made by Sir Thomas Beecham on behalf of Delius in the late twenties and thirties have proved extravagant, and have even stiffened opposition in professional circles. Posterity, I think, will agree with Edward Lockspeiser, that 'Beecham, taking refuge in Delius out of despair at modern developments, overplayed his hand.'

I am certain that Beecham, too, realised this, though he would never admit it. For some years he almost dropped Delius out of his programmes and took up Sibelius, then finally indulged his fancy for novelty in such early works as *Florida* and the opera *Irmelin*.

It is doubtful whether we shall ever hear again performances of Delius's music of such superlative quality as Beecham gave consistently in his prime. *A Mass of Life, Sea Drift, Appalachia, An Arabesque, Songs of Sunset, In a Summer Garden* - all glowed with a lyrical magic 1 have never heard since.

This is not to deny the years of devoted service to the Delius cause by Sir Henry Wood, Sir Hamilton Harty, Sir Malcolm Sargent, Sir John Barbirolli, Sir Eugene Goossens, Leslie Heward, Anthony Collins and Stanford Robinson; nor yet to forget the helpful evaluations of the music and its performance by Ernest Newman and Neville Cardus. May of us have been much influenced in our thinking by their admirable weekly articles in *The Sunday Times* and *The Guardian*.

Though our talented young conductors appear reluctant to tackle Delius, or apparently prefer their music dry and clean, recent compelling performances of the Violin and Cello Sonatas by the remarkably mature teenager Jacqueline Du Pré and Ralph Holmes have shown greater understanding and feeling for the music than I had dared to hope existed among our rising instrumentalists.

It seems unbelievable that Sir Thomas Beecham will not mount the rostrum at St George's Hall, Bradford, to conduct the Centenary performances of his friend's work. In engaging his chosen successor, Rudolf Kempe, we shall not expect him to take Sir Thomas's place - no-one could ever do that - but to bring his sensitive lyrical gifts to reveal new beauties in the strange musical scripts of Frederick Delius.

FREDERICK DELIUS

Born 1862 at Claremont, Bradford - Died 1934, Grez-sur-Loing, France
Freeman of the City of Bradford - Companion of Honour
Gold Medallist of the Royal Philharmonic Society
Hon. D. Litt., University of Leeds - Fellow of the Royal College of Music

The son of Julius and Elise Delius, Frederick was educated at Bradford
Grammar School and the International College, Isleworth. Provincial birth
and parental opposition to his becoming a musician were alike fruitful in
fostering a sturdy independence of spirit which impelled him to seek his
own salvation far from schools and traditional thought. An unwilling
apprenticeship to the wool trade in Bradford and Chemnitz, Saxony, and
so-called business trips to Norway, Sweden and France, ended in his
dismissal from his father's firm. His immediate problem was to find some
form of livelihood affording ample leisure for study. The most attractive
solution, he decided, was orange farming. Eventually Solano Grove, an
old Spanish plantation overlooking the St Johns River, near Jacksonville
in Florida, was rented for him, and he arrived there in March 1884.

A chance meeting in Jacksonville brought him his first vital contact,
Thomas Ward, an organist from Brooklyn, who grounded him thoroughly
in the craft of composition. After a year of intensive training and sport,
shooting alligators and rattlesnakes, Frederick handed over the plantation
to his brother Ernest who, having tired of sheep farming in New Zealand,
had turned up unexpectedly. His next step was to inform his father that he
had occupied himself entirely with music since his arrival in Florida, that
he was now going to support himself as a music teacher in Jacksonville,
his chief aim being to raise enough money to study in Leipzig. From
Jacksonville he moved to Danville, Virginia, where he flourished among
the families of wealthy tobacco planters. Meanwhile his father, who had
had no news of him for months, put detectives on his trail and traced him
to New York where he had secured a post as organist. He was handed a
letter informing him that the past was forgotten, that his father had
relented and would send him to Leipzig. Frederick sailed immediately for
England, spent one night in Bradford, and left the next day for Leipzig.
His studies at the Conservatorium with Jadassohn and Reinecke proved
useless and increased his indebtedness to the admirable Ward, whose
excellence as a teacher he often extolled. At the end of his second year in
Leipzig his father withdrew his allowance and the young composer found
himself at the crossroads. Still in his formative years, he would have been
compelled to return to the wool trade had not his uncle Theodor Delius

offered him a home in Paris. Encouragement from Grieg inspired him to tremendous activity in composing two operas in which he was his own librettist, and a great quantity of orchestral and chamber music revealing little evidence of the highly personal style of his mature work. Cosmopolitan in taste, he read widely in the literature of Scandinavia and Germany. Excepting Busoni, Sinding and Grieg, his friends at this time were drawn from men illustrious in the sister arts - Bjørnson, Strindberg, Gauguin, Munch and other writers and painters. The strong Scandinavian influence of this early period, through literature and friendships, remained with him all his life. In 1897 Delius returned to Florida to set the plantation, now owned by his father, on a surer financial footing. This second visit agitated the growing conflict between his love of solitude and craving for excitement, and after two more restless years in Paris he left its distractions for a country retreat at Grez-sur-Loing, near Fontainebleau, where he married Jelka Rosen, a talented painter, who made him an ideal helpmate.

The first event of importance on his settling at Grez was the concert of his music which he gave in London in 1899. From now on little of outward importance occurred beyond the performance of new works. It was well for him that his music aroused such zeal for his cause, for he had no talent for self-display, nor skill in directing his work. The pioneer efforts of Haym, Buths, and Cassirer in Germany, and Wood and Heseltine in England culminated in the inspired advocacy of Beecham whose superb realisations of Delius's music are unlikely to be surpassed. It remains to be seen whether the traditions of interpretation Beecham sought to establish during half a century will ever take root.

In 1922 there appeared symptoms of Delius's final illness, and he began a round of Continental spas in search of cures. To these were added the first signs of blindness in 1925, and by the following year he was totally blind and paralysed.

Composition was resumed by dictation in 1928 when Eric Fenby offered his services as amanuensis, and eight works including the choral work *Songs of Farewell* were written in 'a feat of technical collaboration without parallel in the history of music'.

The last event of importance was the Delius Festival given by Sir Thomas Beecham in London in 1929, which the composer attended.

A year after his death in 1934, Delius's body was finally brought to England and buried at Limpsfield, Surrey. His wife died that year.

Delius Centenary Festival Bradford programme book 1962

DELIUS AND BEECHAM

A REMINISCENCE BY ERIC FENBY

Record sleeve essay to The Beecham Legacy Volume 3 HQS1126

It is sometimes said that the music of Delius would never have been heard of but for Beecham. The regular inclusion of Delius's works in programmes conducted by Sir Henry Wood, Sir Hamilton Harty, Geoffrey Toye and Leslie Heward in England, and the pioneer efforts of Dr Hans Haym, Julius Buths and Fritz Cassirer in Germany in the first quarter of this century, prove otherwise. What can clearly be claimed for Sir Thomas Beecham on the aural evidence of forty years is that without his marvellous insight, the magical felicities of Delius's lyricism would still be awaiting their full realisation.

This does not imply that there is only one way, Beecham's way, of playing Delius, but that no conductor has yet surpassed him in conjuring up to sheer perfection the hidden beauties of Delius's scripts.

Beecham epitomised for Delius the ideal conductor relationship of which every composer dreams. I ventured to ask him after rehearsal what it was in the music that had first attracted him.

'Here was a composer, Frederick Delius, whom I'd never seen or heard of before; whose music was unlike any other . . or anything that was being written at the time. Nobody seemed to know what the devil to make of it! I found it as alluring as a wayward woman and determined to tame it . . .' He paused to light his cigar and added, '. . . and it wasn't done in a day!'

Apart from a period in his early seventies, the unlettered Muse of Frederick Delius continued to excite him to the end of his life. Some of his most endearing lavishments were made in the privacy of rehearsals when every moment was a performance despite the empty hall. He often sent for me on these occasions, particularly in his prime, merely to share his boyish delight in shaping the music lovingly with the utmost beauty of sound. I cannot recall Sir Thomas Beecham ever rehearsing Delius in the supremely professional and technical manner of, for instance, Rudolf Kempe, who directed the Bradford Centenary Delius Festival in 1962.

Most of Beecham's work had been done beforehand. He would mark in blue pencil every bar of the score, exaggerating Delius's own nuances of expression to make the fullest impact in performance. Copyists would then transfer these markings to each of the orchestral parts of the work. The rehearsal existed in the main to familiarise the players, all of them experts, with the way he wanted the varying textures to sound in balance and attack. His verbal comments, often witty, reinforced the scrupulous observance of these editings, or exploded in humorous reprimand, or in mild rebuke of a player who had somehow missed his entry - 'Cor Anglais! Will you kindly give me some indication of your presence!' Often he would draw attention to the operative note in a phrase, the pointing of which would make all the difference between the effect of telling at once or not at all. 'Clarinet!' he would say, '. . a little more time before you get to the C.' This freedom of play within the beat was the secret of his wizardry.

Why was Beecham so uniquely successful as an interpreter of Delius's music? The two men, superficially, had much in common despite the seventeen years between them. There were certain similarities in their upbringing. Both had come from well-to-do homes in the industrial north of England, and both had fathers who were patrons of music. There was refinement and acute sensitivity in each, though Beecham could be Rabelaisian in speech, whereas Delius loathed the slightest crudity. Both had been exposed to European culture.

The clue, to my mind, lies in Beecham's temperament and the kind of music he pursued when left entirely to his own taste. Even his superb artistry was but the servant of this obsession, and this was the poetry of musical magic.

Some composers have a richer vein of musical poetry than others in their invention. These always kindled an instant response in Beecham. There is a musical magic in Schubert wholly lacking in Beethoven. This was the quality that Beecham adored. He had found it in his incomparable Mozart, though rarefied and impalpable, but nowhere to such excess as in the musical imagery of Delius.

Paradoxically, Beecham the city-dweller, like Oscar Wilde, was 'uncomfortable' with Nature, yet achieved notable triumphs in his imaginative conceptions of Delius's Nature music. In no sphere have Yorkist and Lancastrian rivalries been more completely forgotten than in the complementary artistries of Delius and Beecham.

[1968]

ERIC FENBY IN INTERVIEW
WITH ROBERT LAYTON

In a BBC broadcast on 20 August 1972 Dr Fenby discussed with Robert Layton the way in which Delius dictated his late works, and recalled life in the Delius household. In the course of the programme Dr Fenby illustrated certain points, particularly in relation to the process of dictation, by singing and playing. These, and a few other details, have been necessarily edited out.

R.L.   Mr Fenby, I've heard you described in various contexts as amanuensis, secretary to Delius, and of course the way in which you came to meet with Delius and work with him is well known. But I wondered whether you could clarify the position. Were you ever a secretary or what was in fact your direct relationship with him?

E.F.   My direct relationship with Delius was as his amanuensis, and that solely. I was not his secretary. Delius was like a clam. Nobody knew - with the exception of Balfour Gardiner and his [i.e. Delius's] wife - anything about his personal affairs, not even Beecham. These he managed apparently with great shrewdness. His wife also managed his musical affairs, the business side of his music, again with great shrewdness, writing her 'thunder letters' as she called them to the publishers. But I had no part in any of those dealings. In fact I can't remember ever putting pen to paper on his behalf in a purely business capacity. I was solely engrossed in the enormous problem of getting the music down on paper.

R.L.   I wanted to ask you about the actual mechanics of Delius's dictation.

E.F.   Well, of course, he never could understand how I could be so stupid not to understand him first of all, and he hated anything in the form of repetition. Music to Delius meant sound. It was not a question of how that sound was contrived or whether it would fit in with any canons of musical discipline; he cared not a fig for that kind of thing. All that he wanted was the actual sound as it impinged on his inner ear, and this he had to convey to me. But he always had to have the sound first of all.

      He always called out the orchestration. For example, at the beginning of the *Songs of Farewell* when we first started there, having read out all the score and having told me to take 32-stave manuscript paper, and that he would have 4/4 in a bar, now then - 'Cellos, pizzicato chord - D, A, F sharp.' And I would play that straight away. 'Yes, that's right. Now, put that in: one, two, three, four, "How sweet . . ."'

With the chording, he always called out all the notes from the bottom: A, F sharp, A, A, D, F sharp, B. I knew more or less the noises that he liked in music and I would feel for it all the time. As he called them, A, D, F sharp, I was quick to put the notes down; whatever he said I put down. Then sometimes he called out the wrong note and that had to be put right. But he always thought of it straight away in orchestration: A, violas, D Ist violins, and so on, calling out the instrumentation as it went along. And usually I got the rhythm. He would go [sings], so I knew that was one, two, three, four, one; so I had that rhythm in my mind. Once I got hold of the rhythm, then I had to think in terms of the time factor with each note. And then I would go in for the sound. But first of all it was the rhythm: I found out that I had to get that first or else it was quite useless. I had very great difficulty at the beginning of what was a comparatively easy work when we were doing the Violin Sonata [No 3] because I couldn't get the rhythm: he went [sings] that made six whereas we wanted four in a bar.

Then he would call out quarter-notes. At the beginning I had great difficulty because I always thought that a quarter-note meant a quarter of a beat, in other words a semi-quaver, whereas for Delius in meant of course in the German nomenclature a crotchet.

R.L.   Both you and he must have had absolute pitch.

E.F.   Well no, that was the problem. I had absolute pitch and I am almost now, in my life, at the same age as Delius was when he dictated to me. I'm finding now that through term-time when I am teaching at the Academy and in contact with sounds through my students, my ear is quite accurate. Otherwise in the holiday time, if I'm writing and away from music, the pitch begins to go up.

R.L.   Oh, I see. For me it goes down.

E.F.   It goes upward, and it's going up all the time. And therefore with Delius, particularly when we were doing the 'Depart upon thy endless cruise, old sailor' and in the 'Joy, shipmate, joy' intervals, and Delius takes the sopranos up to top C in the end of 'Joy, shipmate, joy', there's always a tremendous sense of strain. In 'Now finalé to the shore', towards the end of the last chorus of *Songs of Farewell*, again the music goes up to a top B, which is a tremendous difficulty for the sopranos. But most of all, in the third number when we have 'Passage to you, O secret of the earth and sky!' and all the various elements are saluted in turn, and the music gets more and more excited, the poor wretched sopranos have to sing up there [plays up to high C] on the word 'Away'. Delius was always forcing the pitch up, I found, and I had very great difficulty sometimes in keeping it down when we were working on music involving voices.

R.L.   I wonder whether you think his vocal writing in the operas is effective.

E.F.   I think my own feeling is that Delius had a marvellous sense of the colour of voices, just as he had a marvellous sense of the colour of instruments. But of course it is neither colour nor chords that makes the great composer, but in my opinion it is line, and insofar as Delius's lines make musical sense, then I think he understood voices in what was perhaps a somewhat limited but very musical, poetical way. He was always best when he heard voices in the distance, like that marvellous unaccompanied chorus in *The Song of the High Hills*. Where I think he was difficult with voices is in some of the opening choruses of *Songs of Sunset*, where the chromatic part is extremely difficult. It's difficult to sing, it's particularly frustrating to sing. That sort of thing is done over a pedal, and if it has to be sung by people who are only singing from a single part rather than a vocal score, as happens nowadays, it can produce an unsatisfactory effect.

R.L.   Do you think the operas are in any sense effective, or that they will ever take the stage again?

E.F.   No, because of the feeble libretti.

R.L.   Yes. Did he ever talk to you about many other composers? I know the famous anecdote about the Bartók fourth quartet, of course.[17]

E.F.   Yes.

---

[17]   See page 116 and *Delius as I knew him*, 61.

R.L.   Everyone knows that. The story is put about that he was totally impatient, couldn't bear to listen to any other music but his own. And I wonder whether this really was true?

E.F.   I would say of his own contemporaries. But he always liked *Till Eulenspiegel*. And he liked Elgar's *Falstaff*, but he thought it rather repetitious. But still I think that was of the works of Elgar the one he liked best. But outside his own music - it must be conceded at once, and that was one of the most difficult things for me to accept at the beginning - was that he liked no other music but his own. Maybe just a little Wagner, but I often thought that when he asked for the odd bit of *Götterdämmerung* and so on, he would be perhaps living in some episode of the past rather than his specific interest in the music. I am sure that was the same with Grieg. He had very extraordinary tastes. I once remember his asking to hear Barnby's *Sweet and Low* of all things, a piece which apparently he said was very good and which reminded him very much of his youth. That took me back somewhat, I think.

But his main interest in music other than his own was the music of the younger composers. Now at that time Walton was coming to the fore with the Viola Concerto and *Belshazzar's Feast*, and in these Delius delighted. I used to sit by him when he was in bed. The procedure was this: if there was a concert which he thought would interest him, and it was usually a concert in which there was (a) something of his, or (b) there was something by one of these younger composers (Constant Lambert being one of their number - *Rio Grande*, for example, interested him enormously), he would say: 'Well now then, take me up early', and his male nurse used to come after the evening meal and on that occasion there would be no walk outside the village. His customary procedure was to be taken up the Marlotte road where he had pondered most of his works, and this would happen in all weathers but rain. But on these occasions where there would be a concert there would be no walk.

This all sounds rather extraordinary, but the entire drill of the household - and indeed it was a drill, it was of a routine that I have never come across in my life. I could take my watch out at any time of the day when I came over to England and I knew exactly what would be happening in the Delius household. He liked the whole thing like that. He liked his music to be governed by that kind of almost regimental attitude to work. We always worked at precisely the same time every day - if he was able to, of course. But the whole thing was governed by this attitude, the habit of discipline. Habit in Delius was very strong.

I was saying that he would have the doors of his room opened upstairs and we would be invited to sit by the bed and the radio would be set up on a table at the foot of the bed. He would be propped up with pillows after an incredible business: one had to go and ask the baker if he would mind not baking the bread for an hour or so because Mr Delius wanted to hear some music, and we had to go round to various other people in the village, because of the interference. Although it was a very high-powered radio, we always had these local interferences, and the local garage had machinery which upset the apple-cart.

R.L. Were they co-operative? Because Delius wasn't all that popular in the . . .

E.F. Oh no! Delius was not liked a bit in the village. No, I'm afraid not! I used to push him up the village on those evening walks - particularly in the summertime (although these walks went on all the year round, even when it was pitch dark) - and all the lights in the village went out at nine. We used to set off ordinarily at that time. Shielded by an umbrella, and with a lantern, in his little cart we used to push him up the hill, this man who in his own home had had double doors fitted to every room and always a screen round his chair to protect him from the draughts!

R.L. You came from roughly the same part of the world that Delius himself did. And I wondered whether Delius talked to you about his childhood, about his relationship with his parents? Because I think this background, which of course Beecham goes into in some detail in his biography, might well explain some of the facets of Delius's character that puzzle the general reader now.

E.F. Delius was in a sense a man of very few words. I can't remember any particular occasion on which he spoke about his parents, except that from time to time he would drop in an aside about them. And the sum total of that I would think would amount to something like this: that he thought they were admirable parents in the sense that they looked after the creaturely comforts of their children; they provided them with the very best that could be. The second best never obtained in the Delius household. As each child was ready to learn an instrument, it was asked what instrument it would like to take up, and the finest tuition in the north of England would be brought over to Bradford for that purpose.

R.L.   Yet the father wasn't prepared to encourage Delius as a composer?

E.F.   But for no other reason that he thought that music as a profession was beneath the dignity of a gentleman.

R.L.   Would you say that Delius's relationship with his mother was close?

E.F.   His mother, I think, was the chief musical influence in his life at the beginning - her playing was, put it that way. She played the piano apparently very well for an amateur. I remember one night about half-past five we were sitting by the lamp in the living room there. I was reading aloud and Mrs Delius was sewing, and Delius was sitting in his chair characteristically with his head back. Whether he was listening one never knew. At any rate there was silence to my reading. Suddenly there was a knock at the door and the little Saxon housemaid came in and said: 'There's a telegram for you, Mr Delius.' This was then handed to Mrs Delius, who opened it and read. 'Fred,' she said, 'your mother has just died.' I immediately rose for I felt that I should leave the room at that point. But he realised that I was on the point of moving. 'Oh no, sit still, Eric,' he said. And then there was a pause, and he went on: 'Mmm. A strange woman. She never took the slightest interest in my music after I'd left Bradford as a young man. I very much doubt if she ever heard a note of mine played. And after my music began to be played, she made no enquiries about it. She never met Jelka. She never wrote. And once when I tried, in her late 'eighties when she was flying to Cologne and I was still able to get about, I went to Cologne especially to meet her. But she never turned up. There was no explanation. A strange woman. Go on reading, Eric.'

R.L.   This is quite an extraordinary story. Of course, Beecham goes into the finances in his book, the way in which Delius's father apportioned money between the seven of his offspring. But what I wanted to ask you: of course it must seem in a way, from a non-musician's point of view - from the point of view of a Bradford businessman - it must seem quite unreasonable to have to maintain a child, a son, right until his 30s. Do you think that Delius reproached his father in any way? Did he reproach him in your company at all?

E.F.   I think as far as that kind of thing was concerned he did. And I think somewhat unreasonably.

R.L.   Yes, I would have thought so.

E.F.   But - let me be fair to Delius - he always maintained that his father gave him the very best of everything. When he went out to Florida, for example, he fitted him up with the most expensive tropical kit. And as I've already mentioned, nothing but the very best would do by way of tuition or instruments and so on.

R.L.   Tell me about his time in Florida. Did he talk to you about it a great deal?

E.F.   Oh yes, a great deal.

R.L.   It must have made quite an impact on his musical language altogether. And I wonder what kind of impact the atmosphere of the Southern States and the music he heard there made?

E.F.   Tremendous. I think a tremendous impact, more perhaps than has ever been realised, because not only there did he decide to be a composer, you must remember that he went out to Florida to escape the office desk in the family wool business. When he arrived there he'd never before had that tremendous impact on him of silence. He told me that as a boy he loved the silence of the Ilkley moors, and he would ride off for miles often all day in the saddle. He knew there that he was going to do something with his life but he wasn't quite certain what. It was not until he went to Florida and after Ward, the Jesuit organist whom he met casually in Jacksonville, had put him through a course of counterpoint, just the very thing he needed then. Ward understood exactly what Delius required. And therefore we have this extraordinary situation of this young man who wanted to become a musician, marooned as it were on this orange plantation thirty-five miles south of the nearest town, Jacksonville, although there was a small community about three miles away at a little bluff called Picolata on the St Johns River where there were curiously enough enthusiasts, and indeed a woman who was a relative of Grieg's and who for the first time put some of Grieg's music into Delius's young hands.

R.L. When is the Florida period?

E.F. Delius went out to Florida in 1884, that is to say when he was about 22. He was roughly about the same age I was when I went to him. He stayed there roughly about two years. During that time he was for several months quite alone, save for his Negro servant, who was so attached to him that he even slept outside the door on a mat rather than have his room in the loft of the little wooden shack on the plantation. I've been to the plantation; I was there in 1966, and it is pretty much the same as in Delius's day. There were the Negroes tending the oranges and the vast magnolia trees, and the marvellous Spanish moss which drapes from the trees. The light percolates through. Delius so often talked to me about all that kind of thing, on those evening walks up the road to Marlotte about which I've spoken.

R.L. I'd be interested to hear what you think, as a musician, of the *Florida* Suite that Beecham edited. By the way, to what extent did Beecham edit it?

E.F. Dynamic marks only. I think that work is something of an enigma because in it Delius showed his hand as a highly skilled orchestrator - a finer orchestrator than composer. Then in the works which follow it subsequently there is a strange falling-off in his powers of orchestration.

R.L. Could I ask you one thing? One passage in *Florida* has always struck me as being tremendously influenced by Grieg [the passage for horns at bar 15 of the fourth movement *At Night*]. You've mentioned the fact that Grieg's music was shown to him. Had he ever seen any of Grieg's orchestral music at this time?

E.F. Oh yes, he had, the Overture *In Autumn*, and also what I think was really more important, and possibly disastrously so, certain works by Svendsen, because I think it could well be said that this falling off was, I think, due to the fact that he began to place his sounds in a way that to me Svendsen does, producing overall a somewhat muddy effect.

R.L. I see. You think Svendsen's a less than first-class orchestrator?

E.F. Well, that is my own feeling, a personal opinion. I have heard it said that he owed much to Svendsen.

R.L. As in fact did Nielsen for that matter.

E.F. That could be, but . . .

R.L. I think Svendsen's a very underrated composer, but that's neither here nor there.

E.F. It could be. Svendsen's orchestration for himself might have been all right, but in terms of Delius, what Delius was trying to do, it wasn't, because about this time there was an upsurge of Wagnerian influence in Delius's style. In the beginning it was largely Grieg and after a time he began to see that he was getting nowhere by this Norwegian influence. In many ways I think that apart from the natural scenery, the love of the place and so on, the musical influence of Norway or the Scandinavians was somewhat disastrous to Delius. That is my own personal opinion.

R.L. It must have been in a way an odd experience to watch yourself in that recent film that Ken Russell made of Delius.[18] I wanted to ask you not so much about your own self, but whether you thought the portrait of Delius as you knew him was an accurate one as portrayed by Max Adrian, because I think a lot of people will have felt there was a kind of authenticity about it.

E.F. Yes, and I think that comes over in the film. That was exactly as I remember Delius in those last years.

R.L. He spoke like that?

E.F. He spoke like that, yes.[19]

---

[18] As regards the film's opening, in an interview with Robert Secret, *Royal Academy of Music Bulletin* No 3, November 1969, Eric Fenby said: 'I was a church organist before I went to Delius, but once when a cinema organist was ill I had to take his place. When I told Ken about this he immediately decided to put it in the opening of the film, so I had to improvise on the BBC organ to a Laurel and Hardy film, having not touched an organ for twenty-five years! As far as the film was concerned I left it entirely to Russell - I never once went on the set as Christopher Gable, the actor playing me, told me that it would have made him very nervous.'

[19] In a letter, dated 2 November 1974, which serves as a foreword to Christopher Palmer's *Delius: Portrait of a Cosmopolitan*, Duckworth 1976, Eric Fenby adds: 'May I settle a point you raise? Delius's voice was

R.L. Can you imitate him at all?

E.F. Well, it was a slow speech [imitating], it was something like that. It was always as if he was addressing a number of people.

R.L. It was pontifical in other words.

E.F. It was pontifical in that sense, yes. Delius was rather extraordinary in that he would always wait in a conversation or a discussion, and just at the crucial moment top it with something which completely bowled everybody out. He adored that kind of thing.

R.L. As a person he does give the impression of being unkind. Is that a correct impression?

E.F. He was hard.

R.L. Lacking in charity?

E.F. Lacking in charity, yes, but it must never be said that he was unkind because his kindnesses were known only to himself. Nobody who ever came to the door was turned away empty-handed from the village.

R.L. Why was he hated by the villagers?

E.F. Because of his autocratic attitude to life, and to them. He wouldn't speak to ordinary people in the village.

R.L. Why was this, do you think?

E.F. Well, it might be too fanciful to think so but it must never be forgotten that Delius's Bible was *Zarathustra* of Nietzsche.

R.L. Yes. What about Jelka? She emerges in that particular portrait as an almost saintly character.

E.F. Oh no, she was not saintly. She would have hated that. She was no less a Nietzschean in her own way. They were both rabidly anti-Christian.

R.L. Both of them?

---

of light, tenor timbre; pleasant, not harsh, but with a drawl. There was no trace of accent that I could detect.' Fenby, himself a Yorkshireman, would almost certainly not have recognised the accent of his fellow Yorkshireman.

E.F.   Oh yes. And there was a strong sensuality about both of them, but a very healthy sensuality, so to speak. They both loved the good things of life. But she was extraordinarily devoted to him, and he, unfortunately, had the Nietzschean attitude to women to a tee, and he treated her in that kind of way. But she was a woman of great character, great charm, and really great personal beauty.

[First published in *The Delius Society Journal* No 106 Winter/Spring 1991]

BEECHAM AND DELIUS

Eric Fenby's contribution to the 'A Cloud of Witnesses' section of Sir Thomas Beecham, conductor and impresario, as remembered by his friends and colleagues, *compiled by Humphrey Procter-Gregg, (Westmorland Gazette 1973). Revised as* Beecham Remembered *(Duckworth 1976). See Eric Fenby's review on pages 96-98.*

Beecham is generally regarded as excelling all others in the music of Delius: not that his alone is the one way of playing it: Kempe proved that convincingly at the Bradford Centenary Festival. What can clearly be claimed for Beecham is that no-one has projected its poetry more musically. Groves and Sargent may have equalled him in the great choruses of *A Mass of Life*, but in all else Beecham was matchless, especially with the orchestra. Passages such as the marvellous, evocative evening music in the third and fourth movements of the *Mass* have never been given with such artistry since. Beecham always insisted on the finest instrumentalists capable of the utmost beauty of tone colouring the threads of Delius's textures. He would lean forward on the rostrum, shaping his phrases in exquisite flow, allowing the music to breathe and speak as Delius intended with pen and paper, but was unable precisely to convey: the stick often seemingly aimless, but poised to point some pivot chord on which the emotional tension hinged in his control of the melodic line. It was direction as if by mesmerism, his eyes anticipating every inflection.

I remember Oda Slobodskaya, after rehearsing Palmyra with John Brownlee in the title-role of Delius's *Koanga* at Covent Garden in 1935, complaining that she could not follow Beecham because he rarely gave a downbeat.

'But you don't need downbeats from Beecham,' cut in John, 'you can feel where he is!'

Beecham's fifty years' advocacy of Delius in the concert-room, opera house and recording-studio was the sort of which every composer must dream. I ventured to ask him on one occasion what it was in the music that had first attracted him. His reply was hardly what I had expected:

'Here was a composer, Frederick Delius, whom I had never seen or heard of before; whose music was unlike any other, or anything that was being written at the time: that was about 1907. Nobody seemed to know what the devil to make of it! I found it as alluring as a wayward woman, and determined to tame it!' He paused to light a cigar, and added with that characteristic roll of his eyes, 'And it wasn't done in a day!'

He would play through some favourite Delius in rehearsal, the hall empty save for cleaners, and coax the most ravishing sounds from the orchestra as if it were the last time he was ever to conduct it. He often sent for me at these sessions, particularly in his prime in the 'thirties, merely to share his boyish delight in exercising his artistry. There was something endearing about him in such moods, and this is how I usually recall him.

The basic details had been pondered beforehand. He would mark every bar of the score in blue pencil, exaggerating Delius's own nuances of expression, to make the fullest impact in performance. Copyists would then transfer these markings to each of the orchestral parts of the work. The rehearsal existed in the main to familiarise the players, all of them experts, with the way he wanted the design to sound in balance and attack. His verbal comments, often witty, reinforced the scrupulous observance of these editings, or exploded in humorous reprimand or mild rebuke of a player who had somehow missed his entry. 'Cor Anglais! Kindly give me some indication of your presence at four bars after Letter G!'

He would indicate the operative note in a phrase, the pointing of which would make all the difference between telling at once or not at all. 'Clarinet!' he would say, 'a little more time before you get to the C!' Or he would exasperate the first violins by making them repeat a long-drawn melody until he had flighted it to perfection.

His chief concern with Delius was in tending the melodic strands that pass from voice to voice and give the piece its form, and, no less important, the balancing of timbres carrying the supporting harmonies. In the more technical matters arising from errors, he sometimes astonished me. I suspect from his correcting misprints in Delius, that his studies in harmony and counterpoint would appear to have been somewhat perfunctory. I have no recollection of his rehearsing Delius in the highly professional manner of Kempe. I was particularly struck by this at Bradford. Kempe dissects offending passages, and having achieved his purpose, individually reassembles them rhythmically in instrumental counterpoint.

Why was Beecham uniquely successful as an interpreter of Delius? The two men, superficially, had much in common, despite the seventeen years between them. There were certain similarities in their upbringing. Both had come from well-to-do homes in the industrial north of England, and both had fathers who were patrons of music. There was refinement and acute sensitivity in each, though Beecham could be incredibly Rabelaisian in speech, whereas Delius loathed the slightest crudity. Both had been exposed to European culture at first-hand in their teens.

The clue, to my mind, lies in Beecham's temperament, and the kind of music he pursued when left entirely to his own inclinations. Even his superb artistry was but the servant of this obsession, and *that* was the poetry of musical magic.

Some composers have a richer vein of musical poetry than others in their invention; it springs from the quality of their thought. These, it seemed, kindled invariably an instant response in Beecham. There is a musical magic in Schubert wholly lacking in Beethoven. This was the quality Beecham adored. He had found it in his incomparable Mozart, though rarefied and impalpable, but nowhere to such excess as in the musical imagery of Delius.

Paradoxically, Beecham the city-dweller, like Oscar Wilde, was 'uncomfortable' with Nature, yet he was inimitable in his conceptions of Delius's nature music. The Delius Festival in 1929 set the seal on his powers as a peerless exponent of the art of Delius. The entire programmes were conducted from memory, and he barely glanced at his scores in rehearsals. His best recordings date from this time. I doubt if he ever surpassed his performance of *In a Summer Garden* on the old 78s, or of *On Hearing the First Cuckoo in Spring* in the same series. Beecham's recording might well have been labelled 'On Hearing the Last Cuckoo in the Last Spring', so ineffably lovely are the sounds he imparts to it, yet so piercingly poignant is his visionary reading of this little gem among miniatures. In his later years his presentations were apt to be marred unaccountably by sudden erratic fluctuations of tempi. His *Walk to the*

Paradise Garden - his final version on LP records[20] - is markedly inferior in this respect to his earliest 78s. For those who remember his golden years, when each time he faced an orchestra, men knew they awaited an event they were unlikely to forget. His passing ended an era. Lancastrian and Yorkist rivalries, though rampant still in cricket, unite in the complementary artistries of Beecham and Delius.

ERIC FENBY IN INTERVIEW

WITH FRED CALLAND

In January 1974, while in the USA as guest of the St Louis Symphony Orchestra at four performances conducted by Walter Susskind of A Mass of Life, *Dr Fenby gave an interview in Washington with Fred Calland for the Public Broadcasting Service. The interview, which in the resulting broadcast was punctuated with extracts from a number of commercial records, was unscripted, and to preserve something of the informality of the occasion the minimum of editing has been done for this transcript.*

E.F. Curiously enough, I hadn't heard a note of Delius until about the beginning of 1928. One night, just prior to the news bulletin, I was struck by a kind of music I had never heard before, and I was ravished, completely carried away by it. Immediately it ended, the announcer said: 'You have just been listening to *On hearing the first cuckoo in spring* by Frederick Delius. Now the news will follow . .' etc. etc.

I should explain that I had been living as a youth up in a fairly remote part of England on the North Yorkshire coast which was a particularly culturally barren place in most things - but curiously enough not in music. There was a tremendous local interest in music because in the summertime in those days the great London and provincial orchestras were only six-month contract affairs, and so there was a very great urge during the summertime for the very finest players to come to the first-class seaside spa orchestras such as we had at Scarborough. That was again my very good fortune because in those years I picked up a tremendous

---

[20] Eric Fenby must have had another work in mind, perhaps *In a Summer Garden*, as Beecham only recorded *The Walk to the Paradise Garden* as a 78 rpm disc.

amount of practical knowledge in music. They were very leisurely days and a cigarette went a long way with a bassoon player just putting his instrument away if you'd say: 'Now just play that passage and tell me how it sounds and what I must avoid in this.'

My neighbour was the clarinet player in the Scottish Orchestra, and he used to commute over to Scarborough in the summer. He was a librarian and also assistant conductor. He was a chap who liked a drink at the end of the morning. They always played a symphony, and I used to say: 'Now, Mr Fawcett, I will put the music away', because it so happened that I had heard or been struck by a particular progression in a symphony and I wanted to piece the thing together from the score and see how the effect was made. I had made my mind up to be a musician because I had a very fine ear, having had perfect pitch, and since a boy I was articled to a leading organist of the day. That was the choice - between staying locally or going to a musical academy. Because of my ill health at the time I chose the former.

Now that was really an excellent choice, as it proved, because this fellow was an extremely fine teacher - but an extremely idle man as regards music and he spent a very great deal of his time on the golf course. And so it happened that I would be asked on Monday nights to take a choral society, on Tuesday nights an amateur orchestra, on Wednesday nights a madrigal group, and so on right through the week as well as the church duties.

I was a very serious organist, and not a cinema organist as happened at the beginning of the film on Delius in which I was portrayed by Christopher Gable. That was just an episode in my life in that I happened to turn up one day at a cinema and they couldn't start the programme in the old days of silent films, and I was asked to take the thing on. They got me down as a cinema organist. Well, I was a very serious-minded young man in these matters, so that when I read in the *Yorkshire Post* that Frederick Delius, the composer of this piece which had so enchanted me, was blind and paralysed and in very low straits because he couldn't finish his life's work, that he was living in France almost the life of a recluse, I was really quite distressed. But I thought of course no more about it. Then, curiously enough, the thought that perhaps something ought to be done began to become uppermost in my mind. At any rate I would write and say how much I loved his music, because now I had hunted round and was beginning to be more acquainted with some of his larger works.

F.C. How much could you get acquainted with it at that time? He was not too widely known in England, was he?

E.F. He was played by people like Beecham and Sir Henry Wood, and Leslie Heward at Birmingham. Miniature scores of Delius had certainly not been issued in England at that time, and that was a difficulty. But I found by chance that there was to be the publication of the vocal score of the *Mass of Life* .

I wrote to Delius and to my great astonishment received a note to say how delighted he was to hear that a young man liked his music. (This came in the writing of his wife. Obviously he dictated it.) He said that he knew my part of the world; he'd gone there as a boy when he lived in Bradford. And from that moment this extraordinary feeling that I could help him - it was an amazing presumption - got uppermost. I said nothing to anybody, not even my parents. Finally I wrote to him and asked if I might go and help. And he wrote again - or sent me a letter - almost by return, which said they were very touched by my offer, and that if I liked I was to go and spend a few days - a weekend or so - and see if I liked it. He warned me that he was very much living there with his wife on his own, and they had very few visitors, that it was hardly the place for a young man and that it might indeed very seriously handicap my future plans as a musician were I to go to Grez. So anyhow I went. This was 1928, and I stayed there about six years, with, of course, a few journeys home.

F.C. Grez-sur-Loing had been a sort of artists' colony?

E.F. Oh yes indeed. It was about forty kilometres from Paris. just outside the Forest of Fontainebleau. I talked to old men there who remembered seeing old Corot painting down by the bridge, and Cézanne. I remember meeting Lloyd Osbourne, Robert Louis Stevenson's step-son. The one thing that certainly preserved my sanity during an extremely difficult period - because Delius would go for days on end and not speak at all, and I on my part would go months and never see a soul outside that small house - the one thing that saved me was the friendship I formed with an American novelist, Alden Brooks, who lived on the other side of the wall in the old priest's house. He was a delightful fellow. He spent most of his time during the week in Paris, where he appeared to be very interested in collecting works by the 'new people'. He had a remarkable collection of Modigliani, and he had one of the very few wooden sculptures of Gauguin. I always longed for four o'clock on Sunday. That was the time and the day when Delius would receive one or two of his special local friends.

F.C. These were special occasions for him?

E.F. Well, they were special occasions for him because during the week, of course, nobody came. The Deliuses were very much aloof from what went on in the village, and it was a very strange experience for me during the day if Delius said he would like an airing and I pushed him in his little carriage up a road out of the village which led to a village called Marlotte. It was on that road, he told me, that he'd contemplated all his greatest works.

Delius was very strange in that sense, in that he would always lie fallow in the summer time, and he would go up to Norway, where for many years he and his wife had a cottage, and during that time there would be no talk of music whatever. He would then spend most of his days in silence, with a tremendous amount of walking. Of course it's very difficult to think of the invalid of the last years, of the manly adventurer who tired everybody to death, climbing mountains and then coming back and dashing off on a bicycle and all that sort of thing. He seemed to have incredible energy, a great zest for life.

F.C. Is this part of his response to the creative process? Would these things work down deep subconsciously? Would the works, after a period of so-called fallow activity, come out a more or less full reading?

E.F. Well, that's a very interesting point, Mr Calland, very interesting, because Delius would return during the winter months and spend all that time at Grez-sur-Loing, where he would write down what he had meditated. Now, the interesting thing about Delius was that he was completely anti-intellectual. He composed entirely by intuition. And this he did with me just the same as he'd done all his life. For example, in his prime he would begin a piece of work when he felt the urge and would continue with it in full score. He never made a piano reduction or a transcription first like people like Elgar or Vaughan Williams, who used to do four-handed arrangements and then orchestrate afterwards. Delius didn't do that. He ruled the score paper out, decided what instruments he wanted to have - and not always that at the very beginning - he would see how the thing went on, how it was going to shape and what would turn up. He had no idea what was going to happen. He would begin, and supposing he got up to bar 19 or so, and then he found it wasn't going too well, it was a bit strained or enforced, he would put the thing aside in a desk. Now the point is that up to there, that score would be already completed and ready for the copyist down to the smallest detail. That was the way he worked with me too, in full score. I had to sit at the piano and play the sounds as they came out.

F.C.   How would he dictate? For example, if he wanted a woodwind line, would he hum it or call out the notes?

E.F.   Yes, calling out the notes. And the interesting thing is that he never once, during all the work we did together, called a chord by its technical name. It was always given out in actual notation: [singing] A. B. And he sang all pretty well on the same note, and he also dictated with great rapidity, stumbling over his words and so on with an enormous amount of excitement. And he who, down in the living room, would not be able to sit on a chair without arms during those last years of his complete incapacity, completely blind, completely paralysed except for a slight movement of the hands, and couldn't even shake hands. But he could blow his nose. Sometimes he would put a handkerchief over, and then he would raise his hand up to his face. But that's about as far as he was able to do. He couldn't feed himself or anything like that. The whole thing was really most distressing. But the amazing thing was that he could sit there on a chair without arms when he was excited and carried away by these dictations. When Mrs Delius happened to read a poem that she thought might match the mood that she had divined in his music (and this she had been able to do at a very early age in their relationship), she would copy it out, put it on his desk and leave it around in the hope that he might see it. I mean, you couldn't say 'Set this' to Delius. You always had to approach things in an oblique way, because there was no discussion about music.

F.C.   No discussion about music between Jelka and Frederick Delius?

E.F.   No discussion. I was the musician in the house and there was no discussion between Delius and myself. In all the time I was there I don't think we talked twenty minutes' music altogether. He wouldn't discuss music; he wouldn't explain himself.

F.C.   Was he really that much of a loner in the musical world?

E.F.   Oh, completely and utterly.

F.C.   You mean he never rejected, say, Elgar or Harty or some other composers?

E.F.   Oh he would, but the point was he wouldn't listen to any other music but his own.

F.C.   Why was that, do you suppose? Did he feel so defensive or did he feel he had to grasp on to his own individuality?

E.F.   No. I think he just simply disliked it intensely. Of course, obviously a certain amount of music had to come into the house. For example, we would listen to Radio Paris just prior to the news about lunchtime. We always had lunch about half-past twelve, and it would probably come on at that time. And maybe there was a Pasdeloup concert about to finish, or something of that kind, maybe something of Beethoven or the Old Masters. And of course he would be most disparaging in his remarks. 'Scales and arpeggios,' he would say about people like Haydn and Mozart. But I think in many ways that was possibly because as a boy at home he'd had such a surfeit of music of those Masters. He played Beethoven with the family quartet, in which he played second violin.

F.C.   What would you say was Delius's most fruitful period?

E.F.   I would say it was the turn of the century when up to then nobody, not even his most fervent admirers, could have guessed the way his musical mind would go. Up to then he had written the opera *Koanga*, which admittedly stands quite apart from the rest of his work, a strong American influence, and there were the sketches for *Paris* too, which were from about 1899. But then at the turn of the century we get *A Village Romeo and Juliet.* To my mind it comes in a curious influence: it is an American influence, I think, which led the way eventually to what we might possibly come to regard as Delius's most characteristic work. That is the *Appalachia* variations which Delius wrote on a theme he heard in a tobacco factory when he was working his passage home in 1886 from Jacksonville, where he'd been escaping from his father's wrath, pursuing his desire to be a professional musician. He came up from Jacksonville, having felt the need for a more particularly musical environment, and was working his passage home when he heard one of these tunes sung by the leader of the gang of people who ripped out the tobacco veins from the leaves and sang rhythmically. Now, the interesting thing is that in revising that work, Delius inserted a quiet luminous episode for muted strings which has no connection with the theme whatever. In Beecham's hands it was absolutely out of this world, wonderful! I think from that moment Delius became a visionary rather than a mere composer.

This visionary aspect of his personality is reflected very much in the poems and the literature he chose. The *Mass of Life* is quite an enigma to most people. Could anyone else have written *A Mass of Life*? If we just pause at certain periods of his life, we could ask ourselves - who else could have written *Koanga*? - who else could have written *Appalachia*? - who else could have written *A Mass of Life*? I think the most moving works of Delius are those in which he tries to reveal the deeper aspects of transience.

F.C. The *Irmelin* Prelude was a work that you and Delius worked on?

E.F. Yes. That's an interesting thing because right at the end when we'd finished all the works by dictation, he said he would like to look through his life's work, that is to say all that had not been published. *Irmelin* was the second opera, but in those days Delius was having great difficulty in finding librettists and I suppose he tried to outdo Wagner and provide his own. Unhappily it was not very successful. Therefore he wasted a tremendous amount of quite reasonable music.

F.C. I know what you mean. *Fennimore and Gerda* does not read as one of the staggering literary masterpieces of all time. Do you feel it is a viable opera?

E.F. I would think that that's the most characteristic opera of all because there's not a note in that work that could have been written by anybody but Delius. And that's the test, I think.

F.C. How will the *Mass of Life* come out, as a festival piece revived occasionally, or do you feel it will find a wider favour?

E.F.   I think in the end it will probably be lower in the scale than *Sea Drift* and the much-neglected *Arabesque*. But nevertheless it is a work of tremendous power and contains some of the most beautiful nature music that Delius ever wrote. We mustn't forget that Delius was the first great composer, I think, to write nature music on the scale of a Wagner, as he did for example in the *Appalachia* variations.

F.C.   What did he admire in Wagner - the music, the harmonies, the freedom, the length?

E.F.   He admired the flow. Music to Delius was flow; that was the most important thing of all. He said; 'It doesn't matter how you achieve it, so long as you master it. That is the great thing; flow is the essential thing.'

F.C.   Is it not interesting to point out that one of his contemporaries, Richard Strauss, also dipped into the thinking and philosophy of Nietzsche, in his tone-poem *Also sprach Zarathustra*? You could not compare the two.

E.F.   Oh no. Delius would have had a stroke. He couldn't bear it if we'd had to sit through that to the end - the other works like *Don Juan* and *Till Eulenspiegel*, but certainly not *Zarathustra*.

F.C.   It is interesting to point out that they were contemporary and Richard Strauss was in the everyday hurly-burly; he was in the concert hall, he was in the conservatory, he was in the opera house. He was listening to rehearsals and performances and premières, whereas this was not the milieu of Frederick Delius.

E.F.   Good gracious no! Delius was completely hopeless in all these matters.

F.C.   I dare say there are a lot of works that he didn't hear performed. Is that true?

E.F.   When I say hopeless, he was completely hopeless as a director of his works.

F.C.   Lack of discipline, or lack of interest in performing?

E.F.   Delius completely lacked interest in a work once it was finished. He put it in a drawer and never made any attempt to get it published or played; that came from other people.

F.C. In which case you have really done yeoman service in bringing out some things such as the Violin Sonata No 3. What other of those works you worked on do you feel are really essential Delius? *The Songs of Farewell* perhaps?

E.F. Oh yes, I think so. He regarded that as the most important thing that we were trying to tackle, and that everything else was a preparation for it. The *Idyll* too. That was a reconstruction from the early opera *Margot La Rouge*, which was a kind of blood-and-thunder thing he wrote for a competition when he was hard up. When we came to look at that in the final survey, his first thought was that we ought to try and get another libretto, and to get hold of somebody like Robert Nichols, who was a great enthusiast for his music. I went down to see Nichols, who was then living in Winchelsea, taking the score of *Margot* with me. I played it through and Nichols ruminated for a couple of days or so, and then he said he didn't think he could cope with it but that there were some beautiful passages in the music and it was a great shame. I well remember one night he came in, having been out walking in the soaking rain, and said: 'Oh Fenby, I've got it. "Once I passed through a populous city, imprinting my brain with all its shows. Of that city I remember only a woman who detained me for love of me." Fine, we've got it. It's all here.'

F.C. Robert Nichols was instrumental in linking the Whitman text to the Margot music?

E.F. Yes, he was. It was he.

F.C. How did Delius take the suggestion?

E.F. Well, he was greatly shocked at first, I need hardly say. But then he began to see that it was possible. When I got back to Grez, Delius worked on it. All the vocal lines remained the same but with changed words. There were one or two places where obviously we had to tailor the joins and so on, but it all fitted together. It's a oneness of mood that everybody complains about in Delius which is the saving grace which links it all together.

F.C. Did he use all the *Margot* music?

E.F. No. Not all the melodramatic stuff, we just couldn't have that, and in some ways it was fortunate that Nichols, whom Delius had asked to come to Grez so we could work on things à trois, wasn't able to do so. The only solution was my going there, so I was sent in the initial stages just to see what we might do. In the end Delius was delighted with it, of course.

F.C.   What do you think of the Requiem, which is another strange thing that only Delius could have written?

E.F.   Well, I have to admit to being completely wrong about the Requiem.

F.C.   Why?

E.F.   In the beginning when I lived at Grez, I played the thing through. It didn't make any impression on me whatever. I think possibly I was too much prejudiced in the fact that I have been a very ardent and practising churchman, with my life as an organist, and so on. To be thrown straight out of that into this extraordinary house at Grez where with the mention of church you would have been put in the river, it was rather difficult there!

F.C.   Was it primarily the text of the Requiem, the absolutely secular non-liturgical text?

E.F.   Not so much. It didn't seem to me at the time that the music carried any great conviction with it. But obviously when I heard it done by Meredith Davies [who recorded the work for EMI] I had to change my opinion.

F.C.   If you were shocked at encountering the Delius Requiem, what must you have thought of the *Mass of Life* and the moralist problem, and his stated defiance of tradition, religiosity and so forth. Didn't that bother you?

E.F.   No, that didn't worry me in the slightest degree because I began to be a little more attuned, you see, because Delius soon thought he would turn things upside down by giving me *Thus spake Zarathustra* as a Christmas present for my very first year, marking all the passages which he had meditated throughout his life. And I must say I was very moved by the poetic quality of it. I began to understand more of possibly what Nietzsche was trying to do. As far as the *Mass of Life*, I must say that what won me to Delius at that time was not so much *On hearing the first cuckoo in spring*, but I'll never forget standing in the music shop in Scarborough when, having received the postcard to say that the vocal score of Delius's *Mass of Life* had arrived, I called in at the shop for the music. Well, I just opened it at the page of 'O Zarathustra', that marvellous contralto solo and when the men's voices come in, and me standing there reading it in the shop; that won me to Delius, for ever.

F.C.　Someone has written, I think in conjunction with the *Mass of Life*, the following: 'Overcoming the moralist is intended for the deepening and the strengthening of man's experience of himself, which would overcome the need for morality. He dares ask man to evolve out of himself a better, more joyous man, one that can live entirely according to the truth of his own experience.' That seems to touch something about Delius that is to be found in much of his music, is it not?

E.F.　Yes. I'm with you there entirely. The great thing about Delius was courage to speak the truth whether you hurt people or not, and at all levels too. If I hedged when I was asked: 'Do you like that music?' and maybe was in the presence of somebody who was intimately connected with it, and I didn't say exactly what I think, then I got quite a roasting after that person had gone. Or in the performance too if I felt, sometimes like Mrs Delius, it was very much more tactful to be a little kind when well-meaning people came to play their music, and he in the middle of it would say: 'Make the lady and gentleman some tea, and carry me away!', you would be left. And then he would say: 'Why didn't you say it was bad? You must always say the truth.'

　　　　Then the courage to die, that was the great thing, never to be afraid of death, no whimpering, none of this sentiment and nonsense; the courage to face the future and go right out into it. He said that if a man can do that then he's found and won the freedom of his soul. I see Delius in everything that you said in that last remark.

F.C.　His death and his illness; this was as a result of a long case of syphilis, was it not?

E.F.　It was.

F.C.　Now, I'm sure the very thought of this must have upset many of your acquaintances.

E.F.   Oh yes.

F.C.   The very thought of this as short a time as thirty or forty years ago. But now we look upon it as the plague to human beings that it was, especially we even now acknowledge that Schubert, Schumann, Bellini and others died of this dreadful affliction. There were, amongst the German expressionists, some thoughts that this particular disease did affect a person's output and his intensity and energy. Did this affect Delius?

E.F.   I think so.

F.C.   In what way?

E.F.   Well, I think that the peculiar flavour of his music emanates in some mysterious way from that malady, and that was something that I have discussed with no-one. But it was just intimated to me quite briefly by Balfour Gardiner, who himself said he had no doubt about that whatever.

F.C.   They used to say of Robert Schumann, before they acknowledged the nature of his illness, that he was mad and therefore compositions written after a certain onset of the final illness were the result of a madman and therefore incoherent and no good, and it's absolutely not the case. You can study those works and they sometimes have an inner logic and structure that so-called sane people can't even grasp, let alone work out. I gather Delius was not inhibited.

E.F.   To the very last days of his life he saw things with a clearness and forthrightness of vision and expression. He was ever in complete mental control to the very end.

F.C.   But it was a unique, enigmatic, sometimes perhaps very lonely existence. I gather from what you say he embraced life to the very end.

E.F.   To the very end, no question of that. Nor did I ever hear him complain. He said he'd done everything that was worth doing in life; he'd seen everything that was worth seeing. He said: 'I have my imagination, I'm perfectly happy. It doesn't worry me.' He was stoical, he never complained of pain. There was a proud defiance, a hardness which of course I would associate with that kind of superman mentality that could be found in Nietzsche, and of course there again the attitude to women, as well as his attitude to what one might say 'the crowd'. He had no truck with the market-place, whether it was of music or of men. As you said entirely correctly, Delius was a loner. To me I think he was the most unprofessional and the least amateur of all musicians I've known. But to me he was music incarnate.

[First published in *The Delius Society Journal* No 106 Winter/Spring 1991]

DELIUS

(1862-1934)

Eric Fenby remembers the composer and Grez-sur-Loing

(Music and Musicians, May 1974)

When Delius died forty years ago, his private world became public overnight. The rambling old house with its walled garden at Grez-sur-Loing enclosed it no more. There were more people in his garden that Sunday in the hours following his lingering death than in all the years during which I had shared his seclusion. The surviving custodian of this private world, his widow, Jelka, lay ill upstairs. She had just returned from a Fontainebleau hospital after a serious operation.

In response to my telegram that Delius was sinking, Beecham had sent Dora Labbette to see if she might be of help. I was in the music-room when she arrived, and remember her pausing in the doorway, a lovely reminder of another world that seemed so distant from that household, as she gazed down tearfully on the body of Delius lying on the studio couch. I have often been asked whether or not the sprinkling of rose petals over his body was a touch of Ken Russell's fantasy. No, that actually happened at daybreak that morning. Strange, perhaps, to English ways, but it was Jelka's wish, and she did it herself from a wheel-chair.

No one has made a greater and more lasting impression on my mind than Delius. His French burial was true to character: no priest, no prayers, no music, but a silent farewell to the fearless pagan joining the village free-thinkers by the wall in the cemetery on the Marlotte road out of Grez. The Anglican interment a year later, when Jelka was fit enough to travel to England but not, as it happened, to attend the service, was a compromise Delius would never have countenanced. His Requiem is proof of this. Others living in a busy world - Delius, like Nietzsche, had no time for the market-place - may find such singularity embarrassing, but with Delius behaviour was married to conviction, and what to others was of little importance to him was often a moral issue.

There were other attitudes no less singular, and certainly during my time at Grez one was a constant bone of contention between Delius and his wife - namely the future of his music. Jelka had always striven to urge the claims of her husband's work, writing countless letters to conductors, upbraiding publishers, continually exerting every pressure and every influence she could muster to achieve her one objective in life. Delius was supposed to be kept in ignorance of these 'thunder letters' (as she used to call them), although he had an inkling all the same, and scolded her severely when things came to light. But who could blame her? She had sacrificed her painting for him, given him ideal conditions to work and supported him through thick and thin.

Delius, on the other hand, in no sense a careerist, was quite content to let things be, even if hopeful of recognition. He had had his share of broken promises and had realised his ineptitude as a conductor of his music. If conductors wanted to play his work, they would do so eventually without his prompting. He believed implicitly that his music would live, but only by what it was in itself. I have often wondered what on earth he would have thought of the mediocrities of today pushing their scores through publicity agents. Not that he was uninterested in new music: quite the contrary. He was deeply concerned about young composers and insisted that we mark *Radio Times* for performances of their works. He would listen intently by high-powered radio for any sign of natural talent. His comments were dry, sometimes arresting, and his open acceptance of other minds far removed from his own world of thought cured me of any priggish rejections.

It has never failed to astound me, the more I have thought of it since he died, that with this concern for young composers he had made no provision for the future of his own. For years he had looked like a living corpse, and was quite content with a small piece of paper on which, to comply with French law, he had left all his effects to his wife. The document was so old that all the witnesses to his signature were dead.

Then, some days before he died, anxious to show his gratitude to me, he dictated a separate codicil appointing as executor, his closest friend, the composer, Balfour Gardiner. The most important clause in this codicil set down clearly his dearest wish: that his royalties be allowed to accrue and be used to give an annual concert of works by unknown young composers in a programme to include one of his own. Delius died before Gardiner could complete the legal formalities, but his wishes in respect of me were honoured in part subsequently. Beecham then persuaded Jelka to abandon the concert scheme; it was, he declared, an impracticable project. He urged her instead to direct the royalties towards the recording and editing of the main corpus of Delius's work. She agreed, and thus the Delius Trust was born. Beecham called in his lawyer, Philip Emanuel, and appointed him, a bank trustee and two other musical advisers besides himself. Currently [1974] these advisers are Sir Thomas Armstrong, Norman Millar and Felix Aprahamian. No trust can have been more steadfast or inspired more selfless service in those of its members throughout the years[21]. After preliminary surveillance by Rachel Dugmore, a vast amount of work has ensured the safe-keeping of the Delius Archives housed at the Royal Academy of Music in charge of the archivist, Dr Lionel Carley, and music adviser, Robert Threlfall.

A remarkable quality in Delius's music has become more apparent in the past 20 years - its power to arouse affection and fervour for it and its composer in people from all walks of life throughout the English-speaking world. A scientist, for instance, Dr Roland Gibson, founded the Delius Society in 1962. This is a body of enthusiasts who meet in London to share their interest, sustaining that of out-of-town members by a quarterly bulletin containing articles, notices and news of forthcoming Delius events. Older by two years, the Delius Association of Florida Inc is centred in Jacksonville and sponsors the annual Delius Festival, which takes place in January[22] round about the composer's birthday. Its founder members were an accountant, the late Hugh Alderman, whose devotion to Delius's music was boundless, and the late Mrs Henry L Richmond, through whose generosity the shack on Solano Grove (occupied by Delius during his sojourn in Florida from 1884) has now been restored on the beautiful campus of Jacksonville University. Nevertheless, what would

---

21   At the present time the members of The Delius Trust are Trustees: Meredith Davies (Chairman), Helen Faulkner (Musicians Benevolent Fund representative) and Martin Williams; Advisers: Felix Aprahamian, Lionel Carley (Archivist), David Lloyd-Jones, Robert Montgomery and Robert Threlfall; and Secretary: Marjorie Dickinson. Until his death in 1994, Sir Thomas Armstrong was Adviser Emeritus.

22   Later changed to March.

have pleased the composer most is the Delius Competition Contest which almost fulfils his dearest wish: 'In the spirit of the annual Jacksonville Delius Festival the Delius Association of Florida Inc offers five annual awards (a first prize of $100, and four best of category awards of $25 each) for new musical compositions to be submitted according to the following rules etc. . . . ' There is a wide range of categories and no entrance fee. Works selected by the judges from the various categories are performed at a special Delius Composition Contest Concert during the Delius Festival at Jacksonville.

It was said in my hearing repeatedly, often by those whose views I respected, that Delius's music would lose its appeal when Beecham was no longer in action. This inferred an exclusive mastery by one person of a singular idiom, surely unheard of before in an art which waits for life in written symbols even from those who can hear them mentally, and in my experience of students of the orchestra this is not a common accomplishment. Still, it must be conceded, however, that Beecham from around the late 1920s to somewhere about the middle 1940s was matchless in his conceptions of Delius. There are people living in Philadelphia who still rave about his performances. Later he indulged in sentimentalities and erratic outbursts of temperament which sometimes led to impossible tempi and marred certain episodes which could have been masterstrokes. His earliest recordings of Delius are his best. His finest efforts were never recorded and happened fortuitously, as was his mood, at rehearsals or in the concert afterwards.

In the 27 years that yet remained to him after the death of Delius, Beecham developed a rival affection for the music of Sibelius and there were periods of inconstancy to Delius. Sometimes he went for months on end and never conducted a note of the music. Then, as in 1946, he would suddenly give a whole festival of it, or stack up a pile of test-records of a work such as *Songs of Sunset*[23], then drop the whole task in disenchantment. It took courage in those days for a conductor to risk a work by Delius, knowing beforehand his reading would certainly meet with unfavourable comparison with Beecham's from orchestra, public and critics alike. Yet still they persisted, as I can vouch, prompted alone by a love of the music.

---

23   This recording, made on 30 November 1946 at the Abbey Road studios, was issued incomplete in the World Records boxed LP set *The Music of Delius* Volume 2 SHB54.

The real breakthrough came, I am sure, at the Bradford Delius Centenary Festival the year after Beecham's death when, on my appointment as Artistic Director, and backed to a man by the festival committee, I chose Rudolf Kempe to conduct all the concerts. The decision initially caused a stir: it went some way to appeasing a rather disgruntled RPO, none too pleased at the prospect of a week of Delius ahead, but I knew my man. From the first hour of the first rehearsal Kempe restored the mood of the players by the quiet intentness of his practice and their total response to his lyrical phrasing. I was not surprised by their round-robin at the close of the festival: 'Mr Fenby, you can arrange another Delius Festival as soon as you like provided you ask Mr Kempe to conduct us!' I was not so happy with the two fine but rival Bradford choral societies who refused to form a festival chorus, and preferred each society to be responsible for a concert. It would have been more convenient had Delius been born in a neighbouring town over the hills!

Sir John Barbirolli and Sir Malcolm Sargent now gradually came to the fore as champions of Delius. Each appeared to have a special work in which he clearly was thought to excel: Sargent with *A Mass of Life*, Barbirolli with *Appalachia*. Stanford Robinson made his mark with a broadcast concert-version of *Koanga*, whilst the more recent ascendancy of Sir Charles Groves and Meredith Davies have kept Delius before the public in the field of international recording right up to the present day - Meredith Davies with the award-winning *Requiem* and *A Village Romeo and Juliet*; Groves with *Koanga*, *Sea Drift* and *The Song of the High Hills* about to be released. A conductor often overlooked, Anthony Collins, was sensitive in his recording of *Song of Summer*.

I little thought, when I was struggling to take down Delius's music at Grez, that one day I should see the scene enacted in my own home. Ken Russell's film was disturbingly life-like. I had not seen it before its public showing, being myself out of action during the weeks of shooting. Even so, Christopher Gable, playing me, had asked me to spare his feelings and keep away from the set. Eventually I was called to the studios to record the music of the scene where Delius, propped up in bed, listens to Percy Grainger and me playing *The Song of the High Hills* in the music-room. On my arrival I found Russell immersed in directing a 'retake' of my first meeting with Delius which, apparently, had not satisfied Max Adrian. I was ushered into the studio to wait, and was just in time to hear that deliberate and unforgettable greeting 'Come in, Fenby!' I had mimicked Delius weeks before at Russell's suggestion as a guide to Adrian to learning his lines and behaving like Delius, but this was too much for me - the voice, the inflection, the image of Delius sitting there, a rug over his knees, with a great screen about him, slowly extending his hand in welcome. I lived that momentous moment again, I am unashamed to say, and not without a tear. Max Adrian told me later that of all the roles he had ever played he had never before had such difficulty in ridding himself of involvement[24].

The recording proceeded with some interjections addressed to a mysterious character called 'Spud', who functioned unseen behind the sets, in charge of the sound equipment. In shots of the actor playing Grainger, otherwise excellent in the part, the poor fellow's lack of rhythm in simulating a keyboard technique contrived an ingenious solution from Russell. He instructed me to lie on the floor, out of range of the camera, and work 'Grainger's' arms from below appropriately in time with a 'play-back' of the music which Gable and I had recorded previously. Then, when shots of his hands were required, Russell asked me to take his place. The camera revealed a further incongruity as yet unnoticed by us all. His trousers were checked and mine were plain. So mine were whipped off and his put on, and camera and music resumed in unison. This was my active contribution to the film, apart from collaborating with Russell on the script.

The war having intervened and Balfour Gardiner having died after disposing of Delius's house at Grez, I felt no inclination to return. Then in 1967 my wife and I were invited by members of the committee of the Delius Society to accompany them to Grez. I was desolate when I saw what changes had occurred. Alden Brooks, the American novelist, who

---

24   Interviewed by Brian Matthew on BBC Radio 2's 'Round Midnight' programme, 18 November 1980, Eric Fenby said: 'Max Adrian was exactly as I remember Delius. I coached him in the inflexions of Delius's voice, and the way he sat, the way he held his hands. And, of course, what really I think was the most remarkable piece of acting in that very remarkable film, to my mind, was the speed of the dictation, because I had given them various samples from my book *Delius as I knew him* of how to do it. But I didn't think it would be possible for them to do it so remarkably because Delius dictated with the very greatest rapidity.'

Asked about the portrayal of himself in that film, he commented: 'I can only say from what one can judge from that kind of experience, which must be something unique and a great privilege, was to find somebody so sensitive chosen by Ken Russell as Christopher Gable.'

lived as Delius's neighbour on the other side of the church for over thirty years and who knew more about Delius than any man alive, had long been gone and was now dead. He had married one of the Chadwick daughters who were born in Delius's house. Chadwick, who looked like Elgar, was an American painter who had settled at Grez in its hey-day as an artists' paradise. One person alone remained, his eldest daughter, Madame Louise Courmes, and we talked of old times in her elegant home.

A fortnight later, quite unexpectedly, I was back in Grez - this time with Ken Russell. We had been sent for the week-end by the BBC to see if the original settings might be used in making the proposed film. We met the new owner of the house, Madame Merle d'Aubigné, who had asked us to tea in the garden. She was somewhat alarmed at the prospect of a film being made on her doorstep, but I saw at a glance she had no cause to worry. My old quarters had been pulled down, the music-room had been made into bedrooms, the out-buildings and studios had been renovated and the garden bore evidence of much attention. From that moment I accepted the change. The tale of the Deliuses was over, and with it the place where it was lived. And as we walked up the village street with its television aerials on every chimney and modern sports cars parked by the verge, I felt a great relief of mind as if I had laid some ancient ghost.

An opportunity, unprecedented and irreparable, was missed at Bradford after the Delius Centenary Festival in 1962. An exhibition, sponsored by the Centenary Festival Committee with the full co-operation of the Bradford Corporation, had been assembled and mounted to provide visitors with a visual record of Delius's life, the wide cosmopolitan circle of his friends in the worlds of art, music and letters, and the range of his achievements as a composer through the loan of material from numerous sources. Part of it was afterwards shown in London at the Festival Hall through the then director, who rated it highly as second only to the famous exhibition of Proust in Paris. Tentative feelers were put out at the time in the vain hope that it might become permanent, but other exhibitions of more local general interest had already established prior claims and precluded such a possibility in Bradford. For years I regretted what I might have done; that I gave up so soon, and failed to go about it in the proper way. Of late, however, I am really not so sure. After all it is the music that is of his spirit.

In Bernard Levin's amusing game of concocting programmes of music one never wanted to hear again, the first piece of his best effort was *On hearing the first cuckoo in spring*. 'The music of Delius is not an acquired taste. One either likes it the moment one first hears it, or the sound of it is once and for ever distasteful to one. It is an art which will never enjoy an appeal to the many, but one which will always be loved, and dearly loved, by the few.' It is nearly forty years since I wrote that passage; nor have I had reason to change my mind. Delius always will be on the programme of music I want to hear again.

DELIUS AS I KNEW HIM
BBC RADIO 4 'CELEBRATION' SERIES
5 June 1974

INTRODUCTION:
Frederick Delius, whose music for many people sums up the essence of the English countryside, died 40 years ago this week, on June 10th 1934. One of the people who at the end of his life knew Delius best is Eric Fenby. In this programme, which takes its title from his book about Delius, first published in 1936, *Delius as I knew him*, Eric Fenby tells the story of their extraordinary association.

ERIC FENBY:
It began one summer night in 1928. I was playing chess with a friend of mine and I was trapped. My friend as a final gesture got up and turned on the radio. From the loudspeaker came music of exquisite invention, such as I'd never heard before. I remember to this day the precise moment at which I began to listen.

[Music : *On hearing the first cuckoo in spring*]

Later that year I was sitting beside Delius listening to that same music, *On hearing the first cuckoo in spring*, in the tiny village south of Paris where he'd lived for thirty years. I'd heard that he was unable to go on composing. I'd written to him saying that I would do whatever I could to help him, and he'd replied accepting my offer.[25] He was totally blind, and

---

25   In an interview in the BBC Radio Leeds programme, *Beauty and Strangeness*, broadcast on 10 June 1984, Eric Fenby described in greater detail his considerable soul-searching before actually writing to Delius: 'It all comes back to me; not of course my defeat at chess but the extraordinary vision of a new mentality and originality, and great sensitivity, and above all artistry which was to change my whole life. It

to move at all he needed the help of a male nurse. His devoted wife Jelka had met me at the station, and, in the ancient Ford with its yellow curtains, she drove me to the house where they lived. Soon after I arrived, I met Delius for the first time. He sat upright in a chair, gaunt, deathly pale, a rug round his knees. We shook hands and then we talked. He knew Scarborough where I came from. As a boy living in Bradford he'd gone there for holidays. And when we went on to talk about music I brought up the question of English music. He said: 'English music? Did you say English music? I've never heard of any.'

We had lunch, and watching him I wondered how I would be able to help him and to what purpose. And then word came that Sir Thomas Beecham had announced a festival of Delius's music to take place in London. It would cover several weeks of the autumn of the following year. Eventually Sir Thomas appeared in person to persuade Delius to make the journey. Before leaving he drew me aside. Would I look through Delius's manuscripts? He was short of a work for voice and orchestra to include in the Festival programme. I searched through piles of pencilled sketches, all in full score, stacked in a vast cupboard in one of the studies. At last I came upon a likely piece. It was obviously unfinished, though complete in orchestral detail as far as he'd gone. It was for baritone solo. But the sketch was so faded I couldn't make out the words. When I referred to it at supper, Delius dismissed it. 'Play it to me when I have gone to bed.'

---

seemed to me to be the most appalling thing that a man was in such a state and could not finish his life's work. I suddenly got the idea that perhaps I might be able to do something. But immediately I cast it aside as something quite presumptuous. But still it was a nattering thought until suddenly I could stand it no longer, and I remember getting up one night and not saying anything at all to the rest of the family, and writing to Delius, saying how much I loved his music and how much it meant to me. Almost immediately there came back a letter which I afterwards learnt was in his wife's hand. . .

'It was on my second letter that I wrote and said that I'd thought the matter over very deeply, and if it were possible I would like to see whether I could come and help him. And I would give him three or four years of my life to see what could be done. There again came an immediate letter, saying that he was greatly touched by my offer. I must realise that Grez-sur-Loing where they lived almost as recluses was a very tiny village with no young life. Don't bring grand clothes, just come as you are. . .'

I wheeled him up the road out of the village for his customary evening outing, but he was in no mood to talk. And I wondered what his reaction would be when I played the music for him. Later, when he'd been propped up in bed and was ready, his wife held up the manuscript whilst I coped with it as best I could on the upright piano on the landing outside his room. 'Ah! that's Dowson's *Cynara*,' he called. 'Go on, go on.' And when I came to the end he told me that he'd put it aside in 1906, the year I was born. It wouldn't fit the scheme of the choral work *Songs of Sunset* for which it was intended. He'd forgotten he'd ever written it.

The next day he was carried up to the music room and I was asked to play it through again. And when I played the last bar of the manuscript he said: 'Now read the rest of the poem.'

> *But when the feast is finished and the lamps expire,*
> *Then falls thy shadow, Cynara! the night is thine;*
> *And I am desolate and sick of an old passion,*
> *   Yea, hungry for the lips of my desire:*
> *I have been faithful to thee, Cynara! in my fashion.*

'Well,' he said, 'I must try and finish it.' I'll not go now into how it was done or how long it took before he was satisfied, but it was a very painful ordeal for me. And when the decisive day arrived when we were in London and at Queen's Hall to hear the work rehearsed with Sir Thomas, Delius was quite unconcerned as we came to the final section he had dictated to me the previous winter.

[Music : *Cynara*]

There was silence after that performance of *Cynara* and I waited anxiously. 'Eric, lad,' said Delius, 'I can work with you.' That was enough for me. Afterwards, Jelka told me that before leaving for London, Delius had asked her to stitch a £5 note into his jacket lining, and he'd said: 'This is for Eric if it comes off well.'

I was in my element at the Festival. Before then I had not heard one note of Delius's music in the concert hall. What I knew of it had come from studying the scores in the music room and from the actual process of working with him. Very little of his music had been recorded, but now at the Festival I heard all his major works performed to perfection under Sir Thomas Beecham, his great champion; in particular *A Mass of Life*, Delius's grandest choral work, inspired by passages selected from Nietzsche's *Thus spake Zarathustra*. The title suggests a unique nonconformity. It's not a Christian Mass but a passionate affirmation of the will of man to lead him onwards to his final destiny.

[Music : *A Mass of Life*]

Delius was completely exhausted after the Festival and needed rest. So I spent that Christmas at home. He had said that he wanted me to return to him in the new year to take down a violin sonata. About the end of January he dictated a note saying he was ready to begin work. When I arrived at his house I found him racked with pain. We could do nothing but read aloud to him for hours and try and calm him. Eventually a start was made. There was not much to go on: a few scraps he'd jotted down on his last visit to Norway when he still could see; one tune - the first I'd attempted to take down at his dictation. And what a mess I'd made of it at the time now blossomed as he meant it to be. Later, the tune was used in the slow section of the middle movement of that violin sonata. I play it here on Delius's piano at which he composed all his finest music. The violinist is Ralph Holmes.

[Music : Violin Sonata No 3]

Another work which Delius managed to complete by dictation was *A Poem of Life and Love* for orchestra. One hot Sunday morning in August he called for me. He was sitting in the garden in the shade of an old alder tree. He'd thought of a new title and a new opening for the work, *A Song of Summer*.

'I want you,' said Delius, 'to imagine that we're sitting on the cliffs and the heather looking out over the sea. The sustained chords in the high strings suggest the clear sky and the stillness and the calm of the sea. Now, seven-four in a bar, four and three. Now, divided strings. Have you got it?' 'Yes.' 'Chord of D major: A, D, F sharp, doubled at the octave, lowest note the A string of the violas.' And so I wrote down at his dictation the evocative opening.

[Music : *A Song of Summer*]

You may have seen the late Max Adrian as Delius in Ken Russell's television film which took its title from that piece, *A Song of Summer*. He looked and behaved almost exactly as I remember Delius, except that the dry wit which had so endeared Delius to me was lacking. Delius was a very private person, silent by nature but alarmingly outspoken when roused. He loved good food, good wine, good clothes. He always wore white, beautiful hand-made white silk shirts; white suits, everything spotless. He preferred his own music to anyone else's, though he never actually said so, and this without any trace of affectation. Oddly enough, yet characteristically, he rarely worried about having it performed. But I remember one occasion when a publisher enquired if he had anything that he thought might become popular. Delius allowed me to make an orchestral transcription of a vocal dance he'd written called *La Calinda*. I wish Delius had lived to enjoy its royalties.

[Music : *La Calinda*]

I'm unlikely to forget *Koanga*, the opera from which that dance came. Delius's autograph score had been lost for years, and when Beecham announced his long-term plan of reviving the opera at Covent Garden, there was only one thing to do, and that was to reconstruct a new score from the orchestral parts, which had luckily survived. After months of work I was well into the second act when the original manuscript was discovered in an old music warehouse. But the biggest task of all was still to come. This was the choral work, *Songs of Farewell*, for which, as Delius confidently assured me, our previous efforts had now prepared us. I marvel when I think of his courage and stamina, sometimes dictating no more than a bar or two of orchestration a day, never discussing the work but keeping at it day by day with an iron determination and will, retaining details in his mind, and going back, correcting, improving it. It was quite incredible.

Jelka, as usual, had chosen the words. They were from Walt Whitman's *Leaves of Grass*. The sea-scape picture stirs my memory most.

> *I stand as on some mighty eagle's beak,*
> *Eastward the sea absorbing, viewing, (nothing but sea and sky),*
> *The tossing waves, the foam, the ships in the distance,*
> *The wild unrest, the snowy, curling caps -*
> > *that inbound urge and urge of waves,*
> *Seeking the shores forever.*

[Music : *Songs of Farewell*]

When all the unfinished works had been completed, Delius turned to his earliest unpublished manuscripts. He spent long sessions with me in the music room hearing them again. Two works only he approved. The fragments of a one-act opera he'd written for a competition, *Margot La Rouge*, he now shaped into an *Idyll* for soprano, baritone and orchestra.

The other work he approved was an interlude from his very first opera, *Irmelin*, which he now extended and made into an enchanting Prelude.

[Music : *Irmelin* Prelude]

I left Delius in the autumn of 1933. There was nothing more I could do. I promised I would return if he wanted me. And then I had a telegram from Jelka. She was in hospital in Fontainebleau. Delius was in the house alone, except for the servants. Would I go to him? I set off at once and found him deeply distressed. I'd known for some time that Jelka was ill and might die, but not Delius. He'd never looked any different from the day I first met him, and now I saw a change. After some days, and there was hardly a wink of sleep at night, for he insisted that I take the twin bed beside him, he fell into a noisy coma. All Saturday it went on, and in the late evening I fell asleep. When I awoke, there perched at the foot of his bed was a great owl staring first at him and then at me. I don't know how long it stayed there but it seemed an age.

Delius died in the early hours of the next morning. I never hear the end of *The Walk to the Paradise Garden* without recalling the tribute to him after the nine o'clock news on the wireless that Sunday evening. Looking out across the garden, I listened to it in the stillness of the empty house.

[Music : *The Walk to the Paradise Garden*]

ANNOUNCER:
You have been listening to *Delius as I knew him*, presented by Eric Fenby, a celebration of Frederick Delius who died 40 years ago on June 10th 1934. The producer was Alan Haydock.

HONOURING BEECHAM

A review of Beecham remembered *(Duckworth 1976), compiled and edited by Humphrey Procter-Gregg, a revision of* Sir Thomas Beecham, conductor and impresario, as remembered by his friends and colleagues *(private publication, Westmorland Gazette 1973).*

(*Books and Bookmen* Vol 22 No 11, August 1977)

Any knowledgeable musician who has lived through the fifty years ending about 1960 would inevitably name Sir Thomas Beecham as the man who did most for British music in that period. The author of this original book,

Humphrey Procter-Gregg, friend of Beecham's and now Emeritus Professor in the University of Manchester, goes so far as to state that

> to the historian, Handel and Beecham must appear the most potent individual forces in the history of music in England; both operated on a lavish scale . . . both were autocrats of an aristocratic turn of mind . . and both lost a lot of money . . .

All this is true and, as to money, I remember one morning in 1935 finding Sir Thomas strangely serious. 'Look at this, my dear fellow! I have just been calculating the costs of my musical ventures for the year. How much do you think I have made? Thirty-one pounds and ten pence!'

After the death of Beecham in 1961, the author became preoccupied with ways and means of conserving knowledge of the vital influence that Beecham has been for those to whom he was but a name or the subject of extravagant anecdotes. Initially he posed three questions. Why was Beecham a very great man? Why was his contribution to British music so large and valuable? How did he become the superb interpreter of more music than any other British musician in history? The problem was how to present his answers authentically and arrestingly. Eventually he hit upon the brilliant idea of calling upon Beecham's surviving colleagues to recall their personal impressions of the man and his remarkable interpretations, and their professional reactions to his conducting when they had played or sung under him. Almost forty of these colleagues responded with fascinating slants on his character and musicianship. Their comments follow the author's brief outline on Beecham's life and artistic work, his own associations with him in opera, and what I find most relevant of all, his perceptive remarks and his illustrations on two examples of Beecham's technique concerning accent and dynamics in Schubert's 5th Symphony and Rossini's *William Tell.* No rendering I have heard of this symphony since Beecham's has been other than pedestrian by comparison. The same goes too for much of Mozart.

There are several pages of *obiter dicta.* I cannot resist quoting one of the more whimsical to an audience between items at Liverpool:

> Ladies and Gentlemen, in upwards of fifty years of concert-giving before the public, it has seldom been my good fortune to find the programme correctly printed. Tonight is no exception to the rule, and therefore, Ladies and Gentlemen, with your kind permission, we will now play you the piece you think you have just heard . . . This is the so-called *Paris* Symphony of Mozart, composed when as a very young man he was on his first visit to Paris. All I can say about *that* is that the Paris of *his* day must have been

different from the Paris of *mine* when a very young man; or Mozart would certainly never have had the time or the inclination to write a symphony . . .

Not included in an earlier privately printed edition of the book are Beecham's copious programme notes for a concert by the Oriana Madrigal Society in 1906 which Charles Kennedy-Scott conducted and Beecham sang among the basses. Beecham's deep knowledge and love of the English madrigal school represented here by Bennet, Byrd, Dowland, Gibbons, Morley, Mundy, Weelkes and Wilbye are evident in these models of what such notes should be. There is, however, a regrettable omission from the earlier edition - Beecham's scholarly Romanes Lecture which he delivered at the Sheldonian Theatre in Oxford in 1956, disclosing his personal reflections on aspects of seventeenth-century English literature. In expanding this later edition of the book the author has included a transcription from the original tape of a typical 'off the cuff' introductory talk on Mozart which Beecham gave in the same year at the University of Illinois Mozart Festival. His other favourite, Delius, is recalled appropriately,

Whatever the former accomplishments of Professor Procter-Gregg, I doubt if he has surpassed this achievement of his retirement, which is also a labour of love in tribute to his friend. *Beecham Remembered* should be on every music shelf.

COMPOSER WHO LOVED SOLITUDE

A review of Delius: A Life in Pictures *by Lionel Carley and Robert Threlfall (OUP 1977)*

(*Books and Bookmen* Vol 23 No 6, March 1978)

Dr Lionel Carley and Mr Robert Threlfall, archivists to the Delius Trust and leading lights of the Delius Society, have put together a life of Delius, spanning over the turn of the century, in pictures of remarkable range linked by brief biographical notes with apt quotations from Delius's letters and others from notable associates in the arts. How well this medium serves his life! Here, in swift pictorial terms, one grasps the uniqueness of the man and his cosmopolitan milieu in that instant truthful focus often lost in descriptive prose. One or two pictures may seem too peripheral; that, for instance, of 'W G Grace'. But Delius, who saw the great man, and played himself for Bradford Grammar School and later for the English

Eleven in Paris, followed county cricket scores up to his death. The dedication on the fly-leaf 'in memory of Philip Emanuel' - Beecham's solicitor who advised Jelka Delius in setting up the Delius Trust after her husband's death and who, at Beecham's death, became zealous in supporting promotion of the music - accompanies the remark by Delius: 'I don't claim to be a British composer'.

However, on the opposite page, in the phrase 'childhood and youth, 1862-84', we begin in industrial Bradford, then the hub of the wool trade in Yorkshire, where Delius's father, an immigrant from Germany, had established his own wool and noil business. He had married a girl from his native Bielefeld, by whom he had fourteen children. The fourth, his second son, the composer, was known as Fritz until he married, when he changed his name to Frederick. Their home in Bradford, No 1 Claremont, in those days backed onto the moors, but Fritz, always to be the odd man out, was born at No 6 over the road whilst No 1 had the builders in. His parents are shown as a striking pair: Julius, elegant, patriarchal, firm; Elise, bright-eyed, impetuous, aloof. No 1 was a house of music. Julius led the family quartet, and famous musicians visiting Bradford were often engaged to play in his drawing room. yet he despised the profession of music. Joachim, the great violinist, at one of these conservaziones, called upon Fritz, then a youth, to complete an ensemble as second violin with Piatti, the renowned cellist. Joachim's inclusion in characteristic pose foreshadows the breach that was never healed between father and son on the painful issue of music as a career. After attending Bradford Grammar School, and during a reluctant apprenticeship to the wool trade at Chemnitz in Saxony, a tenuous musical link appears in the lesser figure of Hans Sitt, with whom Delius studied the violin. Another figure who lived in Paris and clearly maintained the Delian elegance was Julius's brother, Theodor, who sided with Fritz and afterwards played a decisive role in his musical advancement. Among contemporary postcard photographs of towns in France and Norway is one that was certainly not included in Julius's business itinerary for Fritz as a traveller for the family firm, the casino at Monte Carlo, the consequences of which led to an inevitable break with his father. A curious compromise was reached. Fritz was packed off to Florida to tend a lonely orange farm which Julius had leased for him, Solana[26] Grove, by the St Johns River, some forty miles south of Jacksonville. This was in 1884.

---

[26]   Although the plantation that once was Delius's is known today as Solano Grove, documents of the time leave no doubt that it was then named

There are shots of the Jacksonville of those days and of friends Fritz made two years later whilst working his passage home. Back in Bradford, Julius, impressed by reports of the fees Fritz had earned from teaching the fiddle to the daughters of wealthy tobacco growers in Danville, Virginia, agreed to finance a course of advanced instruction at Leipzig Konservatorium. Fritz accepted, with some unease, knowing that the silence of Solana Grove had confirmed what he felt was in him to do - to devote himself to composition, and entirely different discipline from that of the violin. There was some consolation, however, in that Hans Sitt, his former teacher, was now a professor at the Konservatorium.

The visual biography begins to glow when the focus shifts from Leipzig to Paris, where Fritz acquired the fruitful habit of regular work on composition on a timely allowance from Uncle Theodor. The Scandinavian influence on Fritz in Leipzig nurtured by Grieg and Sinding grew in the coterie of Norwegian artists with whom he made close friendships in Paris, notably with Edvard Munch. Munch's dark effigies of Ibsen, Strindberg, Gunnar Heiberg (for whom Fritz wrote the incidental music to his drama *Folkeraadet*), his Delius, and two self portraits, one a lithograph, the other a glorious flare in oils, are distinctive contributions. Other coloured reproductions are two Gauguins, *Nevermore*, now in the Courtauld Institute Galleries, and once owned by Delius, who bought it through a mutual friend, Daniel de Monfreid, whose evocative painting of Fritz at the keyboard loses too much in black and white. The other Gauguin, a rich canvas, *Slewinski with Bunch of Flowers*, in the National Museum of Western Art in Tokyo, is presumably of a crony of Delius and Gauguin. Also in colour are paintings of Delius by Jelka, his wife, and by her German friend Ida Gerhardi. Jelka's pointillist brushwork is more suited to capturing the play of light in a corner of the garden at Grez than exposing the immediacy of portraiture which Ida's bolder strokes project. The two, as younger women, are photographed as students in an art class at the Académie Colarossi in Paris. There are photographs of Fritz in handsome maturity along with those who in this period contributed variously in furthering his music; the German conductors Buths, Haym and Cassirer; the French composers Ravel and Schmitt, with autograph extracts from their transcriptions; the singer Andrew Black, who was the 'first Koanga'.

Solana Grove. See Lionel Carley's 'Old or New Grove?', *Delius Society Journal* 101, 19-20.

Facsimiles from the autograph MS of Delius's *Sea Drift* and *A Mass of Life* are headed by Munch's sparse lithograph of Nietzsche - *the only free-thinker of modern times and for me the most sympathetic one (Delius)* - no wonder he chose the text of his *Mass* from Nietzsche's *Zarathustra*. These illustrations mark the rise of Delius's fame so long delayed at the great European music festivals under the conductors Fried and Schuricht, and with it the transition to the British phase of Wood, Beecham, Boult, Harty, Heward, Grainger and Heseltine.

The war period till 1918, despite his retreat from Grez to England and then to Norway, caused no abatement in Delius's output:

> I wrote a great deal, almost incessantly; I completed my *Pagan Requiem* [To the memory of all young artists fallen in the war.] A Concerto for Violoncello, Violin and Orchestra. A Violin Concerto - A Cello Sonata - A ballad for Orchestra *Eventyr* (once upon a time) after Asbjørnsen's folklore - *A Dance Rhapsody* (No 2) - A String Quartet - *A Poem of Life and Love* for Orchestra - *A Song before Sunrise* for small Orchestra   4 Elizabethan songs - 2 *a cappella* partsongs -

Munch's affinity with Delius's vision is seen on the cover of the vocal score of his last opera, *Fennimore and Gerda*, in a touching pastel image of the drama based on the novel, *Niels Lyhne*, by the Danish writer Jens Peter Jacobsen.

A postal friendship with an American sculptor, Henry Clews, and his wife, Marie, was a source of strength to Jelka for years with the gradual recurrence of Delius's malady. Pleasant pictures celebrate their occasional meetings at Grez-sur-Loing and the Clews's house, the Château de la Napoule, where Henry made a fine mask of Delius. There are excellent photographs of the cellist, Beatrice Harrison, a noted exponent of Delius in the Twenties, of Grainger with Delius, Jelka with him, but Balfour Gardiner, his closest friend, deserved a likeness of equal quality.

Two British artists are represented: John, by his pencil sketch of Delius done like lightning at the Langham Hotel during the Delius Festival in London in 1929; Gunn, by his full-length portrait painted at Grez in 1932 - true to my memory of his final phase - and now appropriately in Bradford Art Gallery. Over the page is a reprint of columns from a current issue of the *Daily Mirror* announcing the composer's death in June 1934, with the last photograph of him and Jelka also in the Langham Hotel. An apt quotation from Beecham's oration at Delius's reburial at Limpsfield, Surrey, is framed in a faint, riverside view of his house at Grez as seen through the leafless trees in winter from his meadow across the Loing.

There is an explanatory postscript with lists of sources, and the element of surprise is unusually strong in the story of a composer who loved solitude. The authors have succeeded in shaping a miscellany worthy of one of music's originals and clearly of their obvious devotion.

SOME CHANGES OF MIND

In January 1981, on the 119th anniversary of Delius's birthday, Dr Fenby spoke to a large audience, chiefly members of the Delius Society, at Mary Ward House, London. He related something of how he then stood in respect of certain works to which he was not attuned when in the spring of 1936 he wrote Delius as I knew him. *The following is a slightly edited version.*

(*The Delius Society Journal* No 71 April 1981)

There have been many contributing factors in the development of my taste for Delius's music. Initially there was my youthful preference, which has continued ever since, for the *last* works of writers, painters and composers; the Beethoven string quartets, Fauré's string quartet, Verdi's *Falstaff* (the beautifully bound Ricordi full score I bought with my first professional fee now a most treasured possession). There are exceptions - Rossini's *Barber of Seville* and Mendelssohn's string octet, but in the main I have always been fascinated by the wisdom and insight of old age. I little realised that in my early twenties I should be so intimately involved daily with the last works of a contemporary composer, least of all Delius.

In a sense I began with a handicap with Delius. It was like knowing a composer in reverse! My involvement in those last idiosyncratic works of his was scarcely less than his own, largely because of his secluded manner of life to which I had to conform. I looked back on the works that predated them when their rare performances on the radio - and not often good ones - brought them to notice. Little, of course, had been recorded in those days. But it was the work in hand that concerned me most.

Then there was Philip Heseltine, whose years of practical help for Delius in his writings and skilful arrangements of Delius's scores had ended by then in his almost total rejection of all the works he had loved hitherto. *Appalachia* was all that was left on which he could enthuse, and I was very much the target to which his outbursts against the rest of Delius's music were directed when we met. I could not share his fervour for

Appalachia. I admired the exuberant orchestral invention, but there were certain variations that puzzled me in relation to the whole. Prior to the announcement of the tune in D major in the woodwind we have the long, repetitive, static introduction in which nearing the end the trumpet hints briefly in C minor at the first full statement of the tune. Now half-way through the work there is a slow variation of the tune from the horn with strange chromatic harmonies in the strings leading to a mysterious section based on material from the introduction [from letter R up to U]. Now I couldn't see why Delius had extended this static music farther at this point and for so long. It was not until 1966 that I saw in a flash why. It was on my wife's and my first visit to Jacksonville. We had flown via New York to join Mr and Mrs Emanuel there, and had come down many thousand feet on our approach by the Florida coast-line. And flying low over the vast vistas of sprawling forests and swamps bordering the St Johns River, this puzzling music of *Appalachia* welled up in my being after all those years, and when we landed I was so bemused that I could barely answer the general questions about Delius the waiting pressmen put to me. Delius had caught the mood of that tropical landscape uncannily.

I couldn't wait to go to Solano Grove, and when I did I was quite overcome[27]. The inroads of civilisation (so-called) are all too apparent now, and on our visits in the 'seventies we noticed great changes each time. Solano Grove is not now the place of which Delius told me. In his day it could be reached only by cart-track or by boat. But enough of the spirit of the scene remains to confirm its crucial influence on Delius. After all, it was the voices of coloured people in harmony floating at nightfall from neighbouring plantations which, he recalled, induced his first feeble attempts to compose in this very spot. I have never understood why it hasn't occurred to a conductor to use the authentic sounds of a coloured choir in recording *Appalachia*. However that may be, it is not to be wondered at that Delius added voices when he revised *Appalachia*, nor how these early recollections ultimately led him to the highly personal sound of his later choral writing. By the time I came to write that small book in the Faber series of Great Composers, my visits to Florida increased the significance of *Appalachia* for me in Delius's inner

---

[27]   Another Yorkshireman's impressions of Solano Grove a year later - in fact those of a Bradfordian - are recorded in J B Priestley's *Trumpets over the Sea - Being a rambling and egotistical account of The London Symphony Orchestra's engagement at Daytona Beach, Florida, in July-August, 1967*, Heinemann 1968, 90-4.

development. In that melodious variation for strings beginning in the cellos [starting at letter J] in the course of which excitement spreads gradually through the whole orchestra culminating in the theme from the trombones, the music subsides into that marvellous, ethereal passage in the high strings, an incredible afterthought [letter M]. It is here, I am certain, that may be ascribed the transition of Delius from talent to greatness. What it expresses will mean different things of the spirit to each, but I cannot hear it without feeling that it speaks eloquently of the mystery of transience, an experience in life that none can evade.

Another change of mind I have had is in appraising the three violin sonatas. Delius had already rejected an earlier sonata as too repetitious and immature in invention. For some years I felt that in Sonata No 3 the imposition or restriction of dictation had produced a new and refreshing simplicity of utterance, but, granting this and for all the sweep of Sonata No 1, I think that Delius's most original contribution in this genre is No 2. I never tire of that exquisite singing of the violin in the contemplative sections.

Another factor which retarded me strongly in coming to grips with the earlier works in that 'process in reverse' to which I have referred, was the flavour of Scandinavian thought which permeated the Delius household. There was so much talk of Norway, of Edvard Munch, Grieg, Sinding, Jacobsen and others that the *Arabesque* and *Fennimore and Gerda* were known to me and loved long before *A Village Romeo and Juliet*, excepting *The Walk to the Paradise Garden*. Naturally I was inclined to measure the earlier and middle-period works as I came upon them by these musical touchstones, every note of which could have been written by nobody but Delius.

From my first days at Grez I saw that the creative artist, of whatever kind, was the centre of Delius's interest in humanity. He must have known many artists like Niels and Erik in *Fennimore and Gerda* amongst his Scandinavian friends in the late eighteen-eighties and nineties. You will remember how in the Fourth Picture in *Fennimore and Gerda*, Erik the painter and his friend Niels the novelist recall old times and the aspirations they had shared in their teens. Niels is busy on a novel, but admits that he works very slowly. Erik's disillusionment is all too clear. He talks of death: but death of the spirit when a man is wrung to the depths of his soul. In the dialogue between the two, Erik voices his fear that he may have come to the end of his career as an artist. 'The soul of man can be bruised and broken, and no-one knows how deep down in a man his soul extends!' There, in musical terms expressing a profound insight, we have the greatest tragedy that can befall an artist. I was deeply impressed on reading this music for the first time by the economy of orchestral means, the psychological truth and aptness of the musical imagery, its power and well-bred sense of restraint. Thus when I chanced to read another impending tragedy of the spirit when the soul of Koanga is bruised by the treacherous abduction of his bride, Palmyra, at the close of Act II, I was shocked by the uninhibited, full-blooded climax! Sheer grand opera! - I thought. However; when I heard it at Covent Garden in 1935, though John Brownlee as Koanga was dressed like a goal-keeper, I had to admit it was most effective. I was not won over completely until Eugene Holmes, the coloured baritone, brought the house down at Sadler's Wells under Groves in 1972.

The *Requiem* is the work in which my judgement has proved to be the most at fault. Again, nobody but Delius could have written it, but I still think that its musical quality is uneven, especially in those passages when the baritone soloist is moralising and his line is uninspiring in shape. Whenever Delius touches on the mystery of transience, human or in Nature, he always has something beautiful to say in music. The vain cries to an unhearing God of the choruses of Christians and Muslims all yelling their Hallelujahs and La Il Allahs are a vacuous as Elgar's demons in *Gerontius*. I find Delius almost tedious here, as he was when he used to rant against religion, but oh! when he evokes the natural scene of the snow lingering yet again on the mountains and the buds in the valleys breaking forth and the little full-throated birds already singing for the very joy of springtime to come, then Delius really comes into his own kingdom where he is second to none.

DELIUS: THE MAN AND THE MUSICIAN

The Fourth Delius Festival Programme Book, University of Keele
March 1982

A strange dichotomy, to my mind, suffused the character of Delius the man and his singular powers as a musician. As a man he was sociable yet remote; a crisp, demolishing, autocratic wit. Stern, silent yet solicitous, he was sensitive, fastidious and self-sufficient, a gourmet and unyielding stoic.

Sharing his silence in his garden at Grez or on nightly airings on the road to Marlotte, armed with lantern and umbrella when all the village had gone to bed, and even at his table too, proved a confluence for me beyond words, defying our difference of age and outlook. I felt a sense of depth in his presence from which his finest music had welled, at odds with his singular self-willed mind, so hard in everyday mundane matters.

Delius, after years at his craft, came by a tonal rhythm of his own, projecting the expression of inborn gifts all too seldom bestowed on composers: an original imagination and the power of lyric magic in music impelled by an instinct for spell-binding sounds belying the eye in their written characters. The ear was the life of his intelligence, and timbre his ear's intoxicant. He filled his mind with the feel of sounds and tasted timbres as his wine with Epicurean discernment. This relish would fan an inner glow, a poised moment's sudden flash with sometimes no more than a snatch of tune - scarcely ever a rounded thought - or maybe sensuous pairings of chords to ponder and later excite into flow. 'A sense of flow is the main thing' was his sole briefing when, blind and paralysed in old age, he took me as his amanuensis in 1928.

Important, however, as is nuance in Delius, I began to find on working with him and from his remarks as he listened to his music whether by radio or of my own making - for there was little of it recorded then - that a lyric approach to his sense of flow was the source of his notions of musical artistry.

I sensed, too, with growing concern that what was least understood in performance was the fluctuation of the flow. His facial reactions to the flux of the flow - especially when it did not please him - told me what I ought to know and led me slowly to understanding. I saw how contour carried his spirit when shaped in sympathy with his intentions: his pained frustration, even annoyance, when that rapport in effect was broken. 'The fellow has no feeling for my music!' he would say. 'The feel of the sounds tells him how it should go!' I saw how his spirit responded to contour through stress on the operative note in a phrase - often no more than a slight leaning - or in gentle exposure of telling lines running like veins through chromatic textures, or at momentary lifts at cadences.

As to Delius's oral advice, none was forthcoming on musical matters, nor was I encouraged to seek it. I bided my time and soon found that he made himself plain unconsciously in ways such as I have described. Thus in his household over the years I came by much of my knowledge of his music.

It needed more than initiative to launch a new work by Delius. I marvel at the infinite patience alone of those who presented premières - Hertz, Haym, Cassirer, Wood, Beecham, Coates, Mengelberg, Goossens,

Boult, and, more recently, Del Mar. Time allotted for orchestral rehearsal was constantly wasted with irksome halts, sorting out copyist's mistakes in the parts made direct from Delius's manuscripts which Beecham pronounced to be 'progressively unreadable!' Fortunately I could read them myself and he, Sir Thomas, could read my copies. Thus my devotion hardly extends to excusing such laxness in preparing a score for public performance and finally for publication. Once he had ridded himself of the notes with what he considered the essential dynamics, Delius's interest invariably waned. The original score was the master copy jotted down in the faintest pencil swiftly and accurately in full score, and complete in every orchestral detail as far as it went with each day's work composing at the keyboard. Mistakes crept in accountably later in momentary lapses in concentration in the tedium of making a new score in ink, for Delius by now was apt to be bored and meditating the next work to be, or taking up a score put by that had ceased to flow intuitively. This he did rather than try to boost it by solving its next move cerebrally. Again it must be conceded that Delius was not the best of proof-readers!

Piles of these pencilled originals of every work that he had written crammed the shelves of an old French linen cupboard kept in a studio flanking the courtyard. I had access to these private scripts, a rare privilege it transpired, for when I returned to Grez in May 1935 for the exhumation of Delius's remains and their conveyance for reburial at Limpsfield in England, I found no trace of the manuscripts whatever. Was that what Jelka, his widow, had meant when she wrote that she was having 'a great clearance and burning masses of old papers'? Knowing that she was an ill woman but intent on attending the ceremony, I had pressed her to go on ahead to London with Martha, her devoted servant, so that she might rest with friends before going down to Limpsfield the following Sunday. She had left before I reached Grez. The journey, unhappily, proved too much for her and she died in London before I felt it seemly to question her.

If Delius can be faulted most in his judgment of orchestral balance in accompanying solo singers, he had bigger voices in mind than those to be found in England. Here Beecham showed his mastery in adjusting the dynamics of countless passages and adding expressive 'hairpins' where Delius had left his textures blank. Provided that no advance was made beyond these significant liberties Delius was amenable. 'Thomas can edit my scores as he like,' he told me, 'but don't let him tamper with the notes!' That, to Delius, would have been unforgivable. And those were his last words on music.

JELKA DELIUS
A recollection by Dr Eric Fenby

An edited transcript of a talk given to the Delius Society in London on 21 September 1982.

(*The Delius Society Journal* No 79 April 1983)

I first met Jelka on the station at Bourron in October 1928. Had I known it, she was the first wall of defence against intruders into Delius's privacy. In reality I too was an intruder until such time as perhaps I might be able to prove myself. But I had consoled myself initially that if the Deliuses found things about me they didn't like, they would do their best to ignore them if they found I was useful musically.

I have never regarded as particularly accurate Ken Russell's image of Jelka through the acting of Maureen Pryor in the TV film *Song of Summer*. The impression it made, it seemed to me, was of a slight dottiness, whereas Jelka was an extremely assured person. The only time I remember her caught off balance was in the year after Delius's death. We had gone to a recital given in London by Albert Sammons and Evlyn Howard-Jones in which they played the Third Sonata. At the end I was chatting to Jelka when Margot Asquith butted in - 'Jelka Delius! Aren't you sorry you never had a baby by Fred?'

Jelka had a soft, pleasing voice, often amusingly modulated. She loved to play on her foreign inflections of speech when pronouncing English where nine out of ten adverbs were in French! In the day-to-day company of the Deliuses, if one didn't know French, all one would get was the drift of conversation. This marked preference for French adverbs was shared by their American neighbours, Alden and Hilma Brooks. Yet I cannot recall the Deliuses speaking together entirely in French; nor would Delius have anything read aloud to him in French. They spoke Norwegian when they wanted secrecy, and were mildly confounded when Percy Grainger came, because he understood it.

On arrival at Grez I saw how well Jelka managed her household. The house itself was very uncomfortable, especially in winter. There was no heating except in the living room and music room, and nothing at all in the bedrooms. The household at that time consisted of Delius and Jelka, the Saxon housemaid who lived in, and her own brother, who acted as male-nurse. There was also the cook, whose home was in the village, a part-time gardener, and a seamstress and chauffeur who were on call.

My impression of Jelka was of a shrewd, intelligent woman. She could be obdurate in a very German way, and was always looking for flaws in everything, in people's characters as well. But she was firm and steadfast. At times, rather too difficult; at others, particularly with strangers, rather gushing, much to Delius's distaste. But she was uncomplaining with her lot except when driven beyond belief. When I think of what Jelka had to do for Delius, that he never seemed to have the slightest idea of all the constraints put upon her, both emotionally and physically, I am amazed the longer I live. How a man who wrote such sensitive music could be so completely unaware of his hard feelings on occasions I couldn't imagine. It wasn't forgetfulness at all, but his Nietzschean attitude to life even in respect of his closest ones.

Jelka kept a remarkable table. During the week there were home-made soups, a variety of fish and poultry dishes, delicious pâtés, salads, soufflés, and simple but exquisite sweets. On Sundays we always had bouillon soup - I've never tasted better - and invariably brioche and fruit-flan for tea.

Jelka was a punctilious letter-writer and answered all corres-pondence by return. The afternoons whilst Delius slept were given to writing her 'thunder-letters' about the neglect of her husband's music. After tea, should Delius feel unable to work, we would take a walk round the village when she would share her confidences.

She often talked of her unsettled life as the daughter of a German diplomat, moving from one German Embassy to another. Here in the elegant soirées of the day she heard an amount of lieder and the Grieg songs then in vogue, and in her tiny, pathetic voice she would often recall snatches of her favourites whilst going about the house. She knew very little about symphonic music but she was proud of her family connection with Moscheles, the pianist and friend of Mendelssohn. Delius himself was less respectful and apparently sat on a huge volume of the works of Moscheles when composing at the piano. It was still there in my day on the chair at the piano!

'The first time I met Fred was at a party in a girl-friend's studio in Paris,' Jelka told me. 'I had the temerity to sing a Grieg song when somebody said that this young man was a friend of Grieg's. It was received in stony silence! I thought that was the end. I would never see him again, and I'd really taken quite a fancy to him. You can judge my surprise when he came to my studio the next day and played his own setting of the same words which he thought was better than Grieg's! What really brought us together was - in a sense - not music, but because Fred was reading Nietzsche at the time, and so was I. That was our great bond to begin with. I saw him occasionally afterwards, but I was no match against other women!'

Their next significant meeting was at Grez. Delius had visited Keary at Bourron for advice on the libretto of his opera *Koanga*. Hearing that Jelka was painting at Grez and living at the Poule d'Eau, they decided to walk over the fields to see her. Delius had rowed her up the river to land on a derelict garden in which the owner, a crazy Count, had allowed Jelka to paint in his absence. Walking towards the shuttered house Delius had observed with obvious delight, 'Oh! I could work here!' But soon he was off to catch the train to join his boon companions in Paris. As for Jelka, she was already pondering how she might buy the property herself! A national scandal gave her the chance. The Count was in difficulties; the house was put up for sale and Jelka's mother bought it cash down for a very small figure. She insisted on two conditions: that Jelka's German student friend Ida Gerhardi, also a painter, should share the house with Jelka at Grez, and that Marie, a trusted Breton peasant, should look after their creaturely comforts there.

The story has it that Jelka was sure Delius would turn up again, but her hopes were dashed when a post-card came saying he was sailing to Florida! That was the last she thought she would hear of him. But a second post-card some months later told her that he was back in Paris and coming down to Grez for the week-end! Surely the longest week-end in music, for he stayed for the rest of his life. His Florida trip had been a fiasco and he had very little money. Thus Jelka provided the means of establishing him in his work. 'It was wonderful in the early days when the three of us were here,' she recalled. 'Ida and I painting in the garden; we could hear Fred upstairs at the piano in the extraordinary way he would improvise before starting to compose; first in chords which he found by instinct; and then he would decorate them with arabesques and so on!' This man, she felt, had more than talent and, come what may, she would do all she could to help him develop it.

Ida, initially, was the greater help for she knew people like Dr Hans Haym, the civic conductor of Elberfeld, for thus through her contact with him Delius's music was made known in Germany. It is not to be wondered that the inevitable emotional triangle ensued between Fritz (as he was still called), Jelka and Ida. In the end Jelka won him and Ida retired from the scene.

It is often said that it was a pity that Jelka sacrificed her painting to Delius, but in my opinion she had done her best work long before Delius's invalid years. Nor do I think she was as gifted as Ida. Ida's painting had great character and an inner possibility of development which Jelka's work lacked. Jelka's best paintings were almost entirely of scenes from Norway - gorgeous sunsets over mountains. The colourings were bold, contrasting with her Monet-like style in hazy portrayals of lovely young blondes. She had also modelled a fine head of Delius, then in full vigour, cast in plaster. How Jelka must have struggled to take down Delius's music (before my time) in 1922! He had lost the use of his hands but fortunately he could still see to correct his material, as in the Second Violin Sonata. Here she had to write down an original accompaniment to the violin completely beyond her playing powers, and this when she said she was utterly terrified of making the slightest mistake! Her greatest contribution to Delius's music was in finding him suitable texts to set. These she would write out and put on his desk, leave them there and hope for the best. She steered him in this remarkable way till he found his own tone and rhythm in sound. That a woman of scant musical knowledge, who played the piano but at a snail's pace and read music even slower, could listen to Delius improvising and divine in those sounds certain feelings and emotions she could afterwards seek out aptly in words - this to me was her ultimate achievement. We owe to her *Sea Drift*, *Songs of Sunset*, *An Arabesque*, many texts for Delius's songs, suggestions for *A Mass of Life*, and finally *Songs of Farewell*, the words of which she had copied out nine years before its composition.

Her support to me was vital when you think of it. There I was, completely unknown, having to be taken on trust and immediately given an entrée to Delius's music room; before long even entrée to his manuscripts when he discovered I could play from full score when he wished to hear an unpublished manuscript. Jelka, by some uncanny insight, made it clear from the beginning that she believed in me. She didn't expect immediate results. She used to say, 'Now, Fred is the most difficult man you could ever have. You've met a very extraordinary musician . . .' To the very last she always took my side, often against him when things were dark - because she knew that what we had to do was the most important meaning to his life - his music. Nothing mattered so much initially after my arrival at Grez as his making a start after six years of inaction. I shall never forget her coming to me one day in the music room with tears in her eyes: 'Oh! you don't know what it means to me now Fred has told me this morning "Don't read to me; I'm thinking about my music!" And that was wonderful. I thought I'd never hear that again.'

That was the woman Delius married. How fortunate it was for us that he married her and not one of the many women who dangled around him in his early days in Paris.

VISITORS TO GREZ

A talk given by Dr Eric Fenby to the Delius Society at Mary Ward House, London on 22 September 1983. This was an informal, unscripted talk, and the following is an edited transcription.

(*The Delius Society Journal* No 106 Winter/Spring 1991)

I have been asked to speak about the various visitors who came to Grez during the years I was there, that is from 1928 until 1934, when Delius died - and I'm not counting the hundreds who queued in the corridors of the Langham Hotel at the Delius Festival in 1929 in London to file past him and shake his hand when their names were announced.

The first visitor I met at Grez was Alexandre Barjansky[28], the most exciting and most musical cellist I ever heard. To me he was in the line of Paganini, both in appearance and in virtuosity. In appearance he looked like a somewhat dilapidated Anglican dean, always dressed in black, with a great black pork-pie hat, a coat which he wore all through the summer, the astrakhan collar turned up, and black gaiters. He was an extraordinary fellow. And virtuosity? Well, I have never met his equal. He was the first person I heard play the Cello Concerto as written initially by Delius with all the very difficult stopping [after fig.80]; it is fiendishly difficult, and I heard him practise it for nearly three hours one day up in the loft at Delius's during the first period of our encounter. So while Julian [Lloyd Webber] and Jacqueline [du Pré] play the cello line without any of the ornamentations, Barjanksy did - and from memory, which was quite incredible. Virtuosity, yes. He was a friend of Ysaÿe, in fact he very often played chamber music with him. He was also a very close friend of Gabriele d'Annunzio, in whose drawing room in Paris he told me he often gave recitals. Now, with his coming to Grez on about the third day that I took up my residence in Delius's household, I couldn't have had a more propitious visitor, for he gave to me at first hand his deepest insight into Delius's music: his marvellous sense of flow, phrasing, the verve and

---

28 A detailed account of Alexandre Barjansky's visits to Grez can be found in Catherine Barjansky, *Portraits with Backgrounds*, Geoffrey Bles 1948.

authority of all that were of an order I've never heard since. His initial encouragement in the task I had set myself (and of course which we hadn't begun) was just what I needed. Rehearsing with him was the most exhausting but the most rewarding experience.

The next visitors were Alden and Hilma Brooks, Delius's neighbours for over thirty years. On Sundays at Delius's house it was an 'at home' at four o'clock, and people would turn up there, friends in the neighbourhood - there weren't many - but the most usual visitors to be found there would be Alden and Hilma Brooks. They were most delightful, cultivated Americans. Hilma was born in Delius's house. Her father, a very well-to-do American called Chadwick, was the image of Elgar, so it used to be extraordinary when I was pushing Delius up the street to meet 'Elgar' coming the other way! Alden was a novelist, a great collector of pictures, and he used to delight Delius with all the latest art gossip from Paris. He would sometimes work at home, but usually - particularly in the winter months - he would spend the greater part of his week at his most sumptuous flat in Paris where he had Braques, Monets, and Modiglianis (Modigliani was a painter he was greatly keen on at the time). He also had the one Gauguin wood carving too. It was really quite remarkable in those days: we never locked the doors at night, and one could go by at any time during the day and look into what used to be the old priest's house, a rather flat building, set well back in the courtyard, and as one passed there one could see this lovely Gauguin, a little statuette, a quite enchanting wood carving, and this priceless thing stood on a beautiful chest in full view of the street, and nobody locked the door at night!

Brooks occupied himself largely by writing novels, but his most serious work was published after Delius died, in 1937. It was *Will Shakspere: Factotum and Agent* [29] which he sent to me inscribed 'To Eric Fenby, from the window across the wall, his friend, the author, Alden Brooks'. What a book about Delius Brooks could have written from that window across the wall where he observed Delius for about thirty years, and he knew more about Delius than all the rest of us put together! He told me many things he had observed in those years and I will never betray his most intimate confidences.

Another visitor for tea on Sundays who lived in the village was Jesus Maria Joseph Lazard [spelling conjectural]. He was a most

---

[29]   Round Table Press, New York, 1937

extraordinary man, and had apparently invented the English equivalent of the soldier's tin hat in the First World War and various other types of ingenious military equipment. In his younger days he used to discuss his free-thinking philosophies with Delius, but in my time they had both mellowed somewhat and scorned so-called progress in international affairs.

The next people to come were Evlyn and Grace Howard-Jones. Evlyn was a very famous pianist who played the Delius Concerto in the 1929 Festival. He was quite outstanding as an interpreter of Brahms, and Beecham used to say he was one of the best Brahms players he had ever heard. As well as this, he loved the Delius Concerto. Evlyn was quite a 'dry stick' and a bit of a dandy, particularly when he was in London (he lived in Eaton Terrace). He was very precise and when we played together for Delius he would say, 'Now we've got to be perfectly clear in our minds what we are going to do next.' Well, I am afraid I never am, and so it was with great difficulty that we managed to put a concert together! He was very much devoted to Delius, and one summer they came and took a cottage and had two pianos installed where we used to practise and play quite a number of things to Delius. He was a confirmed Anglican and something of a wit, and on dark nights even in the summer when we used to go out and we would meet half way up the village street, I would hear footsteps (there were no lights at all) and then there was a strange noise, and it was him singing 'O taste and see how gracious the Lord is' - which was our meeting call!

I enjoyed quite an interesting friendship with the Howard-Joneses. I felt rather sorry for Delius in many ways because every time they came, Grace would say, 'May I play you one of the Delius [Violin] Sonatas to see if I play it a little bit better?' and Delius used to have to bear all these extraordinary performances. But Grace was quite a good violinist. I met them much later when the Delius episode was behind me because Howard-Jones was one of those people who backed Matthay when he brought out his new method [of pianoforte teaching], and he and many others in certain institutions resigned because the powers-that-be wouldn't accept Matthay's innovation. Matthay started on his own in Moon Street, and the Howard-Joneses, when they lived in Eaton Terrace, thought they would do precisely the same, so they started a school with Howard-Jones teaching pianoforte, Albert Sammons the violin, and Cyril Scott would teach harmony. That went on for some time with Cyril hardly ever appearing on the doorstep because he hated teaching, so John Ireland took it on. When John packed it in, I was asked, so I began my first teaching at the school there. I saw Howard-Jones a little later during the war; I was then stationed at Preston, we had just married, and I had to go to London and I thought, 'Well, let's go and see the Howard-Joneses'. But both Rowena and I were deeply distressed to find them living in the most straitened circumstances because Evlyn had had stroke after stroke and was in a wheel chair. It was a most distressing visit, and that, I fear, was the last I ever saw of Howard-Jones.

Philip Heseltine came next. Beecham had sent him to see whether Delius would be willing that he might prepare the Delius Festival in 1929 (and this was about the spring of 1929). This was a very embarrassing meeting because Delius had known that Heseltine had gone cool on his music. I once saw him coming out of a concert and I said, 'Aren't you staying for the Delius?' He said, 'Oh no, I only came to hear the Haydn.' Delius received him very politely, and he told me, 'Now, I want you to be here, Eric, when he comes', and so I was introduced to Heseltine by Delius.

Heseltine was a most extraordinary person and a very fine speaker - particularly when well oiled! - as were many of them at about that time: Constant Lambert, who again had the most beautiful voice when speaking; Cecil Gray, who spoke most beautifully too. They were an amazing collection of people, and I was more or less admitted into that circle when I was older after that first meeting because of my association with Delius. They could drink me under the table in the first five minutes!

Heseltine had a very remarkable insight into music, and I think I was from his point of view 'accepted' (as I was really by Percy Grainger) in that I was interested in pre-Reformation music. I was never really a Bach man. I was not a particularly good organist - I hated practising. I just managed to get by, so to speak, with Sunday voluntaries. But Heseltine was astounded when he heard that I knew the music of Gesualdo, which in those days was almost a closed book to most people. But Phil had already written a book about him. He had a very sensitive and remarkable mind. He came to his very tragic end which I don't think had anything to do with women or drinking, but simply because he realised that in following the letter of Delius's art instead of his artistic integrity, he came to an intellectual cul-de-sac. I think that is what drove him: there were circumstances which he told me at the time which confirm me very strongly in that belief. It was a very great and tragic loss.

Heseltine came twice only. On the second time, he said, 'Come on, Fenby, let's get out of this,' and he took me on to Moncourt. Both Delius and he were having words on that last visit which was very distressing.

Unfortunately he was trying to plug Bartók's Fourth Quartet and Delius said he had never heard a more excruciating noise in all his life. I was there when this happened. He said, 'Fred, I want you to listen at five o'clock. We're going to hear a broadcast of what I think is a great modern masterpiece, Bartók's Fourth Quartet.' I can just see Delius now. He used to champ in his chair with annoyance, about to explode. 'Well, you call that music!' It was always understood that if things reached that sort of stage, I was to intervene, so Phil and I went on to Moncourt.

Just slightly before that happened we had a visit from dear Lionel Tertis. Tertis had made an arrangement of the Third Violin Sonata and wanted to come and play it on the viola. Poor Tertis had been told that Delius lived quite near to Paris. After an hour's drive from Paris in the snow, poor Tertis arrived. We had to thaw him out, and then I began to worry about what was to happen when the time came to take him up to the music room. We had to suffer the attention of a nearby village piano tuner who was blind. Unfortunately I had perfect pitch in those days and what was Tertis going to say when I gave him an A because it was half a tone down? What did Tertis do? I gave him the A, and suddenly the door opened and Delius's feet came through first as the Bruder carried him in and dumped him in the chair. I played my A and Tertis tuned his viola down. We had no rehearsal, and when we had finished Delius was so delighted. Playing for Tertis was wonderful; after Barjansky the most wonderful thing I'd known in my life. Such an exquisite artist. When it was over Tertis said, 'Would you like to hear another one?' And so we played him the Second Sonata too. It was quite moving when he was well into his nineties and all the viola players in London gave him a send-off at the Wigmore Hall. I was there and he remembered the snow at Grez![30]

For some years the artist Matthew Smith[31] lived at Grez, in quite a small house two or three houses down from the Deliuses, and he used to come often to see Brooks. Every time I think of Brooks and Smith together, I think of the time I went round and there was Brooks prostrate on one sofa and Smith on the other. I said, 'What on earth is happening

---

[30]   See Tertis's own account of his visit in *My viola and I*, Elek 1974, 72-3.

[31]   Halifax-born Sir Matthew Smith (1879-1959) settled at Grez, after his marriage, in 1912. He was in England when war was declared. In 1916 he enlisted in the Army and served in France, not being discharged until 1919 when he returned to Grez, thereafter often dividing his time between London and Paris. He made England his permanent home from 1940.

here?' 'We're trying to give up smoking! We've lasted an hour and ten minutes so far and we're absolutely dying for a smoke!' Smith was again a friend I made and I used to see quite a lot of him in London. After my leaving Delius, I went to live at a little family hotel which my friend Tom Laughton (a hotelier in Scarborough) had told me about, and I was there for some years until the BBC took it over and it's now a BBC car-park. Smith used to come and stay with me there. He was quite an extraordinary person because he always enjoyed his own way, and he was quite unusual in the way he worked. He worked only spasmodically, so-to-speak, and then with tremendous energy and would complete a picture in about half an hour after a long period of gestation. He had an extraordinary attitude to the arts and he was a most delicate and charming man, as the painter friends of mine have often been. Another was James Gunn, about whom I have something to say later on. Smith and Delius always seemed to me as being the two people I thought most unlike their art.

Shortly after Matthew Smith came (and he came several times), Alden Brooks came to see Delius and there was much talk of painting. In fact there was far more talk about painting that year than about music, particularly when Brooks came with all the news from Paris, about Braque, Picasso, and so on. It was a very interesting time then.

Then there was Percy and Ella Grainger. It was the year after their marriage, and they were one of the most handsome couples I've ever seen in my life, in a very unusual out-of-doors kind of way. She looked Swedish all over, with her pile of glorious golden hair on her head, and he with his extraordinary gaiety. He was always in rather strange garb, as if he'd arrived from the backwoods on expedition, and jumping all over the place just exactly as we saw in Ken Russell's film. He never walked down stairs; if he came down stairs, he always took the last twelve in one leap, and he wanted to run with Delius all over the place. When playing he had this extraordinary idea that one must get into the mood [Eric Fenby demonstrated Grainger's habit of warming up at the piano by rapidly patting his knees], and then he would sit down and play the Chopin sonatas to Delius rather impressively. He was a very kind person, and still tremendously attached to the memory of his mother. He did the most extraordinary things, like he always had to have other music going on when he was orchestrating!

We had quite a different visitor after Grainger: Professor Dent, who was writing a book on Busoni and wanted to hear from Delius what he thought of Busoni. Delius was very much on the defensive because he said, 'Busoni gave a performance of my *Paris* which was so disgraceful I couldn't understand most of it. I couldn't believe that I'd written it. He didn't know the score. Sibelius was there too, commiserating with me.' He talked a lot about those extraordinary people that Busoni always had to have round him before he could play properly, one of whom was a dwarf. Delius said, 'What with Busoni and his dwarf, and sitting on the bench with Sibelius who was so "blotto" he couldn't sit still!'[32] And then of course the moment came when Delius could stand it no longer and he said, 'Dent, I really think you have become completely unmusical.' Nevertheless he was asked for tea, and that was always a good sign if they came to lunch and were asked to tea. I walked round the village with Dent after lunch, and he was very charming and delightful, and very interested in the way we were trying to work (then in the early stages).

Another visitor, May Harrison, was charming and an extra-ordinarily good violinist. She was a professor at the Royal College and of course one of the famous Harrison family. May was sent for when Delius had finished the Third Sonata and she came and played it to him.[33] She was a very fine player. Sometimes the intonation used to go a little suspect when she got rather excited. As a violinist at that time she was not quite of the same class as her sister Beatrice [the cellist], but nevertheless a fine artist. She was a very good friend of Arnold Bax. Arnold used to come every year. During the winter months nothing happened at all. Weeks and weeks would go by and nothing happened (except when Tertis drifted in out of the snow!). In the summer, when people were on holiday - and particularly in July and August - many people would be passing through Paris and they would come along and see Delius. It was always a great delight for me when Bax came.[34] When he and May Harrison got

---

[32] At the Beethoven-Saal, Berlin on 15 November 1902. As well as *Paris*, the concert included Sibelius's *En Saga* and works by Mihalovich, Théophile Ysaÿe and Liszt.

[33] See May Harrison, 'Delius', *Royal College of Music Magazine* 1937 No 2, reprinted in *A Delius Companion* ed. Christopher Redwood, Calder 1976, 101-6, and a talk given on 22 March 1945 to the Royal Musical Association, 'The Music of Delius', *PRMA* LXX1, 43-8 and reprinted in *The Delius Society Journal* 'The Harrison Sisters Issue' No 87, 32-7.

[34] In a letter to Colin Scott-Sutherland quoted in his *Arnold Bax*, Dent 1973, 40, Fenby wrote: 'Few ventured on Delius at his home in rural France, but Bax was always welcome. Routine for visitors was usually the same: descent at Bourron or Fontainebleau stations : a drive through the forest in the old Ford to Grez : lunch : a stroll by the river whilst Delius had a nap :

together and recorded the First Sonata, Bax wanted to make a cut and Delius wouldn't allow it at all and said it should be played exactly as written or not played at all. It didn't matter what you did about dynamics, you could alter them, but cuts were anathema to him.

Bax had an incredible piano technique; he was the most marvellous sight-reader I ever knew. I don't think he understood what difficulty was! He just sat there and it all came. I appreciated it the more as the years have gone by, because in the early days after being with Delius I had to earn my living by being a music adviser for Boosey & Hawkes. In those days there were no tapes or anything of that nature. They used to get all these non-musical directors who would sit around while I was brought in and asked to play and try to sell the score.

Bax smoked a foul pipe which neither Delius nor Balfour Gardiner could bear, and he could be rather an embarrassment to some of us: he always had 'that' pianist Harriet Cohen in train, and shortly after he had left on one occasion, Harriet Cohen called in. Apparently she had come to see if Delius would be willing to contribute to an album of [transcriptions of] Bach chorales to which certain of her friends like Vaughan Williams were contributing.[35] Well, Delius refused to see her and would have nothing to do with the Bach chorales. And that was Miss Harriet Cohen!

A charming visitor was Suzanne Haym, daughter of Dr Hans Haym. She was a most beautiful girl. She had come from Germany to Paris to study. I often wondered what became of her. I was asked to go for a walk with Jelka and Suzanne, and I never heard a more unflattering account of what Jelka thought about most men. She may have been trying to warn Suzanne against men and not to marry.

When Beecham came the champagne flowed. (Delius had a very fine cellar with very good wine. When special people came it was champagne, always champagne, and if we had had a good day dictating, out came the champagne.) Both Beecham and Delius were in wonderful form. Beecham was very amusing; he called me 'Master Fenby'. He said, 'Well now, Master Fenby, take me up to the music room and I want to work.' Then he sat down at the piano and played *Songs of Sunset*. He played quite shockingly, like some third-rate Sunday School teacher; I

---

tea : departure. My first impression of Bax remains: Bax in his prime with Delius at Grez: quick, ruddy, shy, untidy, reticent about music, expansive about books, and constantly searching for matches for his pipe. . .'

35 *A Bach Book for Harriet Cohen*, OUP 1932.

could hardly believe my ears. It was really quite dreadful. He would stay on a chord and explain precisely what was in the score.

I think it was on that day that Delius said he'd been asked by a Polish magazine for his views on modern music but he'd felt unable to respond. He mentioned it to Beecham and when we got outside Beecham said, 'What was that you said about the Polish journal?' and Delius said, 'Well, I don't know. . .' Beecham said, 'Master Fenby, go upstairs and get yourself some notepaper.' So Master Fenby went upstairs and got his paper and came down and we began. It all came. Then Beecham said, 'Now read it to me.' So I read it to him, and he changed not one single word, not even a comma.

That was only the beginning. He said, 'I'm going to conduct the entire Festival from memory.' He came day after day and went through each of the works he was going to do. On one occasion he brought Dora Labbette. They stayed until nearly three in the morning and the taxi was still waiting there at three. It had been ticking away all day! And Delius was still up at three in the morning too, going through all the songs. Enormous stamina. Beecham insisted on playing just as badly as ever, one hand after the other. He continued to come as the years went on and Delius, of course, greatly looked forward to these visits.

I remember Cecily Arnold, a soprano and a charming person. She only came once but I'll never forget the occasion.[36] My chief recollection was that we had a delightful lunch, a stroll in the garden, then tea. After tea she sang to Delius. In *The Nightingale has a lyre of gold*, at the phrase 'The lark's is a clarion call, and the blackbird plays but a boxwood flute', I played a wrong note, at which point Delius exploded, 'G flat!' (*The Nightingale* has a very difficult accompaniment and I was playing it from sight.) And they talk about Delius not knowing whether you were playing the right music or not!

Another visitor was R J Forbes, who gave the first performance of the Sonata [No 1] with Arthur Catterall. At that time he was head of the Manchester College of Music.

Almost the next day there followed Granville Bantock's son, Raymond, who was with his new wife on their honeymoon.[37] They came to lunch and Delius talked about the great Birmingham Festival which

---

[36]   See Cecily Arnold, 'A Singer's Memories of Delius', reprinted in *A Delius Companion*, 107-112, from *The Music Teacher*, April 1950.

[37]   See Raymond Bantock in interview, *Delius Society Journal* No 80, 37-41.

Granville Bantock had organised and included Sibelius's Fourth Symphony which Sibelius conducted, *Sea Drift*, and Elgar's *The Apostles*.[38] Raymond Bantock was going to move to some professional post out East to relieve Robert Nichols.

Robert Nichols was a most remarkable person.[39] To go to a concert with him could be quite an alarming experience. I shall never forget at Bournemouth when old Dan Godfrey gave a performance of the *Fantastic Symphony*, Bob got so excited that he jumped on top of the chair and called 'Hurray!' To stay with him was always very alarming because he would wake up in the morning and then shout at the top of his voice all the time. He used to spout reams of poetry. At that time he was writing *Don Juan*, and he was still at it when years afterwards I stayed with him when I was in the Army Education Corps close to Cambridge where he was living. He was remarkable at divining in sounds suitable words.

When he came [to Grez] on one particular occasion - he came several times during the time I was there - Delius wanted him to write an entirely new libretto for *Margot La Rouge*. Delius, I think, was rather ashamed of it, although he thought there was some good music in it. We reached the stage when Delius said, 'Well now, we must start going through all the works that I have written, everything, and play through it. Take your time.' So we went through the whole of the works that had not yet been published. When we turned to *Margot La Rouge*, he said, 'That belongs to my best period, the turn of the century, and so I think something ought to be done.' Bob could not; [when I visited him at Winchelsea] he was going out East and he was only given three days. So he said, 'You can't go back empty-handed. I shall have to give the old man something. But I can't do a new libretto. I think we'll pull the plug on all the dramatic stuff. Never mind about that; we'll just take the best bits. Just you play what you think.' And so I played. Jack Moeran was there as well, and I remember playing some of *Margot* to him - a marvellous page in the

---

38   Bantock wrote in his diary of 1 October 1912: 'Elgar conducted first performance of The Music Makers & Sibelius his new symphony in A minor which was very well received. Delius was also at concert and we three sat together during Elgar's work.' The Festival concluded with *The Apostles*.

39   See Robert Nichols, 'Delius as I knew him', *A Delius Companion*, 113-5, reprinted from *Music Magazine*, edited by Anna Instone and Julian Herbage, Rockliff 1953. See also Nichols' review of Fenby's *Delius as I knew him* in 'The Power of Music', *London Mercury*, January 1937, 270-7.

duet. Jack said, 'I'd give all my music if I could have written that.' It's a quite marvellous, beautiful score, with not a wrong note. Delius could be as marvellous in his own way as Mozart in his, in the sense that there's not a superfluous note in the texture of Delius at his best.

Anyway, I said, 'Bob, we've got two hours. I've got to go in the morning.' Added to which it was very difficult because Bliss turned up, and on the way in, who did I meet going out but Aldous Huxley; he'd been staying there. They'd been having a 'beano' before Bob went out East. So there was hardly time. Bob went out in the pouring rain, came back, gave himself a bath, a bite, and we got this thing knocked out. He'd got the words from all over Whitman's *Leaves of Grass*. His wife, Nora, was a niece of Roger Quilter who was one of the dearest people, a gentle soul.

There were some rather strange visitors. There was a chap called Maynard (a painter), and old Joe Heseltine, who would arrive for a Sunday visit on his tricycle with his entire equipment and his canvases on the back. He was a real card. If one of his canvases got out of hand he would stick bits on. He said he was having a tower put on top of his house up the road in Marlotte so he could see the aeroplanes going by better!

Then there was Norman O'Neill. Norman was a most charming man. His wife said as a young man he was the best looking man in town. When he was 21 he had snow-white hair. He was not a great musician, but he was a very fine organiser and did remarkably fine work, more on the administration side. He was a very good teacher at the Royal Academy of Music - until one day when he was knocked down in the street, just coming out of Trafalgar Square. Norman was, I think, the one man Delius really loved in the sense that he admired him. He was a most engaging person, and oozed charm; a kind person too.

Norman's death quite broke Delius for a while. There were moments sometimes when it seemed as though Delius's life might just be on the wane. But then he'd come bouncing back with incredible resilience as though he could go on for ever. He always looked like a corpse. He didn't seem to change, and on the very day he died he seemed no different than on the day I first saw him six years earlier. There was no reason why he shouldn't go on for ever. Although he was blind, he knew he had the house very much under his thumb. We all had to toe the line.

Earlier I mentioned James Gunn. It was through Norman that we got him to come to do that painting now in the Bradford Art Gallery. Gunn was very like Norman; they were both clubmen, and they both relayed the latest gossip to Delius, and Delius always loved to hear that.

Though he derided London life, he was very interested to hear what was going on. When Gunn came he was completely shattered by the sight of Delius. The first thing he did was the small canvas of Delius's head. I wonder where that has gone; I thought that was absolutely superb.[40] It was the first time he saw Delius. After that the canvases went down hill, so to speak. He couldn't paint a likeness: Delius wouldn't sit, and he couldn't get the chin right. I had to sit with a rug over my knees for hours because Delius wouldn't sit any more. Gunn said, 'Well, how do you cope with this? How do you live in this house?' Delius had a presence which was absolutely sapping; it sapped all your strength. You could even feel him when you were in the garden. There was never any general relaxed conversation; there was no small talk, ever. When he didn't talk there was silence and it could go on for hours. But when talking, he was terse and monosyllabic and entirely to the point. He knew precisely what he wanted, and that was a sign of the genius of the man.

When I was not there at Grez, visitors came and so I missed them. The one occasion I greatly regret was when Elgar came. I had to leave that morning because Boosey & Hawkes wanted me to go through some proofs. It was absolutely imperative and I couldn't stay. But I had a delightful postcard from Elgar, regretting I wasn't there.[41]

---

40 A detailed listing of Sir James Gunn's six sketches, drawings and paintings of Delius is included in Robert Threlfall's iconography 'Delius as they saw him' in *The Delius Society Journal* No 83, July 1984. The sketch in oils to which Eric Fenby refers was the frontispiece (in black and white) to the original edition of his *Delius as I knew him*, Bell 1936, and appeared also (in colour) in the Bradford Delius Centenary Festival programme book.

41 On 24 May 1933, Eric wrote to Elgar from Scarborough:

Dear Sir Edward,

On the morning of my departure for England from Grez-sur-Loing where I have been staying since early January Delius told me of your intended visit.

Need I add that I am most disappointed that I shall not be there to help to make you welcome.

Instead I must content myself by wishing you well for your stay in France.

Let me assure you of my affection and esteem and that I am greatly looking forward to the production of your new symphony.

With warmest greetings,

Yours most sincerely,

Eric Fenby

Florent Schmitt was another man who called on Delius several times over the years, and Delius always enjoyed his visits.

Then there was Philip Oyler, a highly cultivated gentleman whose daughter Soldanella I knew. He managed the millionaire Pitcairn's estate nearby, which included two enormous chateaux. Oyler, like most people in the village, was not accepted by the Deliuses until I insisted that he called, and in the end he became the greatest practical help to them in many ways. I often went to have a drink with him at home, and if he wanted me to go out after dark, he had to put a ladder up to the music room window and throw stones to attract my attention, because Delius wouldn't allow anyone to go out at night. Philip knew nothing about music and used to maintain that I had written the dictated works. In fact, one day he made a colossal blunder and wrote an essay saying that Delius didn't know how much I had done and how much Delius had done.[42]

Dr Heinrich Simon came with his wife and the Art Editor of the *Frankfurter Zeitung* on a glorious summer's day. They stripped off and swam in the river. Then they all went upstairs and stood before Gauguin's *Nevermore*, and the Art Editor began an incredibly eulogistic outburst about *Nevermore*. Jelka and Delius were laughing after they'd gone: they'd not known it was Jelka's copy! Dr Simon was a fine musician who was gunned down in Washington, D.C. by the Nazis. He had done much through his paper's columns [as Editor of the *Frankfurter Zeitung*] to spread the knowledge of Delius.

Finally, Balfour Gardiner, such a central character. I could never have gone on at all without Balfour. I could give you a whole evening about him. He had a heart of gold, and he was a very difficult man, very sensitive, and very fastidious, with such high standards and so little

---

The letter is reproduced opposite by kind permission of Raymond Monk. For an account of Elgar's visit, on 30 May, see *Delius as I knew him*, 123-5; for their correspondence, see *DLL2, op. cit.*, 418-432 (including Jelka's letter to Eric); and for Elgar's own description (slightly cut when it appeared in *The Daily Telegraph* 1 July 1933 and *A Delius Companion*, 94-5) see Jerrold Northrop Moore's *Edward Elgar: Letters of a Lifetime*, Oxford 1990, 470-1.

[42]   See Philip Oyler, 'Frederick Delius in his Garden', reprinted in *A Delius Companion*, 49-54, from *The Music Student*, July 1934; 'Some Memories of Delius', in *Sons of the Generous Earth*, Hodder and Stoughton 1963, 41-54; and 'Delius at Grez', *The Musical Times*, May 1972, 444-7 (and Eric Fenby's letter in the August 1972 issue, 767).

12, Mayville Avenue,
Scarborough.
May 24ᵗʰ. 1933.

Dear Sir Edward,

On the morning of my departure for England from Grez-sur-Loing where I have been staying since early January Delius told me of your intended visit.

Need I add that I am most disappointed that I shall not be there to help to make you welcome.

Instead I must content myself by wishing you well for your stay in France.

Let me assure you of my affection and esteem and that I am greatly looking forward to the production of your new symphony.

With warmest greetings,

Yours most sincerely,
Eric Fenby.

Sir Edward Elgar. Bt. OM.

Fenby's letter to Elgar in 1933.

confidence in what he wrote. He could be easily upset, and it could be over a very small matter. That's why he and Beecham fell out. But he was a marvellous man. I've never heard anyone who could take up a piece of music and discuss it in such positive terms, never with the idiotic analysis of academics, but the quality of thought. He really understood. I learned more from Balfour than anybody else in music, with the exception I suppose of Elgar: Elgar for instrumentation, Balfour for everything else. Nobody I've met could so clearly read a score; he could say where it had gone wrong, and what to do. He taught me quite a lot of things about music, and right at the beginning of my time with Delius, Balfour was behind me. Had he not been . . .

ERIC FENBY ON DELIUS IN FLORIDA

24th Annual Delius Festival, Jacksonville
Programme Book, March 1984

Delius's first mention of Florida to me was revealing. He had asked me to read to him from the Continental *Daily Mail* and, coming upon a headline about something in Florida, I thought it might be of interest to him. I was wrong, for he cut in . . . 'Florida! Ah! Florida! I loved Florida! - the people, the country - and the silence!' I was struck by the way he dwelt on 'silence', and felt immediately that it might be a clue to his unique personality, for I had already discerned its grounding in silence. The ebb and flow of his music, too, often emerges from silence and fades away into silence.

That night, whilst pushing him in his wheelchair in silence with a lantern up the road from the village for his customary airing before retiring, he suddenly said, 'I was your age (twenty-two) when I left Bradford for Florida to escape from the family wool business. I wanted to get away as far as possible from paternal opposition to my becoming a musician. My real purpose - not shared by my companion, Charles Douglas, who wanted to farm - was to try and resolve the conflict in finding my own way in music.' It was clear that the hunch that had impelled him to persuade his father to lease him a small orange plantation by the St Johns River near Jacksonville had had consequences of which he had never dreamed. 'Just think, I met Thomas Ward, an organist, by chance whilst choosing a piano in a Jacksonville music-store! I didn't realise what a good teacher he was until I went eventually to Leipzig

126

Conservatoire. The professors there had no insight whatever compared with his. His instruction was intuitive; just what I needed. He was a fine fellow, too, and I was grieved when he died of consumption some years later.

'Solano Grove, the plantation, was a clearing in the forest, vast and seemingly endless in tropical undergrowth. I used to get up early and be spellbound watching the silent break of dawn over the river; Nature awakening - it was wonderful! At night the sunsets were all aglow - spectacular. Then the coloured folk on neighbouring plantations would start singing instinctively in parts as I smoked a cigar on the verandah.' At magical moments such as these, his youthful intimations of what he might do in life deepened and clarified. The American folk and popular music which he had heard in Bradford as a boy - it was all the rage at the time - and again during his two-year sojourn in Florida, had turns of phrase and emotional impulse which undoubtedly influenced his own music, notably in his opera *Koanga*. Delius could be as brusque as Brahms when these melodic paronyms were pointed out to him!

I cannot remember a week going by without his harking back to his Florida days. Finally, nearing the end, he called for *Huckleberry Finn*, and still to the sound of my reading Mark Twain he sank into unconsciousness.

We celebrate the 50th anniversary of his death with joy and gratitude for the legacy of musical elegies his rare spirit left us.

WARLOCK AS I KNEW HIM

Eric Fenby in conversation with David Cox

(Peter Warlock Society Newsletter No 32 April 1984[43])

D.C. In your book, *Delius as I knew him*, you tell us about meeting Philip Heseltine more than once, when he came over to Grez-sur-Loing to see Delius - and in London at the time of the Delius Festival (1929). Did you see enough of him to form a definite impression of his personality and outlook?

---

43   Reprinted in *Composer* 82, Summer 1984, 19-23, and in *Peter Warlock: A Centenary Celebration*, compiled and edited by David Cox and John Bishop, Thames Publishing 1994, 26-32.

E.F. Oh yes, certainly. During my time at Grez (starting 1928) he first came over to try and persuade him that his presence was vital to the whole project. As usual, I was given my instructions as to what to do with guests. I was particularly interested when Philip came along. Naturally, I had a copy of his book on Delius with me - and I knew some of the 4-handed arrangements he had done of some of Delius's works. But the meeting with Delius was going to be something of an embarrassment, because the youthful enthusiasm for Delius's music which I had had and which Philip had had was no longer the same.

D.C. His views on Delius's music seem to have been very changeable. Actually, you both started in the same sort of way - first of all admiring from a distance, then writing to Delius, out of the blue, and then finding yourself there. In fact, I believe it was suggested previously that Heseltine should go there himself and help Delius as amanuensis in the way that you did. But he would surely never have had the patience, would he?

E.F. No. The life-style which suited me was so absolutely foreign to everything that Philip was doing at the time. He would never have been able to stand the solitude. Anyway, I was very interested when he turned up. I was not at all disappointed in the man. There was a distinction there - so obvious at a first meeting - and he had a brilliant mind; and he was one of that remarkable group of people of his own age who were such wonderful *talkers* about music - Cecil Gray, Constant Lambert, Bernard Van Dieren . . .

D.C. Did you feel that Heseltine was the sort of charismatic personality who, when he comes into the room, becomes the centre of interest and attention?

E.F. I would have thought so. His appearance - the beard and everything - it was like talking to some distinguished chap out of the 17th century. When he spoke, there was a quiet authority, and a sort of twinkle there, which was very engaging. He was indeed one of the best talkers on music that I've ever heard . . Philip had a very beautiful speaking voice - though often the interesting things he was saying were rounded off by some Rabelaisian remark - which was apt to happen too often. He had the most trenchant criticisms for the people who had edited the early music. He could be absolutely livid . . . He was too apt - as Delius was too - to be having an

GREZ-SUR-LOING (S&M)

BOURRON

9. 6. 1928

My dear young friend,

Your sympathetic & appreciative letter gave me the greatest pleasure. I am always so glad when I hear that my music appeals to the young.

I know Scarborough quite well; when a school boy I used to spend my summer holidays at Filey and my memories of all the happy days on that coast are still very green.

Most likely the Phil- harmonic choir will

Part of the first letter, in the hand of Jelka Delius, from Delius to Fenby, June 9, 1928.

Above: Fenby with Delius at Grez in 1932.

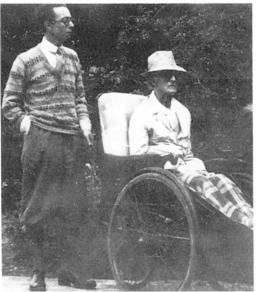

Bottom: Fenby with Delius at Grez in 1929.

Above: Delius with his wife at Grez in 1930.

Left: Jelka Delius.

Left: Sir Thomas Beecham in conversation with Eric Fenby at Delius's reinterment at Limpsfield, Surrey, on May 24, 1935.

Right: Pencil sketch of Fenby by James Gunn in 1932.

Part of *Songs of Farewell* as dictated to Fenby by Delius.

Above: Eric Fenby with Sir Yehudi Menuhin, on a visit to the Menuhin School. (See Tasmin Little's introduction to this book).

Left: Eric and Rowena Fenby on a visit to Florida in the early 1980s.

Above: Thomas Allen and Felicity Lott singing in one of the 'Fenby legacy' recordings made for Unicorn Kanchana in 1981. Bottom left is producer Christopher Palmer.

Left: Another photo from the 'legacy' sessions.

Right: Fenby being made a Fellow of the Royal College of Music by the Queen Mother, the college's President, in 1985.

Below: Fenby, painted by Kenneth Jackson. The painting was commissioned by the University of Bradford, marking its award in 1980 of Honorary Graduateship.

interesting conversation and then suddenly turn the whole thing upside down by some remark which torpedoed the whole thing.

D.C. And were Heseltine and Delius often at loggerheads over music? You mention in your book some differences of opinion - for example, over Bartók's fourth quartet.

E.F. I saw very little convergence in my time. . . Philip was particularly interested in my love of Gesualdo and the early music of the Church - as distinct from Bach.

D.C. In your book you speak of his interest in plainsong and the early music of the Church. With all that, did you gather what his views on Christianity were? He could hardly be described as croyant et pratiquant!

E.F. At times, in fact, *he* found himself the target of Delius's frequent outbursts against Christianity.

D.C. Really?

E.F. He used to say: 'I can't stand Fred when he's in these moods. It's absolutely unbearable. How you stick it here is beyond my understanding.' I (as a Roman Catholic) of course came in for it too. Delius could be extremely tiresome on these occasions. He seemed to think: here's a young chap, he's gifted musically, and he's being ruined by all this Christian business - just in the same way that it's ruined Elgar. . . His main criticism of Philip was - here was a young man of some substance, and his mother wanted him to do nothing but stay in the country home in Wales and write music - and that's just what Delius wanted him to do - whereas it was just the one thing that Philip did not want to do! By the time I came along (1928) it was clear that he was becoming more and more dissatisfied with his own position in music. I think he'd almost come to an intellectual cul-de-sac.

D.C. That was towards the end. I remember you saying he told you that he could not bear to be alone. Was that always so, do you think?

E.F. Absolutely. And he surrounded himself with - I thought - unworthy company. There was a certain nobility in his nature, but he seemed to allow himself to be dragged down. I've been with him sometimes and some girl has appeared and given him the glad eye - and in the middle of a sentence he would break off, take her arm, and off they would go.

D.C.   I imagine he was very attractive to women.

E.F.   Oh yes. Very.

D.C.   Did you meet some of his regular lady friends? Did he bring them sometimes to Grez?

E.F.   Well, no. On one occasion - Delius was quite annoyed about it - he turned up with a whole crowd of people - Anthony Bernard, the young Wordsworth (the composer), 'Old Raspberry' (E J Moeran) - Delius said: 'Why on earth does Philip bring all this crowd of people?' And Jelka asked them all to lunch - a very good lunch!

D.C.   What's your view on the 'split personality' idea, which stems from Cecil Gray's biography? Did you get the impression of somebody who was switching from being a scholarly, very-interested-in-music person to someone who was crudely the kind of character portrayed in Aldous Huxley's *Antic Hay*?

E.F.   Yes.

D.C.   Or was it that everything he did - the high and the low - he did with maximum enthusiasm?

E.F.   I would say that as well. The thing about Philip - you hadn't any idea what he was going to do next. And of course the people he mixed with drank inordinately. And that was a great problem for me, because I was always a person of moderation. I would go out with them and drink - but they would drink pints and pints, and then wait for the pubs to open for the evening session!

D.C.   There was some suggestion in Richard Shead's book on Constant Lambert that if Lambert hadn't known Heseltine, he would not have himself become a victim of drink and drugs.

E.F.   I'm sure. And with Philip, Delius blamed Augustus John.

D.C.   What - as a powerful influence over all of them?

E.F.   Yes, exactly. And Philip got mixed up with models of John. There were all sorts of scenes and love-affairs. A terrible business. . . But with Philip there was a charm. Of that there is no doubt. It was there to the end. It was wonderful. He would bring up some particular motet, say, of Victoria, and we'd talk about it; he would point out some of the beautiful passages that had struck him, and so on. At those times, he was a most wonderful companion. And that's what upset me, because I saw what he *could* have been. He could have been a most remarkable person. . . Towards the end drink was taking its toll. He was tending to be rather bloated, and looking a little rough.

D.C.   Did you ever feel that Heseltine liked to manipulate people? I was thinking of Huxley's portrayal; in one scene he has a youth in tow whom he is obviously leading into debauchery. Did you ever see any signs of him wanting to have control over people?

E.F.   No. . . He was always rather careful in his treatment of me - perhaps because he thought it would all go back to Grez!

D.C.   I remember Steuart Wilson once saying about Heseltine: 'He was the one person I ever knew who was wholly evil.' I wonder what Heseltine had done to make him think that!

E.F.   As an R.C. I have associated with many very remarkable men whom I regarded as holy men - that is to say, remarkable men who had a *presence*. Now Delius had a presence which was quite different from theirs. That wasn't evil. But I had a most uncomfortable feeling when I was with Philip - always this uncomfortable feeling - that there was something there which I couldn't quite put my finger on. There was also something of the same with Percy Grainger. A certain . . . sinister something.

D.C.   Even when you were very simply conversing about music in the ordinary way?

E.F.   Well . . .

D.C.   There was something in the background?

E.F.   Yes. It was a darkness which I was not able to penetrate.

D.C.   Do you think he sympathised with Delius's Nietzschean philosophy?

E.F.   Oh, I think so.

D.C.   More so than with your Christian point of view?

E.F. Oh yes; because he thought that the *Mass of Life* was the greatest of works - infinitely greater than Bach's B minor Mass.

D.C. But that doesn't necessarily tell us about his religious sympathies as such.

E.F. I can't believe that Philip had any spiritual life - what *I* would call spiritual life.

D.C. You think it was all through the music?

E.F. All through the music. Of that I'm quite sure.

D.C. In a foreword to Gray's biography of Warlock, I recall that Augustus John tells of an incident in a church involving something resembling black magic -

E.F. I'm not surprised.

D.C. John speaks of Heseltine's beliefs in 'principalities and powers mustering their unseen array' - or something of the sort. It is of course often said that blasphemy depends for its effect on a background of belief. So it's possible that he was a believer, but was constantly cocking a snook at the Deity.

E.F. Oh yes. I would go along with that. I would say, as regards myself, he always showed respect - he would never say anything that I could take exception to. The fact is, I don't think I would ever have fitted into that particular milieu had it not been for the fact that I was of their opinion as to the enormous value of the early music of the Church.

D.C. Did all of that group show respect for your moderation and your religious beliefs?

E.F. Yes. And behind the whole thing they were very grateful for what I was doing at Grez. They would say 'You're doing something we could never do!' . . .

D.C. With all Heseltine's friends blossoming out into large-scale works - Lambert with *The Rio Grande*, Moeran and Walton with symphonic works, Van Dieren . . and so on - do you think that Warlock felt a kind of inferiority because his own art was small-scale?

E.F. Oh, I think so. My opinion of those terrible days, when he took his life - I don't think it had anything to do with love-affairs at all. I don't think he cared that much [snapping his fingers] about women really.

D.C. He was using them -

E.F. Using them - and the more the merrier. And some of them were very coarse. Oh, he was hopeless in that way! As soon as a pretty girl appeared, he was finished.

D.C. Are you of the opinion, then - which I think was expressed by John Ireland at the inquest after Heseltine's death - that he was disappointed as a composer?

E.F. That is my opinion. I thought he was in distress and almost in despair and that he'd come, as I said, to a sort of musical cul-de-sac. I think he had been influenced too much by the *letter* of Delius's music rather than by the spirit. If he had only imitated the artistic integrity, rather than get into this cul-de-sac where he was strangled and couldn't do any more. His composer friends were all flowering, whereas Philip was just dissipating his whole life. . . Delius was always saying that he should have gone back to his home, or at least established some sort of normal life; but it was useless. He was always complaining about money. But his grandfather once said that Philip was hopeless; if you gave him £100 it would be gone by the evening!

D.C. Of course, if Warlock *had* expanded into large-scale works, as his friends were doing, it would not necessarily have been right for him - whereas what he *did* do is something very perfect, at its best.

E.F. Yes; he was very definitely a miniaturist. He had also that certain magical lyrical quality which is so essential - and which is often lacking - for example, I would say, in John Ireland.

D.C. Heseltine wrote on one occasion that if there had been no Roger Quilter there would be no Warlock. Something of an exaggeration. That came after the Delius influence. And then there was the Bernard Van Dieren influence, which brought with it a kind of artificiality.

E.F. There was that, yes. And it was wrong - that was foreign to his natural tastes.

D.C. It never stifled his natural lyricism, however, did it?

E.F. No, that's true. but it was there . . .

D.C. You say in the book, he always looked you straight in the eye when he was talking to you.

E.F. Yes. That was a very endearing thing about him.

D.C. One person that knew him said he had an odd kind of shyness. Was he perhaps forcing himself to get through that by looking you straight in the eye?

E.F. It could be. I regarded it as part of his sincerity.

D.C. Would you say he was naturally extrovert rather than shy?

E.F. Well, yes. I would think so. But he was obviously a person of moods -very strong moods.

D.C. Which could change very suddenly?

E.F. Oh, yes indeed. But a very endearing soul. Delius was deeply saddened by the way he had simply gone downhill.

D.C. Delius must have felt that he had to some extent moulded him.

E.F. Yes. In those early years - it was almost a father-son relationship.

BEFORE AND AFTER GREZ

For the special Spring 1986 issue of The Delius Society Journal *to mark his 80th birthday, Dr Fenby kindly consented to answer in writing some questions put to him by the Editor, Stephen Lloyd, about the years before and after his time spent at Grez.*

S.L. Eric, as you approach your 80th birthday, you seem in recent years to have been almost as much involved with Delius as you were some 55 years or so years ago. Indeed, you have been astonishingly active in a number of spheres: conducting, recording, filming, resurrecting *Margot La Rouge*, writing and lecturing, to say nothing of the travelling involved. You have always looked upon your time with Delius as a unique privilege, and of course you have memorably recounted this period in *Delius as I knew him* which has become a classic of its kind. But may we instead focus our attention on some aspects of your life that lie chiefly outside your years at Grez?

You were born in Scarborough, where you were a chorister and trained as an organist, becoming much involved in local choirs and choral societies. In the Yorkshire Television film *Song of Farewell* you spoke warmly of the Spa Orchestra's conductor Alick Maclean. How do you remember him, and what were his special qualities?

E.F.   Alick Maclean gave me my first contact with a professional orchestra. He was the conductor of the Queen's Hall Light Orchestra, London, and in summer the Spa Orchestra, Scarborough. In those days contracts for provincial symphony orchestral players did not cover the summer months, so Maclean had the pick of the Hallé, Birmingham and Scottish Symphony Orchestras on the Spa.

Maclean was a gentleman. His commanding appearance on and off the podium was impeccable. He would be in his early sixties. He was a man of few words, who came straight to the point, whose manner was never less than dignified. He was aloof and never seen about the town between performances. He had a beautiful aristocratic-looking wife, said to be Viennese, equally aloof, to whom he was devoted. The pair added great distinction to the social life of the Spa.

Maclean's performances were never dull, always paced with lively rhythms and a flair for the operative notes in phrasing. At that time he was the most musical conductor I had known. There was a hint of the showman in his conducting which suited the Spa and the vast holiday crowds his concerts drew, but he was a strict disciplinarian. He was delightful to me and invited me to conduct my youthful compositions.

S.L.   In *Delius as I knew him* your fondness for Elgar's music is very evident. In fact, you go so far as to say that before you heard of Delius's existence, your strongest musical responses were from Palestrina, Victoria, Mozart and Elgar. What is it in Elgar's music that places him in such company?

E.F.   That rare gift, *musical* personality, is the first, vital essential for me in my response to a composer's sound. If I cannot detect personality in what I hear - and I mean *musical* personality - I reject it immediately. I simply haven't the patience to listen, an attitude that has not changed since boyhood. The moment I heard the *Enigma* Variations as a youth at Leeds Town Hall, I recognised the voice I had known in *Salut d'amour*. From then onwards I asked for miniature scores of Elgar's mature works[44] instead of fees when deputising for local organists. By the time I went to Delius I had studied and absorbed then avidly. My love of Elgar's music still remains, though now more selective than then. His early anthem *Ave, Verum Corpus Natus*, when sung at High Mass at Westminster Cathedral, still moves me to tears.

S.L.   You once mentioned that you offered your services to Elgar when the completion of his Third Symphony seemed doubtful. At what point did you approach Elgar, and what was his response?

E.F.   I wrote to him during the last months of his illness, unaware of its severity, having read optimistic reports in the press which were obviously ill-founded. His daughter Carice answered by return, saying that her father was deeply touched by my offer, adding that now nothing could be done. It is possible that this well-meaning intervention caused Elgar to say to Willie Reed, 'Don't let anyone tinker with it - no-one would understand . . . no-one must tinker with it.' No-one would have respected his dying wish more than I.

S.L.   For a period in between the death of Delius and the outbreak of war you worked for Beecham, a job that cannot have been without incident! What was the nature of your association?

E.F.   First to help in the production of *Koanga* at Covent Garden. Secondly to attend recording sessions and advise on questions of orchestral balance. The association was full of incredible incident, little of which concerned music. Acting on Sir Thomas's precise instruction, Fred Laurence, his faithful orchestral manager, and I recalled certain key players from their first summer holidays for

---

44   He would read his study scores of Elgar while sitting on the great flat slabs of rock at the Wyke, near Cloughton, in all weathers a favourite haunt of his as a youth. 'There were none to be had of Delius in those days; in fact I had never heard of him then! But it was there eventually, on a tiny grassy promontory from the cliff (alas! long since washed away), that I made my decision after days of misgivings to offer my services to Delius.' (Notes for a Delius Society Scarborough itinerary, June 1992.)

some years, and engaged them for a concert in rural Sussex he suddenly had a whim to conduct. They all turned up in white ties with not so much as a toothbrush between them, only to find that the concerts was not until the following night!

S.L.   While music adviser to Boosey & Hawkes from 1936 to 1939, one of your tasks was to prepare the piano reduction for the vocal score of John Ireland's *These things shall be*. What were your dealings with, and impression of, John Ireland.

E.F.   The most finicky musician I have known. He continually oscillated between tying a note or dotting it at the proof stage, which maddened the old-time engravers. He was also an extremely slow worker, and often warned me 'Not so fast, Fenby. You'll have a stroke!' Later I took over from him, teaching written work at the Howard-Jones school.

S.L.   You also assisted Julius Harrison with the scoring of his *Mass in C*. How did this come about?

E.F.   Julius, one of the most charming of men, was an old friend and my daughter Ruth's godfather. Ill and harassed lest he couldn't finish his score in time for the Three Choirs Festival, he appealed to me for help. I had already deputised for him at the Bolton Competitive Music Festival. I agreed, provided he inked in my pencilled scoring in his *own* hand. It was not until years later that the secret apparently was out, though Dr David Willcocks, as he then was, who was to conduct the first performance, may have known from Julius himself.

S.L.   You provided the musical score for Hitchcock's 1939 film *Jamaica Inn*.[45] What was it like to work for Hitchcock? Was there in fact more music written than just the opening and closing sequences?

E.F.   My problem with Hitchcock at the time was that he was going through an anti-music phase with strong preference for realism. For instance, in the cave scenes by the shore, he cut all the music in favour of the sound of wet bare feet walking on straw! And so it

---

45   Daphne du Maurier, authoress of the novel *Jamaica Inn* that was adapted for Hitchcock's film, was fond of Eric Fenby's score and it was at her suggestion that he wrote a military march, her husband being Commander of Airborne Forces. Unfortunately, the music was lost.

went on. Willie Walton was most sympathetic and told me he had had a complete ballet cut in a film with Elisabeth Bergner!

Hitchcock, however, knew what he wanted,[46] hence the slightly Wagnerian sea-music at the beginning - which was his idea. He was much criticised in the press for his sparse use of music. Happily I was paid for my complete score and I was offered two lucrative contracts in Hollywood, but the authorities refused me a permit, and I was called up for national service.

S.L. One of the stars of *Jamaica Inn* was Charles Laughton,[47] whom I believe you knew. What are your memories of that great actor?

E.F. Charles was the brother of my close friend Tom, the Scarborough hotel-keeper, whose family owned and ran two of the finest hotels in England, the Royal and the Pavilion. One night after dinner at the Royal, Tom, Charles and his wife Elsa [Lanchester], John Armstrong the painter and his wife Benita and I were being shown the new Neptune Ballroom and theatrical lighting system John had designed. Somebody mentioned Flecker's *Hassan*, to which Charles enthused about Delius's music. Whereupon I mounted the platform and began to play the incidental music to the exquisite changing colours. Charles then joined me, speaking long passages in that beautiful voice of his which Tom said, combined with music, he had 'never heard used to better effect'.

S.L. During the war you were attached to, among other units, the Army Education Corps, which must have seemed a far cry from your pre-war activities. Where there, however, any amusing moments that come to mind?

E.F. There were amusing moments during the first year when I was in the Royal Artillery. I was posted to a Searchlight Regiment and

---

46   It is surely no coincidence that in a later film, *Saboteur* of 1942, Hitchcock included the character of a blind man who speaks of Delius and his blindness, and plays part of *Summer night on the river* on the piano.

47   Charles Laughton was co-producer, with Eric Pommer, of *Jamaica Inn*, and it was he who suggested that Eric Fenby provide the score. Eric was able to assist in another, very different way. Laughton, in his role as the crooked squire, was having difficulty getting into the part, particularly in adopting a suitably distinguished walk. Eric's suggestion that he thought of part of Weber's *Invitation to the dance* did the trick.

could tell them what note the enemy aircraft sounded on the beam, but that wasn't much use in bringing it down! I formed a garrison military band at Blandford, mostly from Salvation Army players. The only way I could be kept on at Blandford was to be attached to the garrison headquarters in charge of road-making and the camp incinerator! They named one of my road-making efforts 'Fenby's. Folly'![48]

I enjoyed being commissioned in the RAEC. My role was to run 21-day courses at the Army School of Education, Cuerdon Hall, Preston, preparing personnel for civilian life on demobilisation. Single-handed I directed courses in LRAM, ARCM, ARCO, FRCO and Durham Mus. B paper work, in many instances later carrying on study by correspondence. I was ultimately offered a Majority if I stayed in the Army! Previously I much enjoyed conducting the Southern Command Symphony Orchestra when based at Bulford.

S.L.   Your own composition *Rossini on Ilkla Moor* has become quite a favourite. What were the circumstances of its composition? It

---

[48]   In a talk to the Delius Society on 29 September 1988, he related one amusing incident. One Saturday evening, when he and his squad were exhausted after a day's white-lining of some six or seven miles of Dorset roads from his camp to Blandford, there was suddenly a screeching of brakes as a military vehicle pulled up. Fenby, aware of red braid, instinctively swung his right arm to the salute, an arm which happened to be holding a loaded brush, spraying the car and its driver with paint. As a result he was placed under garrison arrest! On his return to camp a letter awaited him from Balfour Gardiner who, living at nearby Fontmell, had invited him to lunch the next day. Fortunately, the Sergeant Major cleared the visit, and on that Sunday Fenby was just relaxing at Gardiner's house after a splendid meal, loosening his collar and tie and putting all thoughts of camp, its duties and his misdemeanours behind him when Gardiner casually announced: 'Oh Eric, I forgot to mention that a chap in the army like you is coming to tea today.' Whereupon the garden gate swung open and to Eric's horror in came his Brigadier accompanied by his wife. 'Yes, we have met,' the guest coolly remarked as they were introduced, and thereafter spoke not a word to Eric.

On Monday morning Eric dutifully presented himself before the Brigadier, who said nothing of their Sunday encounter. But with the formalities over, he asked: 'By the way, what do you do with yourself at week-ends? Do come to tea next Sunday!'

seems you have destroyed many other works of yours, including a symphony. What else of your works have you preserved?

E.F. At the end of my work at Grez with Delius, I returned to Scarborough mentally and physically exhausted and in urgent need of rest. Tom Laughton took me to his farm at Lockton and used to come over whenever he could for walks on the moors. Once he nearly drove me mad repeatedly singing *On Ilkla Moor Baht'at*. 'Not a bad tune,' I said. 'Rossini would have made something of it.' That evening he asked me what I meant by that remark. So I played it in the style of Rossini on his spinet, adding, 'Take another tune, say *Scarborough Fair*, treat it in the same way, and you have a piece.'

    I thought no more about it and two days later decided to go into Scarborough to see a game at the Cricket Festival. Walking down the main street, I came face to face with a poster announcing a new work - '*Rossini on Ilkla Moor* by Eric Fenby to be conducted by the composer'! Within a minute I was confronting Tom in his office:- 'What on earth . . .?' 'Oh. Eric, I'm sorry! I forgot to tell you. Kneale Kelley (at that time the conductor of the Spa Orchestra) is staying here. He's thrilled with the idea. He particularly wanted a novelty for the Gala Concert on Sunday night as the Australian team's coming.' I looked at my watch; it was 11.30 a.m., Wednesday. I wrote the overture and copied the parts, there being no-one to help. I finished the job at 3 a.m. Sunday, rehearsed it at 10 and conducted the performance to a packed audience.[49] I got an ovation, but missed my cricket. The piece caught on, and received over ninety performances within the next twelve months by different orchestras. I have destroyed the rest of my works. Only genius matters in composition.

S.L. Your association with Delius must be known to millions, through your *Delius as I knew him* (which has seen four editions), most recently through the Yorkshire Television film, and of course through Ken Russell's compelling BBC film *Song of Summer* for which you acted as adviser. You were not, I know, happy with the portrayal of Jelka (with no disrespect to Maureen Pryor), but,

---

[49]   Some directors of Boosey & Hawkes were in the audience and they had it published. It is dedicated to its unwitting instigator, Tom Laughton.

allowing for the limitations and necessary compressions of such a film, would you otherwise approve it as a faithful representation?

E.F.   Unfortunately I was ill throughout the whole filming and saw the film for the first time at home. Had I ever been on the set, several things would have been quite different. Ken Russell was very anxious to be faithful to the script. Jelka would not have appeared slightly dotty, nor giggly in describing her mountain descent. She was a highly intelligent woman who came from a family of German diplomats, spoke several languages from childhood fluently, and was remarkably equable in character considering the sustained daily pressures on her.

    My father was portrayed without collar and tie playing chess. I never saw him without collar and tie; he was something of a dandy and couldn't play chess. I was shocked when the scene with the priest was included for it is not in my book. Russell, like me, being a Catholic, it was meant for his ears alone.

    Otherwise it was a remarkable representation.

S.L.   After the war, from 1948 until 1962, the year of the Delius Centenary, you were Director of the music department of the North Riding Training College. This seems in retrospect like a comparatively quiet period during which you might have been charging your batteries, as it were, before the explosion of Delius activity that has come in the wake of the Centenary. Was this a period almost exclusively devoted to teaching?

E.F.   No, the period from 1948 until 1962, though largely devoted to teaching, was not without its many calls on me to give talks on Delius to music clubs up and down the country, at summer schools and provincial music festivals. Most of these were for an expense fee. I gave them all off the cuff to keep myself fresh, but the travelling involved from Scarborough was very trying.

    The most redeeming joy of this time was a delightfully unexpected family life. In 1944 I had married Rowena, who was then nursing at Scarborough Hospital. We met during one of my army leaves. When eventually I was demobilised, I spent my whole gratuity in trying to find a home in London. Then, in despair, we took Quarry House in Staintondale overlooking the sea near Scarborough, till a knock on the door led to my taking a temporary post at the beautiful North Riding College of Education about to be opened locally. Well! I stayed fourteen years, moving into The Crescent, Scarborough, happy in the birth of Roger and Ruth, and watching them grow up contentedly in the most idyllic surroundings, always within 'sound of the husky-voiced sea'.

S.L. The 1962 Bradford Delius Festival was not without its moments of sadness. Beecham had died the year before, and there was also the death of Herbert Bardgett, chorus master of the Bradford Old Choral Society. This latter occurrence must have placed an extra burden on you on top of your duties as Artistic Director. Whose brainchild was the Festival, and at what point did you become involved?

E.F. The instigator of the Centenary Festival was Michael Colbert, the music critic of the *Bradford Telegraph and Argus*. He and a colleague called on me in Scarborough in the autumn of 1960 and outlined his plans. I was kept in touch with every move before the Festival Committee was formed under the chairmanship of the late Sir Kenneth Parkinson.

S.L. In 1964 you joined the staff of the Royal Academy of Music as Professor of Composition. From a teaching point were there any gains from your years with Delius that you could bring with you?

E.F. None whatever. According to Ernest Newman, Delius had the most isolated mind in music. No academic musician I have known would have had a clue how to cope with him. It was only because I was self-taught and without prejudice, and because he said that of all musicians he had known, he saw himself in me. Jelka often remarked on this. She said I played the piano like him: I set about work like him. 'It was uncanny!'

No! The gains from a teaching point of view came from my experiences in the RAEC. When preparing students for examinations I had to toe the line, but I did it in my way.

S.L. Interpretatively Delius does seem to be the most elusive of composers - which is perhaps why so many conductors seem to avoid him. Your revelatory reading of *The Song of the High Hills* makes one feel that many modern performances of Delius seem to miss the essence of the music. If there can be said to be such a thing as a Delius tradition, do you feel there is any danger of losing it when one compares performances of today with those of up to fifty years ago?

E.F. I have come to the conclusion that a Delius tradition is impossible. To imitate Delius's greatest exponent, Beecham, would lead to sterility. I think there were more sensitive performances in the past than today by conductors, notably Leslie Heward, Hamilton Harty, Stanford Robinson, Geoffrey Toye and Anthony Collins.

S.L. Falling a little short of asking you to offer your choices of eight 'Desert Island Discs', could you say what were the most memorable *performances* you have experienced, of Delius or any composer?

E.F. *A Mass of Life, In a Summer Garden, Paris* and *Songs of Sunset* conducted by Beecham at the 1929 Delius Festival; Sibelius's Symphony No 5 at a 1942 Barbirolli Manchester Hallé concert; Sibelius's *Tapiola* conducted by Beecham at Queen's Hall in 1939; motets of Palestrina performed by the Sistine Choir at Leeds in 1927; Mozart's Symphony No 34 in C conducted by Beecham (many times); Janacek's String Quartet No 2 *Intimate Letters* performed by the Vlach String Quartet; Bairstow's imaginative accompanying of the Psalms at Evensong in York Minster in my youth; and Debussy's *Pelléas et Mélisande* at Covent Garden conducted by Boulez.

S.L. It only remains for me to thank you for so patiently and so fully answering my questions, and to wish you on behalf of the Delius Society a very happy 80th birthday.

PART TWO
THE WORKS OF DELIUS

1. Works for Orchestra

MARCHE CAPRICE

see page 150

SUMMER EVENING

Summer Evening is an early work for full orchestra which Sir Thomas Beecham has recently edited and arranged for publication. The youthful sincerity of this music will commend it to the lover of Delius and its sonorous strains should appeal to those who shrink from fuller companionship.

Sleeve note RCA LHMV1050 (1953)

SLEIGH RIDE

see page 150

OVER THE HILLS AND FAR AWAY

In the spring of 1899 an audience had gathered in St James's Hall, London, to hear a concert of works by Frederick Delius, a mysterious Yorkshireman, who lived in Paris. Nobody had heard of him or his music. The first sounds that fell on their ears were the distant evocations of muted strings, clarinet and horns in the Fantasy Overture *Over the Hills and Far Away*, which opened the programme. Little could they have realised that here was a destined visionary whose command of the longer flights of composition was to be matched only by the imperishable beauty of their content. The formative works of an original mind are always interesting if played in the spirit of that mind's increase. Influences worked through, not avoided, are the healthy promptings of a ranging apprenticeship. Delius's influences are easily traceable, for he had no use for the traditional technique of the giants. Excepting Wagner, the lesser men were his models, and in many a page of his early works he beat them at their own game. *Over the Hills and Far Away* presents no difficulties to the listener. Its form as a whole is sectional rather than integrated, though the sudden bracing of the introductory theme in agitated derivatives is purposeful and unifying. We hear, too, in the second subject Delius's early fondness for the waving phrase, and the variation form in the music which follows. There is no dramatic manipulation in the sense of development. The work appeals by its youthful vigour and boyish tunefulness, in which there is that touch of innocence we all read into its title.

Sleeve note Columbia 33C1017 (1954)

PARIS

Delius's long formative period reached fruition at the close of the century when returning to France from his first London concert he finished his tone-poem *Paris*. The sound of his music at St James's Hall had fired his mind anew, and cleared up so many technical problems that, by his own account, he could scarcely wait to get back home to take up his work again. The best of his unfledged works for orchestra aspired to the mastery then in vogue: of the handful of scores he possessed at Grez, half were by Richard Strauss. From Strauss he learnt how to balance great forces and construct on extended time-scale. To apply this insight to his own designs was solely his own concern, and so was his sense of flow.

Delius now met the challenge of the vast German orchestras of the day, and the expectations of his conductor-friends, Haym and Cassirer, were fulfilled in a new work of undoubted originality and power.

Paris is a musical impression of the effect the French capital had had on his mind after twelve years' residence there on leaving the Leipzig Conservatoire. It marked the end of a way of life which Delius realised had to be changed if his aim was to contemplate nature as the source of his inspiration. The break, however, was not complete. Long after settling at Grez-sur-Loing he still hankered in moments of leisure for life on the Montparnasse, and often succumbed to its lure. The city had given him the friendship of Strindberg, Gauguin and Munch - and, at deeper levels, indelible memories of her moods and natural beauties. It is from these that

145

the music was born. The suggestion of any Lautrecian portrayals is purely the listener's prerogative.

For the most part Delius deliberately tones down the colours of his orchestral palette in seeking to evoke the spirit of night brooding over the sleeping metropolis. Exquisite use is made of the mellow darker qualities of the clarinets, violas and bassoons in the play of half-light shadings. Yet all is clearly defined with no hint of the chiaroscuro treatment to be found in his later works. The woodwind figurations based on distant street cries heard in the oboe, bassoons and horns are pointed with a rhythmic subtlety unique in Delius. There are moments in *Paris* which even today still sound quite novel to discerning ears.

The impact of *Paris* on the concert world has remained remarkably consistent since its first performance in Elberfeld in 1901 by Hans Haym, to whom it is dedicated, and the first London performance, in 1908, by Sir Thomas Beecham.

It must have seemed that the romantic qualities peculiar to this virile work were certain pointers to the future. The forthcoming performances at the Delius Centenary Festival of the work on which Delius was next engaged - *A Village Romeo and Juliet* - will reveal that not only was this opera unlike anything he had written hitherto, but unlike any other in music!

Programme note, Delius Centenary concert, RFH 29 January 1962
Bradford Delius Centenary Festival programme book 1962

PARIS (arr. two pianos)

Delius's orchestral nocturne **Paris - *The Song of a Great City*** was first produced in Elberfeld in 1901. In 1903 Julius Buths, a conductor and early champion of Delius, made an arrangement for two pianos which, it appears, was never performed. Later, when the orchestral score was published in 1909, Delius revised many passages, notably in the livelier sections, and these I have recently incorporated into Buths' original arrangement which we are to hear tonight.

Redcliffe Concerts programme 12 December 1977

PARIS
DANCE RHAPSODY NO 1
EVENTYR

Of the three works presented here, *Dance Rhapsody No 1* belongs to a phase in Delius's art midway both in date and style between the two others - *Paris* and *Eventyr*. An unaccountable inner change in the musical essence of his mind had slowly asserted itself in his music round about the turn of the century, and brought into play a mode of composing, intuitive and of singular character. Before the end of the first decade of such originals as *Sea Drift*, *Brigg Fair*, *In a Summer Garden* and *Dance Rhapsody No 1*, there was little trace left of the mind that once had occupied itself with *Paris*. A doubtful reaction to this opinion would not be surprising, nevertheless. The dates of Delius's early works - and even of some later ones - are sometimes misleading. Delius seldom altered a detail; revision to him meant expanding a work. These revisions were pondered well; more often than not they were put in hand leisurely long after first performances; then, and then only, were manuscripts offered to publishers. There were always several scores on the stocks: but the summer months were kept for reflection, usually in the hills of Norway.

Paris certainly had its share of this improving course of action at this stage of Delius's development. The version produced by Dr Hans Haym at Elberfeld in 1901 and Busoni in Berlin in the following year was insufficiently realised compared to that published by Leuckart of Leipzig in 1909. This revised (expanded) version is now assigned to Universal Edition. Delius had made his bachelor home in the Paris of the 1890s. Eventually he settled at Grez-sur-Loing, where, after writing the opera *Koanga*, he indulged in this musical reverie of Paris. This was a crucial work for Delius. The dominance of Strauss, the vast orchestras of the day, and the urge to make his mark in Germany led him to prove his equal skill in instrumental counterpoint. The score includes six horns, three trumpets, with English horn, bass clarinet, double bassoon in addition to triple woodwind. Delius offers no programme other than hints made privately in a letter dated 10th December 1910: 'It is a Nocturne and describes my impressions of night and early dawn with its peculiar street cries and Pan's goatherd, etc. These cries are very characteristic of Paris and the piece begins and closes with them.' Delius rarely depicts in music; but his opening depicts as well as evokes the sense of his own word-picture. The murmur of timpani, the darkness of double bassoon and basses tuned to low D; the eerie, brooding bass clarinet, the fitful stirrings of cellos - a few such strokes were all that were needed. One feels the city gradually awakening and stretching its limbs at the first light of day. Such fancies, however, at best are short-lived. The musical interest soon takes over as mood follows mood in continuous transition with metamorphosis of theme in episodes of lyrical beauty and brilliant invention in scherzo-like incidents. *Paris* is man's music, virile, imaginative, assured, with a painter's sense of orchestral colour. The Delius of *Paris* was the handsome adventurer, the artist, Bohemian and man-about-town with something of the recluse in him even then. The music derives not, as would seem, from his isolation as an artist, or his cosmopolitan way of life, but from the secret adventures of his spirit.

Dance Rhapsody No 1 was written in 1908. The composer was persuaded to conduct it initially at the Three Choirs Festival at Hereford a year later. It follows variation form, English in style, with a middle section as relief. The instrumentation is the same as in *Paris*, except for the inclusion of a bass oboe, heard in the opening dialogue with English horn, then clarinet. Immediately after the French horn entry the conversation is halted abruptly! The dance tune trips from the tongue of the oboe to the pulse of a plucked, rising bass. Note the answer from the flute - a reiterative phrase with a quip from the oboes. Changing facets of this material act as links in the chain of variations. The English disposition of the music yields suddenly to alien rhythms, as if some Spanish influence from Florida had lurked inert since Delius's youth. Eventually the music loses its fire and the variations are resumed with the dance-tune in octaves in flute and clarinet. The emotional peak of the work is reached in the slow, penultimate variation for solo violin and muted-string harmonies of a beauty such as a poet recalled - 'Once, in finesse of fiddles found I ecstasy.' The bass oboe casts its spell and brings the action to a standstill. Strings in unison whirl the dance tune through a labyrinth of chromatics to emerge triumphant in the end.

Norway was second home to Delius. He loved its hills and countryside, its literature and its language in which he was fluent from his early twenties. He made lasting friendships with its artists and writers; he fled to his cottage there in the Great War; he spent his summers lying fallow, and when illness prevented his travelling there he kept in touch through Norwegian newspapers read aloud to him by his wife up to a month before his death. No wonder he relished the folk-tales of Norway taken down by word of mouth and collected by two enthusiasts - Peter Cristen Asbjørnsen and Jorgen Engebretsen Moë over a period of several years. They were published in 1841 under the title 'Eventyr' at a time when national feeling in Norway was gathering strength to assert itself after centuries of dominance by Danes and Swedes in the tangled history of Scandinavian literature. No one has yet attempted to trace which of the tales, indeed, if any, had influenced Delius[50] in 1917 when he came to write his own *Eventyr*. This is his only orchestral piece that clearly suggests narrative, but its musical imagery much more subtly brings out the spirits of the tales. Delius reduces the brass to four horns, but adds to otherwise very large forces, bells, xylophone, and celesta. The musical interest turns on the play and interaction of the two groups of themes. The one, expressing the idea in the strings of the warm-hearted, superstitious country folk; the other, ideas in woodwind and brass of the weird interventions in their lives by the frightening creatures of these legends - the trolls, the giants, demons, pixies. Delius's textures in *Eventyr* are more terse than those in *Paris* and *Dance Rhapsody No 1*. There is also the surprise of attractive new matter as in *Paris* in the reprise. Two powerful climaxes end in shouts which are sometimes omitted in performance. The music moves forward with more compulsion than that which propels the dream-like structures by which he is more widely known. This, and the graphic character of the piece - with its instant feeling of 'Once upon a time . . .' - may account for its clamorous reception abroad in places where hitherto Delius's music has met with some bewilderment. *Eventyr* was first heard in London in 1919. It was conducted by Sir Henry Wood, whose promotion of Delius, now forgotten, earned him its dedication.

Sleeve note HMV ASD 2804 (1972)

LEBENSTANZ (LIFE'S DANCE)

see page 159

---

50   Barrie Iliffe, who shed some new light on *Eventyr* in a broadcast talk on BBC Radio 3 on 9 May 1982, has contributed an article on '*Eventyr* and the Fairy-Tale Element in Delius' to *Frederick Delius: Music, Art and Literature*, edited by Lionel Carley, Scolar Press 1997.

BRIGG FAIR
A SONG BEFORE SUNRISE
MARCHE CAPRICE
ON HEARING THE FIRST CUCKOO IN SPRING
SUMMER NIGHT ON THE RIVER
SLEIGH RIDE
INTERMEZZO FROM *FENNIMORE AND GERDA*

The boyish qualities of Delius's early music, despite obvious influences, are as irresistible to Sir Thomas Beecham as the challenge of the later works. Delius believed in working through his influences, not avoiding them. *Marche Caprice* and *Sleigh Ride*, written in 1888, are reminders that until 1900 there is little in Delius's music to foretell the rapt nature mystic we know today, nor the loaded richness of his subsequent art. The sudden flowering of his genius that year in his opera *A Village Romeo and Juliet* and the astonishing series of works that ensued is without precedent in music. These apprentice pieces are pleasant trifles on which Delius set no store. (Young composers will find in them the importance of keeping their basses moving, a weakness to which Delius was prone.)

In 1907, moved by his friend Percy Grainger's choral setting of a folk-song *Brigg Fair* which he had collected in Lincolnshire, Delius now wrote his own 'English Rhapsody' on the tune. Following a period of prodigious composition in large-scale forms of his own devising, Delius was compelled to centre his musical thought within the contours of the folk-tune and its formal and spiritual projections in a smaller time-scale than that of his previous set of variations - *Appalachia*. But for that propitious necessity the exquisite idylls such as *On hearing the first cuckoo in spring* and *Summer night on the river* on which his fame may ultimately depend might never have been written. Some critics maintain that from *Brigg Fair* onwards Delius merely repeated himself. This view, I think, is mistaken. The new simplicity of the final phase (1928-1934) including *A Song of Summer*, Violin Sonata No 3 and the choral work *Songs of Farewell* was the climax of this growing concentration dating from *Brigg Fair*.

Verses from the old country song run:

> *It was on the fift' of August*
> *The weather fine and fair*
> *Unto Brigg Fair I did repair*
> *For love I was inclined.*
>
> *I rose up with the lark in the morning*
> *With my heart so full of glee,*
> *Of thinking there to meet my dear*
> *Long time I wished to see.*
>
> *The green leaves they shall wither*
> *And the branches they shall die*
> *If ever I prove false to her*
> *To the girl that loves me.*

As usual, Delius goes his own way - an evocative introduction; the folk-song from the oboe with woodwind accompaniment; repetitions that call to mind the early English manner of Byrd's *The woods so wild* (though doubtless Delius had never heard of it); a beautiful meditation unmindful of the tune but akin to it; more variations in which the reins are loosened in pure rhapsody, and finally, after the clamour of the fair, the melting music of the lovers mirrored in Nature. The harmonic and rhythmic changes on the tune ring like varying aspects of the same type of countryside, and Delius was never more English in his feeling for orchestral colour than here. Rarely has he used the dry tones of the bass clarinet to more imaginative effect.

From the vast forces including six horns employed in *Brigg Fair* we turn to the later and more intimate music for small orchestra. Next in order of composition is the **Intermezzo** from the opera *Fennimore and Gerda* (1908-10) based on episodes from the life of Niels Lyhne by the Danish writer Jacobsen. This work is dedicated to Sir Thomas Beecham. The Intermezzo consists of the interludes linking Niels's soliloquy with the rest of the story. It is harvest time, towards evening. Niels, a young poet just returned from the fields, rests thoughtfully on the farmyard wall. He has been unfaithful with Fennimore, his friend Erik's wife. News has come that Erik has been killed and he is stricken with remorse. Friend and lover gone and his poetry come to naught, Niels looks beyond the fields to the distant fjord calmed in the hope of another spring. The music speaks for itself in regretful ebbings and flowings in which time is lost in memories, a quickening of the pulse in a moment of passionate repining, and the heart is stilled in the promise of the Earth.

Summer night on the river (1911) is unique in all Delius's music in the power of its sense of depicting as well as evoking the spirit of the scene. Moments in the Forest Scene in Act III of *Koanga* and *North Country Sketches* too have strong visual suggestiveness, but these are less sustained. Listening to *Summer night on the river* one can almost see the gnats and dragonflies darting over the waterlilies and the faint white mist hovering over willow-tressed banks and overhanging trees. Many a night at Grez-sur-Loing have I lolled over the oars silent with Delius lost in that music. No orchestral work by Delius demands such deep insight and sensitive skill in performance as this. The balance and shading of woodwind timbres in this musical chiaroscuro is imperative to a visionary interpretation of the score.

On hearing the first cuckoo in spring (1912) and *A song before sunrise* (1918) are less exacting. Here the impetus is contained in the chordal flow of many-voiced strings, never turgid but luminous, the woodwind adding their arabesques or pointing the melodic line. This in the former, incidentally, is derived from a Norwegian folk-song.

In the best of Delius we are made one with Nature. No man has given musical utterance to all her moods, but in the expression of her tranquillities he excelled all others.

Sleeve note HMV ALP 1586, ASD357, EM 290323-3 (1958)

Seraphim S-60185 (1971)

Note on *Brigg Fair* in Bradford Delius Centenary Festival programme book 1962

BRIGG FAIR

In 1907, the year *Appalachia* was first conducted in England by Fritz Cassirer, Delius composed **Brigg Fair**, and, like most of his works written before 1910, he revised it after the first performance, notably in the introduction. It, too, is a set of variations, on an English folk-song this time, from Lincolnshire, 'given' to him by Percy Grainger, the opening lines of which run:

> *It was on the fift' of August*
> *The weather fine and fair*
> *Unto Brigg Fair I did repair*
> *For love I was inclined.*

These variations are contained within a smaller time-scale than those of *Appalachia* and with closer adherence to its folk-song theme. Delius himself described them fancifully as of varying aspects of the same type of intimate countryside. There is a magical episode, too, in *Brigg Fair* for solo horn and muted strings and, in the variation which follows it, one of the finest melodic climaxes in lyrical orchestral music. The language of *Brigg Fair* is of exquisite sensitivity, richer and even more personal to Delius than his highly original and youthful *Appalachia*.

Sleeve note HMV ASD2635 (1971)

IN A SUMMER GARDEN
INTERMEZZO AND SERENADE FROM *HASSAN*
A SONG BEFORE SUNRISE
LA CALINDA
ON HEARING THE FIRST CUCKOO IN SPRING
SUMMER NIGHT ON THE RIVER
LATE SWALLOWS (arr. Fenby)

In the spring of 1908 Delius projected his imagination in a musical impression of his garden at Grez-sur-Loing, the tiny French hamlet where his life's work was done. His reveries induced eventually a masterpiece of orchestral fantasy (for he revised it drastically after the first performance in 1909) - *In a summer garden*. Delius's house stood on the village street between an old church and a ruined keep, the high stone walls of his garden sloping down beyond the orchard to the river. He must often have longed for the summer change of landscape swamplike from autumn to spring, his work time, for he would lie fallow in the summer. Then the white courtyard would blaze with myriad flowers, and Nature rim his little world by the great trees at the water's edge. Indoors, apart from works by his friends Gauguin and Munch, all the paintings on the walls revealed colourful studies of the garden in summer mood from the brush of his talented wife, Jelka. But the garden itself was her masterpiece, and the musical imagery it worked in her husband's mind was dedicated fittingly to her.

The texture of *In a summer garden*, despite the full forces employed, has the quality of chamber music, and suggests with exquisite subtlety the sounds and colours of the scene. It opens quietly in chant-like tones for wind quintet, echoed in the strings with a flitting figure from the oboe. To hear this and no more, we are caught up into the composer's dream. Memorise the rhythm of that flitting figure for it, not the opening phrase, is the mainspring of much of the musical action. The development of the salient rhythmic features of this delicate poetry is as masterly as its melodic shaping. For instance, the rhythm at the peak of the flute phrase (following immediately upon the oboe at the beginning of the work) expands in joyous outburst at the first entry of the full orchestra. There is more invention in this man's music than is conceded; it never boasts itself, but mingles naturally in its flow. Delius is rarely given credit for the new type of prose melody he contrived against varying tensions of chromatic harmony. In this work the line is firm, clear and lyrical as in song. A more spacious singing is heard in the middle section from the violas; then, as the current of the passing river deepens, horn and trumpet join in turn to the murmuring of the woodwind till the more animated music of the garden reaches rapture. Gradually the exultant mood relaxes, the opening phrase in the strings brings moments of yearning and reluctance, and the vision of the garden fades.

Delius's brilliantly effective incidental music to James Elroy Flecker's *Hassan: The Golden Journey to Samarkand* was written for Basil Dean's production staged at His Majesty's Theatre in 1923. The original score is for solo wind, harp, percussion and eleven strings (whereas Sir Thomas Beecham's arrangement of the Intermezzo and Serenade employs the normal complement of strings), with the Serenade in the rarely heard version for tenor solo.

A Song before Sunrise for small orchestra (1918) is dedicated to Philip Heseltine, whose early advocacy of Delius in England is apt to be forgotten. As in the better-known *On hearing the first cuckoo in spring* for similar forces (1912), the impetus in *A Song before Sunrise* is contained in the chordal flow of many-voiced strings, never turgid but luminous, the woodwind adding their arabesques or pointing the melodic line. *On hearing the first cuckoo in spring* is more obviously evocative. Its brief introduction in itself is a master-stroke, an epitome of Delius's mature art and, if unfolded imaginatively on the ear, captures in felicitous lyricism his sense of the awakening countryside. But to Delius, musing on the Norwegian folk-song on which his music is based, there is also sadness that the spring of life passes all too soon. The cuckoo notes on the clarinet (in the middle section) do not depict so much as kindle afresh something of that yearly delight which few outgrow.

The nearest that Delius ever comes to depicting is in *Summer night on the river*, also for small orchestra (1911). Moments in the Forest Scene in Act III of *Koanga* (1897) and *North Country Sketches* (1914) too have strong visual suggestiveness, but these are less sustained. Listening to *Summer night on the river* one can almost see the gnats and dragonflies darting over the waterlilies, and the faint white mist hovering over willow-tressed banks and overhanging trees. Here Delius's imagination leads him to an orchestral pointillism unique in his output, but saved from mere artifice by its dependence on melody. For this reason *Summer night on the river* is the most difficult of all Delius's orchestral pieces to realise in performance.

The dance *La Calinda* first appeared in Delius's orchestral suite *Florida* (1886-7). Later he included it in the score of his third opera, *Koanga*, as a choral dance to enliven the wedding festivities of Koanga and Palmyra. This arrangement, made [by Eric Fenby] at the request of the late Ralph Hawkes, the publisher, for a popular piece by Delius, incorporates the vocal parts on orchestral instruments.

When Delius and his wife were forced to flee from France to England during the First World War, the composer put aside his major projects for a time and busied himself with chamber music. The second string quartet (1916-17) dates from this period and, incidentally, contains no material from the rejected string quartet of 1893, as has often been supposed. 'When we were away from home', Mrs Delius told me, 'Fred missed the swallows most!' Thus the third movement of the later quartet which Delius called *Late Swallows* is a beautiful autumnal soliloquy in sound conjured up by thoughts of the swallows darting to and fro from the eaves of the house and studios at Grez now that they were abandoned to the military authorities. This movement, little-known hitherto owing to neglect of the quartet, suggested itself in an arrangement for string orchestra.

Sleeve note HMV ASD2477 (1969)
Note on *In a summer garden* slightly revised from Bradford Delius Centenary Festival programme book 1962 and the sleeve note for Columbia 33C1017 (1954)

DANCE RHAPSODY NO 1

Delius wrote his *Dance Rhapsody* **(No 1)** in 1908 and conducted its first performance the following year at the Three Choirs Festival at Hereford, one of the three occasions on which he was persuaded to direct his music in person.[51] He recalled the event with mixed feelings - 'I had little talent for conducting and, to make matters worse, I caught a severe chill and had my wallet stolen just before the concert!'

The work demands large forces - three flutes, oboe, English horn, bass oboe, three clarinets, bass clarinet, three bassoons, double-bassoon, six horns, three trumpets, three trombones and tuba, percussion and strings. It opens quietly with a short anticipatory dialogue between reed instruments accompanied by string basses ending in a sudden exclamation from the whole orchestra. After a pause, the main theme is heard from the oboe tripping to a mounting bass, an irresistible call to whistle and dance. The flute responds with a pointed figure which the oboes complete in playful quip, and the clarinet takes up the tune. We now dance to harmonic variations of the tune punctuated by changing facets of the flute figure. Soon the pace quickens to a syncopated figure derived from the puckish oboe phrase just mentioned, and heard in the string basses and bassoons. Delius carries us on fitfully in charming rhapsody till the music gradually loses its fire, and we hear again the main tune in octaves by flute and clarinet. More variations lead us to the emotional peak of the work in the slow penultimate variation in which a solo violin soars over ravishing harmonies in muted strings, a magical episode unique in all music. Sir Henry Wood confessed that he never conducted this variation unmoved. A brief reference to the opening dialogue ensues and the music gallops to a martial close.

Bradford Delius Centenary Festival programme book 1962

see also page 148

---

[51]   The three occasions were *Appalachia* at Hanley on 2 April 1908, with the Hallé Orchestra and the North Staffordshire District Choral Society; the première of *In a summer garden* on 11 December 1908 at Queen's Hall, London, with the orchestra of the (Royal) Philharmonic Society; and the première of *Dance Rhapsody No 1* on 8 September 1909 at Hereford, with the London Symphony Orchestra.

ON HEARING THE FIRST CUCKOO IN SPRING
SUMMER NIGHT ON THE RIVER

see pages 154-5

NORTH COUNTRY SKETCHES

North Country Sketches, dedicated to Albert Coates, was written in 1913-14 and first performed by Sir Thomas Beecham with the London Symphony Orchestra at a London concert in 1915. It is Delius's one instrumental work in which he recalls expressly his impressions of the Yorkshire countryside he had known as a boy, though it may be of interest to add that years later before dictating the new opening to *A Song of Summer*, in his garden in France, he told me to imagine we were sitting among the heather on the Yorkshire Moors overlooking the sea.

The orchestral colours of these musical symbolisations of our wilder northern landscape have sharper and more bracing qualities of timbre than are to be heard in *Brigg Fair*, which, I always think, Delius placed much further south than Lincolnshire in his music. There is more pictorial suggestion in the first two movements than is usual in Delius despite his nature titles. The division of the strings into twelve parts, the imaginative preoccupation with texture rather than tune, the astringent harmonies drooping in motion, the lyrical oboe all but silent, now joined by two others in bleak figurations with icy fingerings from the harps, call up the visual *Winter Landscape* whilst 'cellos, horn, then clarinets and bassoons lament the lifeless scene.

Delius is not easy on his performers. The right sense of colour and weight on the right note in the right place for the instrumentalist. A flexible hand, firm yet unprejudiced, with a flair for balancing rhapsody in the singing phrase from the conductor. A helping hand, too, in dance movements when Delius, resisting modulation, and defying the laws of musical gravity, expects to achieve dance motion continuously from phrases static on strong beats often ending where they began. The *March of Spring*, light and lively, throbs rhythmically in hope of the Summer Garden through quiet ruminatings to joyous outburst culminating in the march-like tune which gradually dies in the distance - the most difficult movement to bring off successfully in all his orchestral music.

Bradford Delius Centenary Festival programme book 1962

NORTH COUNTRY SKETCHES
LIFE'S DANCE
A SONG OF SUMMER

Delius loved the northern scene. There were years when he seemed possessed by it whenever he took up his pen to compose. A perusal of a catalogue of his works will show the extent of his passionate interest, notably from 1908-14, when his mind ranged in musical accord with the nature poetry of the Dane, J P Jacobsen, in the opera *Fennimore and Gerda*, the choral *Arabesk*, and the wordless *Song of the High Hills* of Norway. It will also hint at his working habits. The moment he felt intuition wane he would put aside the main task in hand and take up something entirely different - *Summer night on the river*, for instance, an exquisite parenthesis to the *Arabesk*; or he would work at the seemingly intractable *Life's Dance* which had defied his efforts at a convincing solution ever since 1899, when the first version, *The Dance goes on*, had been based on an extravagant Danish drama, *Dansen Gaar*, by Helge Rode. It was England, not Scandinavia, however, that impelled his major orchestral impressions of the northern scene he had known as a boy when riding his pony on the Yorkshire moors - *North Country Sketches*, written at his home in rural France between 1913-14. There were yet to be two more northern tokens - the strangely improbable Ballad for Orchestra, *Eventyr* (Once upon a time: after Asbjørnsen's Norwegian folk-tales) which had occupied Delius during World War 1 whilst living at his cottage in Norway, and the physically improbable English epilogue which brought this northern phrase to a close - the gentler *Song of Summer* which followed in 1929.

I cannot pretend to know what Delius sought to convey precisely beyond the purely musical content of his **North Country Sketches**. In the six years that on and off I was his musical amanuensis and one of his household, I doubt if his conversation about music exceeded twenty minutes all told; and this mostly at my initiation. Otherwise talk about music was taboo. What insight I have into Delius's music I learnt through his dictations; by noting his reactions when I played them to him with varying accent or phrasing; from a comment on radio performances of his music, or the rare remark about his ponderings. There is no programme as such to *North Country Sketches*. The clues, I think, to his mind here, apart from those given in the titles of the movements, are his observations on life. 'Man is nothing! Nature alone recurs!' This was the nub of his thought at all times. Despite a degree of pictorial suggestion unusual in Delius in the first two movements, we surely hear the *spirit* of the wind sighing at the falling of the year and man's irremediable hold like a leaf. The marvellously imaginative colourings of texture enclosed in the familiar 'Delius sound' are projected with aptness and acute sensitivity. The Mazurka-like Dance, characteristic of Delius, is again, I feel, a dance of the spirit rather than feet; fitful, wayward, changeable in turn, as if only with thoughts of recurring Spring can the heart in Winter exult in dance. The last impression, The March of Spring, throbs to the rhythms of 'Spring's awakening', the original title of this movement. The downward progression of drooping lines that shape the impression of languishing Autumn and the static bareness of Winter are gone. The impression of Spring is of upward movement exhilarating in bravura passages with meadowland dallyings in oboe arabesque which lead to rapture in the strings until the march ends in serenity. The score, inscribed to Albert Coates, was first performed by Sir Thomas Beecham at a London Symphony Orchestra concert in London in 1915.

Delius made three versions of *Life's Dance* before he was finally satisfied. The first, *La Ronde Se Déroule (The Dance Goes On)*, a symphonic poem based on the drama already mentioned, began its course under Alfred Hertz at St James's Hall, London, in 1899. The development section was not convincing so Delius, preserving the original opening, set about revising and expanding it. The second version, entitled *Life's Dance*, by now dissociated from the drama, was introduced by Julius Buths in Düsseldorf in 1904 and met with success in Germany - even more than did *Paris*, it seems. But Delius found the coda weak and reorchestrated several passages. The third version, with the same title, was brought out by Oskar Fried in Berlin in 1912. Delius was delighted with the result and dedicated the work to Fried. He wrote to his publishers Tischer & Jagenberg: 'I think the Dance of Life (Life's Dance) is my best orchestral work. I have had it in my file for some years for the ending did not please me very much but at last I have found what I was looking for and it is now complete.' Though Tischer & Jagenberg published it at once, the work still remains almost unknown. In the hope of a performance in 1933, Delius told me: 'I wanted to depict the turbulence, the joy, energy, great striving of youth - all to end at last in the inevitable death.'

Whereas in *North Country Sketches* Delius uses double woodwind and sub-divides his strings throughout, often into as many as twelve parts, in *Life's Dance* he has triple woodwind but rarely divides the strings. The score of *Life's Dance* is an immediate rebuke to those who accuse him of lack of skill in manipulating traditional counterpoint. If anything he is too inventive at times for the rapid pace of his figuration. These, when chromatic and widely spread, provide as severe a test for players as any tone-poem by Richard Strauss, whose scores Delius had carefully studied. The rondo-like form of *Life's Dance* certainly owes much to this attention. The work is not without idiosyncrasy. The reflective passages in compound time beginning in the duet for violas and cellos call to mind the *Mass of Life*, but the affinity between the opening phrase of the dance and that of Elgar's Violin Concerto is indeed a remarkable coincidence. *Life's Dance* is the culmination of Delius's power in this type of invention before he found the unique and unmistakable voice of his own.

In *A Song of Summer* the same large forces are deployed as in *Life's Dance*, but how differently the ear can tell. The work is based on material salvaged from an earlier tone-poem, *A Poem of Life and Love*, dating from 1918 with transitions and new material dictated to the writer by Delius, now blind and paralysed, in 1929: 'I want you to write down this new opening for the new work. Bring your score-paper and sit beside me . . . I want you to imagine that we are sitting on the cliffs in the heather looking out over the sea. The sustained chords in the high strings suggest the clear sky and calmness of the scene . . . 7/4 in a bar (four and a three: divided strings, chord of D major - A, D, F# doubled at the octave, lowest note the A string of the violas . .)'. The work was heard for the first time under its new title at the Promenade Concerts in 1931 conducted by Sir Henry Wood.

Sleeve note HMV ASD 3139 (1975)

AIR AND DANCE

see page 163

EVENTYR

see pages 148-9

A SONG BEFORE SUNRISE

see page 152 and 154

A SONG OF SUMMER

My work for Delius began the day I joined his household at Grez-sur-Loing, a village to the south of Paris, beyond Fontainebleau, where he had lived for thirty years. Upstairs awaiting completion on his desk in the music-room was an arrangement for two pianos begun by his close friend Balfour Gardiner of his last orchestral score, *A Poem of Life and Love*, written, I gathered from his wife, before blindness and paralysis took their toll. Gardiner was expected to arrive within the week[52], and her plan was that we should play it to Delius to try and reawaken his interest in music in the hope that he might start to compose again, now that I had come to Grez.

Well, we played it. Our performance was received in silence. We repeated it - still with no comment. Delius seemed quite listless but jovial later at supper.

When Gardiner left, I felt some unease, being conscious of Delius's cautious probing, and I dreaded the inevitable question I fear he would put to me. Well, it came all too soon: what did I think of the piece? Now Delius was a very difficult man despite a certain charm and dry humour; a very private man; awesome and given to silence. And had I known how much he resented criticism of his music, I should never have dared to say what I did of the invention of some of the weaker sections of the work, which I thought might have been written by a student, and very much in Delius's early manner too. And here was I, little more than a student myself. However, my opinion had already been approved in private by his wife Jelka, and I gave it when asked with more candour than tact, and Delius was taken aback. Eventually he conceded. 'Then select the good material and make a piece out of it yourself. Take your time. I'll hear it when you're ready.' And with this he was carried away.

Eventually the next dreaded moment came, but not without praise for my written effort. Delius said he could work with me; now he would see what he could do. I tore up my manuscript in triumph. I had managed to rekindle his interest.

I'm not going to touch on the technical problems we encountered in the process of dictation, but listeners may remember Ken Russell's BBC documentary television film *Song of Summer*, with Max Adrian as Delius and Christopher Gable as me. We are shown working in the music room

---

52   Eric had arrived at Grez on 10 October 1928; Balfour Gardiner was
      expected on 20 October.

exactly as it happened; Delius in his chair beside me, as I play back his dictations at the piano and scribble them down in full score. And another sequence shows Delius dictating out of doors. This was the new opening to *A Poem of Life and Love* which he renamed *A Song of Summer*. Here he tells me to imagine we were sitting on the Yorkshire moors in the heather, gazing out to sea. The quiet high divided strings suggest the calm of the scene; the cellos and basses the waves lapping the cliffs below; and the fluttering flute figure the seagulls gliding overhead, again just as he described the new opening in real life before dictating it to me.

> Spoken introduction to BBC broadcast, recorded 17 October 1978,
> broadcast 24 November 1978.

see also page 160

FANTASTIC DANCE

The last of the dictated works was the *Fantastic Dance* for orchestra which was given a delightful first performance by Sir Adrian Boult at a BBC Symphony concert in 1934, the year Delius died. It is brief, as might be expected, for Delius, though mentally alert to the end, was exhausted by the gruelling daily effort expended on the choral work *Songs of Farewell*, and several other projects too, such as shaping the *Irmelin* Prelude and the *Idyll* for soprano, baritone and orchestra from material that already existed. Yet knowing the fondness for a dozen bars of score he had sketched in his own hand years before, he decided to extend them and to complete a short work to dedicate to me. I was privileged enough as it was to help him, without this touching gesture he made me in the *Fantastic Dance*.

> Spoken introduction to BBC broadcast, recorded 17 October 1978,
> broadcast 24 November 1978.

MUSIC OF DELIUS arranged by Eric Fenby

All but one of these arrangements were made by the writer of this note at the suggestion of the Delius Trust and others, dating from the early sixties. The exception was the *Dance*, originally for harpsichord, adapted especially for Elena Duran's recording début on this disc. Delius was induced to write the piece by the celebrated English harpsichordist Violet Gordon Woodhouse, who claimed to be the first to record the instrument.

The archaic touch of melodic charm and the rich chordal flow of the dance prompted this arrangement for flute and strings.

When the inimitable James Galway asked for 'something to play by Delius, and one piece must be *La Calinda*!', the somewhat neglected *Air and Dance*, written initially for string orchestra, seemed to be an appropriate foil. *La Calinda* is a remarkably assured excerpt from Delius's first apprenticeship work, the suite for orchestra *Florida*, composed in his student days at Leipzig in 1886-7. It is only in the middle section, however, that he hints at the erotic slave-dance that was banned from public performance and from which this extract takes its name. It is arranged here for flute and strings. In the third arrangement, the *Air* merges into the *Dance* in slowly undulating lines ushered in gently by the flute which move diversely to a thrilling climax. The pace quickens in sprightly rhythms, eventually subsiding reflectively, and a solo cello recalls the *Air*. Its reverie is but short-lived, cut off abruptly by a jaunty fling.

By 1922, Delius was unable to write but could see to correct five pieces for piano he was contrived to dictate to his wife. These were included as a novelty in a concert at Oxford in 1964 when David Tall, the then conductor of the Wadham College Orchestra, requested a version for flute, oboe, two clarinets and bassoon, two horns and trumpet, timpani and strings. Thus, under the title of *Five Little Pieces* for small orchestra, a delightful *Mazurka*, Delius's favourite rhythm in dance, had readily invited orchestration. *A Waltz*, child-like on the piano, seemed unaccountably to reach adolescence when the same notes were dressed instrumentally. Both these pieces were dedicated to Yvonne O'Neill, daughter of the composer Norman O'Neill, now Mrs Derek Hudson. *Lullaby for a modern baby* is an enchantingly original cradle-song requiring the pianist to hum the tune or enlist the services of a violin when it is played on the piano. Here it is given to the solo flute, paired briefly to the solo viola, with gentle lullings in muted strings. A second *Waltz*, elegant and thicker in texture than the first, was begun at Croissy in 1891 and finished at Grez-sur-Loing in 1922. It expands with an almost Brahmsian expressiveness, lilting to a forceful climax. Finally, in an enigmatic *Toccata*, a lively but rather pensive theme in flute, clarinets and first violins enters to arpeggios in the low strings. Oboe and clarinet - in turn - strive to soar and maintain flight and dip to a hovering theme in the strings. The mood is continued in risings and fallings and mounts, supported by the brass, to a crowning flourish of the opening theme which quite unexpectedly peters out. This last movement was encored at Oxford.

Delius, like so many composers, found that writing a string quartet laid claim to the most exacting discipline inescapable from its constraints. The string quartet was the one medium in which as a youth he had practical experience as second violin in his father's quartet at their home at Claremont in Bradford. It is not surprising, therefore, that despite the surfeit he had in those years of Haydn, Mozart and early Beethoven, he should hanker to write his own quartet by 1888, when he was twenty-six. This and other attempts he made - the next was in the following year and again three years later - were all dishearteningly abortive. In each instance he retrieved some material and carried it forward to the ensuing bid, even to the quartet in three movements he composed in 1916 which was performed that year in London by the London String Quartet. After the performance he added a scherzo, reinstating a nimble theme from the 1888 attempt, and thinned out several passages heavy with double stoppings. This now conclusive solution was presented by the same quartet, also in London, in 1919 and published in 1922.

In 1962, the centenary of Delius's birth, Sir John Barbirolli proposed that an arrangement of the slow movement, *Late Swallows*, should be made for string orchestra, and in 1977 the Delius Trust decided that the three other movements should be realised similarly with the title **Sonata for Strings**.

Matchless as is the expressive power of the string quartet in its intimate weavings, passages occur in Delius's quartet which rarely avoid a sense of strain in maintaining the momentum and sweep of phrase, when rests are few in any one part, and textures tend to be chordal and passive. An arrangement for string orchestra, though losing the directness of smaller focus, imparts a more spacious ease in the playing. Patterns of awkward figurations at speed can be shared between players at the same desk, and the sound of small groups of soloists can be set against that of larger forces playing at the same or different dynamic, and niceties of phrase can be pointed by telling means of divisi.

The crux of composition is a convincing continuity and Delius achieved it here, as so often, relying on flowing lyrical line moving forward purposefully, constantly looking back on itself and harping on prominent rhythmic features ripe for further onward propulsion. It is quite clear that he had in mind a near approach to sonata form, but his first subject, centred upon G, leads to a second subject upon C, and not as might be expected on D. A theme reminiscent of Ravel follows. Contrast comes in excitable bravura; and a recapitulation, though conventional, ends surprisingly in the relative minor. The nimble 1888 theme propels the scherzo in C minor, slowing to a lyrical section in the major, and resuming to end on the same minor chord as that which closes the previous movement. Delius is the elegist in *Late Swallows*, written when he had fled from his home at Grez during World War 1. Memories of Florida haunt him again in an interlude voicing his longing for home in the emotional context of the slave tune from his opera, *Koanga*. A rousing introduction to the last movement quickly collapses in calm, till a perky pentatonic theme in the basses emerges to recur, rondo-like, between episodes interspersed in its action. A rustic feeling finally asserts itself.

Sleeve note EMI ASD3688 (1979)

2. Works for Solo Instrument(s) and Orchestra

CONCERTO FOR PIANOFORTE AND ORCHESTRA

Delius sketched the first version of this concerto in three separate movements during his return to Florida in 1897 to dispose of his orange-farm. It was first performed in Elberfeld in 1904 by Julius Buths as soloist under the direction of Hans Haym. Some years later the composer recast it in one movement. This version was heard eventually in London in 1907 with Theodor Szántó as pianist who annoyed Delius by substituting passages of his own invention in the solo part. The present printed score, however, is as Delius intended.

Critical opinion would appear to be almost unanimous in agreeing that no work by Delius displays the ineptitude in handling free treatment of sonata form more plainly than his pianoforte concerto. In the later double, violin and cello concertos he approaches a solution to the problem in the only way it was given him to essay, having regard to the essentially lyrical and contemplative qualities of his art. By balance of mood through nature music he achieves a sense of growth through similar types of texture rather than by contrast and expansion of design. Obviously he could not resist the conventional demands upon him to write concertos, even though to accept them was clearly against his temperament.

Towards the end of his life his dissatisfaction with the work increased, not from a realisation of its formal weakness, as might have been imagined (indeed, he was not in the least concerned about this!), but through embarrassment by its content.

Having criticised the pianoforte concertos of Mozart and Beethoven for years as 'scales and arpeggios', he recoiled before the discovery that the 'fillings' he had put in their place in his own work were not in good taste.

Can the first-rate performance of third-rate music justify its survival? Few works beg the question more pertinently than this Pianoforte Concerto of Frederick Delius.

Programme note, Delius Centenary concert, RFH 29 January 1962

CONCERTO FOR VIOLIN AND ORCHESTRA

Within the limits of an exceptionally personal attitude to music, Delius's most enduring achievements have been made as in *Sea Drift, In a summer garden,* or *An Arabesque,* when idiosyncrasies of form and content have been satisfied anew with the growth of each masterwork. When, however, he attempts works styled Sonata or Concerto which carry musical and formal implications foreign to his nature, and substitutes in their place his own particular brand of rhapsody, he not only poses great problems for himself, but invites strong criticism for his pains.

Delius wrote four concertos: a Pianoforte Concerto (1897, revised in 1906); a Concerto for Violin and Violoncello (1915); a **Violin Concerto** (1916) dedicated to Albert Sammons and first performed by him at a Philharmonic Society Concert in 1919, conducted by Sir Adrian Boult; and a 'Cello Concerto (1921). By his own rather than traditional standards, the violin concerto is regarded as the best, though Delius himself preferred his 'cello concerto. He obviously realised the importance, even necessity, of certain types of invention in writing concertos; for instance, the introductory theme of the double concerto would not be inapt in any classical concerto, yet he relapses into formalism in its use. Nevertheless, in the violin concerto the orchestral reiterations of the opening theme plainly reveal his feeling for the need of some form of free ritornello. It is largely by making such concessions to the importance of contrasts (as in classical procedure) in the persistent fanfare motives in the brass, that the violin concerto sounds more concerto-like than either the 'cello or the double concerto. Again, the stuff from which it is made attains more formal cohesion than the material of his other concertos. His dislike of his early pianoforte concerto in later years was due not, as might have been expected, from dissatisfaction with its formal weaknesses, but embarrassment by its content, and lapses of taste were anathema to Delius!

Six introductory bars and the solo violin enters magnificently in unceasing song through bravura, meditation, accompanied cadenza and dance, to end in the dying cadences of Delian dreams.

Bradford Delius Centenary Festival programme book 1962

CELLO CONCERTO

Delius's **Violoncello Concerto**, completed in 1921, received its world première in Frankfurt in 1924 by the Russian cellist, Alexandre Barjansky. Both he and Beatrice Harrison were its chief exponents in the 'twenties and 'thirties, since when it has suffered neglect. It is the last of Delius's four concertos. Of them, by his own rather than traditional standards, that for violin is considered the best, a view not shared by the composer. Asked why he preferred his cello concerto - 'Melodic invention' was the laconic reply.

Though regarded primarily as a harmonist, Delius was drawn in later years to the problems of developing lyrical line in terms of extended melody. His flights of melodic prose, notably in the Sonata for Cello and Piano composed in 1917, aspire to a long-spanned freedom of phrase rare in British music. Again, in the cello concerto, he came nearer fulfilling that ideal than in his other works labelled 'concerto'. He never surpassed in craftsmanship the glorious sweep of D major melody (announced by the cello against climbing strings) at the *Allegramente* sequel. Yet he hardly sustains its promise for more than a dozen bars. Apart from florid passages for the soloist, Delius makes little concession to the usual devices of Concerto. The effect is an idyll for cello and orchestra played without break, with no cadenza. A brief preamble, then an A-B-A scheme with an interlude of slower song braced by thematic interplay of woodwind arabesque. No composer but Delius would have relied on means so similar to provide his contrasts of texture. The basic pulse is slow throughout. It is the rhythmic detail within the pulse that changes each episode, often in trochaic movement (-U-U-U). Adventure gives place to felicity in this luscious autumnal reverie. The solo part in this recording was edited and revised by Herbert Withers with the approval of the composer.

Sleeve note HMV ASD644 (1965)

Two names will always be recalled in the singular history of Delius's **Concerto for Violoncello and Orchestra** - the Russian cellist, Alexandre Barjansky and the English cellist, Beatrice Harrison. It was Beatrice Harrison in response to whose plea the concerto was written initially, and from whom Delius sought advice whilst working on the score in London in the spring of 1921. It was not she, however, but Barjansky who gave the world première. Induced by its publisher, Emil Hertzsche of the Universal-Edition, Vienna, Barjansky presented the concerto successfully in that city in January 1923, and repeated it in March at a much acclaimed Delius concert in Frankfurt. There he met Delius and the two remained friends. Barjansky and Harrison were the concerto's chief exponents and devotees in the nineteen twenties and early thirties, since when it has suffered neglect. It should be noted with gratitude that the soloist in this recording [Julian Lloyd Webber] has done his utmost recently in making the concerto known. I offer two reasons for the former neglect: the exacting nature of the solo part and the unusual shape and content of the work.

As to the unusual shape of the concerto, it differs essentially from his other concertos, the piano, the double and the violin, in that following as they do an A-B-A scheme, its recapitulatory A group of themes is suddenly curtailed, and a sequel of entirely new subject matter is introduced marked *Allegramente*. One can but guess but not explain the mystery of Delius's motive here. It is even more puzzling than a similar surprise which occurs towards the end of his early tone-poem *Paris*. This sequel poses problems of balance marring performances of the concerto when the *Allegramente* is taken too slow, whereas Delius felt it to be impassioned on entry, a glorious sweep of D major melody heard in the cello against climbing strings. To attempt to describe this musical adventure would be unreadable were it desirable. Who but Delius would have believed in employing means so closely alike in providing contrasts in his textures? In general terms the pulse is slow until the *Allegramente* entry. It is the rhythmic detail within the pulse that changes each episode, often in trochaic movement. The music flows without a break with moments of solo recitative as in the declamatory opening *Lento*. Themes linked by orchestral narrative are announced by the solo cello complete with partnering counter-subjects which tend to expand in melodic prose. There is no cadenza, nor any dynamic duality between soloist and orchestra, but a felicitous instrumentality of sound braced by woodwind arabesque. The effect is an autumnal reverie, evocative not depictive, a *i* music deeply felt. No wonder Elgar told Delius when they met in old age at Grez-sur-Loing that the work by Delius he longed to conduct was 'the beautiful cello concerto'.

The edition of the solo part used on this reading was edited by Herbert Withers with the composer's consent.

Sleeve note RCA S9010 (1983)

CAPRICE AND ELEGY

In the same year, 1930, as the completion of *A Song of Summer*, Beatrice Harrison, the cellist, asked Delius to write two little contrasting pieces suitable for her American tour. Within a month he had dictated the *Caprice and Elegy* for cello and chamber orchestra.[53] These miniatures are gems; simple as only genius would dare to offer in old age. They are object lessons, too, in skilful writing in the medium. Even in simple textures as these, dictation was seldom easy. Although I could often guess the next mood, the element of surprise was always there, especially in the shifting harmonies. Slips in nomenclature infuriated Delius. 'No! No! No!' he would blaze at me when in my haste to jot it down I played inadvertently the note to be written instead of the note to be heard when dealing with transposing instruments. It was easiest, of course, when he had pondered beforehand the orchestral disposition of his many-voiced textures, but hardest of all when he invented on the spot, without premeditation.

Spoken introduction to BBC broadcast, recorded 17 October 1978, broadcast 24 November 1978.

---

[53] In November 1930 Eric conducted a recording of the *Caprice and Elegy* for HMV, with an unnamed orchestra and Beatrice Harrison as soloist. It was issued on B3721. This was his only recording for the gramophone until the 1981 *Fenby Legacy* sessions for Unicorn-Kanchana.

3. Works for Voices and Orchestra

APPALACHIA

From 1900-06 Delius was occupied at Grez-sur-Loing with a succession of large-scale works of undoubted genius - *A Village Romeo and Juliet, Appalachia, Sea Drift, A Mass of Life* and *Songs of Sunset*. No composer working at this time can match the quality, range of content or variety of treatment revealed in this astonishing series for voices and orchestra. *Appalachia* stands apart from these and other choral works by Delius, as *Paris*, in the purely orchestral sphere, from *In a summer garden, North Country Sketches* and the rest. It is as if Delius, replete with the luscious wine of his musical lyricism in *A Village Romeo and Juliet,* now took up his sketches of *Appalachia* begun in 1896 and in their completion refreshed himself at the mainstream of music before turning his back on it for ever. *Appalachia* is the answer to those who regard Delius as a gifted amateur lacking technique enough to write vital music, and mooning his life away in chromatic slitherings, deftly coloured in atmospheric suggestiveness. No composer deficient in craftsmanship would expose his weakness more certainly than in a long work the musical interest of which is sustained in cumulative development of a theme in variation form. Add to this the resources of a vast orchestra including triple woodwind, bass clarinet, double bassoon and six horns suffusing a texture in strange beauties of convincing melodic, rhythmic and harmonic ingenuity, *Appalachia* proves that Delius, in his own way and when the subject demands, can play the technicians at their own game. Two operas, *The Magic Fountain* and *Koanga*, had already shown his deep feeling for primitive peoples, their intuitive accomplishments and the landscapes of their environments. Delius loved to recall the scenes of his youthful days as an orange-planter in Florida, and even waited upon death to readings from the books of Mark Twain. This is not strange in a man who lived for music, for what he became as an artist was prepared technically and spiritually on that plantation; his thorough grounding in counterpoint, as his note-books attest, under the expert guidance of a rare teacher, Thomas Ward, the local organist at Jacksonville, encountered by chance in this distant spot; his gradual rejection of academic invention as useless to his particular expressive purpose; his resolution to be himself at all costs. *Appalachia* gave Delius the freedom to brood upon, expand and communicate orchestrally his mature impressions of the New World which lack of experience in his apprentice-work, *Florida*, and time-space of the two early operas named had prevented hitherto. His note on the title-page of the score reads: 'Appalachia is the old Indian name for North America. The composition mirrors the moods of tropical nature in the great swamps bordering on the Mississippi River which is so intimately associated with the life of the old Negro slave population. Longing melancholy, an intense love for Nature, child-like humour and an innate delight in dancing and singing are still the most characteristic qualities of this race.'

A horn call echoes through the plantation groves in the still twilight as the music unfolds in a long-drawn introduction leading to variations on a Negro folk-tune with choral epilogue. Some critics have dubbed the introduction 'untidy', yet the great vistas of sprawling vegetation become articulate in its immediate sounds, and converge as the vision narrows to the more human focus of the slave-theme announced in full eventually by the English horn accompanied by bass clarinet and three bassoons. No useful intention is served in describing the musical stuff of each variation, which is often linked to the next without a break. A surer guide is to regard the introduction as evoking the natural scene of the first part of Delius's note, and not merely the sensuous impressions but the emotions it arouses, and to react in one's way to the psychological implications in the transformations of the slave-tune as symbolising the drama of the slaves. Delius's sparing use of the human voices in the variations cannot fail to convey a sense of man's insignificance in the scheme of things nor, as he expresses it in the haunting wordless interpellations of the chorus, the poignancy in the lot of many. Yet humour lightens the way in engaging turn of phrase. The slave-tune moves to its final metamorphosis, a slow march, proud and majestic in its drummed lament. We then share the emotion of one of Delius's keenest recollections distilled through the medium of his own instinctive art, the distant sounds of naive Negro song in improvised harmony so often heard from the verandah of his shack:

> *After night has gone comes the day,*
> *The dark shadows will fade away;*
> *T'ords the morning lift a voice,*
> *Let the scented woods rejoice,*
> *And echoes swell across the mighty stream.*

The great river rolls on its way, and the emotional climax of the work comes in the pathetic cry of the baritone to wife or child far beyond the 'sad waters of separation':

O, honey, I am going down the river in the morning.
Heigh ho, heigh ho, down the mighty river,
Aye, honey, I'll be gone when next the whippoorwill's
*   a-calling;*
And don't you be too lonesome, love, and don't you fret
*   and cry,*
For the dawn will soon be breaking, the radiant morn
*   is nigh,*
And you'll find me ever waiting, my own sweet Nelly Gray!

Delius leaves the scene with the voices of an oppressed people stilled in the heart of the Mississippi.

Sleeve note Columbia 33CX1112 (1954)

When Delius was working his passage home from Florida to England in 1886 with the aim of studying at Leipzig Conservatorium, he stayed some months in Danville, Virginia, to replenish his funds by teaching the violin to the daughters of prosperous tobacco planters. Here at Danville he was attracted by a song he often heard sung by coloured people in the tobacco factories where, in those days, a 'leader' of a 'singing bunch' would start such a song and hundreds would take it up in harmony as they shredded the tobacco leaves; it was a song not unlike Verdi's well-known refrain in the famous quartet in *Rigoletto*, a touch of European influence maybe in the rapidly changing industrial scene. Ten years later Delius recalled it and transformed it in attempting a set of orchestral variations with the title *Appalachia*, the old Indian name for North America; but he lacked the capacity in this his first draft to solve the technical problems involved in writing extended music without words. He therefore put his sketches aside and completed an interesting miscellanea including three more operas and, what were of greater importance still to his subsequent development as a composer at this stage, two purely orchestral pieces, *Paris* and the second revision of *Life's Dance*. Not until 1902, however, did he return to the score of *Appalachia* in earnest. By now his conception had deepened insight; it was to be nature music on a grand scale embracing the human situation. The gist of his note on the music reads: 'The composition mirrors the moods of tropical nature in the great swamps bordering on the Mississippi River which is intimately associated with the old slave population . . . '

Delius, as far as is known, never saw the Mississippi countryside. The music of *Appalachia* welled up in his mind from the haunting impressions of the St Johns River and the coloured folk who lived by its banks round Solano Grove, his orange plantation near Jacksonville, Florida.

Those who are interested in the tonality of music should listen intently to the following chords played quietly on the piano or guitar. They form the basis of his lengthy introduction and give a sense of the unusual perspective of his singularly imaginative approach to the eventual key of his variations. E flat, G, B flat - the vast, sprawling vistas of river and forest are projected before us, the trees mysterious and grey with Spanish moss; E flat, G flat, C flat - banjo-like strains hint at the lively dance-loving black communities, and trumpets and horns open a dialogue to be summed up vocally in the epilogue; E flat, G natural, C natural - the first intimations of the slave song emerge from trumpet with oboe through the texture, and come to rest on C, E, G, for our initial hearing of the song from English horn with woodwind accompaniment. This leads to the first variation, a minor aspect of the song in F, A flat, C for French horn and strings; he moves without break to the second variation with the tune in clarinet and bassoon to a waving motion in the strings in F, A natural, C. Thus he establishes F as the key-centre of his scheme.

The next variation is in A-B-A form and oscillates gently between minor and major in the statement from the cellos and comment from the violins, as if Delius had suddenly remembered England in the pastoral quality of his writing for strings. But something of greater moment comes presently in a magical passage for high muted strings - an episode irrelevant to the slave song melodically - but deeply committed to it spiritually; it is vitally prophetic, to my mind, of the ultimate fulfilment of his genius in its obsession with the transientness of life in ways that no one could have predicted. This, to me, was his moment of revelation; at last he knew what was in him to do. Delius's more vigorous powers of invention are then revealed in two variations that exploit more virile and active sonorities in triple woodwind and six horns with athletic counterpoint from the strings. The childlike humour of the slaves is suggested by a curious effect. Cellos play in their high register doubled by the E flat clarinet in cross rhythms with the bassoons against a background of harp glissandos. Wordless human voices sound from afar at the end of this and the next three variations - pathetic reminders of man's insignificance in his dreaming and dancing amid nature's extravagance. A side-drum disturbs our reverie and the slave song is roused to militant purpose, then slumps dejectedly into a solemn march which moves to the emotional climax of the work in the doggerel of a ditty:

Chorus:

> *After night has gone comes the day,*
> *The dark shadows will fade away,*
> *T'ords the morning lift a voice,*
> *Let the scented woods rejoice,*
> *And echoes swell across the mighty stream.*

The river heaves in the sticky heat - marvellously evocative of Solano Grove - and a brief lament for the lot of the slaves from flute and woodwind quickens impulsively:

Soloist:

> *O Honey, I am going down the river in the morning.*

Chorus:

> *Heigh ho, heigh ho, down the mighty river,*
> *Aye! Honey I'll be gone when next the whippoorwill's*
> > *acalling.*

Soloist:

> *And don't you be so lonesome, love,*
> *And don't you fret and cry.*

Chorus:

> *For the dawn will soon be breaking,*
> *The radiant morn is nigh,*
> *And you'll find me ever waiting*
> *My own sweet Nelly Gray!*
> *T'ords the morning lift a voice* etc.

and Delius's sound-picture of a bygone age fades in a poignant coda.

Sleeve note HMV ASD2635 (1971)

[A brief note appeared in the Bradford Delius Centenary Festival programme book 1962, beginning: '*Appalachia*, a remarkably free and fluent set of variations on an old Negro slave song revealing the extent of Delius's isolation from the contemporary trends of composition of his time, has long been esteemed by many who dislike his later work. . .']

FENBY ON *APPALACHIA* WHEN VISITING FLORIDA IN 1966

. . . Much of the journey south is over the sea, but as we neared the Atlantic coast and descended gradually to lower altitudes it was clearly possible to follow the route from the excellent maps provided for all passengers, and I saw the vastness of the forests and swamps as we approached Jacksonville. Above all I was fascinated by the colour of the trees, a dull milk-chocolate brown through the grey of Spanish moss in which they are enveloped. I scarcely remember the landing: I was so bemused by that blend and its singular effect on my mind. Even through the bleak wind as we made our way from the plane and through all the welcoming handshakes I could think of nothing but that colour. Then, in a flash, as we drove to our hotel I understood for the first time why there are sounds in *Appalachia* quite unlike any other of Delius's works. I was to be made aware of this during our visit. . .

. . . We piled into our hostess's car and bounced from rut to rut up the muddy track which led to a dense wood of high trees till we came to a clearing in which Negroes were working. Here we walked through a narrow strip of land matted with luxurious undergrowth past orange trees bearing fruit, and then I saw the giant magnolia tree Delius had described near the place where his house had stood overlooking the St Johns River. It is this piece of land within the old orange grove, fenced off from the rest, that Mrs Richmond has bestowed in perpetuity to the University.

The landscape over the river seems boundless and there was that same brooding peace in the grove that Delius had so often recalled. Despite my friends I could have wished myself alone, for so much that has mattered most in my life began here. Nor could I rid myself of the ethereal passage for high strings which comes in *Appalachia* before the return of the six-eight cello variation in D minor. Whatever Delius may have meant by it in the context of the work, to the end of my days it will conjure up the mysterious peace of Solano Grove, the spiritual birthplace of his most personal art.

from 'Revisiting Solano Grove: Delius in Florida'
Composer No 21 Autumn 1966

SEA DRIFT

BBC Home Service Interval Talk
Friday 20 August 1943 8.21 - 8.33 p.m.
Rehearsal 7.20 p.m.

ANNOUNCER:
During the interval, Eric Fenby will talk about Delius's *Sea Drift*.

FENBY:
I remember that a few days before Delius died, I told him that a certain choral society was rehearsing his *Sea Drift*. 'Good,' he said, and then

added rather thoughtfully, after a pause - 'Yes, I think if I had anything worth saying, my boy, I said it in *Sea Drift*.' Most of us, I'm sure, would agree with him. Certainly, *Sea Drift* is one of those great lyrical utterances of his maturity, so curious, so novel, so individual, that it seems to have little or no connection with any music that went before it. No wonder that conservative circles in music were dismayed when confronted for the first time with those unusual markings in sounds of this rare mind. And no wonder, too, that *Sea Drift* has suffered so many bad performances! All his life as a composer Delius was continually perplexed to discover why so many well-meaning interpreters of his music failed to realise in performance what to him were the obvious intentions of his expressive purpose. It is easy to reply that the fault was often his. That is true, but in his more inspired pages - as here in *Sea Drift* - few, if any, have excelled him in putting down on paper precisely what he wanted to say, strange as the notation may often appear. In this unique world of sound Delius has opened up for us and exhausted regions of feeling which do not seem capable of being further explored.

The words, by Walt Whitman, are a collection of extracts from the first of a group of sea-poems first published in 1860, and forty years later Delius set them to music once and for all time. The poet tells us that in his boyhood 'when the lilac scent was in the air', he was walking on the sea-shore on Long Island, or Paumanok as he called it, using the old Indian name - and observed two birds, migrants from the south, nesting in the briars at the edge of the sands. So much did they interest him that he returned every day to watch them and listen to the singing of the 'he-bird'. 'Till of a sudden,' he says, 'maybe killed, unknown to her mate, one forenoon the she-bird crouch'd not on her nest, nor return'd that afternoon, nor the next, nor ever appeared again. And thence forward all summer in the sound of the sea . . . I saw, I heard at intervals the remaining one, the he-bird, the solitary guest from Alabama.' The poet, as a lover who has lost his mate, tells us what depth of meaning this boyhood memory has for him. The 'hoarse surging of the sea', the fluttering of the lonely bird and its vain callings on its lost mate over the waters - all seem to interpret for him his own feelings of profound and everlasting loss. This drama of the sea, and the sky, of the rising and 'drooping' moon which Whitman uses to enhance the sense of fierce and heartbreaking sorrow, Delius has known how to present in music of unexampled accuracy, suggestion and poignance. Listen to the waves rocking softly under the noon-light of a May day. Feel the serenity of the scene in the opening strains of the orchestral prelude:

PART TWO : THE WORKS OF DELIUS

[Record]

The mood is now set and the voices of the chorus enter in quiet reminiscence followed by the unobtrusive entry of the baritone solo describing the poet, as a curious boy, 'cautiously peering' at the birds, 'never too close, never disturbing them.' The sun shines on their mated joy, as 'singing all time, minding no time' they keep together. Then tragedy falls, and the remaining one is left to its sorrowing.

Here is the space, sunlight and a great wind blowing, and the bird calling on the wind, 'Blow, blow up sea-winds . . . I wait and I wait till you blow my mate to me':

[Record]

Now mark a contrast to that sunlight and space in the music of starlight, the grieving sea, the sinking moon and the 'despairing carol' of the bird - 'O rising stars, perhaps the one I want so much will rise, will rise with some of you.'

[Record]

The work reaches its climax in a passage unmatched in all music for poignancy and intensity of human feeling. The solo baritone, who has served throughout the work to blend the feelings of the lonely boy with those of the lonely bird, sings:

> *O past! O happy life! O songs of joy!*
> *In the air, in the woods, over fields,*
> *Loved! loved! loved! loved! loved!*
> *But my mate no more, no more with me!*
> *We two together no more, no more!*

Then, as if all mankind were joining in this mystery of separation, we hear the hushed voices of women in the lover's cry, 'No more, no more!' and with the men's answering whisper 'No, no more!' - the sad music dies away in silence. Not every-day music, but truly, a great masterpiece.

[Record]

SEA DRIFT

Sea Drift, composed in 1903, and first performed at Essen (Germany) in 1906, is a setting of words selected from Walt Whitman's *Out of the cradle endlessly rocking* from his anthology of poems *Leaves of Grass*.

Introduced to English audiences by Sir Henry Wood at the Sheffield Festival of 1908, *Sea Drift* established itself through subsequent performances by Sir Thomas Beecham as one of the few great choral masterpieces of this century.

A young bird-watcher by the sea, the she-bird that never returns, the he-bird's cries for its mate, and the boy's share in its grief - these everyday experiences Delius pondered and transmuted into deeply emotional lyrical music symbolising the boy's first awareness of the mystery of separation and death. The soloist identifies himself in turn with the boy-narrator, the anguished bird, and the chorus intensifies the drama by sharing the narrative or in poignant re-echoings of the text.

Bradford Delius Centenary Festival programme book 1962

A MASS OF LIFE

'It would be possible to consider all *Zarathustra* as a musical composition,' wrote Friedrich Nietzsche, pondering the great riddle-like prose poem he had finished in 1885. Clearly, no sound-board was more attuned to deepen the ring of Nietzsche's metaphors than the musical imagination of Frederick Delius. The suggestive power of its first response to poetic fragments from *Zarathustra* - the *Midnight Song* given at the Delius concert in London in 1899 and later to become the spiritual axis of *A Mass of Life* - is so compelling that progression to the work in its present dimensions can be seen to have been inevitable. Zarathustra is Nietzsche's conception of man at his highest as an individual. His sayings, biblical in style (sung tonight in the original German with an English translation by Edward Travis preferring 'you' to the archaic 'thou') affirm his doctrine of the man of the future; man as Superman; proud, energetic, dominant, exceptional in his truthfulness, disdaining as weakness, as Delius did, the old values of Christianity. 'I want to make myself very plain to you as regards religions and creeds. Personally I have no use for any of them. There is only one real happiness in life, and that is the happiness of creating.' Thus Delius to the writer.

A Mass of Life - and I can imagine Delius's dry remarks on framing the title - is a choral celebration of the Will of man to say 'Yea!' to life in certain joy of the 'Eternal Recurrence' - Nietzsche's perennial theme - in face of the Christian slaying of self to gain the promise of Life Eternal. This is the music of that Nietzschean joy as felt by Delius in virile manhood; spontaneous and careless of Wagnerian inflections that still continued to haunt him momentarily; the music of a sensitive, restless adventurer, a tireless walker and climber of mountains; not yet the perpetual harper on transience who reached uniqueness in its musical expression in the full ripeness of his later years.

The *Mass* is divided into two parts in a balanced sequence of eleven soliloquies devised for Delius by his friend Fritz Cassirer, the German conductor who gave the first performance of *Koanga* in Elberfeld, *A Village Romeo and Juliet* in Berlin and *Appalachia* in London.[54] Cassirer, like Delius an ardent lover of Nietzsche's poetry, selected such passages from *Zarathustra* as seemed most apt to the lyrical expression of those singular traits he had divined in Delius's musical temperament. The singers share the words of Zarathustra, personified in the baritone soloist, now declaiming, now meditating or mingling dynamically as human instruments in the quieter orchestral textures. The score calls for four soloists, double chorus and large orchestra.

Part 1 opens without preamble with a passionate choral invocation to Zarathustra's ruling compulsion. He longs to transcend all the pettiness of life, so that in his prime he may face in his soul whatever his inmost Will may demand. The music gathers a massive strength and holds it in determined purpose, briefly relaxing for further effort which Delius braces his powers to sustain in urging Zarathustra's plea.

II. In a short, lilting baritone solo Zarathustra exhorts all men to lift up their hearts and limbs and dance as the wind rushes and the sea rises each to its own music. All greater men should learn to laugh, for laughter is holy.

---

54   The occasion of the first performance in England of *Appalachia* on 22 November 1907 was, in the opinion of Beecham who attended, 'one of the half-dozen momentous occasions I have known' and 'one of the few red-letter days in English music, an occasion that the majority of the Press failed to appreciate' (*Frederick Delius*, 146-7). Beecham, who had first met Delius five weeks earlier, was 'startled and electrified' on hearing his music for the first time. 'It seemed that if there was one thing above all else for the orchestra and myself to do at once, it was to acquire all of [Delius's] music that we could lay our hands on . . . and play it often and everywhere' (*A Mingled Chime*, 64).

III. Tenor, soprano and contralto soloists comment on Man as lover, pursuing his loved one, Life. Life dances enticingly before Zarathustra to the swaying rhythms of female voices; the pulse quickens and the double chorus joins in fugue-like impetus rare in Delius. The chase gives way to more tranquil mood and, in a moving contralto solo, Life appeals to Zarathustra that they should love each other. The basses enter in a hushed intoning of the Midnight Song and the bell tolls faintly in horns and harp. Life and Zarathustra look tearfully on each other as the cool evening shades fall on the green meadow to exquisite harmonies in the strings.

IV. Misgivings, even despair, follows upon these ponderings as Man shrinks before the Riddle of Life. His misgivings are heightened by dark forebodings in the orchestra and doleful interjections and a loud questioning outburst from the choir. He must 'listen to what the solemn midnight hour is saying!' Baritone and basses close with this murmuring.

V. Cold tones of clarinets, astringent bass oboe and bass clarinet blend with French horns in evoking the mood of mysterious night. The basses whisper and soon the warmth of string tone glows as the baritone feels his very soul to be one with the awakening songs of lovers. The contrast between his light of heart and the dark of night persists in the imaginative writing for strings and the alternation with wind timbres which merge in a glorious emotive climax that ebbs to a snatch of a song of a lover in the fading voices of the choir.

Part Two begins with an orchestral prelude: *On the Mountains*. Zarathustra is alone with his thoughts in the stillness: horn calls echo over the distant valleys. Then, like a sudden storm at sea, the chorus erupts extolling the freedom of Man's prime of life. The soloists exult in summer's stillness 'close to the eagle, to sun and snow', and the sea music is heard again in a great longing, 'O harden yourself, my heart!'

II. In a moving song for baritone, Zarathustra now communes with his lyre in sad reflections from the past evoked by dream-like melodic lines and musing harmonies in the orchestra.

III. It is evening and the philosopher is wandering through the forest. Presently he comes upon a clearing where young girls are dancing. Their charming intricacies of step and gesture are suggested in the rhythms of their four-part song, wordless in laughter and fluttering delight. The girls are startled on seeing Zarathustra. Reassured, they resume in wilder dance, then tire, leaving Zarathustra to his thoughts. Their voices come from afar and his reverie dims with a sigh in strains of haunting poignancy.

IV. Zarathustra, in the felicity of noon-tide, lies down on the grass and falls asleep under a tree. Shepherd pipes sound from beyond in a four-part canon for oboe, cor anglais and bass oboe, and the sense of timelessness pervades the scene at the quiet chorus entry. Zarathustra stirs and eventually soloists, choir and orchestra stretch their limbs in joyous outburst. Nowhere is the genius of Delius more subtle and sensitive than in the visionary significance of the winding passages for strings that ensue. The myriad voices of Eternity seem to live again in the hovering chords of the choir's 'O happiness! O happiness! the ancient noonday sleeps!' and the music dies in mystical calm.

V. Zarathustra, now in the evening of life, ponders the past and the indifference of men. The chorus pursues this mood of regretfulness and the climax comes in the great unison at the close, 'Joy is deeper than sorrow!'

VI. The music of this final sequence resolves the spiritual and emotional issues of the *Mass* with overwhelming grandeur. The orchestra tells of approaching midnight. Zarathustra calls his friends to wander in the cool air, and when the loud clamour of the heart is stilled he will whisper what the solemn old midnight bell has revealed. The bell tolls in the violas and cellos (so: ray: doh: soh) continuing in the higher strings as Zarathustra reveals its message - 'Joy is deeper than the heart's unease! Joy longs for time without end!' The paean to Joy rises, transporting in sound to die away rapturously into the night.

Delius completed the score of *A Mass of Life* in 1905. The second part only was performed at the Tonkünstler in Munich in 1908. The first complete performance was conducted by Sir Thomas Beecham in London in 1909.

> Programme note, RFH RPS Concert, 5 December 1984. Revised version of notes for EMI SLS 958 (1972) which was also used in Programme for Washington (USA) Cathedral Choral Society performance 15 May 1983.

A Mass of Life (1904-5), the grandest of Delius's major choral works, was inspired by passages selected from Nietzsche's *Thus spake Zarathustra* (1883-6). The title suggests a unique non-conformity. Delius, though a man after Nietzsche's heart, achieved a balanced synthesis by the choice of such poetical fragments as he felt apt to the full expression of his musical idiosyncrasies rather than the deliberate dissemination of philosophical ideas. The text, which in this performance is being sung in the original German, is biblical in style: poetry, metaphor and irony blend in the revelation of Nietzsche's gospel of the 'Eternal Recurrence'. Four soloists and large choral forces share the words of Zarathustra, Nietzsche's Superman personified in the baritone soloist in a sequence of 11 soliloquies, declaiming, meditating, questioning or mingling as human instruments in Delius's characteristic orchestral textures. The first complete performance of the *Mass* was directed by Sir Thomas Beecham in London, in June 1909.

The score of *A Mass of Life* calls for soprano, alto, tenor and baritone soloists, double chorus and an orchestra comprising three flutes and piccolo, three oboes, English horn, bass oboe, three clarinets, bass clarinet, three bassoons, contrabassoon, six horns, four trumpets, three trombones, tuba, timpani, bass drum, cymbals, triangle, glockenspiel, glocken, side drum, castanets, gong, two harps and strings.

Programme note (with brief synopsis and full text in German),
Saint Louis Symphony Orchestra, Carnegie Hall, 24 January 1974

SONGS OF SUNSET

Writers on art are constantly drawing attention to the preoccupation of certain artists with some central theme which recurs again and again throughout their work. For instance, the Mother and Child theme which dominates the inspiration of Henry Moore. Similarly with Delius. This record contains music which illustrates varied aspects of the theme from which he rarely strayed whenever he set words to music; a theme which obsessed him increasingly from his early opera *Koanga*, through the choral works *Appalachia, Sea Drift, Songs of Sunset* to *An Arabesque* - the transience of creaturely love, its partings, frailties and separations. The two poets on whom he has drawn here are Ernest Dowson, who like Delius was happier in France than in England, and the Dane, Jens Peter Jacobsen, who assuaged Delius's passion for what he regarded as his spiritual home - Norway and its mountains where, in his prime, so much of his final music was contemplated before being written down on his return to his rural retreat in France.

It is doubtful if Dowson is much read these days, but his poetry, if now as faded as the pressed flowers in Delius's well-thumbed copy of his verse, lives in *Songs of Sunset* through the rays of Delius's own musical poetry which penetrate far beyond the verbal imagery to the very essence of the mood which we could divine in the singular quality of the music itself, even without the use of words. The work, which is continuous, is unified by an inner compulsion difficult to define but inevitable in effect. Its texture is relatively simple; the choral writing is duplicated in the orchestra more than is usual in Delius, particularly in the opening choruses, where the downward pull of chromaticism combined with pace and tone does not make for ease; yet the orchestration is an object lesson in the sparing and imaginative colouring by the instruments. The trombones and tuba make but five short entries in the whole piece.

A dominant pedal (Delius began *A Village Romeo and Juliet* in exactly the same way) and the chorus enters on the second beat and sings of the day that is almost done for lovers. On the word 'lies' (at the cadence 'Faded it lies in the dust') can be heard from flute and English horn a little love-call (lah soh lah me) which is never long absent from one's ear in some form or another throughout the invention. This is followed by a passionate duet, paraphrased from Propertius, 'Cease smiling, dear, a little time be sad', and the chorus sighs of love, the twilight of the heart in dreamful autumn. The mood is sustained in the beautiful soprano lyric, 'Exceeding sorrow consumeth my sad heart' and the baritone's song of the 'waters of separation'. Gaiety is restored momentarily in the lovers' hearts in the ensuing chorus which extols the blitheness of nature in full bloom. But the lovers realise that the spring of the soul for them is over; their love can never bloom again. The baritone then reflects on the weariness of love - 'I was not sorrowful, but only tired of everything that ever I desired', and the work closes in a choral epilogue 'They are not long the days of wine and roses', and fades characteristically 'within a dream'.

Sleeve note HMV ASD2437 (1968) and DKP(CD)9063 (1987)

No composer has ever invented more haunting musical symbols to suggest the transience of human life reflected in the autumnal twilights of nature than Frederick Delius. Almost all he wanted to do in music was held in that one theme. It was not the theme in itself that counted, but what he put into it musically. The limitations and very uniqueness of his music arise from this deliberate restraint. Often these symbols are of extreme simplicity and yield melodically to emotional permutations as does the tiny four-note figure introduced into the orchestral accompaniment of the duet 'Cease smiling'. Sometimes they are even echoes from other works, as the *Appalachia* quotation in the violins at the words 'the sound of the waters of separation surpasseth roses and melody' in the baritone solo.

In *Moritura* and other lyrical poems by Ernest Dowson, Delius found the verbal overtones attuned to his musical purpose, and by careful selection and arrangement of verses he produced a song-cycle sustained in continuity of mood in richly imaginative vein.

Appropriately, *Songs of Sunset*, one of Sir Thomas Beecham's favourite works, was first performed by him at a Delius concert in London at Queen's Hall in 1911.

Bradford Delius Centenary Festival programme book 1962

THE SONG OF THE HIGH HILLS

From his early friendship with Grieg, which dated from the 'eighties, till the time of his final affliction, Delius contrived whenever possible to spend his summers in Norway. This was his spiritual home where the best of his works were pondered, often through weeks of silence, to be realised later in France. Such was his tireless energy that, before he took a house there overlooking the Norwegian hills, he usually went alone, occasionally with his wife, and once with 'Mr' Beecham.

One year, his fiftieth, he was compelled to remain at Grez. The work he had on the stocks, *The Song of the High Hills*, was not going too well. Parts eluded his grasp, and one in particular, the wordless chorus, resisted his efforts for weeks. Eight years were to pass before the new piece was first performed by Albert Coates with the Philharmonic Choir at a concert of the Royal Philharmonic Society in London.

This vivid evocation of mountain scene belongs with *Summer night on the river*, *On hearing the first cuckoo in spring* and *North country sketches* to the last great period of instrumental music inspired by the contemplation of nature. It is the mood of landscape rather than its pictorial image that Delius seeks to evoke. If tonal structures can be the source of such insights, the attraction of Delius's music for those whose aesthetic awareness is not bounded completely by music is readily understood. In no other work does Delius convey the sense of 'wide open spaces' more imaginatively than in *The Song of the High Hills*. Through the use of his wordless chorus he extends the spiritual range of his forces and, one is tempted to think, fuses his orchestral and human voices in a blend of musical pantheism which, in this particular context, symbolises his vision in sound.

We set out with him in good heart till the pace slows before immensities of peak and cloud in the growing orchestral rapture of the hill-song. Then through cooler heights of mist and snow we climb to full sublimity. A myriad voices emerge from afar till the grandeur of nature is matched in song. The vision fades as the human voices are lost in the hills and are heard no more. We begin the descent the way we came, still musing on life and its mystery.

Programme note, Delius Centenary concert, RFH 29 January 1962

Bradford Delius Centenary Festival programme book 1962

AN ARABESQUE

This superb work was completed in autumn 1911, revised in 1915 (when Delius was the guest of Sir Thomas Beecham at Grove Mill House, Watford) but not performed till 1920 in Newport. Since then it has been played little and understood less. (He had been compelled to leave his home at Grez before the German advance; had fled to England with his wife and was awaiting permission to cross the North Sea from Newcastle to Bergen and remain in Norway at his cottage in the hills until the end of the war.) Jacobsen's poem is a strange utterance in which human passion is personified in the God Pan; a lover's rhapsody on the briefness of bliss. Delius composed to his wife Jelka's German version. Philip Heseltine's English translation, I suspect, is a little extravagant here and there. Jacobsen (1847-1885) was, it seems, very much the countryman, a botanist whose translation of Darwin's *Origin of Species* won him far greater renown than his poetry. There is ample power here in Delius's music and to spare; and effortless virtuosity in deploying his voices and orchestra in a refined and masterly means of expression. The opening sounds, reminiscent of the last movement of the First Violin Sonata, rise mysteriously from the depths in divided violas and cellos to flower in an expressive, descending, sequential figure in the violins which plays an important role in the eventual course of the music. Delius delights in arabesques in the woodwind and maintains independent divided string parts in great freedom throughout, so that the chorus has its own autonomous life in the texture and breaks the convention that the chorus basses must double the orchestral basses. The same size orchestra is made to produce richer and fuller sonorities in more copious designs than those of the more intimate *Songs of Sunset*, whilst the role of the chorus is reduced to effective commentaries on or re-echoings of the sentiments expressed by the baritone soloist. Yet Delius never surpassed the sheer magic of the final pages evoking a northern winter landscape.

For me, *An Arabesque* exemplifies the best of Delius. To the question posed, the merest sigh, by the chorus in the closing bars - 'Knowst thou Pan?' - I am moved to reply: 'Yes! I have known him - in the spirit of Frederick Delius.'

Sleeve note HMV ASD2437 (1968), revised for DKP(CD)9063 (1987)

REQUIEM

Half a century has passed since Delius completed this choral work. In the forty-four years since its first performance at a Philharmonic Concert in London conducted by Albert Coates, it has proved to be the most neglected of all Delius's major compositions. The reason is not far to seek. This is not a Requiem in the traditional sense as understood in Latin Christianity, but Delius's own singularly personal lament for all that in his judgment cramps the human spirit on its all too brief, meaningless life here on earth - the 'tale of falsehoods and golden visions', the 'houses of lies' of religion as Christian and Mohammedan cry in vain for God.

The love of woman, courage to live fearlessly and then, still more, die fearlessly though death be total extinction, this for Delius is the crown of life. Man, he always insisted, is a mystery; Nature alone is eternally renewing.

It has taken another World War and a revolution in insights into the meaning and purpose of life without parallel in our culture to admit a more tolerant attitude to such notions through the medium of music and his own text of biblical quotation and characteristic outspokenness.

In the fourteen years between the composition of *Margot La Rouge* and the Requiem, Delius had developed unpredictably. The Requiem, the strangest in the line of nonconformity, stems from the almost equally neglected *Arabesque* rather than *Sea Drift*, notably in such passages of evocative beauty as 'The snow lingers yet in the mountains'. Such moments as these win Delius lovers invariably in the remotest parts of the globe!

Delius deploys his huge orchestral forces in a manner unique in his entire output. Triple woodwind often sound in pairs, and six horns are used with more restraint and discrimination than, for instance, in *Brigg Fair*. He mixes his orchestral timbres where normally he prefers pure colour, and disposes his melodic and harmonic strands, especially in the strings and brass, with telling acuity, sureness and skill. There is a sudden astringency in his harmonic thought from which he was to recoil in later works. He was deeply seared by the wastage of youth in the carnage of the First World War, which involved him painfully in conflicting loyalties when relatives and the sons of friends faced each other as unwilling foes.

The vocal lines of his soloists are less memorable than in the *Idyll* with its immediate surface appeal, and the angular phrases of the baritone part when restricted in lower levels of pitch are often difficult to project above the orchestra. Delius is particularly hard on his tenors when called upon to sing, as it were, against the musical grain of a progression in the lyrical commentary of the chorus 'Among her fragrant blossoms. . .' The mystery of Delius will always remain that, despite such asperities, his choral writing is supremely imaginative in original sounds, and often thrilling in effect.

In no other work is the character of the man Delius more clearly revealed - even betrayed - than in this curious Requiem.

Sleeve note EMI ASD2397 (1968)

SONGS OF FAREWELL

Songs of Farewell was first performed by Sir Malcolm Sargent and the Royal Choral Society in Queen's Hall, London, at a Courtauld-Sargent concert in March 1932. 'Concerning the proud spirit of these Whitman settings,' observed Professor A Hutchings in his biography of Delius, 'there is little to say, except that they were the last choral legacy of the composer who wrote *A Mass of Life*, and that, when the arrival of his amanuensis made possible an Indian Summer after the main musical harvest, nobody could have dared hope for grain so rich and vital as *Songs of Farewell*.'

Least of all me. In 1928 Delius had accepted my offer to try to help him find a way to resume composition after two years inaction through blindness and paralysis. The orchestral work *A Song of Summer* and the Sonata No 3 for Violin and Pianoforte were the chief fruits to date of that collaboration. When, however, I had read the text that Mrs Delius had selected and copied out previously from Walt Whitman's *Leaves of Grass*, and seen the paucity of musical material Delius proposed to use as a basis for a work for double chorus and orchestra - a few odd phrases jotted down on billheads on his last walking-tour of Norway, and groups of chords ringed 'good' - my heart sank.

He had already insisted on dictating orchestral music into full score without a preliminary piano draft. Yet, realising his dislike of treating the choir and orchestra as separate entities complete in themselves, I could not conceive how eight vocal parts were to be shaped and threaded into the orchestral texture in a balanced whole. Nor how, working so slowly from bar to bar, he would prevent disorder and lack of tension between the parts.

Instinct gradually led the way. After months of trial and error, with never more than a few bars to show for hours of work, and only then when Delius felt well enough to be carried up to the music-room to dictate, the score was finished.

The combination of passing notes and arpeggio notes is a device known to students of elementary harmony. But the combination of passing notes and arpeggio notes at the line 'Seeking the shores forever' (II) is transmuted by genius beyond the sense of words, of voices and orchestral timbres to the frontiers of Illumination.

Sleeve note EMI ASD644 (1965)

[Eric Fenby's brief programme note for the Delius Centenary concert in the Royal Festival Hall on 29 January 1962 and the Bradford Delius Centenary Festival 1962 programme book consisted of the above opening paragraph to which he added: 'All I will add is that after thirty years I marvel at my presumption and technical assurance in offering myself for so great a task.']

IDYLL

DELIUS LOVERS WILL NOT BE DISAPPOINTED

A new Idyll *by Frederick Delius, which will have its first performance at the Proms on Tuesday, is here described by Eric Fenby, who, as Delius's devoted amanuensis, had, next to the composer, most to do with its creation. This photograph is of Delius at the summit of his powers, the Delius who has never yet disappointed his listeners.*

The Radio Times September 29 1933

In the spring of 1902 Delius composed his one-act opera *Margot La Rouge* for a competition. It has since remained unpublished and unperformed owing to the unfortunate nature of its libretto. How Delius came to write music to such a deplorable text is a mystery, which deepens when it is remembered that in the two years immediately preceding this lapse he had written the healthy and invigorating *Life's Dance* for orchestra (a work that has had very few performances in England for some unknown reason), his lovely and intimate opera *A Village Romeo and Juliet*, and in the two years immediately following it was to give us *Appalachia* and *Sea Drift*.

The opening prelude to *Margot La Rouge*, evoking, as it does, the distant presence of a metropolis, brought to mind Walt Whitman's retrospective idyll, 'Once I passed through a populous city', and an entirely new work was conceived. Use was accordingly made of the opening of that poem and such extracts from the poems of Whitman and the music from *Margot La Rouge* as were deemed suitable, and this work gradually assumed its present form.

Here, in making these selections from Walt Whitman's *Leaves of Grass*, Delius had the valuable assistance of Mr Robert Nichols, whose enthusiasm for the composer's music is well known. The original orchestration has been preserved throughout except at such places where minor adjustments were necessary. A short introduction leads us to the baritone entry:

> *Once I passed through a populous city,*
> *Imprinting my brain with all its shows.*
> *Of that city I remember only a woman,*
> *A woman I casually met,*
> *Who detained me for love of me.*
> *Day by day and night by night we were together -*
> *   all else has been forgotten by me.*
> *Again we wander, we love, we separate,*
> *Again she holds me by the hand, I must not go.*
> *Day by day and night by night together!*

Then, in his musing, he hears the voice of the woman:-

> *Day by day, night by night we were together.*

he crying:-

> *I hear her whisper.*

and she singing again:-

> *I love you, before long I die.*
> *I have waited long merely to look on you,*
> *For I could not die till I had once looked on you.*

They extol the contentedness and solemnity of their ascent to the sphere of lovers, and the music becomes more and more impassioned:-

> *O to speed where there is space enough and air enough at last!*
> *We are two hawks, we soar above and look down.*
> *What is all else to us who have voided all but freedom*
>   *and all but our own joy.*

But, as in *Songs of Sunset*:-

> *They are not long, the days of wine and roses.*

the dread of separation darkens as a cloud:-

> *Face so pale with wondrous eyes, gather closer yet, closer yet.*
> *Perfume therefore my chant, O love, immortal love.*
> *Make me a fountain*
> *That I exhale love wherever I go.*

The work ends with a beautiful yet poignant passage:-

> MAN: *Sweet are the blooming cheeks of the living.*
>   *Sweet are the musical voices sounding,*
>   *But sweet, ah sweet, are the dead*
>   *With their silent eyes.*
> WOMAN: *I ascend, I float to the regions of your love, O man.*
> BOTH: *All is over and long gone, but Love is not over.*

The *Idyll*, I fear, may bring to an end that series of compositions which Delius has written despite the almost unbelievable difficulties imposed on him by his blindness and physical weakness. Some small thing such as a song may yet come into being. A few words about those difficulties will not be out of place here, and will reveal something of the iron nature and the quality of the man.

To dictate a simple and symmetrical melody, sixteen bars in length with interesting four-part harmony, is not an easy accomplishment for a man in full possession of his faculties. It requires great concentration lest some misunderstanding arises between dictator and amanuensis. To be blind and physically incapable of concentrating for any length of time, and yet feel the urge within to dictate that simple melody with its implied harmony increases the many possibilities of misunderstanding.

From this stage we pass to the dictation of this melody in five, six, even eight-part harmony - for the texture of Delius's harmony is usually full and rich - and score the result (by dictation) for strings, woodwind and horns. Here we meet with more difficulties - questions of spacing in the harmony, of range in the part-writing, the blend and balance of the instruments employed. All these problems then must be weighed in the mind of the dictator.

So far we have been discussing the dictation of a melody of an ordered or measured type, with its harmonisation and applied orchestration. But Delius's melodies are purely rhapsodical, most of his phrases irregular, and the chief interest by no means centres on the melodic line - or what most people would call the 'tune' - but rather in the ever-changing harmonic implications of his melodies. (Delius once remarked to the writer, 'Regard the harmonic background of a melody as the varying aspect of the same type of countryside.') His orchestration is never applied. When music comes to him he hears it in terms of the orchestra; most of his sketches are in full-score from the beginning.

A little thought will now give some idea of the labour and sustained effort necessary for the dictation of such works as *A Song of Summer* for orchestra, and *Songs of Farewell* for double chorus and orchestra when nothing but the headless skeletons existed in sketch form. Delius usually sang or called out the notation and orchestration of his musical ideas and always knew exactly what he wanted putting down on paper. His dictations were afterwards played over to him on the pianoforte.

Sometimes at certain points he found great difficulty in explaining precisely what he meant, and his hatred of verbal repetition tended to complicate matters when the musical threads of a previous day's work had to be taken up again. His vocal gifts being of a somewhat limited nature, humorous incidents often arose, but never once was there a hasty word or the slightest sign of impatience.

There is something approaching greatness if not greatness itself in the manner in which the composer of *A Village Romeo and Juliet*, *Appalachia*, *Sea Drift*, the *Mass of Life*, the *Song of the High Hills* placed himself in the hands of a young musician whom he had never seen, and will never see, and with whom he was willing to struggle for hours to complete works that in his heyday he would have written without effort in as many minutes.

Few people can imagine the tragedy of such a situation or the feelings of that young man.

I wonder, too, what Delius felt about it!

It must not be supposed that his afflictions have made him an unhappy man. Recent photographs are largely responsible for that erroneous opinion. Delius is ever cheerful and never bemoans his misfortunes. He still remains profoundly interested in everything - his memory is amazing; he is still a passionate lover of Nature, a gourmet, a great wit (one should hear him tell the story of his mountaineering expedition in Norway with Beecham when the latter forgot to bring his lunch!).

There is little music that gives him pleasure nowadays, and he has no use for what he calls the 'wrong note' music of some of his contemporaries. Music for him is an outburst of the soul. His mind is occupied chiefly in the succession of English, French, German and Norwegian books read by the various members of his household.

No praise is too high for Mrs Delius, for whom the last twelve years have meant endless self-sacrifice. She will have a prominent chapter in that book as yet unwritten, 'The Wives of Great Composers'.

Delius lovers will not be disappointed in the *Idyll*.

4. Works for Solo Voice

SONGS

'I have always felt a compulsion to set words to music' - thus remarked Delius to me in 1931. The first phase of that compulsion - from the mid eighteen-eighties in Florida to the end of the century in France - saw the completion of three operas and miscellaneous instrumental works, and the bulk of some sixty cosmopolitan songs to Norwegian, Danish, English, French and German poems, a selection of which is presented here. Delius, though fluent in Norwegian and Danish, set many of these Scandinavian poems in German, in which they were known in translations throughout Europe. In effect several songs are more singable in German than in the published English versions, and are so sung here.

SCANDINAVIAN SONGS

TWILIGHT FANCIES

A young princess sits alone in her summerhouse. Stirred by the horn-calls of a boy minding sheep, she dreams of love as the sun goes down. Perhaps the most popular of Delius's songs, certainly one of the best of his earlier works, it was also a favourite of his wife, Jelka, who herself translated his songs into German from 1900 onwards.

PART TWO : THE WORKS OF DELIUS

THE VIOLET

This ditty makes a charming effect: its overall curve is skilfully shaped, and its harmonies still hold surprising freshness especially at the cadences.

IN THE GARDEN OF THE SERAGLIO

An Eastern fancy notable chiefly for the phrase in the accompaniment which Delius quoted four years later in the third movement of his *Mass of Life*, in which female voices float in rapt wordless adoration of life on 'night's still silent waters'. J P Jacobsen was one of Delius's favourite poets and inspired one of the masterpieces of his later 'Scandinavian' period, the choral-orchestral *An Arabesque*.

SILKEN SHOES

Delius incorporates melodic verse with lines of sequential melodic prose in keeping pace with this poem's emotion. It was this type of melody Grieg had in mind when he warned young Delius against Wagner's influence.

AUTUMN

There is verve and imagination in this song, and a sense of intuitive depth; and with it a prediction of the poignancy we find in Delius's later works, suggested here in the moving sequel with its questioning of the unknown.

YOUNG VENEVIL

This lively yet callous little episode, neatly told in two verses and as skilfully dramatised, is too often sung like a dirge. The singer almost needs to act the song.

IRMELIN ROSE

Jacobsen's narrative poem wherein bold medieval knights vie in wooing Princess Irmelin is based on a similar legend to that of Delius's opera *Irmelin*, for which he wrote both music and libretto in 1890-2. Inevitably there are echoes of Irmelin's theme from the opera in the course of this song and as late as 1930 Delius still thought well enough of it to make, with my help, an exquisite lyric for small orchestra, the *Irmelin* Prelude. The girl with the snow-cold heart is, incidentally, a major part of the complex imagery in the same poet's aforementioned *Arabesque*.

LET SPRINGTIME COME

This joyous evocation of the coming of spring suggested in the accompaniment is not for the singer. 'Springtime cannot bring me joy. I must await my own Springtime. When? When?' Delius thought well of this song, and voiced precisely the same sentiment in the sixth song of his superb Dowson sequence *Songs of Sunset*.

FRENCH SONGS

Delius's sensitively wrought French songs are French in spirit, without affectation, yet truly Delian. They were written at intervals between 1895 and 1919, when the last song, *Avant que tu ne t'en ailles*, was left unfinished and completed eventually by dictation in 1931. The songs [*Il pleure dans mon coeur*; *Le ciel est, par-dessus le toit*; *La lune blanche*; *Chanson d'automne*; *Avant que tu ne t'en ailles*] are all to poems by Verlaine and evoke, with unusual precision in Delius, a correspondence in sound and mood implied in the poet's imagery.

ENGLISH SONGS

It was not Philip Heseltine, as supposed, but Lady Cunard who in 1914 introduced Delius to Elizabethan verse by giving him her own American editions of the 'Queen's Garland' and the 'King's Lyrics' with suggestions of those he might care to set. The ones he chose were by Shakespeare, Jonson, Nashe and Herrick, two of which follow [*To Daffodils*; *So white, so soft, so sweet is she*].

I-BRASIL

The Celtic *I-Brasil*, surely Delius's most haunting song, evokes the sorrow on the wind calling us far away to the legendary islands of peace. The key of D and the long-drawn cadence with its deep pedal-point irresistibly recall the end of the Requiem, whose paean to the eternally renewing powers of nature - similarly Nordic-Celtic in tone - fades, likewise, beyond all horizons of mortal perception. D major, a long pedal-point and a gradual sinking deep into a dim distance are also common to Delius's ultimate musical statement, 'Now finale to the shore' in *Songs of Farewell*. Coincidence? There are depths of the creative unconscious which lie past the range of plummet.

Sleeve note Unicorn DKP9022 (1983)

SONGS FOR TENOR AND CONTRALTO

Throughout his career Delius wrote altogether about fifty songs in five languages: Norwegian - in which, notwithstanding his upbringing, he was more proficient than in German; French - the sound of which he grew to dislike and spoke very rarely in later years, nevertheless, he insisted that the Verlaine songs should always be sung in French; Danish; German and English. An admirable little booklet *The Songs of Delius* by A K Holland in 'The Musical Pilgrim' series (OUP) treats the subject with penetrating insight. He would often pause in a major task to set some lyric when its moods and feelings were akin to his own, and projected a musical poetry he felt unable to resist. The exquisitely turned French songs are French in spirit, without affectation, yet truly Delian. They were written at intervals between 1895 and 1919 and capture with unusual precision in Delius the now faded sentiments of the eighteen-nineties. Distinct from these, the English songs, written in 1915-16 at the suggestion of Lady Cunard, though fresh, charming and spontaneous, demand more lively, flexible and delicate treatment and are more difficult to perform successfully for both singer and accompanist. The Celtic *I-Brasil*, perhaps his most haunting song, evokes the sorrow on the wind calling us far away to the legendary islands of peace.

Bradford Delius Centenary Festival programme book 1962

CYNARA

In the spring of 1929, Sir Thomas Beecham wrote to Delius asking if he had an unpublished work for voice and orchestra to include as a novelty in the programmes of the festival of Delius's music which he was proposing to give in the autumn of that year. I was instructed accordingly to look through the piles of faded pencil sketches (all in full score) that had accumulated from a lifetime's work. Along with the sketches of *Songs of Sunset* was one I could not place. On playing it over to Delius, he recognised it immediately as a setting for baritone and orchestra of Dowson's best-known poem *Cynara* which he had abandoned, indeed quite forgotten, after judging its inclusion inappropriate in the scheme of *Songs of Sunset* for which it was intended initially. It was quite complete in every detail up to the words 'Then falls thy shadow, Cynara', at which there was a blank. Delius decided to fill it, and, after some painful and frustrating hours of work, managed to complete the remaining bars by dictation. I shall never forget my thrill when I took down the telling chord on the trombones on the final word 'Cynara'!

The success of this dictation was as crucial to Delius as to me. If it failed to sound well in performance he would give up trying to compose altogether. When at last I sat beside him somewhat apprehensively in Queen's Hall at the orchestral rehearsal, I had no idea that before leaving Grez-sur-Loing for England he had told his wife, Jelka, to sew three fivers into the lining of his jacket 'for Eric, if it comes off well'. I got my fivers and Sir Thomas his novelty, which was first sung by John Goss at one of the festival concerts. Subsequently, before it was published, Delius added the present ending with its reference to the opening bars.

Sleeve note HMV ASD2437 (1968)

5. Chamber Works

SONATAS FOR VIOLIN AND PIANO

Delius wrote four violin and pianoforte sonatas. The first, still in MSS, and dated 1892 was, for some reason, broadcast five years ago by special permission, an experience unlikely to be repeated. The second (published as No 1) was sketched as early as 1905, but not completed until 1914. No 2 followed in 1924 and No 3 in 1930. These three sonatas show astonishing diversity of texture for a composer of so singular a mind. Though regarded primarily as a harmonist, Delius's flights of melodic prose, notably in the cello sonata, aspire to a long-spanned freedom of phrase rare in British music. To sustain spontaneous rhapsody in convincing and inevitable flow even in one single line is still the most difficult feat, I think, in the trade of writing music. If the main function of the piano in Delius's conception of sonata is to 'load every rift with ore', such chordal highlighting of the melodic line serves but to increase our scrutiny.

Bradford Delius Centenary Festival programme book 1962

Delius wrote, in all, four sonatas for violin and piano, the earliest in 1892 and the last in 1930. The sonata of 1892, a work in three separate movements, remained in MS, being rejected as derivative and immature. Thus we are left with three sonatas numbered as on this record in order of composition and publication. No 1 was begun in 1905 and put aside (as was his habit) when the music did not come naturally. It was not until

PART TWO : THE WORKS OF DELIUS

World War 1, however, when major projects were abandoned, that he took up the sonata again. Like No 2 it plays without a break; there are traces of influences not yet absorbed, but there is a bigness and spaciousness of design not to be found in Nos 2 and 3.

No works by Delius have been more maligned: they are treated as oddities unworthy of notice. They belong to a time when the term sonata still aroused certain expectations of dramatic interplay of themes. These expectations are not fulfilled in Delius's conception of sonata. Pedantry is much to blame in presenting sonata form as a blue-print which is sacrosanct. Haydn and Mozart would have scoffed at this notion! Delius, approaching and withdrawing as he pleased from the periphery of this enclosure of thought, is obviously not to every taste. Whereas classical composers have sometimes replaced development of themes by bringing in completely new subject-matter in movements purporting to be sonata, Delius relies almost entirely on a succession of episodes to give continuity. This, and the element of surprise in some of these lovely byways of music, make these sonatas, to my mind, unique. It has been said that 'it is one thing to make an idea clear, and another to make it affecting to the imagination.' Now there are innumerable sonatas with clear ideas, but how many are affecting to the imagination? This, I feel, is where Delius excels. We may tire, perhaps, of his oneness of mood. But if we ourselves are in that mood, he never fails to project that mood in sounds so unmistakably his own that by his very genius he makes them our own. All these sonatas reveal his gift in sustaining lines of lyrical flow, more akin to prose than verse. His melodic direction is sure and firm and moves with that unconscious skill which comes when genius has found itself. There are passages of weak invention, but the cumulative effects of his paragraphs evoke a genuine musical experience of differing quality in each sonata. We hear, too, as in No 3, that he could write a good tune when he chose. The 3rd Sonata is interesting in the key-relationships of the movements. I remember thinking as he finished dictating the final bars of the first movement, 'Surely he has ended in the wrong key!' Not till we came to the close of the last movement did I sense the truth of his intuition centering, diverging, then centering again on two adjacent notes - D and E! The juxtaposition of keys is less elusive in No 2 and radiates from a central C. There is even a hint of recapitulation in his harking back to the opening theme at the close of this single-movement work. The slow sections, to me, are sheer magic; simple and telling in exquisite play with reiterated notes and the leap of a fourth! And they say that Delius was lacking in craftsmanship!

Nevertheless, the lay-out and figuration of his piano parts can be exasperating to performers. I saw that his own long elegant fingers must have had an enormous stretch. This probably accounts for the particular problems to be faced in No 1. Tactful suggestions (prompted by the smallness of my own hand-stretch) induced him to shape more manageable arpeggios at awkward places in No 3. Delius was not a pianist - nor am I - but had been an accomplished violinist in his youth. Apart from some terrifying leaps from the depths to the highest reaches of the instrument, the writing for violin is deftly placed. Great players of the past - Sammons and Tertis - have told me of their love of the purely musical qualities of these sonatas and how, on returning to them again and again, they have always found them fresh.

It was typical of Delius that he felt it rather an insult to players to plaster his scores with dynamics or bowings; provided they played the notes he had written, he preferred to leave such matters to them. There is no one way of playing his music, but I have often heard him condemn a performer as having no feeling for his phrasing. In this he must bear some blame himself for he gives little guidance to the player in making his sense of flow as clear and meaningful as he intended it. 'But, surely,' he would say, 'a really musical person must feel it my way!' Inflection is the secret of phrasing in Delius, as Beecham discovered to our delight. Moving to the operative note in a phrase; a little lingering without breaking the continuity and the poetry at once begins to bloom.

These three most singular sonatas would themselves, in my opinion, have made the reputation of a lesser composer. There is a peculiar power about them - for instance, the sweep of the opening of No 1 - which could only come from a mind that had already achieved excellence in the larger forms of composition.

Sleeve note Unicorn RHS310 (1972)

THE THREE VIOLIN SONATAS

A maxim of Delius was 'Never explain. To explain is always weak.' Hardly a fillip for one about to become his amanuensis! Yet these sonatas, especially the first, seem to bewilder many an ear confused initially in making sense of their singular ways of musical progression. To such the writer offers a guide, avoiding entirely all technical terms in construing the unusual form of the first movement of Sonata No 1. The gist of the matter is this: Delius tends to announce a theme and develop it instantly on stating it, merging statement and expansion into one, a propensity shared by Schubert himself, though, of course, in lesser degree; for instance, in the woodwind theme at the opening of the *Unfinished Symphony*. And when the flow of the melodic line is more akin to prose than to verse, rhythmic sense may elude the ear in the fitful pace of Delius's rapture:

theme 1 - violin in melodic prose + short expansion

theme 2 - piano with interjection from the violin + brief connecting passage to

theme 3 - violin, melodic verse couplet + expansion leading to

theme 4 - violin with counter-melody in piano curtailed by forceful intervention of

theme 3 - violin statement + expansion continued in piano subsiding to

theme 4 - piano with counter-melody, now in violin, + expansion leading to quick dance episode with rapid passages in the violin falling to a tranquil anticipation of

theme 1 of the reprise - at the same pitch as the movement began, centering on D

theme 2 - violin + expansion merging into new expansion of the connecting passage mentioned initially with violin counter-melody based on theme 1. (Note that theme no 4 is omitted.)

theme 3 - violin, statement now at a different pitch from that at which it was first heard, + expansion preparing the mind expressively for the coming of the slow movement.

Thus Delius suggests yet evades the effectuation of sonata form as understood traditionally.

The brief blend of pentatonic, modal and chromatic inflections that inform both line and harmonies of theme no 1 contrasts with the wholly chromatic textures evoked by theme no 3 - which centre on shifting chords rather than any particular key - whereas modal affinities persist throughout the entire slow movement. The violin's singing reverie is not an untroubled flow. Six descending parallel chords, a questioning impulse from the piano, gradually develop a dialogue between the two instruments in which the piano is eventually persuaded. Quiet accord is reached in the rapture of those altitudes in which the violin excels. At this point in 1905, Delius put his manuscript aside, and not until 1914 did he add the last movement. This has the drama of a march of moods, the irremediable moods of Life symbolised in the fickle play of a musical trochaic rhythm beginning in the key of B minor. Jaunty, self-satisfied, alert, with lyrical dallyings on the way, the pace quickens and the heart lifts in a five-note snatch of thoughtful song till the march rhythms falter and go, and restless, tortuous fancies become stark realities. The mysterious music that follows may cause some to read in its sombre mood a composer's reflections on the tragic events that tore Europe apart that year, a notion not without truth. This dark but stirring episode gathers in resolution and power, surging to an emotional climax of overwhelming intensity, and then unwinds to calmer mood letting in the light of day in returning hopefully to the reprise. The march is resumed, earlier diversions are recalled., till noble expansions of the snatch of song prefigure excitedly a clarion of joy extolling the Sonata's prelusive phrase, and the Life-rhythm, in the briefest of epilogues, triumphs on a chord of B major. The work was first performed by Arthur Catterall and R J Forbes in Manchester in 1915.

Nine years elapsed. Delius had become an invalid and was now unable to write legibly. But that most remarkable woman, his wife, who had long since abandoned her painting to devote herself entirely to him and the massive correspondence involved in his music, had acted already in transcribing his seven little pieces for piano. Delius, happily, still could see to correct her work where necessary. Such was her zeal to assist him in their isolation from possible help that 'in fear and trembling' - as she said - 'I managed to write down the second sonata!' This indeed was an achievement, for though she could read music, but at her own pace, the piano part that Delius dictated was quite beyond her skill as a pianist, not to mention the twenty-eight bars for violin without a break, and this in subtle melodic phrase, at the start of the sonata. Marvellous too, for it rises in curves like a bird in flight, swooping and winging higher and higher till, following a drop almost to earth, a swift and terrifying sudden ascent shatters the analogy completely, Yet in these twenty-eight bars are merged melodic fragments and their expansions, each in turn implying the next in one continuous flowing line, balanced, imaginative, apt and direct, with not one note misplaced or too many, a demonstration of craftsmanship concealed by lyrical charm. How Delius must have loved the violin! Listen to the slow movement. Surely this music holds what Virginia Woolf was seeking in words: 'Art is being rid of all preaching: things in themselves: the sentence in itself beautiful: multitudinous seas: daffodils that come before the swallows dares'. The sonata is the most personally idiomatic of the three, but unlike No 1, though cast similarly in form, it begins and ends in the same key. Albert Sammons and Evlyn Howard-Jones gave the first performance in London in 1924.

By the middle of 1925, Delius was totally blind and almost completely paralysed. However, in 1928, the will to work, though gone for some years, now revived in last efforts, one being the Sonata No 3, which he dictated in the spring of 1930. It was clear from what scanty sketches there were - the opening bars of three separate movements barely decipherable in his own hand - that these had predated much of the music of Sonata No 2, except in those passages in that work previously written in his normal hand. It was also a revelation to find that Delius, who is usually regarded as a composer distracted with harmony, was invariably four or five bars ahead in shaping the violin's melodic line before he appeared to give a thought to the chordal tensions of the accompaniment. These were disposed surprisingly, and here he reverted to his former habit of composing with the aid of the piano, but now with the writer as his hands and eyes. The sonata was finished in a few weeks, and later that year, May Harrison, its dedicatee, partnered by Sir Arnold Bax, produced it in London at the Wigmore Hall.

The romantic nature of these sonatas, in which his affections and inborn gifts appear overmasteringly lyrical and reflective, may seem to belie their claim to what is expected of 'sonata', but Delius, despite his sensuous textures, was deeply concerned to achieve in sound a balanced synthesis of musical design, however the action of its content, or whether its material was accommodated in three separate movements or one. Delius was, above all else, an artist in the poetry of sound.

Sleeve note EMI ASD 3864 (1980)

STRING QUARTET

This work, actually Delius's second quartet, was written in 1916-17 and bears no relation to the quartet of 1893 which Delius rejected. It was first performed in London by the London String Quartet in 1919.

The first of the four movements begins with animated sweep of phrase in typically Delian texture which flows to a second subject of quieter character. Interest is then sustained through melodic development of fragments of these subjects chiefly in the first violin, sometimes with a counter-melody in the second violin, but always changing in musical meaning as the ever-shifting chords vary their tensions on the melodic thread leaving the viola and cello to fill in figurations of the harmony.

In the Scherzo, Delius achieves lightness despite the sluggishness of chromatic harmony moving at pace, but is really true to himself only in the song-like slower section which breaks the dance.

The third movement, *Late Swallows*, is a beautiful autumnal soliloquy in sound conjured up from thoughts of the swallows darting to and fro from the eaves of the studios at Grez, now that Delius and his wife had had to abandon their homes to the military authorities and flee from France in the First World War. 'When we were away from home, Fred missed the swallows most', Mrs Delius told me, and I well remember his 'Tell me, lad, are the swallows late this year?'

Critics condemn the last movement as inferior. Some hold that it should be omitted from the performance.

Note in Bradford Delius Centenary Festival programme book 1962

Delius was cradled to the sound of chamber music, his father's daily recreation, and eventually played second violin in the family quartet. Yet already by his middle teens he was indulging a distaste for the music of the classical masters and their chamber works in particular. Ultimately, after rejecting his own early violin sonata and at least three string quartets which he had written before the turn of the century, that singular instinct of his was to produce four unique duos labelled Sonatas, of which three are for violin and piano and the quartet recorded here. Its music derives initially from the juxtaposition of pentatonic and contrasting chromatic elements sometimes (as in *Late Swallows*) reminiscent of Negro folk-song, with metamorphosis of phrase linking all four movements.

A quiet opening and the music flows in the poetry of lyrical curve to a second subject sustaining the same mood. Continuity is then maintained through melodic fragments of these subjects chiefly in the first violin, sometimes with a counter-melody. Musical meaning changes subtly as varying tensions of chromatic harmony play on the main melodic thread. All the movements, especially the first, reveal concessions to sonata form unusual in Delius's mature work. The mood of the sudden, abrupt coda - immediately before its beautiful close - is then resumed in the second movement in gayer, lighter accentuation. But Delius soon tires of this flippancy and relaxes into song to end - even more pertly - in a remote key! This movement is based on the final bars of all that survives of a scherzo from another abandoned early quartet of which two movements only were completed.

Late Swallows - the third movement - is a lovely autumnal soliloquy inspired by thoughts of the swallows darting about the eaves of the studios at Grez-sur-Loing, Delius's home in rural France, after he had been compelled to leave when German occupation of the village seemed imminent. Beyond the disturbance of his normal routine there is no suggestion in the quartet that war had affected him personally. A spirited introduction leads after a pause to the finale when a jaunty, pentatonic tune is heard from the cello and subsequently the first violin. Another tune, equally sprightly, emerges gradually - adding a rustic dance-like touch. The course of tonalities is surprisingly unpredictable whilst achieving a sense of instinctive rightness as in the whole of this peculiar Delius work. Its first performance was given by the London String Quartet in London in 1919.

Sleeve note Pye GSGC14130 (1970)

see pages 164-5 for Fenby's arrangement of the String Quartet for string orchestra

CELLO SONATA

Sixty-two years ago, almost to the day, the first performance of this sonata was given in this hall by Beatrice Harrison and Evlyn Howard-Jones.

No work by Delius has been more misread through failure to grasp the sense of flow in the subtle inflections of the cello lines which he found he could not convey on paper, but left to the soloist's intuition. The pianist's role upholds the flow and underlines its musical sense in a rich poetry of chordal textures characteristic of Delius's art.

Wigmore Hall programme note 19 November 1980

There is a touch of rapture already in the cellist's opening phrase of this remarkable duo if played with rubato as Delius intended it. In fact I contend that this free interpretation of flow is essential to a definitive performance of his music, being mindful of its basic tempo.

The listener unfamiliar with this work may well be confused by its unusual progress. A long preamble composed of short flightings of irregular phrases of melodic-prose from the cello combine eventually in a sweeping contour to full rapture. The cellist, with the exception of a few bars' rest whilst the pianist is introducing a second subject, plays without a break throughout the whole work, whereas the pianist's role calls for perception in relating to the cellist's fluid line, and in judging the play of chordal tensions integrating its musical sense. Only twice is the cellist's function secondary to the pianist's climactic melodic curves, and these occur at the most vigorous moments of the work.

The second subject, recalling Grieg in its quaver tailpiece, makes a vigorous contribution to the formal scheme until features of the main theme assert themselves again.

The kernel of the work is a lovely interlude, typically Delian in mood, leading to an impressive recapitulatory finale which crowns the work in a coda of triumph.

The Sonata was completed in 1917 for the English cellist Beatrice Harrison, to whom it was dedicated. She gave the first performance later that year with Evlyn Howard-Jones at the Wigmore Hall in London.

New York recital programme 14 November 1991

6. Works for the Stage

THE STORY OF KOANGA

upon which Delius based his opera, is here told by Eric Fenby, who worked with Delius as his amanuensis during the last years of the composer's life. The first performance in England of Koanga *will be relayed from Covent Garden on Monday.*

The Radio Times 20 September 1935

The novelty of the short season of opera to be given this autumn at Covent Garden and afterwards in the provinces is Delius's third opera, *Koanga*, which is to receive its first performance in English. It was composed between 1895-1897, and after repeated efforts to interest people in its production in London, Delius returned home to France, disheartened and discouraged. *Koanga* was eventually performed in Elberfeld in 1904 under the direction of Fritz Cassirer, and was greatly enjoyed by the townsfolk there, especially by the small children who acted as piccaninnies! The only serious criticism came from their parents, who complained bitterly of the havoc caused by black grease-paint in tiny garments, and on one occasion the performance was held up for a considerable time by a deputation of infuriated mothers.

Delius had written his own libretto for his first two operas, *Irmelin* and *The Magic Fountain*, but realising by now that he had neither the time nor the literary gift for such thankless tasks, he commissioned his friend C F Keary to make a libretto from Cable's novel of Creole life, *The Grandissimes* - selecting the story of Koanga as the basis of his opera. It will be remembered that Delius had lived as an orange planter in Florida from 1884 to 1886, and to the end of his days he used to talk about the wonderful instinctive feeling for harmony possessed by the Negroes, and how he used to sit on his verandah far into the night smoking cigar after

204

cigar as he listened to their subtle improvisations in harmony. In the meantime Delius had returned to Europe to study, and it was not until January 1897 that he decided to go out to Florida again, this time not to seek solitude, but to put his estate in order, for the Negro in charge of it had gifts for pocketing Delius's profits that far outshone the Negro's excellent gift for music. It was on this second visit that much of the music for *Koanga* was composed.

The scene of the prologue is a typical southern orange grove. It is evening and dancing is going on in the house. Four young girls, Renée, Hélène, Aurore and Olive, tired of dancing and playing all day, beg Uncle Joe, an old Negro slave, to tell one of his stories. They are joined by Jeanne, Marie, Hortense and Paulette, and all sit round the old man whilst he tells them the story of Koanga and Palmyra. Clouds descend and cover the stage, and after a brief orchestral interlude they clear gradually and disclose the garden of a plantation in Louisiana, with slave huts and distant fields of sugar cane, edged by a stretch of the forest. It is dawn and the beginning of yet another day in the life of a slave.

Act One. Palmyra, the beautiful half-caste maid of Clotilda, wife of the planter Don José Martinez, but really the natural daughter of Clotilda's father, is sad and lonely and her thoughts are interrupted by the call of the cow-horn summoning the slaves to their work, and by the appearance of Simon Perez, the detested slave-driver whose repeated advances make her life intolerable. The slaves, half-asleep, appear at the hut door, the lazy ones are roused with the whip, and soon they are off to their work, singing in unison as they go:

> *Come out, niggers, come out to cut the waving cane;*
> *The moonlight shadows are faded and the day is back again,*
> *The humming-bird is waking, good niggers don't complain,*
> *So come once more and hasten to the fields of sugar cane.*

Perez persists in his love-making, and from the fields the same chorus is heard, now in harmony. Palmyra is about to go, when Don José comes upon the scene. He complains that the last load of slaves was hardly worth the whip; Perez replies that this time they have sent a splendid prize: 'a noble warrior of ancient race, a prince of his realm'. Don José orders him to be brought before him. Koanga enters, in chains, guarded by two Negroes. He calls upon his fathers from the grave to revenge him and heaps curse upon curse on the traitors who have made him captive. No more will he see 'the slow Inlanga River, nor the wide, shady forest where the serpent crawls at ease, nor hear again the arrow speeding home'. He vows that he will die rather than be a slave. Don José threatens to use the whip, and Palmyra cries out in horror, recognising in Koanga the signs of a Joloff Prince and Voodoo priest. This for the first time draws the attention of her master to Palmyra, and he entices her to use a 'woman's wiles' to subdue him. She falters. Something of the past awakens in her, and almost in spite of herself offers to share Koanga's fate if he will 'bow his back'. To Perez's chagrin, her charm works too well and Koanga agrees.

Act Two opens with the Negroes celebrating their Master's birthday and the wedding day of Koanga and Palmyra. Clotilda, unable to bear the thought of Palmyra being given in marriage to a pagan - she has brought up the girl as a Christian - does her best to dissuade her, and Perez, mad with jealousy, kidnaps Palmyra with the aid of a few servants during the merry-making. Koanga, astonished and enraged, demands his bride from the indignant Don José. They fight; the planter falls to the ground, and Koanga, calling upon Voodoo to rain his curses on the plantation, escapes into the forest.

Act Three opens in the heart of the forest. Koanga has established himself as the Chieftain of fugitive slaves. A sacrifice is prepared, the dark forms dance around the fire, gashing themselves with knives. The fire dies down, Koanga prays to Voodoo and a vision of Don José's plantation appears. Amid the dying slaves he sees Palmyra and hears her cries of distress. He returns to the accursed plantation and, finding Perez importuning the unhappy Palmyra, he slays him, and is himself done to death by the spears of Don José's men. Palmyra, overcome, stabs herself. The Epilogue brings us back to Uncle Joe and the girls listening to the story.

KOANGA

A Talk by Mr Eric Fenby

BBC National Programme Monday 23 September 1935

I hope it will interest you on this occasion to hear something about Frederick Delius and the circumstances under which he composed his opera *Koanga*. The Frederick Delius that I should like to talk to you about for a few minutes is not the tragic figure and relic of a man most of you have come to know by the awful photographs taken of him during the last years of his life, nor the Delius some of you saw in the flesh when he came over to attend the festival of his music given in his honour by Sir Thomas Beecham in 1929; - no, I want you to forget all this, and allow me to give you some idea of the sort of man he was at the time of the composition of *Koanga* - I mean the Delius of the late nineties.

Judging by one or two unpublished photographs taken about this time, and by chance remarks made by the composer to me when I caught him in reminiscent mood, I am able to piece together a picture of him in those days, a necessarily imperfect picture, of course, but a picture by which I should prefer you to remember him; for the picture by which he is most likely to be remembered is but the shadow of the man. Now Delius must have been a tall, handsome young fellow, aristocratic in bearing, meticulous in dress, fond of sports - he was a very keen cricketer, a good change bowler and useful 'bat' and often played for an English XI in Paris.

He had done what I too had done as a small boy; gone to the Scarborough Cricket Festival, and sat on the cheap benches with his sandwiches and his bottle of 'pop', and even in his old age his interest in the game did not wane. When he used to be brought downstairs before lunch he would send for me to read the latest scores and to wheel him round the garden in his chair and discuss the prospects of the various teams, particularly at Test Match times. He must have been a very wilful, restless, self-centred young man; very sure of himself - a man who knew all there is to be known about food, about wine, and, to complete the delectable trinity - the fair sex! A prodigious reader, a stimulating and entertaining talker with a dry wit curiously his own, often, I am sure, a very trying companion - in short, a most unusual young man.

I have mentioned his restlessness. The moment he had finished his work he would rush off for a long walk, or a long cycle ride, or a strenuous holiday climbing mountains in Norway, and thirty years later with blindness and paralysis fast creeping upon him, he insisted on being carried up a high mountain in Norway to see the marvellous sunset on the great hills in the distance. Percy Grainger helped by Mrs Delius and two servants bore the brunt of that seven hours' ascent, and then as they neared the summit it all seemed in rain, for clouds obscured the view. But at the great moment, the clouds dispersed, Delius revelled in his sunset, and, within a few minutes, a dense mist settled over the scene, and they began the perilous descent.

This little incident will also reveal something of the youthful grip on life which was manifest so often in his old age. But we are concerned with the young Delius, the young composer who set to work on the score of *Koanga*. He had contemplated the idea of writing a Negro opera for some considerable time and even tried to make his own libretto. It will be remembered that his previous attempts in this direction had failed, and that consequently he had wasted a good deal of beautiful music, particularly in the case of *Irmelin*, his first opera, in which much of the music has an unmistakable charm and freshness about it. I shall refer to *Irmelin* for a moment later on. Delius realised by now that he had neither the time nor the necessary literary gift for such thankless tasks. What was more natural than that he should commission his friend Keary, with whom he shared a flat in Paris, to make a libretto for him?

Keary, already at work on it, had gone down to the country, and was staying at a little village near Fontainebleau called Bourron, about twenty minutes' walk over the fields from Grez, the village where Delius was to settle down for life the following year. When the 'book' for the first act was completed, Keary sent for Delius, who was then in Paris, asking him to come to Bourron on the next day to read it through. Trivial though it may seem, this incident influenced the whole course of the composer's life.

It must be explained that shortly before this, Delius had met a young painter, Jelka Rosen, at the home of a mutual friend in Paris where the young woman had come to study painting. Miss Rosen appeared to be very enthusiastic about Delius's music and not a little solicitous for his future well-being. Delius had confided in her that as his father had refused to make him a small allowance on which to live, and thus devote himself entirely to composition, he would have to earn his living by teaching. All his creative inspirations would come to nought! However, he was able to jog along for the time being thanks to the generosity of an uncle in Paris.

Miss Rosen was now in Grez staying with her girl friend Ida Gerhardi, another young painter, at the Hôtel Chevillon, then a great rendezvous for artists, and hearing that Delius was at Bourron with Keary, she invited him over to lunch. It was a lovely summer's day, and those of you who have not seen Grez on such a day can hardly realise anything of the beauty of the old church, the light on the lines of poplars, the plain edged by a distant stretch of the wood. Robert Louis Stevenson has described it beautifully somewhere in his writings, but I am away from my books and cannot remember the passage.[55] The young couple took a boat from the hotel landing-stage, and going under the bridge landed and

---

[55]   'Forest notes' chapter in *Essays of Travel*, London, 1905. See also Christopher Redwood's article 'Grez before Delius - Part One', *Delius Society Newsletter* 42, 14-17.

walked up what appeared to be an overgrown garden. Skirting the pond they eventually found themselves in the courtyard of a rambling house looking onto the street. The young woman, with astonishing intuition, decided that this was the very place for Delius to work in. There he could concentrate undisturbed to his heart's content, and from that moment she resolved that by hook or by crook she would buy that property.

Meanwhile, Delius returned to Paris and worked hard on the first act of *Koanga*. It was his habit in those days to work through the night and sleep during the day. He used to tell me that he smoked incessantly as he worked, that a bottle of red wine was never far out of elbow's reach, and how sometimes he would leave his work in the middle of the night and steal out for a chat at some café table with his painter friends. Much interesting correspondence passed between Delius and Keary on the subject of the libretto, Delius all the while complaining that Keary's words were too 'high-flown'. The music for Act 11 was finished by the end of that year, 1896, and in the New Year Delius decided to return to Florida for a few months to put his orange-grove in order. Keary, having completed the libretto, handed over the last act to the composer, who wrote the greater part of the music for it on that second visit to Florida. Miss Rosen, in Delius's absence and unknown to him, had persuaded her mother to buy the property at Grez. She was now installed there, but had had little or no news of Delius. However, the day after he returned to Paris from Florida she received a postcard announcing his intention of coming down for the week-end![56] From that week-end Grez became his home and it was here that *Koanga* was completed and all his finest music conceived.

[As you have been told, Sir Thomas Beecham is performing the opera in two instead of three acts. That is to say Act 11 becomes Scene 11 of Act 1, and Act 111 becomes Act 11.] For the purposes of this production Sir Thomas has found it necessary to interpolate two little unpublished pieces. The first you will hear before this next act. It is an extract from a suite *Florida* written in 1889 from which Delius borrowed the theme for the merry-making scene at the wedding feast of Koanga and Palmyra. Perhaps you will be able to catch the words?

Dansons la Calinda, Ha, ha, ha, ha, ha, ha, ha.

---

56 The reader is also referred to Jelka Delius's 'Memories of Frederick Delius', Appendix VII in Lionel Carley's *Delius: A Life in Letters* Vol 1, Scolar Press 1983, 408-415.

Now the second piece will be played in the last act, after the vision of Don José's plantation fades away, and the scenery is changed. It is a charming little flight for small orchestra which Delius dictated to me and which he developed from a few musical ideas that particularly appealed to him in his very early opera *Irmelin*. It therefore receives its first performance tonight. You will easily recognise it as it clears away the somewhat depressing atmosphere created by the music for the long-drawn-out scene at the beginning of the third act - a swamp in the heart of the forest where Koanga has established himself as chieftain of fugitive slaves.

Now I will leave someone else to tell you something about the next act . . .

KOANGA

Delius finished the score of *Koanga* in Paris, 1897. He was 35 and still unknown. Two years later he used a legacy to give a whole concert of his music in London; the second part of the programme consisted of excerpts from *Koanga*. He still had to wait another five years to hear it in its entirety when Dr Hans Haym, of Elberfeld, at last persuaded his reluctant committee to stage the opera at the Stadttheater. Haym himself prepared the music and conducted several performances.

Koanga is one of those singular works that attract attention in Delius's development but which stand apart from the rest of his music. Usually, once a work was written, Delius's interest in it would wane. It would then be renewed and be relived temporarily every time he heard it again. For *Koanga*, however, he showed concern as though it held some secret bond that bound him to his youth in Florida. It was the one work he deplored in old age he was never likely to hear again. And so it proved. A dark grandeur pervades the score which, whilst yielding to hankerings after Wagner, recalls the tragic gusto of Verdi. The elements of time, place and plot allowed him a range of textures and moods wider than in his other operas.

In a lively prologue, planters' young daughters breathless from dancing beg an old servant, Uncle Joe, to tell one of his much-loved yarns. He agrees. Delius takes us back two centuries by projecting an orchestral picture in sound of a moonlight scene on a sugar-cane plantation on the Mississippi in Louisiana, the Southern setting for Uncle Joe's tale.

PART TWO : THE WORKS OF DELIUS

Act 1

Palmyra, a mulatto slave-girl, sings of her troubled spirit. A cow-horn wakes the slaves for work. Men and women stretch and yawn and the orchestra flexes its muscles too. Simon Perez, the plantation foreman, begins his daily pestering of Palmyra until Don José Martinez, the owner, appears. A new batch of slaves arrives and others sing as they work in the fields. A handsome specimen, Koanga, an African prince and Voodoo priest, is dragged in chains before Don José. He refuses to work, and with just pride bewails his fate. Palmyra feels the power of his spell and he in turn is drawn to her. Don José encourages this attraction and offers him Palmyra if he will submit. The bargain is struck and the wedding arranged. Perez is furious. The characters combine their various reactions in a vocal quintet of harmonic complexity. But only Don José's wife, Clotilda, knows the truth about Palmyra's birth, a secret she keeps to herself for the present as slaves add their voices in good-humoured song in one of the rich ensembles in the opera.

Act 11

Delius delighted in distant voices and indulges in charming offstage effects as the slaves prepare for their master's birthday and the wedding celebrations. A banjo strums its part in the score (surely anticipating *Porgy and Bess* by at least a quarter of a century). Emotional tension begins to rise between the child-like songs of the holidaying slaves, their itch to dance, the anger of Perez, the anguish of Clotilda and the joy of Koanga and Palmyra. In a fine aria 'The hour is come', written after a rehearsal at Elberfeld, Palmyra gives her soul to Koanga and he, in most expressive tones, renounces his people and his lands far away to be a humble slave for love of her. They plight their troth to the seductive rhythms of the Creole dance 'La Calinda'. The excitement increases; Palmyra, parted momentarily from Koanga, is seized by Perez and his men and rushed away. Koanga is affronted and demands her back. Martinez refuses. Koanga, enraged, threatens to bring down the curse of Voodoo and dashes off into the deep forest. A remarkable passage for woodwind in unison over a pedal in the basses reaches its peak as the voice of Koanga calls in the distance to his gods, and the orchestra clinches the emotional climax

Act 111

The prelude evokes a swamp at nightfall. An uncanny sense of the eerie scene deepens with each change of key as slaves await Koanga's coming to cast the magic spell with Rangwan, another Voodoo priest.

Impressionist touches in the woodwind blend with weird incantations of the men. Blood from a gourd is poured on a fire, the slaves gash themselves with knives and a wild dance subsides in a vision of Don José's stricken plantation which has fallen under Voodoo's curse. The men bemoan their homeless plight and Koanga imagines he hears Palmyra lamenting her love. In a marvellous outburst of dramatic splendour he calls on the morning star to lead him to her. Meanwhile, on the plantation, Christian slaves pray for deliverance. Don José, indignant and bewildered, promises revenge on Koanga if only they will get back to work. Perez still pursues Palmyra, and Koanga appears as he tries to embrace her and chases him into the forest, where he kills him with his spear. Koanga is set upon by Don José's men and suffers excruciating torture. He is carried in on a litter and dies by his bride, who, renouncing her faith, stabs herself and joins him in death.

In the charming epilogue, we return to the girls sitting on the verandah listening to Uncle Joe. They stay up and watch the coming dawn. The day breaks, and sunlight floods the scene of a soft May morning.

Sleeve note EMI SLS 974 (1974)

LA CALINDA

The boyish tunefulness of what is known publicly of Delius's early music has endeared itself to many, due in no small measure to the frequent performances of this dance, *La Calinda*.

Two versions exist. The first, made at Delius's request by the writer of these notes, is selected from the Negro opera *Koanga* (1895-7), and includes the vocal dance music from the wedding scene of Koanga and Palmyra transferred from voices to orchestra.

The second, edited by Sir Thomas Beecham and usually performed by him, belongs to a later date, and is based on the original material from the *Florida* Suite (1886-7) afterwards incorporated in *Koanga*.

Programme note, Delius Centenary concert, RFH 29 January 1962

see also pages 155 and 163

A VILLAGE ROMEO AND JULIET

Composed in 1900-1 at Grez-sur-Loing, *A Village Romeo and Juliet*, Delius's fourth opera, was first produced at the Komischen Oper in Berlin in 1907, under the direction of Fritz Cassirer. It was given its first London performance in 1910 under Sir Thomas Beecham, and for a long while it was he alone who directed subsequent performances in England, notably the second Covent Garden production in 1920, that given by the students at the Royal College of Music in 1934, and several broadcast performances. More recently there was the successful revival by Sadler's Wells Opera Trust Ltd, conducted by Meredith Davies, at the Delius Centenary Festival in Bradford in 1962. The musical kernel of the opera, the poignant interlude known as *The Walk to the Paradise Garden*, has been heard frequently in concert programmes during the past forty years. Delius, acting on Beecham's suggestion, prolonged the original interlude to its present form prior to the last scene for the London production of 1910.

The libretto which Delius set, often concurrently in English and German, is based on a simple tale from Gottfried Keller's *People of Seldwyla*. It was prepared by Jelka Delius in the original German and lost something of its quality in her English translation. Several attempts have been made to improve upon this: the present recording uses that made by Tom Hammond for Sadler's Wells. As the title suggests, the story has features common to Shakespeare's play, but instead of a feud between aristocratic families, there is ruinous strife between neighbouring farmers over an unclaimed strip of land separating their farms. The rightful heir is a nameless vagabond, the Dark Fiddler, who, for his own reasons, haunts his land but never demands it. The real drama bears upon the frustrated love of Sali and Vrenchen, the boy and girl of the rival farmers, a tragedy of the spirit rather than incident.

The gigantic score reads: 3 flutes (the 3rd interchanging to piccolo); 3 oboes; English horn; 3 clarinets and bass clarinet; 3 bassoons and double bassoon; 6 horns; 3 trumpets; 3 trombones and bass tuba; percussion including 2 harps, xylophone, bells and gong; and the usual strings. In the stage production a solo violin, 6 horns, 2 cornets, 2 alto trombones, tenor drum, bells and organ are required on or behind the stage.

The instrumental counterpoint in *A Village Romeo and Juliet* reveals greater freedom of melodic flight in longer curves of cantilena, and finer shades of blend in the use of timbre, pure or mixed, than any work he had written before. There are combinations of woodwind and horns which in beauty and range of suggestion he rarely surpassed, save in such moments as the opening bars of the slow movement of the Double Concerto which are clumsy on paper, ravishing in sound. And yet the progressions in Act 111 of *Koanga* (1895-7) which contributed most strongly to his development in the imaginative use of these sections of the orchestra are not to be found in the excerpts from the opera which were played at the Delius concert in London in 1899, one of the few occasions on which he had been able to hear his music. Another feature of the orchestration of *A Village Romeo and Juliet*, considering the size of the forces and the age in which it was written, is the sparing use of instruments, particularly the heavy brass. From first to last Delius's touch is assured and imaginative, with some inclination to paint rather than draw, as when, to take the simplest example, one woodwind timbre reinforces a vital note in a chord in the course of a progression played by strings, and then is silent. This was but another means of evoking the spirit of things, not depicting them. All this he did in his personal way, careless of rule or procedure, and prompted alone by his feelings. This absence of manner in applying his colours to a texture never predictable, enchants in its freshness. Nor did he ever descend to the level of 'professional orchestration'. He was an artist in sound always.

The intensity of Delius's expression warmed to the subject in *A Village Romeo and Juliet* in a contemplative attitude which no composer, past or present, could have equalled, and he had the power to communicate his vision. This contemplative attitude goes far beyond the reach of time, and far beyond the personal tragedy of Sali Manz and Vrenchen Marti of Seldwyla. The Dark Fiddler still hangs about his land, and his playing bodes no good. Our Paradise Garden is overgrown, and we too are children of strife. Delius was often criticised for his detachment and a self-absorption which lured him into musical by-paths which few can follow. This new kind of beauty he discovered may not please all, but in *A Village Romeo and Juliet* it ranges over experiences familiar to all.

First Scene

It is a calm day in September. Manz and Marti are out with their ploughs. Marti, eyeing the disused land dividing their farms, takes in another furrow for himself as he turns, wagering that Manz on his side will be doing the same. Presently Sali and Vrenchen bring their fathers' mid-day meal, spread it out in the shade and run off to play in the wood. The ploughmen pass the time of day and take their lunch. Their children soon return, attracted by a man's voice singing in the distance. The singing ceases and in a while a fiddler hobbles into sight. Marti recognises him as the trumpeter's grandson and heir to the waste land. Being of doubtful parentage he has no rightful claim, so his land is to be sold. Sali and Vrenchen are alarmed, but the stranger bids them play on his land and leaves assuring them that no harm will come until the plough has levelled his plot. The farmers begin to accuse each other of filching strips of land. With tempers rising, Manz and Marti each take their child roughly by the hand and forbid them to play together.

Second and Third Scenes

Six years have passed. The quarrels of the two farmers have led to lawsuits leaving both families ruined. Sali, longing to see Vrenchen again, returns to Marti's derelict farm, and the two catch sight of each other. They regard one another in silence, then clasping hands impulsively they recall their happy childhood and bemoan the feud that has wrecked their lives. Vrenchen is in despair, but Sali is hopeful and begs to stay awhile and say what is nearest his heart. She pleads with him to go lest her father return from Seldwyla and find them together.

Both realise they are children no more, and their feelings for each other are plain. Sali tries to embrace her but she resists, bidding him go and meet her towards evening in the wildland between the farms.

Later the Dark Fiddler comes upon the lovers and quickly reveals his part in their lives, and the curse his land has brought. He bears them no ill-will now they are all beggars. They may come, if they care, and share his wanderings.

He goes and Vrenchen is afraid. She remembers full well what followed their last meeting. Sali, however, assures her that the man means no harm. Their idyll is short-lived for Marti, spying on his daughter, confronts them in anger. He attempts to drag Vrenchen away, but Sali opposes him. Marti sneers and the youth fells him to the ground. Vrenchen rushes to her father's side, believing him dead.

Fourth Scene

Vrenchen, sitting alone by a dying fire, prepares to spend the last night in her old home. She has just returned from taking her father to Seldwyla. The blow from Sali has crippled his mind. Shortly afterwards Sali appears, looking pale and dejected. The painful sequel to their last meeting has deepened their love, their sense of reliance on each other, and they decide to face the world together. It is now dark and their elation subsides. Vrenchen draws Sali to the bench by the fire and they fall asleep in each other's arms.

They dream they are being married in the old church of Seldwyla. The bells peal and the choir and organ join in a chorale in blessing on the pair. Dawn breaks and the lovers wake to realise their joy was but an illusion.

Presently peasants are heard yodelling in the distance. Sali remembers that it is the day of the great fair at Berghald, and begs Vrenchen to forget all cares and share in the fun.

Fifth Scene

The fair is in full swing and a side-show is about to begin. Dancers appear on a platform outside the tent, the circus band strikes up and the crowd takes up the refrain. Sali and Vrenchen arrive on the scene and are soon recognised by a couple coming out of the inn as they stroll arm in arm round the booths. Sali buys Vrenchen his token, a cheap little ring. The lovers are now conscious of staring eyes, and the enticements of the show people add to their embarrassment. People begin to stream out of the tent as the show ends, and Sali and Vrenchen elbow their way through the throng out of the fairground. Hand in hand and lingering to kiss, they walk to the spot where Sali imagines they will be unknown - the Paradise Garden.

Sixth Scene

We enter the Paradise Garden. Everything has run wild. A dilapidated little country house overlooking the winding river in the valley is now an inn, and lighted lanterns hang from the verandah in the soft summer twilight. A barge full of hay is moored at the water's edge. The poor horn-player, hunchbacked contrabass player and other vagabonds sit drinking with their women at a table in the garden, and standing in silence away from the rest, the Dark Fiddler watches the last glow of evening on the high snow mountains. In a while he joins the others who have been enquiring about his land. He tells them why it was judged to be heirless and put to sale; of the hatred it has caused.

During his tale Sali and Vrenchen saunter into sight. The fiddler hails them and bids them join him and his friends. They all drink to the health of the lovers and Sali and Vrenchen are tempted to think that life might be kinder with these wanderers. The Dark Fiddler continues to press them and is joined by a female companion who, with an eye on Sali, jeers at Vrenchen and advises them to get married. They are much too respectable for the likes of her. Her sort of life would never do for them.

Sali and Vrenchen realise that what the woman says is true. Vrenchen kisses him tenderly and with the rising moon flooding the valley in soft and mellow light, the Paradise Garden is touched as if by a mysterious enchantment. A bargeman is heard approaching from a distance and his song finds responsive echoes in the lover's hearts -

> *Passing strangers drifting by,*
> *Ho, passing strangers drifting by!*

They choose to be happy one fleeting moment and then to die. The Dark Fiddler appears upon the verandah playing wildly on his violin, and sounds of singing and laughter come from within. Sali beckons Vrenchen to their marriage-bed of hay, assists her into the barge, and withdraws the plug from the bottom. He throws it away, and the barge drifts slowly down the river.

The Dark Fiddler, now joined by his friends, points meaningly in its direction. If ever there were moments when music expresses the inexpressible in words they are these, as the orchestra rises to a climactic chord, the boat sinks, and all is calm.

> SLS966 1973. Synopsis and Introduction much expanded from Bradford 1962 Delius Centenary Festival programme book, the Introduction being developed from the Foreword in 'The Delius Fellowship' booklet, October 1948, accompanying the two-volume set DB6751-62 (see below)

A recording of Delius's operatic masterpiece *A Village Romeo and Juliet* in its entirety is long overdue, for not only is it important that his finest works should be presented to the public through the medium of the gramophone in the lifetime of the conductor most faithful in feeling and interpretation to the inner spirit of the music, but also because this opera loses less than any other in being divorced from the stage. It is, in fact, what Percy Grainger would style the 'Room Opera' par excellence. The keynote is intimacy and this can be best enjoyed in the home. Delius's personal view of lyricism illumines a drama of a hundred years ago which unfolds in six pictures of a kind most minds delight in - the Swiss countryside. The characters are such as all can imagine, farmers, vagabonds, show people, and two dream children who fall in love.

Composed in 1900-1 at Grez-sur-Loing in France, *A Village Romeo and Juliet* was first produced at the Komischen Oper in Berlin in 1907 under the direction of Fritz Cassirer, and was given its first London performance under Sir Thomas Beecham in 1910. Sir Thomas Beecham alone has directed subsequent performances in England, notably the second Covent Garden production in 1920, that given by the students at the Royal College of Music in 1934, which would surely have rejoiced the composer's heart, and several broadcast performances of more recent date. The musical kernel of the opera, the poignant interlude known as *The Walk to the Paradise Garden*, has been heard frequently in concert programmes during the past twenty years, and there have been occasional broadcast performances of the whole or portions of the work at the Delius Festivals organised by Sir Thomas Beecham, and Hallé concerts under the late Sir Hamilton Harty and John Barbirolli. An orchestral suite in three movements has also been arranged by the writer of this note.

A *Village Romeo and Juliet* is Delius's fourth opera, and there is little to suggest in the musical behaviour of its comparatively undistinguished forbears, *Irmelin* (1890-2), *The Magic Fountain* (1893-4), and *Koanga*, excepting Act 111 (1895-7), that three years later they would be followed by a series of major works of full vigour and breadth of mood on which Delius's fame as a composer largely depends, *Appalachia* (1902), *Sea Drift* (1903) and *A Mass of Life* (1904-5). It will be remembered that Delius's unusually long apprenticeship, or first period, came to an end not, as might have been expected, in a work of masterly advancement for voices and orchestra, but in a purely orchestral triumph - *Paris, The Song of a Great City*, completed in 1899. To the two friends who were watching Delius's development with affectionate and practical interest, Haym and Cassirer, it must have seemed that the romantic qualities peculiar to this virile work were certain pointers to the future. Little can they have imagined that the new opera on which he was working with such zest was to be not only unlike anything he had written hitherto, but unlike any other in music. The composition in 1898 and performance at the Delius concert in London 1899 of *Zarathustra's Midnight Song* for baritone solo, men's chorus and orchestra (later incorporated into *A Mass of Life*), had wrought a mysterious inner change. Delius was not yet ripe for his conception of Nietzsche's masterpiece. It was a happy circumstance for him and for us that he now found in a libretto based on a simple tale from Gottfried Keller's *People of Seldwyla*, the almost perfect outlet for his natural development.

As the title suggests, the story has features common to Shakespeare's play, but instead of a feud between aristocratic families, there is ruinous strife between neighbouring farmers over an unclaimed strip of land separating their farms. The rightful heir is a nameless vagabond - The Dark Fiddler, who, for his own reasons, haunts his land but never demands it. The real drama bears upon the frustrated love of Sali and Vreli, the boy and girl of the rival farmers, a tragedy of the spirit rather than of incident. The narrative unfolds scene by scene. The chief point to make about the libretto is that Delius set it in German, and that the English translation is no better and no worse than most.

It has always seemed to one person at least that, given the barest outlines of the story, and a performance of merit with singers of fitting timbres, the impressionable listener would be no less moved though the opera be sung in Chinese. It is the orchestra which talks to best effect. This may be 'bad opera'; by certain standards it is, but not in the art of Delius. And whilst it must not be assumed that all the interest is confined to the orchestra, the vocal instruments, solo and chorus alike, are no more important than those of the orchestra. Few there are, if any, vocal phrases sung by the principal characters in *A Village Romeo and Juliet* which will live in the memory in that passionate fusion of music and words as in 'wonderful, causing tears' from *Sea Drift*, 'Cease smiling, dear, a little while be sad' from *Songs of Sunset*, Zarathustra's 'Abend ward es, vergebt mir, dass es Abend ward' from *A Mass of Life*, or even the phrase of a minor character in *Koanga*, 'No fear, no troubled thought shall grieve our mind'. The wash of lovely harmony does not always add lustre to a phrase. Nevertheless, the vocal lines in *A Village Romeo and Juliet* are more incisive in nature than those of the earlier operas, and a growing fondness for rhythms in 12/8 and 6/4 time already noticeable in these works now attains greater expression. It is the receding voice of the unseen boatmen caught from the far distance as the drama reaches its emotional peak that will fire the imagination for ever once it is heard, the epitome in sound not only of the whole opera, but Delius's outlook on life - 'Heigh ho! - travellers we a-passing by'. The hushed, unearthly sounds of plainchant falling on the ear a few steps from the bust street could scarce hold more pregnant suggestions of Infinity. Apart from these unforgettable moments in opera, experience is likely to prove that one's deepest impressions arise from the orchestra.

The music flows in continuous rhapsody often emanating from the expressive interplay of short, telling phrases heard in ever differing orchestral timbres as at the entrance of Manz, when the melodic development of an interesting rhythmic 'fingerprint', to quote Ernest Newman, the collective effect of which is:

will not fail to fascinate the student of Delius in comparing this passage with a similar development of the same pattern, modified thus:

in the score of *In a summer garden* written eight years later. The varied unities of the texture bring many surprises. It is enough to cite one at the opening of the third scene which follows the second without a break. This third scene unfolds in an orchestral change of penetrating brightness from the high register of the piccolo and clarinet playing in octaves what portends to be a return to the main theme of the opera after its subtle transmutations; but again the two familiar steps downwards in the melody surprise in an unexpected flowering leading to new growths. (The clarinet has already hinted at this coming enrichment in its short solo [near the end of Scene Two]). The main theme, however, is there after all, but held back momentarily in the quieter tones of first violin as two of the six distant horns enter in free imitation of the novel turns in the melody. Most composers would have come to grief in attempting a further transformation of the thematic material at such a point, and at so slow a pace. Yet the invention is astonishingly true to the sense of pace, grandeur and cold brilliance which Delius wishes to evoke in this sound-picture of mountain scenery. His invention does fail, even so, in the short orchestral passage [Scene Six] during which the vagabonds drink to the health of the lovers. Here Delius, who took his wine with the best and could toast like a Will-o'-the-wisp, lapses into feeble academic wit. Nor does he recover himself completely until the last vagabond has departed, and Sali and Vreli are alone. Then the sheer genius of the man transports us in a master stroke to the end of the work, and we are left in wonder. Was the reason for this fall his impatience to conquer the heights? - a tendency noted by the writer in his passage with the composer, who, having reached the summit, so often lost himself in his gaze as to forget his faltering ascent.

The instrumental counterpoint in *A Village Romeo and Juliet* reveals greater freedom of melodic flight in longer curves of cantilena, and finer shades of blend in the use of timbre, pure or mixed, than any work he had written before. There are combinations of woodwind and horns which in beauty and range of suggestion he rarely surpassed, save in such moments as the opening bars of the slow movement of the Double Concerto which are clumsy on paper, ravishing in sound. And yet the progressions in Act 111 of *Koanga* which contributed most strongly to his development in the imaginative use of these sections of the orchestra are not to be found in the excerpts from the opera played at the London concert in 1899, one of the few occasions on which he had been able to hear his music. Another feature of the orchestration in *A Village Romeo and Juliet*, considering the size of the forces and the age in which it was written, is the sparing use of instruments, particularly the heavy brass. From the first to last Delius's touch is assured, poetic and original, with some inclination to paint rather than draw, as when, to take the simplest example, one woodwind timbre reinforces a vital note in a chord in the course of a progression played by strings, and then is silent. This was but another means of evoking the spirit of things, not depicting them. All this he did in his personal way, careless of rule or procedure, and prompted alone by his feelings. This absence of manner in applying his colours to a texture never predictable, enchants in eternal freshness. Nor did he ever descend to the level of 'professional orchestration'. He was an artist in sound always.

The intensity of Delius's expression warmed to the subject of *A Village Romeo and Juliet* in a contemplative attitude which no composer, past or present, could have equalled, and he had the power to communicate his vision. This contemplative attitude goes far beyond the reach of time, and far beyond the personal tragedy of Sali Manz and Vreli Marti of Seldwyla. The Dark Fiddler still hangs about his land, and his playing bodes no good. Our Paradise Garden is overgrown, and we too are children of strife. Delius was often criticised for his detachment and a self-absorption which lured him into musical bypaths which few can follow. This new kind of beauty he discovered may not please all, but in *A Village Romeo and Juliet* it ranges over experiences familiar to all.

> Foreword and Analysis to 'The Delius Fellowship' two 78rpm record volumes of *A Village Romeo and Juliet* October 1948

MARGOT LA ROUGE

When Frederick Delius left Leipzig Konservatorium as a student in the late eighteen-eighties he was destined to spend eight years in rented rooms in the little villages on the outskirts of Paris. Practical support from his father was to cease and, but for the foresight and generosity of his uncle Theodor, a well-to-do art-loving bachelor resident in Paris, his heart's desire to be a composer would have languished in an unthinkable return to the servitude of the family wool business in Bradford, the West Riding of Yorkshire.

Though he found Paris 'ten times more beautiful than London' he was drawn instinctively to the countryside for inspiration in his work, as other young artists were seeking to do in that period of vision and extravagance that was stirring the arts of the day in France. From the hamlet of Ville d'Avray he wrote to Grieg in the autumn of 1888: 'So I am at work again. Next door is a little restaurant where I eat. It is really wonderful here. Nobody comes and all around are woods and hills. One would think one is a hundred miles from Paris!'

Yet the attractions of Paris were not far from mind. He would drop his pen and enjoy to the full the high life of his uncle's salons, then change to old clothes and romp with the friends he had made amongst young painters and writers. These diverse experiences were eventually to yield some fragmentary sketches, *Scènes Parisiennes* and *Episodes et Aventures* - and the tone-poem *Paris (The Song of a Great City)* dated 1899 which, incredibly, has never been heard in France at all![57]

Again the French phase erupts surprisingly in the composition of Delius's fifth opera, *Margot La Rouge* (1901-2), and continues fitfully in his settings of the French orientated English poems of Ernest Dowson in *Cynara* for baritone and orchestra (1907) and *Songs of Sunset* for soprano, baritone, chorus and orchestra (1906-8), ending in 1919 in the last of the Verlaine songs for voice and piano, *Avant que tu ne t'en ailles*, which appear intermittently in the Delius canon from 1895.

Delius describes *Margot La Rouge* as a lyric drama in one act to words by Rosenval. Who Rosenval was nobody seems to know, nor is there any evidence of any other work attributable to him. It has been established, however, that Rosenval was the pen-name for a certain Berthe Gaston-Danville, presumably long since dead. (It would have been useless my asking Delius even if I had thought of it. He would have said 'Don't ask questions! To explain is weak!' Thus what I know of him he told me of his own accord.) The opera, it is affirmed by Delius researchers, was written for and submitted as an entry in the 'Concorso Melodrammatico Internationale of 1904 sponsored by the publisher Sonzogno of Milan'.

Delius never referred to it even when, in 1932, he based his *Idyll* for soprano, baritone and orchestra on words adapted from Walt Whitman's *Leaves of Grass* by reworking with my help selected lyrical passages from *Margot La Rouge*! In this reworking process we used Delius's original full score, beautifully written in his own hand,

---

57   This work has since been performed in Paris, on 25 January 1990, Michaël Schönwandt conducting the Orchestre Philharmonique de Radio-Paris.

maintaining the initial orchestration, but reshaping the vocal lines when required appropriate to Whitman's verse in accordance with the scheme Robert Nichols had drafted, after he had heard the selected music played over and over again to him. Since then I have never seen Delius's MS and when, in 1980, the Delius Trust commissioned me to make a new orchestration of those passages not contained in the *Idyll*, using Ravel's vocal score which he made for Delius in 1904, I wished I had read through Delius's autograph score of *Margot La Rouge* more often. But that was fifty years ago. My task now was to reproduce on paper as faithfully as I possibly could the sounds Delius had in mind when first conceiving the music. Music, he told me, invariably came to him complete in timbres and thus I pondered each progression until I felt sure I was near the truth. It may be that my use of the brass in the storm scene and later excitements may be more dramatic than Delius's original, but my zeal might be heard as a pardonable liberty!

The opera opens with a prelude which is one of the most perfect and inevitable pieces of music, in that not one note is more than is needed to convey its direct simplicity in expressing the mystery of Nature's nightfall, and what that nightfall might bring in the tale we are about to hear. Those who know the *Idyll* may find interest in the way Delius turns the same music to different account in *Margot La Rouge*. This is most obvious in the prelude which in the *Idyll* is taken at the slow speed of an old man's reverie of a past love affair; whereas in the opera the prelude has the speed and expectancy of youth. As might be expected, the love-duet is the most sustained piece of lyrical invention in both works, and it will be noticed that Delius gives the male part in the *Idyll* to a baritone rather than to a tenor, as in the opera. The duet is thus the nub of each work. In *Margot La Rouge*, which concerns us most here, it reveals the chance meeting of a man and a woman who were once lovers, and their brief bliss in being reunited.

There is much fine music in this singular opera which belongs to what many would consider to be 'Delius's best period'. It follows by one year *A Village Romeo and Juliet*, was finished in 1902 with *Appalachia*, and predates *Sea Drift* also by one year. Such weaknesses as there are occur in the vocal lines of the narrative, but these are more than offset for me by this melodramatic aspect of Delius, then forty years old, and settled in the village of Grez-sur-Loing, some forty kilometres south of Paris on the edge of the forest of Fontainebleau where *Margot La Rouge* was written.

Sleeve note BBC REGL458 & CD3004X (1982)

FENNIMORE AND GERDA

Fennimore and Gerda, Delius's last opera, was completed in 1910. It was a remarkable conception of opera at the time, anticipating much that has happened since in the theatre and on television in dispensing with musical and scenic unessentials. 'Short, strong emotional impressions given in a series of terse scenes' was how Delius described his intentions. He had dedicated the opera to Sir Thomas Beecham hoping, no doubt, he would bring it out. This, unhappily, was not to be. Sir Thomas had revelled that very year in his fine production at Covent Garden of Delius's *A Village Romeo and Juliet*, a work he loved with all his heart, and was quite alarmed by the improbable path his favourite contemporary composer was taking. He could not warm to the new opera. Its conventional happy ending appalled him, an opinion later to be shared by Delius's friend and biographer Philip Heseltine. And when in October 1916 Delius had remarked in a letter to Heseltine that 'realism on the stage is nonsense, and all the scenery necessary is an impressionistic painted curtain at the back with the fewest accessories possible' - this, indeed, was too much for Beecham. So the work had to wait until 1919 for its première in Frankfurt. A glance at the libretto will show that Delius had had to compromise. In the 1914-18 war-years, the Deliuses had fled to their cottage in Norway, and despite their German origins, were somewhat nervous of their reception when attending the final rehearsals. But their fears were groundless and Delius took several curtain-calls on the night. Back at their home in rural France, they were further encouraged to hear from Frankfurt that the opera was still running successfully.

The libretto of *Fennimore and Gerda* is based on central episodes from a novel, *Niels Lyhne*, by the Danish writer Jens Peter Jacobsen, a kindred spirit whom Delius admired for his firm rejection of Christian beliefs. The novel itself hinges on predicaments of deep concern to Delius: artistic disillusionment and its consequences; a love of - yet Nietzschean contempt for - women; the futility of striving for happiness through passion; and 'the lonely burden of unbelief that needs must develop stronger individuals than those accepting Christianity'. It is this latter predicament intensified to a harrowing climax in Jacobsen's prose from which Delius recoiled in planning his opera. Admitting his own fearless unbelief and occasional sorely trying outspokenness, Delius was a very private person and must have flinched at the problems of adding this crescendo of incredulity, the gist of which is as follows. The triangle of love between Niels, his friend Erik, and Erik's wife Fennimore has snapped in tragedy. Niels, the atheist, now in middle age, is eventually ogled into marriage by a teenage flapper, Gerda. Their bliss is brief; Gerda dies and their baby son later. Niels is left shattered but defiant. War is declared and he enlists in the army. He is wounded in battle and dies in hospital 'the difficult death, babbling of his armour and how he must die standing!' This conveys no hint whatever of the powerful tensions deployed by Jacobsen. The reader's solution is simple enough. The opera consists of eleven mood-pictures with pauses to mark the passage of time. Those who agree with Beecham and Heseltine may lift up the needle from the disc at the pause before the tenth picture. It may well be that, had Delius chosen to end the opera here and called it *Niels Lyhne*, its public impact would have been greater. However, the nature-preludes in the tenth and eleventh pictures are gems in themselves.

Each of the eleven pictures is a separate musical movement developed concisely with economy of means in textures original in colour and design from a large orchestral palette. Nothing could be farther from the ways of grand opera than the tragedy of these ordinary people made pathetically insignificant by reflection in Delius's autumnal orchestral imagery. There are the familiar ingredients of his art - the intimate phrase indelibly drawn, usually from instrumental voices, but first vocally immediately the curtain rises on Fennimore and Niels, 'How peaceful! I wish I could always sit beside you and watch you' - the perfect timing of a commonplace remark in Erik's 'Sit down and have a cigar' - the inevitable operative passionate duet between soprano and baritone - the overwhelming emotional outburst, 'No one knows how deep down in a man his soul extends!' - the simultaneous use of foreground and background in the wordless tenor voice on the water, or the dirge in its crowning orchestral climax as Fennimore awaits Erik's body being borne back from the fjord over the snow, or the wordless choruses from the village evoking a sense of Niels's contentment in managing his farm.

Delius's vocal lines, though angular, allow convincing characterisation and freedom of interpretation to the soloists. But as always with Delius the orchestra expresses what words cannot tell nor feelings make known. No work by Delius, apart from his Requiem, reveals the man more faithfully as I knew him than this laconic Danish opera.

SYNOPSIS

First Picture

Two young friends, almost brothers from boyhood - Niels Lyhne, a writer, and Erik Refstrup, a painter - are staying with Consul and Mrs Claudi and their daughter, Fennimore, at their country home at Fjordby in Denmark. Erik goes off to the fjord to paint whilst Niels is content to be with Fennimore. They sit at her window, she working at her embroidery and he curious about her childhood. She tells him of her boring existence and how she longs for life: Copenhagen, artists, Italy! Niels is saying how much he loves her when Erik returns at the threat of rain, and asks Fennimore for a song. She sings a ballad about a girl pining for excitement.

Second Picture

It is evening. Erik and Fennimore are sitting in a boat by the Claudis' landing stage. They hear a voice singing in the distance as another boat approaches rowed by Niels. Erik and Fennimore disappear in the darkness before her father's party land. Niels is left to moor the boat and catches sight of Erik and Fennimore embracing passionately in the garden. Her song, he now knows, was not meant for him!

Third Picture

Three years have passed. Erik and Fennimore have married. Alone at their house on the Mariagerfjord, their marriage is on the verge of breakdown. Erik has lost interest in his work and has written to Niels inviting him to visit them. No answer has come; then Niels remembers the telegram in his pocket. Meanwhile, Niels and his baggage arrive, and while Erik shows the porter out, Fennimore pleads with Niels to help Erik, who returns with glasses and bottles of wine. The three drink each other's health.

Fourth Picture

Later that evening, over wine and cigars, Erik and Niels recall old times and the aspirations they shared in their teens. Niels is busy on a novel, but admits that he works very slowly. Erik's disillusionment is all too clear. He talks of death: but death of the spirit when a man works on and achieves nothing, when travel abroad is of no avail, and a man is wrung to the depths of his soul.

PART TWO : THE WORKS OF DELIUS

Fifth Picture

It is later summer afternoon. Erik sits despondently at his easel. There is a commotion outside. Some of his companions have come to take 'the great painter' to the fair at Aalborg. There will be women! actors! Fennimore begs him not to go. Surely he has Niels for companionship? But he leaves her weeping on the sofa. Niels, seeing her distress from the window, tries to console her with memories of Erik as he was as a boy. Niels gives her his word he will be her friend always.

Sixth Picture

Fennimore stays up for Erik, dozing in an easy chair. She stirs, yearning to recapture their first days of love. Erik comes home sodden with drink, twits Fennimore for not being in bed and falls on the sofa in a stupor.

Seventh Picture

Autumn comes and Niels and Fennimore are out for a walk. Niels discovers a bird's nest and Fennimore bends over the bush to see it. Niels clasps her hand and kisses her passionately. For a moment she is horrified by the consequences, but when Niels reassures her he has loved her all along she yields and vows to be his for ever.

Eighth Picture

It is now winter. Niels and Fennimore have become lovers. Fennimore awaits him impatiently in the twilight. Her maid enters with a telegram: Erik is dead! thrown out of a cart! His body is being brought back to her. Fennimore is distraught. Niels must never enter the house again. She rushes out to meet him.

Ninth Picture

Niels looks at Fennimore in disbelief. He is stunned. They both feel the sting of remorse which in Fennimore is fired to hatred. She rails on Niels nevermore to come near her. Niels slinks away towards the fjord while she watches the approach of Erik's body being borne back sadly and slowly to her. The sight of it is too much: she flees and collapses in the snow.

Tenth Picture

Three years have passed. Niels has given up his writing and returned to Lønborggaard where he played as a child. It is harvest-time. The farm-lads and land-girls, still busy in the fields, sing happily in the evening light. Niels has found contentment on his farm.

Eleventh Picture

The following spring Niels calls on Councillor Skinnerup. The object of his visit soon becomes apparent. Councillor Skinnerup has four teenage daughters who are playing a hoop game in the garden. Gerda, the eldest, seems preoccupied and is not concentrating on the game. The others tease her till she ceases to play. When Niels joins them from the house they scatter giggling out of the way. Niels greets Gerda with a little present, a book with a pressed ivy leaf plucked in Verona from Romeo and Juliet's grave. He proposes, is accepted and the councillor gives them his blessing. He leads his delighted daughters indoors, leaving the new pair of lovers to kiss.

Sleeve note EMI SLS991 (1976)

Historical note and synopsis used for Opera Theatre of St Louis programme book, June 1981, and for Edinburgh Festival Complete Programme Guide, September 1983

APPENDIX ONE

A CATALOGUE OF SOUND RECORDINGS OF ERIC FENBY

This discography lists all commercial recordings, and those held in archives and private collections, of Dr Eric Fenby as either conductor, accompanist, speaker or composer. Recordings made by others of his arrangements or completions of the music of Delius are not, with one exception, included here. The sequencing of works is in accordance with Robert Threlfall's *Catalogue of the Compositions of Frederick Delius*, Delius Trust 1977.

*   playing on Delius's own Ibach three-quarter grand piano bequeathed to Eric Fenby by the composer
+   introduced by Eric Fenby
**   *The Fenby Legacy* recordings
P   Recording held in private collection
♠   Text reprinted in this volume.

A. WORKS OF DELIUS

LA CALINDA (arr. Fenby) [I/4]
RPO, Fenby
  rec. 31 March 1981 Barking Assembly Hall **
      DKP9008/9 RT9008-9 DKP(CD)9008/9 UKCD2073
[arr. Fenby] Elena Duran (flute), Bournemouth Sinfonietta, Fenby
  rec. 1 September 1978 Guildhall, Southampton   ASD3688 TCASD3688

THE WALK TO THE PARADISE GARDEN [I/6]
LSO, Fenby
  Royal Festival Hall 11 July 1982   [P]

INTERMEZZO from FENNIMORE AND GERDA [I/8]
RPO, Fenby
  rec. 2 December 1983 Barking Assembly Hall, London
        DKPC9063 DKPCD9063 UKCD2076

SERENADE from HASSAN [I/9]
Lloyd Webber, Fenby (pno)
  BBC Radio 3 b/cast 30 July 1981   [P]

APPALACHIA [II/2]
London Symphony Chorus, LSO, Fenby
  Royal Festival Hall 11 July 1982   [P]

SONGS OF SUNSET [II/5]

Sarah Walker, Thomas Allen, Ambrosian Singers, RPO, Fenby
    rec. 29 December 1986 All Saints Church, Tooting
                DKPC9063   DKPCD9063   UKCD2073

THE SONG OF THE HIGH HILLS [II/6]

Ambrosian Singers, RPO, Fenby
    rec. 5 & 6 April 1983 Walthamstow Assembly Hall
                DKP9029   DKPC9029   DKPCD9029   UKCD2071

AN ARABESQUE [II/7]

Thomas Allen, Ambrosian Singers, RPO, Fenby
    rec. 29 December 1986 All Saints Church, Tooting
                DKPC9063   DKPCD9063   UKCD2076

REQUIEM [II/8]

Jonathan Summers, Felicity Lott, Goldsmiths' Choral Union, RPO, Fenby
    Royal Festival Hall   25 January 1984   [P]

SONGS OF FAREWELL [II/9]

Ambrosian Singers, RPO, Fenby
    rec. 10 & 11 February 1981 Watford Town Hall **
                DKP9008/9   RT9008-9   DKP(CD)9008/9   UKCD2077

IDYLL [II/10]

Felicity Lott, Thomas Allen, RPO, Fenby
    rec. 30 & 31 March 1981 Barking Assembly Hall **
                DKP9008/9   RT9008-9   DKP(CD)9008/9   UKCD2073

SEVEN DANISH SONGS [III/4]

    1. Silken Shoes   2. Irmelin Rose   3. Summer Nights
    4. In the Seraglio Garden   5. Wine Roses
    6. Red Roses   7. Let Springtime Come

[1]   Anthony Rolfe Johnson, Eric Fenby (pno)*
    rec. 28 & 29 September 1982 Rosslyn Hill Unitarian Chapel
                UKCD2041   DKP9022   UKCD2075

[2,4] Felicity Lott, Eric Fenby (pno)*
    rec. 28 & 29 September 1982 Rosslyn Hill Unitarian Chapel
                UKCD2041   DKP9022   UKCD2075

[5]   Sarah Walker, RPO, Fenby
    rec. 2 December 1983 Barking Assembly Hall
                DKPCD9029   DKP9029   DKPC9029   UKCD2075

APPENDICES

[7] Sarah Walker, Eric Fenby (pno)*
>> rec. 28 & 29 September 1982 Rosslyn Hill Unitarian Chapel
>>>> UKCD2041 DKP9022 UKCD2075

[7] Felicity Lott, RPO, Fenby
>> rec. 2 December 1983 Barking Assembly Hall
>>>> DKPCD9029 DKP9029 DKPC9029 UKCD2075

CYNARA [III/5]
Thomas Allen, RPO, Fenby
>> rec. 30 March 1981 Barking Assembly Hall **
>>>> DKP9008/9 RT9008-9 DKP(CD)9008/9 UKCD2077

A LATE LARK [III/6]
Anthony Rolfe-Johnson, RPO, Fenby
>> rec. 2 April 1981 Barking Assembly Hall **
>>>> DKP9008/9 RT9008-9 DKP(CD)9008/9 UKCD2072

TWO AQUARELLES [IV/5]
RPO, Fenby
>> rec. [No 1] 31 March & [No 2] 2 April 1981 Barking Assembly Hall **
>>>> DKP9008/9 RT9008-9 DKP(CD)9008/9 UKCD2077

Scottish Baroque Ensemble, Fenby
>> Edinburgh Festival, Queen's Hall 29 August 1982 Radio Forth b/cast [P]

SONGS FROM THE NORWEGIAN [V/9]
>> **1. Cradle Song   2. The Homeward Journey 3. Twilight Fancies**
>> **4. Sweet Venevil 5. Minstrel   6. Love Concealed**
>> **7. The Birds' Story**

[3] Sarah Walker, Eric Fenby (pno)*
>> rec. 28 & 29 September 1982 Rosslyn Hill Unitarian Chapel
>>>> UKCD2041 DKP9022 UKCD2075

[3] Sarah Walker, RPO, Fenby
>> rec. 2 December 1983 Barking Assembly Hall
>>>> DKPCD9029 DKP9029 DKPC9029 UKCD2075

[4] Felicity Lott, Eric Fenby (pno)*
>> rec. 28 & 29 September 1982 Rosslyn Hill Unitarian Chapel
>>>> UKCD2041 DKP9022 UKCD2075

[7] Felicity Lott, RPO, Fenby
>> rec. 2 December 1983 Barking Assembly Hall
>>>> DKPCD9029 DKP9029 DKPC9029 UKCD2075

DEUX MELODIES [V/16]
1. Il pleure dans mon coeur 2. Le ciel est, par-dessus le toit
[1] Anthony Rolfe Johnson, Fenby (pno)*
  rec. 28 & 29 September 1982 Rosslyn Hill Unitarian Chapel
          UKCD2041 DKP9022 UKCD2075

[1] Anthony Rolfe Johnson, RPO, Fenby
  rec. 2 December 1983 Barking Assembly Hall
        DKPCD9029 DKP9029 DKPC9029 UKCD2075

[2] Felicity Lott, Eric Fenby (pno)*
  rec. 28 & 29 September 1982 Rosslyn Hill Unitarian Chapel
          UKCD2041 DKP9022 UKCD2075

[2] Felicity Lott, RPO, Fenby
  rec. 2 December 1983 Barking Assembly Hall
        DKPCD9029 DKP9029 DKPC9029 UKCD2075

TWO SONGS FROM THE DANISH [V/21]
1. The Violet 2. Autumn (Whither?)
[1] Felicity Lott, Eric Fenby (pno)*
  rec. 28 & 29 September 1982 Rosslyn Hill Unitarian Chapel
          UKCD2041 DKP9022 UKCD2075

[2] Sarah Walker, Eric Fenby (pno)*
  rec. 28 & 29 September 1982 Rosslyn Hill Unitarian Chapel
          UKCD2041 DKP9022 UKCD2075

LA LUNE BLANCHE [V/26]
Anthony Rolfe Johnson, Eric Fenby (pno)*
  rec. 28 & 29 September 1982 Rosslyn Hill Unitarian Chapel
          UKCD2041 DKP9022 UKCD2075

Anthony Rolfe Johnson, RPO, Fenby
  rec. 2 December 1983 Barking Assembly Hall
        DKPCD9029 DKP9029 DKPC9029 UKCD2075

CHANSON D'AUTOMNE [V/27]
Sarah Walker, Eric Fenby (pno)*
  rec. 28 & 29 September 1982 Rosslyn Hill Unitarian Chapel
        DKP9022 UKCD2041 UKCD2075

I-BRASIL [V/28]
Anthony Rolfe Johnson, Eric Fenby (pno)*
  rec. 28 & 29 September 1982 Rosslyn Hill Unitarian Chapel
        DKP9022 UKCD2041 UKCD2075

Anthony Rolfe Johnson, RPO, Fenby
    rec. 2 December 1983 Barking Assembly Hall
            DKPCD9029 DKP9029 DKPC9029 UKCD2075

FOUR OLD ENGLISH LYRICS [V/30]
1. It was a lover and his lass   **2. So white, so soft**
3. Spring, the sweet spring   **4. To Daffodils**
[2] Anthony Rolfe Johnson, Eric Fenby (pno)*
    rec. 28 & 29 September 1982 Rosslyn Hill Unitarian Chapel
            DKP9022 UKCD2041 UKCD2075
[4] Sarah Walker, Eric Fenby (pno)*
    rec. 28 & 29 September 1982 Rosslyn Hill Unitarian Chapel
            DKP9022 UKCD2041 UKCD2075
[4, orch. Fenby] Sarah Walker, RPO, Fenby
    rec. 2 December 1983 Barking Assembly Hall
            DKPCD9029 DKP9029 DKPC9029 UKCD2075

AVANT QUE TU NE T'EN AILLES [V/31]
Felicity Lott, Eric Fenby (pno)*
    rec. 28 & 29 September 1982 Rosslyn Hill Unitarian Chapel
            DKP9022 UKCD2041 UKCD2075

AIR AND DANCE [V1/21]
[arr. Fenby] Elena Duran (flute), Bournemouth Sinfonietta, Fenby
    rec. 1 September 1978 Guildhall, Southampton   ASD3688 TCASD3688
Scottish Baroque Ensemble, Fenby
    Edinburgh Festival, Queen's Hall 29 August 1982 Radio Forth b/cast [P]

A DANCE RHAPSODY NO 2 [VI/22]
RPO, Fenby
    rec. 29 December 1986 All Saints Church, Tooting
            DKPC9063 DKPCD9063 UKCD2071

A SONG OF SUMMER [VI/26]
BBC Concert O, Fenby +
    rec. Golders Green Hippodrome 17 Oct. 1978 BBC b/cast 24 Nov. 1978.
        BBC Sound Archives T38611; National Sound Archive T2581BW
RPO, Fenby
    rec. 10 & 11 February 1981 Watford Town Hall **
            DKP9008/9 RT9008-9 DKP(CD)9008/9 UKCD2072

IRMELIN PRELUDE [VI/27]
RPO, Fenby
>   rec. 31 March 1981 Barking Assembly Hall **
>>   DKP9008/9   RT9008-9   DKP(CD)9008/9   UKCD2072

FANTASTIC DANCE [VI/28]
BBC Concert O, Fenby +
>   rec. Golders Green Hippodrome 17 Oct. 1978   BBC b/cast 24 Nov. 1978.
>>   BBC Sound Archives T38611; National Sound Archive T2581BW

RPO, Fenby
>   rec. 31 March 1981 Barking Assembly Hall **
>>   DKP9008/9   RT9008-9   DKP(CD)9008/9   UKCD2071

CAPRICE AND ELEGY [VII/8]
Beatrice Harrison, Orchestra, Fenby
>   rec. 25 November 1930 Small Queen's Hall, London
>>   HMV B3721   SH224   SBT1014

Julian Lloyd Webber, BBC Concert O, Fenby +
>   rec. Golders Green Hippodrome 17 Oct. 1978   BBC b/cast 24 Nov. 1978.
>>   BBC Sound Archives T38611; National Sound Archive T2581BW

Julian Lloyd Webber, RPO, Fenby
>   rec. 2 April 1981 Barking Assembly Hall **
>>   DKP9008/9   RT9008-9   DKP(CD)9008/9   UKCD2077

Julian Lloyd Webber, Fenby (pno)
>   BBC Radio 3 b/cast 30 July 1981   [P]

VIOLIN SONATA NO 1 [VIII/6]
Ralph Holmes, Eric Fenby (pno)*
>   rec. 20 & 21 March 1972 St Giles Church, Cripplegate, London
>>   RHS310   UNS258   UKCD2074

Ralph Holmes, Eric Fenby (pno)+
>   St John's, Smith Square, London 3 June 1972 Westminster Festival
>   BBC Radio 3 b/cast 28 January 1973   BBC Sound Archives T35660

Yehudi Menuhin, Eric Fenby (pno)
>   rec. 10-11 October 1978 EMI Studio No 1 Abbey Road   ASD3864

CELLO SONATA [VIII/7]
Julian Lloyd Webber, Eric Fenby (pno)*
>   rec. 12 January 1981 Rosslyn Hill Unitarian Chapel
>>   DKP9021   UKCD2074

Julian Lloyd Webber, Eric Fenby (pno)
>   BBC Radio 3 b/cast 30 July 1981   [P]

SONATA FOR STRING ORCHESTRA (QUARTET arr. Fenby) [VIII/8]
Bournemouth Sinfonietta, Fenby
      rec. 1-2 September 1978 Guildhall, Southampton ASD3688 TCASD3688
- LATE SWALLOWS only
BBC Concert O, Fenby +
      rec. Golders Green Hippodrome 17 Oct. 1978   BBC b/cast 24 Nov. 1978.
        BBC Sound Archives T38611; National Sound Archive T2581BW

VIOLIN SONATA NO 2 [VIII/9]
Ralph Holmes, Eric Fenby (pno)*
      rec. 20 & 21 March 1972 St Giles Church, Cripplegate, London
                        RHS310 UNS258 UKCD2074
Ralph Holmes, Eric Fenby (pno)+
      St John's, Smith Square, London 3 June 1972 Westminster Festival
      BBC Radio 3 b/cast 28 January 1973   BBC Sound Archives T35660
Yehudi Menuhin, Eric Fenby (pno)
      rec. 10-11 October 1978 EMI Studio No 1 Abbey Road   ASD3864

VIOLIN SONATA NO 3 [VIII/10]
Ralph Holmes, Eric Fenby (pno)*
      rec. 20 & 21 March 1972 St Giles Church, Cripplegate, London
                        RHS310 UNS258 UKCD2074
Ralph Holmes, Eric Fenby (pno)+
      St John's, Smith Square, London 3 June 1972 Westminster Festival
      BBC Radio 3 b/cast 28 January 1973   BBC Sound Archives T35660
Davyd Booth, Eric Fenby (pno)
      Samuel P Mandell Theater, Drexell Univ., Philadelphia 27 Jan. 1974   [P]
Yehudi Menuhin, Eric Fenby (pno)
      27 May 1977 Malvern Festival   BBC Radio 3 b/cast 3 January 1978 [P]
Yehudi Menuhin, Eric Fenby (pno)
      rec. 10-11 October 1978 EMI Studio No 1 Abbey Road   ASD3864

DANCE FOR HARPSICHORD [IX/6]
[arr. Fenby] Elena Duran (flute), Bournemouth Sinfonietta, Fenby
      rec. 1 September 1978 Guildhall, Southampton   ASD3688 TCASD3688

FIVE PIANO PIECES [IX/7]
   1. Mazurka   **2. Waltz for a little girl**   **3. Waltz**
   4. Lullaby for a modern baby   **5. Toccata**
[4, arr. violin & piano] Ralph Holmes, Eric Fenby (pno)
      St John's, Smith Square, London 3 June 1972 Westminster Festival
      BBC Radio 3 b/cast 28 January 1973   BBC Sound Archives T35660

- arr. Fenby for Orchestra as **FIVE LITTLE PIECES**
Bournemouth Sinfonietta, Fenby
    rec. 2 September 1978 Guildhall, Southampton   ASD3688 TCASD3688
BBC Concert O, Fenby +
    rec. Golders Green Hippodrome 17 Oct. 1978   BBC b/cast 24 Nov. 1978.
        BBC Sound Archives T38611; National Sound Archive T2581BW

B. WORKS OF OTHERS

PURCELL Sonata in G minor
Ralph Holmes, Eric Fenby (pno)
St John's, Smith Square, London 3 June 1972 Westminster Festival
    BBC Radio 3 b/cast 28 January 1973   BBC Sound Archives T35660

GRAINGER Shallow Brown
David Wilson-Johnson, Scottish Baroque Ensemble, Fenby
    Edinburgh Festival, Queen's Hall 29 August 1982 Radio Forth b/cast [P]

C. FENBY AS COMPOSER

FENBY Rossini on Ilkla Moor
BBC Midland Light Orchestra, Stanford Robinson
    BBC b/cast date uncertain   [P]
BBC Northern Ireland Orchestra, Terence Lovett
        BBCTP 30 September 1965; National Sound Archive M534R
BBC Concert Orchestra, Ashley Lawrence
    BBC b/cast 2 February 1974   [P]

[Files at the BBC Written Archives Centre, Caversham, list 19 broadcast performances between 14.1.45 and 2.4.66, with other records indicating at least three further performances of an earlier date]

FENBY Jamaica Inn
Title music and opening sequence (3') and end-title music (0'15") for Alfred Hitchcock's 1939 film.   Video

orch. Fenby DELIUS Margot La Rouge (sung in French)
Lois McDonall, Kenneth Woollam, Malcolm Donnelly, Ludmilla Andrew, Richard Jackson, Dennis Wicks, Anne Collins, Margaret Field, Phyllis Cannan, David Wilson-Johnson, Alan Watt, BBC Concert O, Norman Del Mar
    f.p. rec. 9 December 1981 Golders Green Hippodrome
    f. b/cast BBC Radio 3 21 February 1982
                REGL458 NB9134 Z6546 CD3004X

D. ERIC FENBY TALKING

a) Commercial recordings

1.　*A talk by Eric Fenby, OBE*: 'In this talk about the man [Delius] and his work, recorded specially to accompany the issue of *A Village Romeo and Juliet*, Mr Fenby ranges widely over Delius's art, illustrating his points with music examples drawn from existing EMI recordings' [27'07"]. He also illustrates at the piano the completion by dictation of *Cynara*. EMI Studio No 1, Abbey Road. 23 October 1971. EMI SLS966, 1973

2.　Eric Fenby describing his first attempts at dictation as an introduction to his recording with Ralph Holmes of three violin sonatas [5'10"]. Unicorn UNS258, RHS310, 1972

3.　Eric Fenby reading an extract from *Delius as I knew him* [6', adapted from pp.21-7] in which he describes the visit of Barjansky and playing with him the Cello Concerto and the Cello Sonata.　Unicorn-Kanchana DKP9021, 1983

b) Film recordings

1.　*Song of Farewell*. Yorkshire TV documentary, directed and produced by Nick Gray, in which Eric Fenby returns to Scarborough and Grez and talks about his time with Delius, and visits the Menuhin School of Music [56']. First televised 1 August 1982

2.　*Discovering Delius: A Portrait of Frederick Delius 1862-1934*. A Landseer Production for the Delius Trust in association with RM Associates 1993 [59']. Numerous brief contributions from Eric Fenby, intercut with music and pictures, totalling 4'45".

c) Archive recordings (those held in private collections denoted by P)

1.　*As I knew him - a personal portrait: Delius*. Eric Fenby talking about the routine in the Delius household and the problems of the process of dictation. Recorded 20 November 1951, first b/cast 26 November 1951. BBC Sound Archives 17132-3. ♠

　　　　a. Extract, 2'43", in Jack de Manio's *Today* programme. Centenary b/cast 29 January 1962. [P]

　　　　b. Extracts, 8'45", in *Frederick Delius 1862-1934: a portrait of the composer drawn from the writings and recorded memories of those who knew him*, an hour-long programme in which Fenby describes life in the Delius household and the method of dictation in *A Song of Summer*. BBC b/cast 20 February 1969. [P]

2. *Delius - One hundred: a radio portrait written by Colin Shaw to mark the centenary of the birth of Frederick Delius in Bradford on January 29 1862*, with the recorded voice of Eric Fenby, Robert Harris (narrator), and John Cameron (baritone), BBC Northern Singers and BBC Northern Orchestra, cond. Stanford Robinson. BBC Home Service b/cast 28 January 1962. [P]

3. *Man of Music: a programme about the life of Frederick Delius who was born in Bradford, a hundred years ago*, written by Bertha Lonsdale and introduced by Eric Fenby [40']. BBC Home Service b/cast 30 March 1962. [P]

4. *A Lifetime of Music*. Eric Fenby talking with Irene Slade about his musical career and the years when he worked for Delius and Sir Thomas Beecham [c.20']. BBC b/cast 26 May 1965. BBC Sound Archives LP29774 & 29775. National Sound Archive M399W

5. Eric Fenby talks with John Amis about Delius in *Talking about music no. 18*. BBC b/cast 13 February 1968. BBC Sound Archives LP27566. National Sound Archive 6888WR & 8005W

6. Eric Fenby reminiscing about Grainger. BBC recording [1'25"] as part of a programme on Grainger introduced by John Amis. B/cast 30 June 1968. [P]

7. Eric Fenby interviewed by John Amis on Delius in BBC's *The week ahead*. B/cast 17 June 1971. BBC Sound Archives LP34185 bO2

8. Eric Fenby talking in *The week ahead* to John Amis about *Koanga* at the time of the Sadler's Wells production [7'50"]. BBC Radio 3 b/cast 13 May 1972. [P]

9. Eric Fenby talking to Ronald Eyre about *Koanga* in BBC Radio 4 Arts programme *Scan*, and comparing the different approaches taken by Groves and Beecham to the score [6']. B/cast 18 May 1972. BBC Sound Archives LP34624 b02

10. Eric Fenby talking about the structure and interpretation of the three violin sonatas. An interval talk between his performances of the works with Ralph Holmes at the 1972 Westminster Festival [12½']. St John's Smith Square, London 3 June 1972. BBC Radio 3 b/cast 27 January 1973. BBC Sound Archives T35660

11. Eric Fenby talking with Robert Layton [34½'], dealing with the methods of musical dictation illustrated at the piano, and describing life in the Delius household. BBC Radio 3 b/cast 20 August 1972. [P] ♠

12. *Eric Fenby in conversation with Fred Calland.* Public Broadcasting Services (USA) January 1974, re-b/cast WJCT-FM Stereo 90 1 March 1977. [P] ♠

13. *Delius as I knew him:* Eric Fenby talking to the Philadelphia Branch of the Delius Society and the New School of Music. Samuel P Mandell Theater, Drexell University, Philadelphia 27 January 1974. [P]

14. *Delius as I knew him:* on the 40th anniversary of Delius's death, Eric Fenby retells, with recorded music examples, the story of his time at Grez [44']. B/cast 5 June 1974 in BBC Radio 4's *Celebration* series. [P] ♠

15. Eric Fenby considers reasons for the neglect of the Cello Concerto, and discusses the work with particular reference to both Jacqueline du Pré's recording with Sargent (who reshaped certain passages) and memories of Barjansky's interpretation, with recorded extracts and examples played at the piano [14'20"]. BBC Radio 3 *Music Weekly*, introduced by Michael Oliver, b/cast 21 March 1976. BBC Sound Archives LP37464 f01

16. Eric Fenby talking to the Delius Society at Limpsfield on Delius the man and musician, with recorded music examples [57']. 26 May 1977 [P]

17. *The Frankfurt Group:* Eric Fenby reminiscing on Percy Grainger, Roger Quilter, Norman O'Neill, Cyril Scott and Balfour Gardiner [4 extracts, 5']. BBC Radio 3 *Music Weekly*, introduced by Michael Oliver, b/cast 23 October 1977. [P]

18. Eric Fenby interviewed by Robert Seager on Pennine Radio 1978. [P]

19. Eric Fenby in conversation with Ellen Frank, during which he 'reflects on the beginning of his collaboration with Delius. He speaks frankly about Delius the man and comments about the [Jacksonville] Composition Contest and Concert being in accord with the composer's wishes'. WJCT-FM Stereo 90 b/cast 1 & 2 March 1978 and 15 March 1980. [P]

20. *Delius as I knew him:* Eric Fenby introducing and conducting the BBC Concert Orchestra in a programme of works either dictated to or arranged by him: *A song of summer, Caprice and Elegy, Late swallows, Five pieces* and *Fantastic dance* [50']. Recorded Golders Green Hippodrome 17 October 1978, BBC Radio 3 b/cast 24 November 1978. BBC Sound Archives T38611; National Sound Archive T2581BW ♠

21. Eric Fenby, prior to his Wigmore Hall performance of the Cello Sonata with Julian Lloyd Webber, interviewed by Joan Bakewell about his decision to work for Delius [5'50"]. BBC Radio 4 *PM* 17 November 1980. [P]

22.	Eric Fenby talking to Brian Matthew in BBC Radio 2 *Round Midnight*, discussing, amongst other things, the Ken Russell film, his arrangement of *La Calinda*, his re-orchestration of *Margot La Rouge* and the genesis of the *Idyll* [21']. Also including Julian Lloyd Webber. B/cast 17 November 1980. [P]

23.	Eric Fenby appearing with Julian Lloyd Webber and Kate Bush in Russell Harty's BBCTV programme, with extracts from the Ken Russell film, and Fenby and Lloyd Webber performing part of the Cello Sonata [18']. Televised 25 November 1980. [P]

24.	*Delius - some changes of mind*: Eric Fenby talking to the Delius Society at Mary Ward House, London, about his changed attitude towards certain works. 29 January 1981 [P] ♠

25.	Eric Fenby contributing, with Lord Boothby and Felix Aprahamian, to a Beecham Symposium following the Delius Society annual dinner at Bloomsbury Crest Hotel (see *Delius Society Journal* 77, 20-1). 12 June 1982 [P]

26.	Eric Fenby interviewed by Veronica Gordon Smith during the Edinburgh Festival (in which he conducted the Scottish Baroque Ensemble in a Delius-Grainger concert), with reference to his work with Delius and to Percy Grainger [12'40"]. August 1982 Radio Forth. [P]

27.	*Jelka Delius*: Eric Fenby talking to the Delius Society at Mary Ward House, London. 21 September 1982. [P] ♠

28.	*Fenby looks back on Delius*: interview with John Amis in *Talking about Music no. 284*, throwing 'new light on Delius and his work and on Sir Thomas Beecham's mistrust of Fenby, believing that Fenby imposed his own ideas on Delius', and including excerpts from *The Fenby Legacy* recordings [17'13"]. BBC Transcription Service CN04101.02/S; National Sound Archive LP151562

29.	*Visitors to Grez*: Eric Fenby talking to the Delius Society about Delius's various visitors chiefly during his time there, at Mary Ward House, London. 22 September 1983. [P] ♠

30.	Eric Fenby interviewed in *Beauty and Strangeness: a portrait of Frederick Delius* [sections totalling 20'20"]. BBC Radio Leeds 10 June 1984. [P]

31.	*That boy's no good*: Independent Local Radio hour-long documentary on Eric Fenby's years at Grez, narrated by Lyndon Jenkins with substantial contributions from Eric Fenby, and also including the speech recording from Unicorn UNS258 (RHS310) and a brief extract from EMI SLS966. Various regional broadcasts 1984. [P]

32.   *Conductors I have known:* Eric Fenby talking to the Delius Society at Mary Ward House, London (see *Delius Society Journal* 93, 3-6). 22 October 1986. [P]

33.   *The missing years:* Eric Fenby talking to the Delius Society at Mary Ward House, London, about the years following Delius's death (see *Delius Society Journal* 97, 7-10). 27 October 1987. [P]

34.   *The war-time years:* Eric Fenby talking to the Delius Society at Mary Ward House, London, about his war years (see *Delius Society Journal* 100, 21-22). 29 September 1988. [P]

35.   Eric Fenby discussing his recording of *An Arabesque* and Delius's current standing, with reference also to their working together [7'28"]. BBC Radio 3 13 February 1988. [P]

36.   Brief recorded comments from Eric Fenby (from different sources) on performing Delius, in *Composer of the Week* 9-13 July 1990 (repeated 16-20 July). BBC Radio 3 [P]

37.   Eric Fenby talking briefly about Percy Grainger and *Brigg Fair* [3'57"], interviewed by Lyndon Jenkins as part of a Henry Wood Promenade Concert interval talk, BBC Radio 3 31 July 1992. [P]

ADDITIONAL BBC PROGRAMMES

The following is a summary of other BBC programmes as listed at the BBC Written Archives Centre, Caversham, some of which may exist as recordings. Details of the programme content are not to hand, and a number of the entries may be repeats of BBC Sound Archive recordings. In many cases only the title of the programme in which a Delius item appeared is given.

9.11.41   *Music Club* [programme not located]
24.1.43   *Music lover's calendar* [talk c.20']
8.3.46   Introducing records of Delius
?.4.47   *English musicologist - Delius:* talk for BBC Latin-American Service [30'] [date of b/cast not given and programme not located]
21.11.48   *Music Magazine*, Home Service
29.1.53   *Revue musicale: Frederick Delius* [programme not located]
29.1.59   Light programme *Roundabout: Delius as I knew him*
2.2.62   In *Pick of the week*, extract from b/cast of 28.1.62
26.2.62   Home Service *A world of sound*, from b/cast of 26.11.51
30.3.62   *Today*
7.6.63   Home Service *A world of sound*, from b/cast of 26.11.51
13.7.63   From b/cast of 26.11.51
28.5.65   Extract from b/cast of 26.5.65 in *Pick of the week*
29.9.66   Repeat of b/cast of 26.5.65

7.3.67	*Concert Calendar*
23.9.67	*Portrait of Frederick Delius* [possibly Sound Archive recording]
6.10.67	Interviewed by John Twitchin, Radio 4, on the death of Sir Malcolm Sargent
25.2.68	Radio 4 *Music in London* with John Amis
7.11.68	Radio 4 *Home this afternoon*
9.1.70	Radio 3 *The week ahead*: talking about Grainger
29.3.70	Interval - *Composer at work* [possibly from b/cast of 26.5.65]
19.6.71	Radio 3 *The week ahead*
14.5.76	Radio 3 *Music Weekly*
26.7.76	Radio 4 *Kaleidoscope*: interviewed on Christopher Palmer's book on Delius
18.10.79	Repeat of b/cast of 24.11.78
29.1.80	Radio 3: talk in RHS310 and Violin Sonata No 3 from same source
9.7.82	Radio 4 *Today*: interview in connection with RFH performance of *Appalachia*
9.7.82	Radio 2 *Round Midnight* interview with Brian Matthew
22.5.85	Radio 4 'PM': in connection with Delius Festival week in Bradford
31.1.86	Extracts from b/casts of 20.8.72 & 21.3.76 in Radio 3 *This week's composer*

ADDITIONAL

Song of Summer. BBC Television *Omnibus* dramatised documentary [75']: 'The strange story of the blind composer Frederick Delius and the young organist from Scarborough, Eric Fenby', with Christopher Gable portraying Fenby, Max Adrian as Delius, and Maureen Pryor as Jelka Delius. Written by Ken Russell and Eric Fenby from *Delius as I knew him*. Directed by Ken Russell. First televising 15 September 1968.

APPENDIX TWO

A FENBY-DELIUS SUMMARY

A summary of Dr Fenby's association with the music of Delius, briefly detailing his work on the scores and his many arrangements, those works he has recorded or performed in public, and his writings and recorded talks on specific scores. Transcripts in Eric Fenby's hand of scores other than those he has either completed by dictation or arranged have not generally been included. For further information the reader is referred to the Delius catalogues by Robert Threlfall listed below. Commercial and private recordings are detailed in the discography above. While the list of performances, especially of chamber works, cannot claim to be exhaustive, it is hoped that the most significant occasions have been included.

Most abbreviations are standard, e.g. FS Full Score, VS Vocal Score, SS Study Score, MS Manuscript. B&H and Univ. denote the publishers Boosey & Hawkes and Universal Edition respectively, and cond. a conducting engagement.

THE MAGIC FOUNTAIN [I/3]: VS 1953 (facsimile publication, Delius Trust)

KOANGA [I/4]: VS 1935 (B&H), FS copy (MS, Delius Trust)

> Talks: BBCNatP 23.9.35♠, BBCR3 13.5.72, BBCR3 18.5.72
>
> Writing: *Radio Times* 20.9.35♠, *Daily Telegraph* 19.10.35
>
> Notes: EMI SLS974♠, SS B&H 1980

* selection arr. for reduced orch. (MS)
* **LA CALINDA**: arrs. for orch. (B&H 1938) / flute & pno 1976 (B&H) / flute and string orch
  commercial recordings (vers. for orch. and flute & orch.)
  Talks: BBCR2 17.11.80; Notes: RFH 29.1.62♠, ASD2477♠, ASD3688♠

FOLKERAADET [I/5]: see note on Collected Edition

A VILLAGE ROMEO AND JULIET [I/6]:

> Notes: Delius Fellowship 1948♠, Bradford 1962, EMI SLS966♠, SHB54
>
> Writing: *RAM Magazine 204* 1973

* Wedding Music arr. for chorus & organ 1933 VS (Univ.)
* Suite 1948 (MS)
* **WALK TO THE PARADISE GARDEN**: cond.: LSO RFH 11.7.82, LSO Daytona Beach, Florida 28.7.82, LSO Cardiff 5.12.82

MARGOT LA ROUGE [I/7]: re-orch. 1980 (MS, Delius Trust)

> cond. première (orig. vers.) St Louis June 8, 11, 17, 23 & 26 1983
>
> Talks: BBCR2 17.11.80
>
> Notes: REGL458♠, CD3004X

FENNIMORE AND GERDA [I/8]: see note on Collected Edition

> Notes: EMI SLS991♠, St Louis 1981, Edinburgh Internat. Festival 1983
>
> Writing: *RAM Magazine 211* 1976

* **INTERMEZZO** (arr. Fenby c.1936): FS (B&H 1945); arrs. for oboe and string quartet 1978 / oboe and piano (B&H 1980) / flute, oboe and piano (f.p. 1987)
  commercial recording
  Notes: ALP1586♠, ASD357, Seraphim S-60185, EM2900323-3 & -5

HASSAN [I/9]

* Suite 1931 (MS)
* **SERENADE**: arrs. for cello and chamber orch. 1929 / cello and piano 1931 (B&H) / organ 1934 (B&H)
  private b/cast recording (cello & pno)
  Notes: RCA LHMV1050, LVT1020, EMI ASD2477♠

APPALACHIA [II/2]:

> cond. LSO RFH 11.7.82 & Daytona Beach, Florida 28.7.82
>
> private recording (11.7.82)

Notes: Columbia 33CX1112♠, Bradford 1962♠, EMI ASD2635♠, ESD7099, EMX412081 etc.
Writing: *Composer* 1966♠
* reduc. in choral score (with Dent's reduced orch.) 1975 (B&H Hire)
SEA DRIFT [II/3]:
Talks: BBCHS 20.8.43♠
Notes: Bradford 1962♠, EMI ASD2958
A MASS OF LIFE [II/4]:
Notes: EMI SLS958; New York, St Louis and Washington Jan. 1974♠; Cleveland November 1977; RFH 5.12.84♠
* reduc. in wind 1980 (B&H Hire)
SONGS OF SUNSET [II/5]:
commercial recording
Notes: Bradford 1962♠, EMI ASD2437♠, UK DKP(CD)9063
Writing: *Delius Society Newsletter 31* 1971
THE SONG OF THE HIGH HILLS [II/6]:
commercial recording
Notes: RFH 29.1.62♠, Bradford 1962, EMI ASD2958
AN ARABESQUE [[II/7]:
commercial recording
Talks: BBCR3 13.2.88
Notes: EMI ASD2437♠, UK DKP(CD)9063
REQUIEM [II/8]:
cond. RPO RFH 25.1.84
private recording (25.1.84)
Notes: EMI ASD2397♠
SONGS OF FAREWELL [II/9]: completed by dictation 1929-30: VS & FS (B&H, 1931)
cond. Jacksonville 22.2.75, 5.3.83
commercial recording
Notes: RFH 29.1.62, Bradford 1962♠, EMI ASD644♠
IDYLL [II/10]: arranged and completed by dictation 1932: VS (B&H 1933), SS (B&H 1976)
commercial recording
Talks: BBCR2 17.11.80
Notes: *Radio Times* 29.9.33♠, SS & VS note

SEVEN DANISH SONGS [III/4]:
commercial recordings (nos. 1,2,4,5 & 7)
Notes: UK DKP9022♠
* **Let Springtime come**: orch. vers. completed by dictation 1929 (OUP Hire)
commercial recording

Notes: UK DKP9022♠

CYNARA [III/5]: completed by dictation 1929: FS (B&H, 1931)
commercial recording
Talks: EMI SLS966
Notes: EMI ASD2437♠

A LATE LARK [III/6]: completed by dictation 1929: FS & VS (B&H 1931)
cond. Jacksonville 5.3.83
commercial recording

PART-SONGS [IV]:
cond. *On Craig Ddu* and *The splendour falls* Bradford 29.1.62
* **TWO AQUARELLES** (arr. Fenby 1932) [IV/5]: FS (B&H, 1938)
cond. Edinburgh 29.8.82
private b/cast and commercial recordings

SONGS WITH PIANO/ORCHESTRA [V]:
commercial recordings
Notes: RCA LHMV1050, LVT1020, Bradford 1962, UK DKP9022♠
* **To Daffodils**[V/30.4] orch. 1983 (DT)
commercial recording (pno. & orch. vers.)
Notes: UK DKP9022♠
* **Avant que tu ne t'en ailles** [V/31]: prepared for publication 1931 (B&H
1932)
commercial recording
Notes: UK DKP9022♠

MARCHE CAPRICE [VI/6.1]:
Notes: EMI ALP1586♠, ASD357, EM290323-5 etc.
SUMMER EVENING [VI/7.1]:
Notes: RCA LHMV1050♠, LVT1020
SLEIGH RIDE [VI/7.2]:
Notes: EMI ALP1586♠, ASD357, EM290323-5 etc.
OVER THE HILLS AND FAR AWAY [VI/11]:
Notes: Columbia 33C1017♠
AMERICAN RHAPSODY [VI/12]:
Corresp.: *The Times* 10.12.86, [see also *Independent* 10.12.86]
PARIS [VI/14]:
Notes: RFH 29.1.62♠, Bradford 1962, EMI ASD2804♠
* arr. Buths for two pnos. rev. Fenby 1977 (MS)
Notes: QEH 12.12.77♠
LEBENSTANZ (LIFE'S DANCE) [VI/15]: see note on Collected Edition
Notes: EMI ASD3139♠, ED290026-1, CDM763171-2 etc.

BRIGG FAIR [VI/16]:
>   Notes: ALP1586♠, ASD357, EM290323-5 etc., Bradford 1962, ASD2635♠, ESD7099, EMX412081-1 etc.
>   Talks: BBCR3 31.7.92

IN A SUMMER GARDEN [VI/17]:
>   Notes: 33C1017, Bradford 1962, ASD2477♠

DANCE RHAPSODY NO 1 [VI/18]:
>   Notes: RCA LHMV1050, LVT1020, Bradford 1962♠, ASD2804♠, CDM763171-2

ON HEARING THE FIRST CUCKOO IN SPRING [VI/19.1]:
>   cond. LSO Cardiff 5.12.82
>   Notes: LHMV1050, LVT1020, ASD2477♠, ALP1586♠, ASD357, EM290323-5 etc.
>   * arr. for organ (OUP 1934)

SUMMER NIGHT ON THE RIVER [VI/19.2]:
>   cond. LSO Cardiff 5.12.82
>   Notes: LHMV1050, LVT1020, ASD2477♠, ALP1586♠, ASD357, EM290323-5 etc.

NORTH COUNTRY SKETCHES [VI/20]:
>   Notes: Bradford 1962♠, ASD3139♠, ED290026-1 etc.

AIR AND DANCE [VI/21]:
>   cond. Edinburgh 29.8.82
>   private b/cast recording
>   * arrs. for pno. (B&H, 1931), for flute and pno./strings 1976 (B&H 1977)
>   commercial recording
>   Notes: ASD3688♠

DANCE RHAPSODY NO 2 [VI/22]:
>   commercial recording

EVENTYR [VI/23]:
>   Notes: Bradford 1962, ASD2804♠, CDM763171-2

A SONG BEFORE SUNRISE [VI/24]:
>   Notes: ALP1586♠, ASD357, EM290323-5 etc., ASD644, ASD2477♠
>   * arrs. for organ (MS, Fenby) / for piano (Thames 1982)

POEM OF LIFE AND LOVE [VI/25]: completion of Balfour Gardiner's arr. for two pnos. 1929 (Delius Trust 1992)

A SONG OF SUMMER [VI/26]: completed by dictation 1929-30: FS (B&H 1931); arr. for two pnos. 1929 (MS, Delius Trust)
>   cond. Jacksonville 22.2.75, (lecture/perf.) Bracknell 23.7.78, BBC Concert O 17.10.78, LSO Cardiff 5.12.82, Jacksonville 10.3.84
>   private b/cast and commercial recordings
>   Talks: BBC 8.3.46, BBC 20.2.69, BBCR3 24.11.78♠
>   Notes: ASD3139♠, ED290026-1, CDM763171-2

IRMELIN PRELUDE [VI/27]: arranged by dictation 1931: FS (B&H 1938)
  commercial recording
 * arrs. for piano (B&H 1938) / for organ (B&H 1938)
FANTASTIC DANCE [VI/28, dedicated 'To Eric Fenby']: compl. by dictation
  1931: FS (MS, Delius Trust), pno. cond. score (B&H 1933)
  cond. BBC Concert O 17.10.78, Jacksonville 5.3.83
  private b/cast and commercial recording
  Talks: BBCR3 24.11.78♠

LEGENDE [VII/3]:
  pub. perf. (pno.) Westminster Theatre 4.6.67
PIANO CONCERTO [VII/4]:
  Notes: RFH 29.1.62♠
VIOLIN CONCERTO [VII/6]:
  Notes: Bradford 1962♠
  cond. Jacksonville 22.2.75
CELLO CONCERTO [VII/7]: see note on Collected Edition
  Talks: BBCR3 21.3.76, DKP9021
  Notes: ASD644♠, ASD2764, RS9010♠, RD70800, RK70800
CAPRICE AND ELEGY [VII/8: completed by dictation 1930: FS (B&H 1931)
  cond. BBC Concert O 17.10.78, BBC b/cast 30.7.81 (pno.)
  private b/cast and commercial recordings
  Talks: BBCR3 24.11.78♠
 * arrs. for cello and pno. (B&H 1931) / [*Elegy* only] for 5 cellos 1974 (MS,
  Fenby)

VIOLIN SONATA NO 1 [VIII/6]:
  pub. perf. St John's Smith Square 3.6.72
  private b/cast and commercial recordings
  Talks: BBCR3 27.1.73
  Notes: Bradford 1962♠,RHS310♠, UNS258, ASD3864♠
CELLO SONATA [VIII/7]:
  pub. perf. Westminster Abbey 13.5.78, Wigmore Hall 19.11.80, BBC
  b/cast 30.7.81
  private b/cast recording and commercial recording
  Talks: DKP9021,
  Notes: Wigmore Hall 19.11.80♠, New York 14.11.91♠
STRING QUARTET [VIII/8]: see note on Collected Edition
  Notes: Bradford 1962♠, GSGC14130♠
 * **LATE SWALLOWS**: arrs. for pno. 1929 (Thames 1982) / for string
  orch. 1962 (Galliard 1963)
  cond. BBC Concert O 17.10.78
  private b/cast recording
  Talks: BBCR3 24.11.78

Corresp.: *Delius Soc. Newsletter* Dec 1963
Notes: ASD2477♠
* **SONATA FOR STRINGS** (arr. Fenby): 1977 (Stainer & Bell)
commercial recording
Notes: ASD3688♠
VIOLIN SONATA NO 2 [VIII/9]:
pub. perf. St John's Smith Square 3.6.72
private b/cast and commercial recordings
Talks: BBCR3 27.1.73
Notes: Bradford 1962♠, RHS310♠, UNS258, ASD3864♠
VIOLIN SONATA NO 3 [VIII/10]: completed by dictation 1930: (B&H 1931)
pub. perf. Bradford 29.1.62, Jacksonville 4.2.66, Westminster Theatre 4.6.67, St John's Smith Square 3.6.72, Philadelphia 27.1.74, Malvern 27.5.77, Chicago 18.5.79
private b/cast and commercial recordings
Talks: BBC 1.1.47, RHS310T11, BBCR3 27.1.73
Notes: Bradford 1962♠, RHS310♠, UNS258, ASD3864♠

DANCE FOR HARPSICHORD [IX/6]
* arr. for flute and strings 1978 (B&H Hire)
commercial recording
Notes: ASD3688♠
FIVE PIANO PIECES [IX/7]
private b/cast recording (no. 4)
* arr. for orch. 1964 (B&H Hire)
cond. BBC Concert O 17.10.78
private b/cast and commercial recordings
Talks: BBCR3 24.11.78
Notes: ASD3688♠

Eric Fenby also collaborated in the Collected Edition by editing certain works which Beecham had not prepared in this way: viz. *Margot La Rouge*, *Fennimore and Gerda*, *Folkeraadet*, *Life's Dance*, Cello Concerto and String Quartet.

In compiling the above list, acknowledgement is made of the following sources, all by Robert Threlfall, to whom thanks are also due for additional assistance:

A Catalogue of the Compositions of Frederick Delius: Sources and References, Delius Trust 1977
Frederick Delius: A Supplementary Catalogue, Delius Trust 1986
Frederick Delius: Complete Works - Editorial Report, Delius Trust 1990
'Delius in Eric Fenby's MSS', *Composer*, 31 Spring 1969, pp.19-21 and 57 and Spring 1976, pp.33 & 35

APPENDIX THREE

THE PUBLISHED WORKS OF ERIC FENBY
(with British Library catalogue reference)

FOR MUSIC ON THE EVE OF PALM SUNDAY
unacc. chorus, SATB, poem by R Nichols, B&H 1933 (in The Winthrop Rogers Edition of Choral Music for Festivals) E.602.ss.(7.)

FOR MUSIC ON THE EVE OF PALM SUNDAY
unacc. chorus, SATB, B&H 1938 (Winthrop Rogers Church Choral Series No 11) F.1147.

MAGNIFICAT AND NUNC DIMITTIS
B&H 1937 (Winthrop Rogers Church Choral Series No 15) F.1147.

ROSSINI ON ILKLA MOOR: Overture for Orchestra (1938)
Hawkes 1941   g.727.m.(4.)
 2(II = picc.).2.2.2 - 2.2.1.0 - timp. perc. cyms / BD - strings   8'

ROSSINI ON ILKLA MOOR (arr. for military band by Norman Richardson)
B&H 1948   h.3211.b.

THE ABCA, ARMY BUREAU OF CURRENT AFFAIRS, SONG BOOK
(with C Hassall, musical arrangements by Lieut. E Fenby), 1944 B.934.

John Ireland **THESE THINGS SHALL BE**, piano reduction by E Fenby, 1937 (Winthrop Rogers Edition, B&H 8003) F.1267.t.(5.)

APPENDIX FOUR

ARTICLES ON ERIC FENBY

'Eric Fenby, Amanuensis, Teacher and Composer' ('Thursday Portrait'), *Scarborough Evening News*, November 2 1950

'Delius film revives Scarborough friendships for Eric Fenby', *Scarborough Evening News*, November 1 1968

'Eric Fenby's fond farewell' [farewell Wigmore Hall concert, 11 November 1980], *The Sunday Times*, 16 November 1980

'Thanks for the memory: Holy Trinity Church clergy and choir, 1914' [photograph including Eric Fenby and his father, Mr H H Fenby], *Scarborough Mercury*, October 12 1985

Adrian Cruft, 'A profile: Eric Fenby', *Composer*, Spring 1968, .2-3

Christopher Palmer, 'Indian Summer of a Genius - Fenby's work for Delius', *Country Life*, September 9 1976, p.658

Christopher Palmer, 'Eric Fenby - A Biographical Sketch', as an introduction to the 1981 Faber reprint of *Delius as I knew him*, xv-xxii

Christopher Palmer, 'Recording the Fenby Legacy', *Delius Society Journal* 73, October 1981, 6-10

Christopher Palmer, 'The Fenby Connection', *Records and Recordings* Number 289, October 1981, 16-18

Frank Peters, 'Opera Theatre Awaits Original Delius Score' [*Margot La Rouge*], *St Louis Post-Dispatch*, 8 May 1983

Patric Standford, 'Quiet man of note', *Yorkshire Post*, January 2 1990

David Tall, 'The Fenby Legacy', *Delius Society Journal* 56, July 1977, 6-10 & 15-17

Robert Threlfall, 'Delius in Eric Fenby's MSS', *Composer*, 31 Spring 1969, 19-21 & 57 and Spring 1976 33 & 35

James Wierzbicki, 'Discovery of score makes OTSL scramble' [*Margot La Rouge*], *St Louis Globe*, 4-5 June 1983

John White, 'The Meditation of Old Times Resumed' [A visit to Grez with Eric and Rowena Fenby], *Delius Society Newsletter* No 18 October 1967, 1-2

Shorter references in *The Delius Society Newsletter* and *The Delius Society Journal* (see Index 1-100), the *Scarborough Evening News*: 1.11.62, 19.11.80, 25.11.81, 4.12.84, 29.1.86, 6.5.87, and the *Scarborough Mercury*: 20.12.86

INDEX

INDEX

INDEX

Printed in the United Kingdom by Hobbs the Printers Ltd,
Brunel Road, Totton, Hampshire SO40 3YS